GIRL

AT MY

DOOR

THE
GIRL
AT MY
DOOR

REBECCA GRIFFITHS

Bookouture

Published by Bookouture in 2021

An imprint of Storyfire Ltd.
Carmelite House
50 Victoria Embankment
London EC4Y 0DZ

www.bookouture.com

ISBN: 978-1-80019-892-0
eBook ISBN: 978-1-80019-891-3

For my husband, Steven.
Without you, there would be nothing.

… I got a stocking and tied it round her neck to put her to sleep.

Extract from the testimony of British serial killer and necrophile
John Reginald Halliday Christie, June 1953

PROLOGUE

He could almost taste her anxiety. Brackish. Moist. Anxiety that had nothing to do with him. Not yet, anyway. Neat and ordinary in his brown trilby and raincoat, he was one of the invisible people, no different from the thousands of others who moved about these city streets after dark. It was his ordinariness that allowed him to walk close on her heels, silent in his soft shoes, listening to the tantalising rasp of her stocking tops as thigh rubbed thigh. Close enough to reach out and touch the tender skin behind her ear, if he wanted to. And he did want to, very badly. He licked his lips and leered into her shadow. Women knew what they were doing; they knew their power. Arousing his masculinity and then stifling it, mocking it... humiliating it. It was why he committed such bestial and revolting crimes against them.

London cowered behind the fog. The vapour curling up off the Thames and thickening in his lungs made it difficult to breathe. Buildings, rising taller than trees from the wet pavements, melted into the murkiness as he trailed the woman down street after street, his eye fixed on the glittery diamante trinket pinned to the folds of her hair. The only thing of interest amid the gloom, in a city where everything was filmed in the greasy hue of gaslight and choked in smog.

When she reached a busy thoroughfare, she stopped and turned. For a terrible moment he thought she was on to him but the gesture was nothing more than a reflex: something carried from childhood and the automatic drill of road safety lessons. Things he'd needed to learn in adulthood when he arrived here twenty-five years ago, unfamiliar with the tempo of London traffic. Her face was as pale as the moon that rose above the moors back home, and looking at her more closely, he appreciated how young and beautiful she was. It made his heart beat faster.

Hurry, she seemed to tell herself, crossing briskly from kerb to kerb through the grind of buses and taxicabs and the rain that had begun to fall. He was guessing this route she'd decided on was a shortcut and now she wasn't sure. Shame he wasn't wearing his special constable's uniform, with the bogus authority it gave him – bogus because his role in the Emergency Reserve had ended in 1943. It would have allowed him to march right up to her and offer his assistance. Women in distress were always happy to trust an officer of the law.

'Are you lost, lass?' He chuckled to himself, delighting in her panic as she scanned the stretch of pavement, the whites of her eyes caught in passing headlamps. 'You look as if you are.'

Now.

Do it now.

He knew his persistence would be rewarded. Like the trapping of the small yet exquisitely beautiful tortoiseshell butterfly on Swales Moor when he was a boy. These chances were just as rare, so he needed to go easy.

Then, a passing bus and the woman's expression brightened. *Too fast, surely?* Pulse thumping and oddly concerned for her safety, he gasped when she stepped into the road and thrust out a hand to seize the pole.

He watched her swing aboard, whiplashed by the tail of her coat. He had gone and missed his chance, but there would be another. He only had to be lucky once, he consoled himself; she had to be lucky every time.

CHAPTER ONE

Queenie Osbourne stepped back from the microphone and slipped, slinky as a mermaid in her sequin-scaled gown, beneath the wave of applause. It was as if the appreciation in the smoky nightclub was going on in another room. For another singer. And had nothing to do with her. She noticed the cigar-sucking bulk of Cyril Bream, the Mockin' Bird's owner, a man everyone called Uncle Fish, watching from the wings and beckoned to him. He swayed towards her: an overloaded cargo ship negotiating the sea of music stands, drum kit and piano, his Humpty Dumpty appearance belying the intellect of a man who had made his fortune in the cotton mills of Manchester. He reached for her hand inside its satin glove and lifted it into the air while she stared out at the members seated at tables adorned with tasselled lamps.

'They love you.' Cyril kissed her hand, his white Edwardian moustache prickling the satin. There were tears in his eyes. Tears like he'd had the day of her audition. 'Pop in and see me before you go,' he said, then disappeared.

Queenie left the stage and trailed the cheers of appreciation down to the dressing room in the fishtail of her dress. Once inside, she drew back the red velvet curtain, making it clatter on its rings. The curtain was there to partition the room and give her privacy when she needed it. Most of the time she didn't. It was her dressing room, and apart from Terrence, the other boys in the band rarely came in here. She sat before the mirror, unclipped her hair and fanned it over her shoulders, loving the loose, long waves. Who else had hair like this? She appreciated its glassy sheen, its rich brown tones. Close to the mirror, melting into her image, Queenie failed to notice Terrence Banks standing by the door.

'You coming for a drink?' Tall and dapper in his pinstriped suit and polka-dot tie, his question slid beneath her vanity.

'I was only…' Her excuses died in her mouth. What was she doing? Admiring herself, loving herself? 'Sorry.' She blushed.

'What for?'

She shrugged – there was nothing to say. She'd been caught out and now she was ashamed.

'You're beautiful, darling. And if you've got it, flaunt it.' Terrence fiddled with the handkerchief ruched in his breast pocket. 'Another full house tonight. It's that write-up in the *Standard*, calling you the next Billie Holiday. It echoed what that Herbie Weiszmann said. Lucky, on his visit from New York, he walks into our little club. Who'd have thought it? Our Queenie, singing on Broadway… Let's go celebrate.'

'I won't be a tick.' She turned away, strangely embarrassed, not quite knowing how to deal with the prospect of stardom. 'I just need to sort my face out.'

'Pretty necklace – who gave you that?'

Queenie pressed a hand to the emerald pendant swinging from her neck. 'Digsby.'

'Not that old chrome dome?'

She winked and applied a fresh coat of red lipstick.

'God, Queenie, you don't let him touch you?' A horrified look.

'Don't be silly. I never let any of them touch me.'

'How come? They must want something in return.'

'I know how to play them, that's all.' She blotted her mouth.

'You worry me. Everything's a game to you.'

Another wink. 'Silly old duffer gave me these too.' A flash of her earrings.

'You and your sparkly things. You're such a magpie.'

'But I don't steal things.'

Terrence undid his top button and loosened his tie. 'No, you just steal their hearts, darling.'

They left the dressing room and walked up the narrow flight of stairs, made their way to the bar with its dimpled stools and banks of glasses. Aside from the rest of the band, the Mockin' Bird was empty.

'What'll you have?' Terrence waved a hand over the optics.

'Port and lemon. Easy on the ice.'

'Our singer's such a star, isn't she, lads?' The click of his lighter and he lit one of Queenie's slim white Sobranies. 'She told you about Broadway?' He passed it to her and took another for himself.

'*Shh*, Terry. I've not signed the contract yet. I might stay here.' She drew on her cigarette.

'You can't pass up on that.' He exhaled smoke in two grey tusks. 'Weiszmann's fixing you a recording deal with Atlantic Records, too. This is the chance of a lifetime.'

'I'm with Terry,' Dick, the saxophonist, piped up. 'You've gotta go for it.'

Buster, the band's drummer, sat at the bar wearing his haunted look and a suit that had probably belonged to his late father. Prone to angry outbursts, he was a man racked with anxiety and Queenie had always found him a little unnerving. Not that she could blame him if he ranted at the likes of her: someone who hadn't heard a shell fired, or seen a friend blown to pieces, who didn't have nightmares and hear dead men screaming in the dark. As a girl, she'd been packed off to her grandparents' farm to be safe during the Blitz because this man, along with thousands like him, believed it was his job to protect her and others like her.

She watched as he took a last leisurely pull on his fag and fumbled for the edge of the counter. It was obvious he was drunk, that he needed its support to get to his feet.

'Come on, Buster, tell us a story.'

Queenie thought he was at his best when he told stories, on nights like these when they sat around listening to him pluck things from the air. Frightening things that made the hairs stand up on the back of her neck.

'I'd best be off.' Buster downed what was left of his pint and pocketed his Woodbines.

'Want a hand? Can't you reach?' Terrence, teasing, lifted Buster's army overcoat down with ease. A coat which, although carefully dyed, still betrayed its origin in every line.

They waited for their drummer to leave, for the outer door to bang shut, then an outbreak of chortling and adenoidal snorting.

'He was out again tonight.'

'What d'you mean?' Queenie looked at Dick, who nodded, letting Terrence explain.

'He's missing the beat all the time.'

'I didn't notice.'

'He drinks too much.'

'You can't say anything – the poor guy thinks the world is against him as it is.' She lit another of her cigarettes. 'He told me he still has nightmares because of the war.'

'We all have nightmares. Everyone's lost something, someone… We're all half of what we were before the bloody war.'

Surprised by the bitterness in Terrence's voice, she thought of her brother who never came home from the South China Sea.

'You're smoking a lot.' He changed the subject.

'No more than you.'

He leant over the ashtray. 'Excuse me. I don't wear scarlet lipstick, it's not my colour, darling.'

Queenie broke into song. '... A cigarette... a lipstick's traces...' Her voice, caramel-sweet with its sexy rasp, circled the empty club.

Terrence hummed along to the tune of 'These Foolish Things', his fingers working the burr oak counter of the bar: an imaginary piano.

At that moment the main door of the club swung open and a tall, loose-limbed black man in a smart coat and hat hovered unsure on the threshold. His row of beautiful white teeth gleamed like an advertisement.

'Who's that?' Queenie liked the look of him.

'It's Malcolm. He must've finished early. Blast it, I told him to wait for me outside.' Terrence fumbled for his overcoat.

'That's him, is it? I'd love to meet him.'

'You will, Queenie. Soon.'

'Why not now? Go on, Terry, invite him in. We can have a drink, all of us.'

Terrence shot her a look that said this was impossible.

'Where are you going? Can I come with you?'

Another look, sheepish, his cheekbones flushing cherry-pink. 'Not this time, Queenie. Sorry.'

It was almost three in the morning and Cyril Bream, his ledger open on his desk, was poring over the bills. A cigar smouldering at his elbow, his round face illuminated by the desk lamp. The increase in taxes and business rates was beyond his comprehension. He tallied the incomings and outgoings, wrote his findings in pencil in the corresponding columns. The next few weeks were going to be lean. He let his big soft body sag into his chair. At least with the invention of the NHS, he no longer had his wife's hospital bills to pay. If he was careful... if he could hold on to Queenie, they would get through. But who was he kidding? She wasn't going to pass up a chance like that and stay in this little place.

He rubbed his eyes and got up to lift the blackout curtain he'd yet to take down. Revealed a sky full of stars. There would be a frost tonight, he predicted, before dropping it again. On the sideboard, a bottle of single malt the band had bought him for his birthday a fortnight ago. Sixty-five. He was a relic in a dead world. He poured himself a compensatory fingerful and gulped it down. All very well playing the jolly old buffer, but the truth was that he nurtured a real dread of the future. There was hope when he'd still had his sons, but neither George nor William had come home from the front, and now Cyril felt he was nothing more than flotsam in a world that had no room or use for him any more. He sat down again and tried to focus on his accounts, but instead his mind wandered to his wife. Not the bedridden woman she had become in the last few years, a woman too ill to leave hospital, but the way she had looked when they'd first met. Barely twenty, her long legs muscular like a tennis player's. Her bobbed blonde hair and beaded headband, the swish of the braided fringe on her flapper dress when she danced the Lindy Hop.

Queenie left the bar and knocked on the office door.

'My dear girl, come in.' Uncle Fish motioned her to one of his easy chairs. 'Would you like a drink?'

She shook her head and sat down tidily. Her fingers coiled around the strap of her evening bag. 'How's Gloria?'

Queenie looked at a framed photograph on the desk: a family snapshot of her employer with his wife and sons. Terrence was right – everyone had lost someone.

'As well as can be expected. They're looking after her very well at the Royal Brompton.'

'I could visit her?'

'Would you?' He sucked on the end of his cigar. 'Poor darling could do with cheering up.'

'You said you wanted to see me?'

'I did, my dear.' He pushed a poker deep into the fire. A fire so low it was nearly out.

Queenie watched the flames lick, one then two, until it was ablaze.

'I think it's about time we upped your wages.' If this was his way of stopping her from leaving, it was feeble and touching and made her feel worse than she already did. 'You should at least be earning the same as the boys.' He plumped down on his chair with a leathery creak.

'Sounds fair.' *Isn't Uncle Fish going to ask me about Weiszmann's offer? Evidently not… head in the sand.*

'On top of your clothing allowance, of course.' He downed another mouthful of cigar smoke.

Queenie smoothed her dress over her knees and shared nothing of her need to use this allowance to supplement the shortfall in housekeeping. That her father's emphysema had worsened and meant he had reduced his hours at the bottle factory.

'Should be easier now clothing rationing's ended. Although I must congratulate you, my dear.' He tugged on his moustache. 'That's another wonderful outfit. You are good at giving your public what they want.'

My public?

It seemed farcical to someone of her origins. She couldn't seriously believe she had a public. Returning, as she did, to the bleak-bricked monotony of that rented terraced house and her room squashed under the eaves. Whatever her evenings here brought with them – adoration from the audience, a stream of male admirers – it all melted into nothing when she was back at the Belfast sink.

Uncle Fish counted out money from his cash box and she took the bundle of notes, thanking him.

'Just one other thing.' He picked up his cigar and filled his cheeks again.

'Yes?' She breathed in the rich, spicy smoke.

'Gladys is leaving to get married and I need a new waitress. Someone personable, happy to muck in. You wouldn't happen to know anyone?'

CHAPTER TWO

It had stopped raining by the time Joy Rivard reached the top of Great Russell Street. But the damage had been done. Her old green school coat was blackened by rain and her stout shoes mud-encrusted. Even her hat in fawn velour had failed miserably. The brim collected water so that when she tipped her head, icy rain slid down inside her collar. Refusing to travel by Tube, if it rained, she would usually pick up a bus but had been caught on the hop today. Never one for heels like her best friend Queenie, the walk from her lodgings in Gloucester Road and up through Hyde Park wasn't a problem. The interest she found along the way helped energise her for a day cooped up inside the British Museum, where it was her job to classify and catalogue the thousands of books, journals, patents, prints and ancient manuscripts in the Reading Room.

Since first arriving in London from Northern France, the ink still wet on her bilingual secretarial certificate, Joy found she shared the same fears as her father, who wouldn't go underground either. Whenever recounting tales of Paris, his youth spent working the kitchens of Maxim's, he would say it was only rats and those with something to hide who went beneath the paving slabs. A distressing irony, coming like a stab to the heart, to think her father had been buried in the churchyard of Arras's Saint-Géry these last three years.

Tilting her nose to the sky, where a glimmer of sun found a space between a dip in the rooftops, she pushed the sadness about her father away. Today was her birthday and to celebrate she was meeting Queenie before work. Work was another thing to feel good about. Joy knew she was lucky to have a job; the labour market was flooded. For every man that returned after the war, there was a woman who refused to be shooed back inside the home. Her mother used to say it was a mistake to be born a woman – a woman needed to earn her own living. But Joy didn't see it like that. After leaving school at sixteen, an aunt had paid for her to attend college, where she learnt how to be useful in the business world of men. And even though she was always short of money – after paying rent, there was barely anything for food and nothing for luxuries – she refused to go back to her mother's house in Arras.

Joy was on the last leg of her journey and she loved this street. As long and straight as a corridor, the lofty buildings engulfed the pavements in shadow. Great Russell Street was made up of ubiquitous pubs and laundries, drapers and tobacconists with windows advertising everything from Neapolitan ice cream to Old Holborn tobacco. When she came upon a fruiterer, its wares set out in crates on the pavement and looking as colourful as jewels, she opted for a large apple and stepped inside to present it at the till.

'Just this, please.'

'Those are display only,' the shopkeeper barked at her.

She shrugged inside her wet coat and breathed back the musty shop smell. 'I'd still like to buy one,' she said, allowing the offending fruit to be snatched away.

The man in a starched apron pulled a face, but Joy stood firm, forcing him to go behind a curtain and return with a paper bag heavy with an apple.

'Thank you.' Joy dropped the necessary coins on the counter and left the shop.

The people running the outlets in this part of town had an air of hostility that made her feel – as many Londoners did – the foreigner on foreign soil. Something she supposed she was, as this wasn't her country, and despite her impeccable English, the moment she opened her mouth, her accent made people suspicious. The indigenous population of this city evidently had trouble differentiating a German accent from her French one.

When the tall black railings encasing the British Museum came into view, she peeped through the gaps and sighed at the Greek Revival façade that never failed to impress. A miracle, surely, when so much of London had been bombed, that this remained relatively intact. The clip-clop of hoofs on the road and she turned to a horse hauling a cart. It pulled up in front of her, and a dusty-coated man jumped down and began humping coal sacks to the pavement. She went over to the horse, stroked its muzzle and was sorry for the drooping head, the matted mane. She supposed the animal never galloped in grassy meadows, free of its harness and cart. A flash of her wartime childhood at Bugbrooke Farm: sun-kissed and dirty-kneed, sauntering the lanes around Goldchurch aboard a Suffolk Punch belonging to Queenie's grandfather.

She took the apple she had been saving for lunch out of the bag, nibbled off pieces to feed the horse from the flat of her palm. Listened to the jolly jangle of metal bit.

'All gone,' she told the long-lashed eyes behind the blinkers.

'Joy!' a woman's voice called from across the street.

Queenie. Her hourglass silhouette cut from the gloom. But for her dark hair, she was the image of Betty Grable. Joy raised an excited hand and with a final goodbye left the horse behind.

'Happy birthday.' Queenie kissed Joy's cheek. She smelled of Californian Poppy.

They linked arms and set off along the pavement, passing a lone policeman who couldn't stop himself from turning to admire Queenie from beneath the peaked cap that looked too big for him.

'What were you doing with that horse?'

'Feeding him my apple.'

'You're a one, you are.' Queenie gave her an affectionate squeeze.

'I am?' She didn't understand.

'You decided where we're going?' Leading, steering, Joy kept pace with Queenie's positive strides.

'You look lovely.' She stole a glance at her friend.

'As do you,' came the quick reply.

Do I? Really? Joy didn't believe her. In her drenched coat and muddy shoes, her imitation panama with its thin blue ribbon, limp and ruined. Queenie obviously wasn't looking at her. No one looked at her. Compared to Queenie, Joy believed she was nothing. Queenie was exotic and not quite of this world. With her dark eyes and bounce of hair, she had always cast Joy in the shade.

'What about trying down here?' Queenie piloted them into a side street.

Joy waved a hand in the direction of a Lyons Corner House. She had been envisaging a breakfast of bacon and eggs and had counted the shillings and pence out ready.

'This looks nice.' Queenie, as assertive as her heels striking the cobbles, led her on towards the candy-striped awning of a tea shop. 'We'll go in here.'

They dipped inside, pushing beyond the tinkling bell and into a space confused by mirrors, packed with women of all shapes and sizes. The smell was of roasted coffee, almonds, perfume: expensive things. They chose a table by the window, to have what was available of the daylight.

'Marie Antoinette.' Queenie twisted away to read the name of the shop, while a ginger cat beside the till eyed them with suspicion. 'Didn't she come to a sticky end?'

'Her fault for telling the starving population of France to eat cake.'

'Talking of cake, what d'you fancy?' Queenie cocked her hat at a better angle in the mirror then removed her coat to reveal a bold red dress beneath.

Joy admired the way it flowed from the waist and swayed when she moved to the counter to choose tea for two with apple cake and shortbread. Embarrassed about her ready-made suit bought on credit from Oxford Street, she kept her coat fastened and picked up the menu, saw they served cream of chicory soup at lunchtimes. The remembered bittersweet tang of this, one of her father's specialities, in her mouth.

'You look miles away.' Queenie sat down opposite.

'I was wondering what happened to Papa's recipes after he died.'

'Have you asked your mother?'

'She probably burnt them.'

'Burnt them?' Queenie, appalled.

'She burnt his clothes and books.' A memory of her mother poking them down into the hot hungry mouth of the brazier her father had fashioned out of an oil drum to incinerate leaves. 'She made sure there was nothing of him left.'

'That's horrible, Joy, I'm so sorry.' Queenie reached over the tabletop and put a hand on hers.

When their rather odd breakfast arrived, Queenie lifted her hand away and the warmth of her was replaced with a strange cold feeling.

'You heard from your mother?' Queenie's eyes shone from a face that was as flawless as the inside of her porcelain cup.

Joy groaned over the clatter of crockery. 'She's threatening to visit in the summer.'

'I've some news that'll cheer you up.' Joy listened to her say the Mockin' Bird was looking for a waitress. 'You'd be perfect. I've told Uncle Fish all about you.' Queenie passed her a cup of tea. 'How about it? You're always saying you could use some extra cash.'

'I don't know.' Joy squirmed. 'What would I wear?' She was thinking of Queenie's lustrous gowns.

'I can lend you something.'

Joy was conscious of the other customers sitting close by: the clink of their china, the delicacy of their conversation.

'Don't look like that. It'll get you out of that crummy bedsit, and we'll get to spend more time together. Look, I know you said you were doing something with Amy tonight, but why don't you come to the club?'

'It's too late to let Amy down. I'll come another time.'

'You've been saying that since forever.' Queenie rolled her eyes. 'It's lovely there. I don't know what you've been imagining. Uncle Fish wouldn't let any riff-raff in.' Queenie ate a square of shortbread, dabbed crumbs from her mouth. She transferred her customary red lipstick to the damask napkin Joy thought too beautiful to even unfold.

'Don't tell me you're still feeding that pigeon?'

Queenie had noticed Joy take the last corner of cake and fold it into the paper doily. 'Yes, I am.' She ignored the look she was getting. 'I can't disappoint him; he's come to expect it now.'

'Oh, I nearly forgot.' Queenie dived for her handbag. 'I hope you like them.'

The gloves were beautiful. The leather was the colour of the purple plums her father used to grow. She put them on and tilted her hands to admire the tiny button at the wrist, the flawless stitching.

'Queenie.' She gasped. 'This is too generous.'

'Do you like them?'

'*Like them?* I love them. Thank you.'

'I'm so glad.' Queenie lifted her teacup and toasted her. 'Happy birthday, Joy.'

CHAPTER THREE

Terrence Banks didn't seem to need sleep. However late leaving the Mockin' Bird, he would make the short journey from Mayfair to Soho for the shadowy after-hours café life because he happened to love the wrong person.

'Here will do. Thank you.'

He wasn't stupid; he never took the same taxicab twice and always asked to be dropped a few streets from his intended destination. Even the most affable of cab drivers could be working for the police, and he needed to be vigilant. Handing over the necessary fare, he stepped out into the night. The piercing cold sharpened to a spike in his throat as he adjusted his homburg and buttoned his overcoat for the walk ahead. A glance at the moon. Full and rare and hanging in the night sky. It silvered the pavement and the dejected bomb-blasted metropolis as he tracked down one dilapidated street after another.

This area of the West End that would never quite reach the dizzy heights of neighbouring Mayfair or Bloomsbury certainly had its uses. With its cheek-by-jowl townhouses, taverns and gaming rooms, it served as a gathering place for refugees and the dispossessed and was, since the end of the war, becoming known for its raffish, unregulated air. But only if you knew where to look. Because the endless parades of Georgian buildings gave no hint of the seedy goings-on below the paving slabs. Up here, in daylight or gaslight, Terrence could be the decent man society believed him to be. He had always been frightened of the law, but his need to mask his proclivities was driving him further and deeper into

London's murky underworld than he ever meant to go. Terrence hadn't chosen his sexuality. He hadn't asked to be born to love men. How was it his fault he needed to mix with the con men, prostitutes and petty thieves?

Brought up a Catholic, it wasn't only the police he feared. Homosexuality, in the eyes of God, was an abomination, and if his illegal practices were discovered, his mother would never forgive him. It would knock his self-respect clean overboard – a pretence he had managed to maintain all his adult life. He knew what he and Malcolm did was risky; it was why he needed to keep their relationship secret. If they were discovered, it would mean his family, friends, colleagues at the bank, the band would shut him out in the cold – well, maybe not Queenie, but his reluctance to put her in a compromising position was why she and Malcolm still hadn't met. It was hard for others to understand how repressive the atmosphere surrounding homosexuality was. How fears of his impending disgrace and imprisonment haunted his every waking hour. Because no one ever spoke of it, it wasn't until he was into late adolescence that he realised it was a crime. He'd tried talking to his headmaster about it, but because the man couldn't bring himself to mention it, Terrence supposed he was lucky he'd managed to work out what was going on before anyone else did. Using the dictionary to formulate his feelings, the one thing he did establish was the ugly aura of criminality, degeneracy and abnormality that surrounded it, and this was why he had remained mostly solitary until he'd met Malcolm.

On his left, a gap appeared between two high buildings – blink and you'd miss it. A furtive look over his shoulder before slipping between them, down into an unlit passageway narrow enough for the shoulders of his coat to graze the wet brick sides. Accompanied by the hollow sounds of his shoes bouncing through the dark, he aimed for the farthest end and the innocuous black door. Heralded by a grimy portico and sliver of light from a rectangular panel, he squeezed inside. Was hit by a wall of voices and the penetrating heat of those who came to gamble and drink after hours.

'Welcome to Albert's Cavern…' he mouthed through the veil of cigarette smoke. 'The sleaziest dive in town.'

He shut the door behind him and swung his head around, looking for his boyfriend. Searching the dark-beamed space, he recognised, along with the faces of his nattily dressed friends, the faces of those he knew to avoid. Like that high court judge Albert had identified for him. Secreted inside a candlelit booth, his heavy arm looped around a prostitute, claiming her. Terrence considered the recent court case this judge had presided over: a young man charged and convicted of gross indecency and given a five-year prison sentence. He had followed the story in the papers, and this judge's closing statement – 'These are the most sordid and depraved crimes I have ever come across in my thirty years on the bench' – chilled him to the core, especially as the previous week this very same judge had officiated at the trial of a child killer.

How was exploiting women not a crime, but it was a crime for a man to be in a loving, consensual relationship with another man? The hypocrisy was breathtaking. Terrence turned away to pinpoint the owner of this den of immorality: the head of the wasters, buggers, hypocrites and thieves. Albert's tall and bulky figure was manning the bar as usual. A Romanian gypsy who had reputedly fled the Nazis, he was hailed as Soho's very own Oscar Wilde with his foppish ways and velvet frock coat. He was a terrific showman and, from a distance, as tempting and bejewelled as a Christmas tree. Much like his establishment in that the padded couches and armchairs looked inviting from afar but up close were greasy-skinned with pinhole burns.

At last, Terrence saw Malcolm huddled with unknown others at the bar. Cool inside his pinstriped zoot suit, his mocha-skinned face fixed in concentration. He looked like one of those film noir detectives, and the fist Terrence carried in his chest squeezed a little tighter around his heart. A reminder their love could only be a transient thing and that like some men he had known in the past, Malcolm would no doubt end up conforming to the pressures of society by finding himself a wife. Some unfortunate woman who didn't object to her husband's lukewarm advances, and in exchange for a child or two would cover for him.

When Malcolm saw him, he smiled his great white smile. Like a row of lights in the darkness above his crisp, striped shirt. Terrence was about to cross the floor to greet him when someone came in from outside and crept past. A man, small and ordinary, in a brown trilby and raincoat. His eyes fidgety behind horn-rimmed spectacles. Terrence didn't know why, but he disliked him on sight and rubbed his sleeves to rid himself of the sudden goosebumps prickling his arms. He followed him to the bar and stood alongside. Up close, the man reeked of Tube trains and the unpleasant damp of unaired clothes. And something else. Harshly astringent and belonging to his schooldays. Slippery, he couldn't bring it to mind. It was then he noticed the odd sucking movement the man did with his mouth and the way he kept looking around him as if searching for something. His fretful fingers tugged on his collar, pulled at his ear, as he exchanged words with Albert. Words Terrence couldn't hear. But seeing him single out a prostitute and push a tumbler of something towards her, it was obvious what he was there for.

A hand on his shoulder. He swivelled to receive it. Malcolm. His smile cutting a hole through the sleaze.

'Man, you jumpy, Terry.' The smile faded and the two of them kissed.

'Now then, my dears, what can I get you?' It was Albert who pushed between them.

'Scotch and a splash for me and whatever Malcolm's having, thank you.'

Albert reached to the optic. A hiss of soda. Only half-listening to Malcolm's reply, Terrence had refocused his attention on the man in the trilby and noticed he was wearing plimsolls. Odd. Who wore plimsolls with a suit, coat and hat? The man was as loathsome as he was fascinating, and Terrence was still watching him when he unexpectedly returned his interest. The look was one of self-righteous disgust as he eyed Terrence and Malcolm with obvious contempt. Ashamed to have been caught staring, Terrence turned away, but not before noticing the man knock back his drink and creep downstairs with the prostitute.

'Who was dat?' Malcolm put a protective arm around him.

'I don't know, but I didn't like the look of him.' Terrence threw his gaze to the ceiling to fling off the sense of unease the stranger gave him. It was then he identified the smell.

Jeyes Fluid.

And his sense of foreboding intensified.

CHAPTER FOUR

The house at the top end of Rillington Place was quiet and mostly dark. The lower end of the passageway, bathed in the cloudy light of the fading day, disturbed him. Disturbed him because he knew he was running out of time. All afternoon, he'd been keeping watch for her through the peephole he'd fashioned in the door of his ground-floor flat and had just about reached the point of giving up when, to his absolute delight, there she was.

Beryl Evans.

With her pretty face and tumble of hair. Appearing, as if by magic, at the foot of the stairs with her baby in her arms. Transfixed, he trained his eye behind its horn-rimmed lens on the young mother as she laid the baby in the pram and arranged its blankets, bending and stretching to check the things she needed were in the basket between its wheels. It wasn't long before he became aware of the budding erection going on in his underpants.

'One day, lass… I'll have you one day,' he muttered, wiping his wet mouth on the back of his hand.

Fixed on Beryl, he admired her slender elegance afresh and replayed the contents of their agreeable little chat earlier in the week. The way she made him feel when she touched his arm. It took his breath away. How many more signs did he need? It was as plain as day she was as attracted to him as he was to her. It was why he'd invited her to call him Reg – the name he went by with friends and family – the moment she and her husband, Timothy, had moved into the top-floor flat, and why he didn't mind in the least about her flouting his house rules by leaving the baby's pram in the hall.

'I'll be finding a way to bend you to my will before long.' He breathed his menacing intent. 'Aye, you mark my words, lass. I'll be partaking in a little something of you, one way or another.'

Then, pushing down on the handle, he opened the door and tiptoed into the darkened hall, where he stood, still as a post and cloaked in shadow, watching Beryl from his hiding place below the stairs. He could often be found here, spying on those he shared this house with, but since the arrival of Mr Evans and his alluring young wife, his surveillance routine had ratcheted up a notch.

He was about to step forward, to place a hand on Beryl's shoulder, when the scratch of a key in the lock and the front door opening stopped him dead.

'Hello, dear. Lovely evening. You off out with Geraldine?' It was his wife, and swallowing his disappointment and anger, he saw Ethel sidestep the pram to allow Beryl the space to manoeuvre her baby out into the street.

'Hello, Mrs Christie. Tim's mum's doing our tea tonight.'

'Well, you have fun.'

Sensing their conversation was coming to a close, he shuffled backwards, soundless in his canvas shoes.

'Is that you, Reg?' Ethel threw her voice along the dingy passageway. 'I weren't expecting you home. Why aren't you in work? Reg? Don't walk off.' She trotted after him, spoiling his mood with her questions. 'I asked you why you aren't in work.'

'Dr Odess signed me off sick.'

'Again? What's wrong with you now? You want to watch it; you'll be getting yourself a reputation.'

'Give over, woman. Get in here, we don't want all and sundry knowing our business.' Seizing her roughly, he manhandled her into their kitchen with its squalor, its damp-stained walls and dripping tap.

'What's that funny smell?' She sniffed the air and dumped her bag of groceries on the draining board. 'You had a woman in here?'

Refusing to answer, he closed the door behind them with a decisive snap.

'And what've you been doing with this?' His wife, keeping on with her questions. 'You know how tight we are for space. It needs to be shoved right up against the window.'

He watched in silence while she fussed with the rope chair, shifting it this way and that until she was happy it had been returned to its usual position.

'She's very pretty, don't you think?'

'Who is?' His wife turned to him, wide-eyed.

'Beryl.'

'Oh no, Reg.' She pressed a nervous hand to her mouth. 'You'd better not be getting ideas. You're to stay away from her, d'you hear?'

He gave her one of his crooked smiles.

'I mean it.' She wagged a finger. 'You stay away from that girl.'

'Or what?' he challenged, an evil gleam in his eye. 'There's nowt you can do to stop me. I do what I want, with whoever I want. And you'd do well to remember that fact, Ethel Christie.'

CHAPTER FIVE

Carrying a bag of groceries and wearing an outfit copied from *Vogue*, Queenie was on her way home from her dance class. She knew all the shortcuts, and swinging along on her heels, down the lanes that led off Wimbledon Broadway, she reached Pelham Road in no time. A movement caught in the tail of her vision made her look back to a row of terrace houses that dropped away to a valley of rubble. These were the carcasses of homes, what was left after the Blitz. The sight of timbers poking through the bricks like broken ribs was as distressing as the evidence of wallpaper and fireplaces: the relics of people's lives. There were signs of workmen and machines today. The growl of an engine and a sudden crash as a wall was flattened. Now they had made a start, it wouldn't be long before new houses went up; she'd seen it happening in other parts of the borough. It meant that South Wimbledon was becoming little more than a route between one place and another. The ancient outpost of Mitcham eaten away by the slow expansion of London that, creeping ever nearer, was eroding the lavender fields of her childhood.

A weak April sun glinted on the pavement. Up ahead was another leftover from childhood: the curve of her old school railings and a crumple in the asphalt where the walls used to be. Her brother, Harry, had stayed on at school until he'd left to join the navy. Queenie, pulled out at thirteen to go to her grandparents' farm, never went back. Her father saw little point in educating girls. Girls would get married and another man would benefit from their education. It didn't matter that Queenie had won a place at the grammar school; they couldn't afford the uniform, never mind the textbooks.

The wind gathered along this route, trapped by the tunnels of grey-brick houses that competed for sunshine and air. In a rush of activity, the Chapman twins raced by showing teeth too white to be real. Lugging sticks the lengths of men, they dragged them over the slats of Mrs Clark's fence. Naughty boys – she should tell them to stop, but she wouldn't. Mrs Clark was no friend of hers.

She took out her keys ready. Mrs Wilson, opposite, was down on her hands and knees, scrubbing the front step of her house with a brush and a galvanised bucket. She lifted her gaze as Queenie strode past.

'Good day to you.' Mrs Wilson spoke in an overly controlled way and eyed her with suspicion.

Always the object of curiosity, Queenie – called the Duchess and accused of believing herself special by those who gathered to gossip, but never with her – supposed she invited it with her fabulous figure and fashionable clothes. She turned the corner into Balfour Road and saw the usual knot of women up ahead. It was obvious they were talking about her. Their resentment swelled and flapped like the washing on their clothes lines. If she were a horse – a memory of the childhood game she'd played with Joy – she would clatter her hooves against the ground to scare them away. But Queenie wasn't a horse. Any more than she was a child. So, she did all she could to brace herself for what was to come.

'Good morning, ladies. Lovely day.'

Smiling into the stream of insults this triggered, she swerved between the gap in the privet and up to her green front door. Pleased to see the rosebush planted in memory of her mother was covered in buds that would soon flourish into milky-white flowers. Weaving through the shadows and dustbins kept down the side of the house, an unexpected image of Tommy came to her as she slipped the bolt on the garden gate. Kissing her. His hands exploring her body as she resisted, then yielded. Then resisted again.

'Be a sport, Queenie.' His breath on her ear. 'Let me up to your room.'

A shaft of sunlight broke through the cloud to illuminate the green of springtime leaves and she looked up in time to see a blue tit, a beakful of dry grasses, dip between a gap in the eaves.

She exchanged the remembered face of her first love for one of her eighteen-year-old self, home from Goldchurch after the war with no idea what to do with her life. Until her ailing mother heard her singing along with the wireless. 'Queenie, love. With your looks and talent, you could go anywhere.' And with the seed firmly planted, it began to sprout. Spikes of green, like shards of snowdrops after a hard winter, pushed through the wreckage left behind after the war. It was her mother, alerted to an advert in the *Evening Standard*, who encouraged her to take singing and dancing lessons with Dulcie Fricker. A woman who saw there was money to be made by representing her and so pushed her in front of Uncle Fish.

Inside the kitchen, she dumped the groceries on the draining board and hung up her dance shoes beside the gas masks no one had bothered to put away. She looked over at the framed black-and-white photograph of Harry dressed in his naval uniform and searched his smile for any sign he knew what was marching towards him on life's horizon. Was thankful to find nothing. The photograph was taken three months before his battlecruiser, HMS *Repulse*, was bombed.

She put the ration books away in the Oxo tin and listened to her father moving around in the room above. The sound of his cough forking through the floorboards. Her fear his emphysema was worsening reared its head again, but she refused to dwell on it. She'd lost too many family members; her father was all she had left.

The scuff of his slippers on the hall rug and her father was there. 'Ta for fetching this,' he wheezed, taking his paper from the bag.

'They're finally getting around to clearing that bomb site at the top of Pelham Road.'

''Bout time.' He coughed again. 'Ruddy eyesore.'

'I hope they don't go finding poor Violet Tanner.' A shiver as she unwrapped a block of margarine. Added it to what remained of last week's butter – there weren't enough points to have butter again this week.

When the kettle came to the boil, she made them both a cup of tea. Her father checked the shallow boxes of seedlings on the windowsill, then sat down at the table and shook out his paper. Decently muscled for a man his age, with the sleeves of his shirt rolled back to the elbows, she could tell he'd been working in the garden. She'd spotted the tin bucket and the crop of new potatoes by the door.

'We could have these for tea. Go nice with spuds.' He pushed a bowl containing three brown hens' eggs towards her. 'The girls are laying well.'

The clunk of potatoes as she tipped them into the sink. The crash of saucepan lids. She turned on the tap and snapped on her orange Marigolds. Unlike her mother, Queenie looked after her hands and was glad to find rubber gloves in the shops last year. She groped the muddy water, the bank of grit that had formed at the bottom of the Belfast sink, and stared out at the garden. At her father's vegetable beds that, like the tittle-tattling tongues of neighbours, were just as industrious.

'You know I've been offered a part in *South Pacific*, on Broadway?' Potatoes scrubbed, she set them to boil.

'Wimbledon Broadway?' He coughed his cough. A sound that had featured throughout her childhood.

'No, *Broadway*. New York.'

'America?' Her father licked a finger and turned the pages of his newspaper. 'You want to be settling down.'

Thoughts of London's old, cold, bombed-out streets butted up against the pictures she'd seen of New York with its glamour and modernity. Her mother would have been right behind her if she was here, but she wasn't. Dying five months after the end of the war with something that could probably have been treated had the NHS been around.

'They're building skyscrapers.' She lifted the saucepan lid, steam hot on her hand as she tested the potatoes with the tip of a knife. 'There's no rationing, people have got money.' She put one in her mouth. *Hot, hot...* Her teeth snapping through its skin.

'If that's what you want.' He dropped his head; he'd found the sports pages.

She set the frying pan on the flames and, with the smell of sizzling margarine in her nostrils, cracked one egg, then another, against the lip of the pan. Stood back to watch the whites harden. Fat stung her wrists and the whiff of burning margarine fired off a memory of when the factory down the road was hit, splattering the nation's supply of Stork against the blackened pan of the night sky. Thought about the camaraderie that came with the blackout. When sirens squealed like slaughtered pigs and people scrabbled to the Tube and lay side by side like oiled sardines.

It had been on such a night Queenie hooked up with a group of older boys who taught her to play rummy and poker for money; that because she didn't have money, they required a flash of her knickers as a forfeit. Not that it was much of a forfeit; she loved the attention until her father put his foot down and sent her to stay with his in-laws. Claiming London wasn't safe. But neither was the Essex coast. What about that time a German plane crash-landed in her grandad's fields? Not that the excitement compensated for being ripped away from Tommy, whose skin smelled of toffee apples on Bonfire Night. It nearly broke her heart. In the same way it nearly broke her when she came back five years later to discover he'd married that prissy Flora Miller from around the corner.

'I've something to tell you.' Her father burst in on her deliberations. 'I've met a woman.'

'*A woman?*' Queenie dropped the spatula with a clatter. 'W-when did that happen?' She gawped at the back of his head.

'We just got talking. She's an usherette down the Odeon.'

'That's nice for you, Dad.'

'And the thing is, we're to get married in the autumn. We've plans to move to the country. Norma—'

'*Norma.*' Queenie repeated the name of her soon-to-be step-mother. 'Married? Bloody hell, Dad, isn't that a bit sudden?' Tears stung her eyes.

'Her family own a smallholding in Norfolk. It'll be better for my chest.' He coughed again on cue.

Wiping away a tear she didn't let him see, she lifted out the eggs and slid them sunny-side down on a plate with a spoonful of potatoes. Pushed it in front of him.

'I can't take these blessed pea-soupers no more.' He coughed into his balled-up fist. 'You're a good girl, Queenie. I knew you'd understand. I've paid the rent on this place till February next year, so there's no need to worry.'

'Will they let me take over the tenancy?'

'I should think so.'

'Really? An unmarried woman, living alone?' Queenie knew things were starting to improve for women, but not as quickly as she might need them to.

'You're on good money at the club and there's your little tailoring sideline. Anyway, didn't you say you were off to America?'

She stared at him while he talked about Norma. About how he would invite her over so the two of them could meet. She was being selfish, she told herself as the world turned a bruised yellow with the setting sun. He was still a relatively young man, he deserved a second chance; if clean country air helped his health, who was she to stand in his way? Her father placed his dirty crockery on the drainer for Queenie to wash and she put an arm around him, kissed his stubbly cheek. She felt him change when she did this. Felt him stiffen and pull away.

She left him and the dirty plates; they could wait. Went up to the landing and looked out of the window that gave on to a tumble of roofs. She had nothing to say to her father. If she did start talking, she would only end up saying the wrong thing. A pigeon swooped down through its shadow and landed on the window ledge. It pecked at its reflection, the sound of its beak against the glass. She listened to it until she could no longer stand it, then clapped it away.

CHAPTER SIX

His mother's house, four streets away from Camden Town Tube, was not like other houses. The front garden was more or less wild, and there were no pretty borders to turn the head of the passer-by.

'Sorry, mister.' A boy and girl with chapped cheeks bumped against him as they careered past.

Terrence smiled after them. It wasn't so long ago that he'd played in this street, bouncing along the pavement with hoops and balls. He was the only one of his siblings still living in London. His younger brother, Colin, like his five older sisters, had moved to Halifax, where their parents originated from, leaving him the responsibility of their mother. He didn't begrudge them; they were busy with their own families and visited when they could.

Terrence had his own latchkey. Necessary because his mother refused to answer the door. Whenever someone came to the house, she would hide on the stairs and hiss, 'You get it.' He had no idea what she did when he wasn't here.

Opening up, he peeked into the living room with its hulking furniture and heard the voice on the wireless, but not what it said. The house was filled with the warm smells of baking. And something else. Something that thrust him back to childhood Sundays when his father was alive.

'Mum, are you there?'

Nothing. But she had to be home; she never went anywhere. Terrence shook off his coat and pegged it up in the way he would when home from school. A sideways look at his mother's plaster *Madonna and Child* figurine nailed to the wall. The image had dominated him since he could crawl, and it wasn't one he liked. Turning from it, he found his mother standing before him, as solid as one of her armchairs and tied into an apron on which she had embroidered a pink flower. Bigger than anything in nature, its luxuriant petals spread out over her comfortable middle.

'Happy birthday, Mum.' Terrence bent to give her the obligatory kiss she tilted her head for. His lips bumping against her powdered cheek. 'Here you go.' He handed her a box of sugared jellies.

'My favourites. You are a naughty boy.' She beamed up at him. 'Wherever did you find them?'

Terrence tapped the side of his nose. 'I've got my sources.' *Thanks, Albert – the go-to man who can get you anything.*

'Clever boy. Not that I want you wasting your money on me…' Her objection fizzled out. 'I've made a pie. And there's roast chicken for later.'

'Lovely.' That's what the smell was. Terrence kept to himself the news he wouldn't be staying.

'I'll go and put the kettle on.' Her rings flashing. 'Won't be a minute.'

The front room faced east and the sun had passed over the house long ago. Left alone, he listened to his mother bumping about in her kitchen, shooing the cat from under her feet. He looked around the space that had remained unchanged since childhood. His father's cello gathering dust against the wall. A permanent fixture that, like his mother, didn't go anywhere either. He sidled over to place a hand on its gloriously curved shape that was just like Queenie's figure. The comparison might have been evoked, he thought, by Man Ray's iconic 'Le Violon d'Ingres' with the painted-on f-holes on the buxom woman's back. He moved away from the cello and lifted the lid on the upright piano he had learnt to play. Its sound was impaired and the keys were chipped like a rat had gnawed the ivory. He closed the lid again.

He circled the room, dragging his fingers over the spines of paperbacks and a rubber plant with dusty leaves. The cabinet heaving with china ornaments bought on holidays to Dorset and presents from his sisters. A jam pot of wax flowers faded to the colour of onion skins. He sat down in the armchair, its sides shredded by cat claws, and tilted his head to the cornice, where a damp patch had stained the ceiling brown. Mr Tiddles jumped into his lap and began tenderising his thighs, purring like a pigeon.

'Hello, old boy. Nice to see you.'

Terrence stroked the cat with a steady determination and watched grey hairs fall on his trousers, float to the floor. The back door slammed. He imagined his mother going outside in her slippers to scrape the breadboard for the birds. The families of finches and tits she had tamed in from the wild to feed at the tables his father had made before suffering a fatal stroke.

His mother appeared, pushing her little brass trolley into the room, its wheels protesting against the bumps in the rugs. Mr Tiddles jumped down.

'Don't sit there, Terry.' Clattering noises as she laid out cups and saucers. 'That's Dad's chair.'

He shifted to the couch. 'You should give Dad's cello away.' He said this because he couldn't say how ridiculous she was about his father's chair – the man had been dead for nearly twenty years.

'I'm not ready to part with it yet, lad.' Another flash of her rings as she raised a hand to the headful of curlers under her headscarf.

A rather self-conscious gesture. Not that Terrence was looking at her hair that, despite his mum being in her seventies, was still as sandy-brown as his. He was more interested in her choice of lurid blue eyeshadow, her drawn-on eyebrows, the faint moustache.

'How's about a slice of pie?' She spoke as if to a stranger. 'Home-made pie's such a treat.'

There was nothing of the woman Terrence had known as a child, and he worried how much longer she could manage to live here on her own. He watched as she cut a wedge of the golden-topped pie and slid it onto a plate.

'Cream?'

There wasn't time to answer, it was already being poured, thick and yellow, from a jug off the trolley. He didn't ask where she had it from. The pie crust had been patterned with pastry leaves and he picked out a chunk of apple, ate it with his fingers. It was sweet and sharp all at once. He was hungrier than he realised.

'Aren't you having any?' The inside of the crust was white and gluey. Thinned at the top so the red of the blackcurrant jam showed through. He spooned up a pond of cream. Sugar gritting his tongue.

'I cooked it for you. I only ever cook for you.'

He swallowed his mouthful and watched his mother shelling peas. Her hands, mapped with rope-like veins, were as busy as her garden birds.

'Where did you get those?' Terrence couldn't remember the last time he'd seen peas, apart from in a tin.

'Ivy Sutton. A glut, she said, so I took them. Waste not, want not.'

He liked watching her. Her automatic movements were comforting. The transference of pea pod from newspaper to her chipped enamel colander. The room filled with their raw, green smell.

'You're quiet today, our Terry. Is anything the matter?'

'I can't stay for dinner.' He scrunched his face in anticipation of her disappointment. 'I'm sorry, Mum, but I'm due at the club in an hour.'

'Y-you and that c-club,' she started, sputtering, an engine warming up. 'What d'you need to work there for? You've your job at the bank. When are you going to settle down and find yourself a wife? It's not natural, living like you do, the hours you keep... You need someone to look after you.'

'I look after myself.'

'Aye, you've your army training to thank for that. Mind you, I still say you were too young. Signing up at sixteen, then going off to war... if your dad had still been with us.'

'Don't start that again.' He lifted a hand and looked at his nails.

'I'm not starting nowt. I'm only saying. You'll be twenty-seven, next birthday; don't you want to find a nice girl?'

'A nice girl? I'm not sure I know any. Apart from Queenie.'

'Queenie?' His mother's frowned response. 'I don't like her sort. She's not wife material… Whatever would Dad say? He wouldn't have liked her.'

I think you'll find he would, and for all the reasons you don't.

'Oh, no, Terry, you haven't gone and set your cap at her?'

Pie finished, he put down his plate. Glanced over at the *Madonna and Child* in the hall. He wished he could tell her what he was, own up to what he suspected she knew but couldn't admit to. But he wouldn't, it was too risky; if push came to shove, she might choose her God over him.

Neither spoke. The only sounds were the ticking clock on the mantelpiece. The hum of the wireless. The sipping of tea. He turned his head away, reluctant to let her see his tears.

The band picked up the pace. Changing to another song. Queenie, with her usual command, swayed to the rhythm and opened her throat to the mic. Her dress was one with the back scooped out, showing an opaque window of her skin. Terrence adored her. Shimmering and silvery as moonlight, she was like no one else. But not as a lover. Her charms in that department were wasted on him. It was why the two of them could speak plainly; theirs was a relationship unmuddied by hormones and desire. His hands flowed over the piano keys like sea over sand while he peered beyond the dazzling stage lights, seeking the softer, rosy tint of the Chinese lanterns strung along the club's far wall like fake moons.

When the band broke off at half-time, Terrence, saying he needed to sort his music, asked Queenie to fetch him a Scotch and soda. Buster was already slouched on a bar stool; he'd been hitting the sauce before they'd even opened and was out of rhythm again.

He was chatting up that new waitress friend of Queenie's. Joy, he thought she said her name was. Sweet little thing and clever, the way she slipped between French and English and Italian and talked books. He couldn't do that with Queenie; Terrence had never known her to finish a book. But however clever Joy was, she was having trouble telling Buster to keep his paws to himself. Couldn't the twerp see he didn't stand a chance? Evidently not. It must be dreadful to be a woman sometimes, to have to fend off types like Buster. He was about to rescue Joy when she ducked away with a tray of drinks to a nearby table. Terrence couldn't imagine anyone being interested in Buster romantically. Squat and graceless, with his thinning gingery hair. He could almost feel sorry for him. Almost.

Returning to his sheet music, marking in pencil about phrasing and tempo, little chimes of laughter had him looking over at Major Charles Gilchrist, who had pulled up a bar stool beside Queenie. The silver-topped cane he was sometimes seen with was propped against him, and when he removed his peaked cap, the pendant lighting gleamed off his blue-black hair. What a contrast to Buster, this elegant man was the quintessential English gent and, going by the squeals of gaiety, Queenie was obviously flirting – and who could blame her? Charles Gilchrist, a decorated officer, was movie-star quality.

Realising he wasn't going to get his drink any time soon, Terrence descended the stairs to the dressing room and flopped into the velvety embrace of the chaise longue. He shoved a cigarette from Queenie's packet of Sobranies into his mouth and, while he smoked, his gaze wandered the dusty surfaces, the red curtain Queenie pulled across when she wanted privacy.

'There you are.' The door burst open and Queenie handed him a tumbler. 'I've been looking everywhere.'

He thanked her and watched as she positioned herself in front of the mirror, kicked off her green suede slingbacks.

'The two of you have met?' Queenie swung an arm to the auburn-haired girl hovering on the threshold.

He winked to put her at ease and encouraged her inside. 'Joy and I are quite well acquainted, thank you.'

'*Acquainted*... I told you he was posh.' Queenie set about dabbing Californian Poppy on her cleavage, under her hair.

Posh wasn't something Terrence considered himself to be; he was as working class as she was. Cigarette finished, he stubbed it out and settled back with his drink to listen to their chatter.

Queenie wriggled up to make room for Joy and talked to her reflection. 'Have a try of my lipstick. Not like that, silly... let me do it for you. Us girls have to make the most of ourselves.'

Queenie shook out one of her white cigarettes and lit up. 'Hey! You been smoking my fags, Terry? You're naughty, you know they cost a fortune.'

'You cadge enough of mine.' Terrence caught the look of amusement on Joy's face and winked at her again.

'They're for ladies. Keep your mitts off.'

By God, Queenie was clever. His thoughts as he watched her smoking as if in a film. Even those elegant cigarettes were props. The girl was one big act, and Terrence was grateful he wasn't like other men and under her spell. He'd noticed Joy was a little under Queenie's spell, however, and would have struggled to understand how these two could ever be friends had he not been told of their shared wartime childhood.

Joy had looked lost to start with tonight, but Queenie was showing her the ropes, and provided she kept out of Buster's way, Terrence supposed she was safe enough. But serving drinks to these sophisticated types, with their status and money, people who were nothing like her? He wasn't sure it suited Joy any more than the dress Queenie had lent her. And yet, there must be more to the girl than he gave her credit for. What was she, barely twenty? Coming to London from France on her own, no family. That took guts.

'Try a little rouge. Uncle Fish likes us to be glamorous and the punters tip better if you look nice,' Queenie started up again. 'At least you're wearing that hair clip I gave you. You need a bit of sparkle.'

'Who got you the roses, darling?' Terrence, sipping his Scotch, thought the diamante trinket pinned to Joy's hair was delightful.

Queenie pushed her nose to the petals. 'Card just says, "An admirer".'

'And you've hundreds of those.'

'She certainly has,' Joy agreed, eyes downcast.

'What's wrong with you?' Queenie was on to her.

'It's that Lawrence man. He's pestering me to go out for dinner.'

'Cor, I wish he'd ask me. The old duffer's loaded. Let him spoil you, if that's what he wants. What d'you say, Terry?'

'I think it's up to Joy.' He bent over his knees to re-lace his toffee-coloured Oxfords.

'But supposing he wants more?' Joy pulled a face.

'Saving yourself for Mr Right?' Queenie teased her.

'I'm not going to jump into bed with any old person. I'm not like you.'

'What?' Aghast. 'I don't sleep with them. This...' Queenie looked down at herself. 'Out of bounds, Joy. I just let them spoil me. Meals out, the odd knick-knack.' A flash of her bejewelled fingers. 'You've got to know how to play them. That way you can get what you want without giving anything of yourself.'

'You make it sound like a business.'

Terrence, listening, had to agree.

'Well, it is. Marriage is the same. Not that I want any part of it. Can you see me with a string of nippers... tied to the sink for the rest of my life?' Queenie yawned and stretched, abandoning herself to the yawn with a judder. 'This is a new age for us, Joy. Thanks to those wild women suffragettes, we've got choices. We don't have to be like our mothers. You wait around for Prince Charming if you want but with so many men lost in the war…' She tapered off, letting them fill in the gaps. 'And we all have to eat. So, if dear old Lawrence wants to take you for a blowout—'

'I'm not going.'

Queenie looped an arm about Joy's shoulders; so much of the way they were reminded Terrence of the sisters he rarely saw. 'You're too sweet for your own good. You'll drive them all crazy.'

'But I don't want to drive anyone crazy.'

'You know Buster's mad for you?'

'I don't like him. He scares me.' Joy looked desperate. 'I didn't do anything to encourage him. I was only being kind.'

'I know that; you're kind to everyone.' Queenie took back her arm and powdered her nose. 'Don't worry about Buster. Whatever fixation he's got on you, he'll get over it.'

CHAPTER SEVEN

There she was again. Waving goodbye to her freckly friend through the weekend crowd. He'd seen her earlier but had lost her. It was miraculous. Heaven-sent. He had to admit, he really wanted this one; she was his absolute ideal. The only disappointment was that she'd hidden her willowy figure under a shapeless green coat and her beautiful auburn hair under that cut-price panama.

Chancing upon her a few weeks ago, he had taken to following her whenever the opportunity arose. It meant he was coming to know something of her haunts and habits. Although, the Lyons Corner House at the top end of Kensington High Street had been a new one. Walking past earlier with his dog, Judy, keen to get to the park, he saw the girl had met up with a plain little friend for an unbuttered scone and a cup of hot milk. He added these little details to the growing list of things he was gleaning about her. He had a superb mind for detail and loved being privy to the minutiae of people's lives; he felt it gave him power over them. His love of detail was why he'd volunteered as a full-time special constable with the Met in 1939 – well, this and the uniform he still liked to parade around in. For a man who had often been in prison, it was an astonishing piece of impudence; not that he saw the irony – had he done so he would be a different person. But in the same way he was able to delude himself about his own integrity, he was, by some uncanny stroke of luck, able to delude others also.

Something else he'd gleaned about this young woman was that she never took the Tube, and only caught a bus if it rained; that the rest of the time she liked to walk, and at a brisk pace. It was one of the first things that attracted him to her. Unlike his wife, Ethel, who was a slouch by comparison and someone he needed to jab in the ribs to get her to pick her feet up, this girl walked on air.

'Come on, Judy.' He tugged the lead and pulled the dog away from a lamp post she was sniffing. 'I can't be losing her again.'

Walking like this reminded him of Sunday afternoons and the ten-mile hikes his father would take him and his sisters on. Occasions when he was instructed to hold his shoulders back and swing his arms and walk like a guardsman. It wasn't a happy memory. His father had been what he termed a manly man who had a violent temper. He would often thrash him for trivial offences like stealing a tomato from a plate or rocking on a park bench with his sister, Dolly.

Hurrying along behind with his dog through the assault of car horns and burn of exhaust, he saw the girl take the next right into Queen's Gate, where the sonorous throb of a cello found them through the crowd. Drawn by its plaintive, almost human sound, he watched as she looked up to where a first-floor window had been thrown open to allow music to spill onto the street. To the bowing arm behind chiffon curtains. Bach. He identified the melody and, humming along, watched the girl close her eyes to it and sway a little. What a sensitive soul she was, the realisation stirring something dark inside him.

Then someone barged past her. Rudely bumping her off the pavement. With her hat tipped forwards into her eyes, the girl almost lost her footing.

'Out of the way... out of the way.' A sharp voice, the accent not unlike the girl's. Obviously stunned by the discourtesy, she stood mouth agape, waiting for the woman – chic, with a blonde chignon, towing two fair-haired boys – to turn the corner before threading her way along Kensington Gore.

It had been raining, and a bright spangle of light flooded the city and hung on everything. Voices rang out in the fresh air that smelled of the earth. He watched the girl moving ahead of him, avoiding puddles and pedestrians and, with the Royal Albert Hall at her back, she slipped between a gateway in the railings and into Hyde Park, where she opted for a bench, sat down and pulled a book from her bag.

Continuing to observe her through the railings, his dog sniffing around his ankles, he fondled the silk stocking filched from Beryl Evans' washing line that he kept in his pocket. His thoughts becoming black and deadly and coated in the heavy dark loam of his back garden where the rotting bodies of Ruth Fuerst and Muriel Eady lay buried. He smiled. Killing them had been easier than imagined, and the fact he'd got clean away with it gave him the confidence to think he could do it again. His method of rendering them unconscious with the gas he'd persuaded them to inhale – he'd expected them to struggle when he'd positioned the mask over their faces and pressed it down. But to his wonderment and awe, neither Ruth nor Muriel had moved, such was their trust in him.

He wondered when he should try to gain the trust of this one. And with a thought occurring, he pushed his glasses up his nose and strolled into the park, his face growing hot with excitement.

CHAPTER EIGHT

Joy arrived at the bench where she'd arranged to meet Queenie and sat down to monitor the steady progress of dog walkers and families pushing prams along the network of paths. In a break in the rain, the park gleamed under the pale May sky. A couple ambled past, deep in conversation as they folded away their umbrellas. Their sense of togetherness heightened her feelings of estrangement and her mind swam back to her lonely bedsit. To the weekend stretching ahead that, apart from her breakfast out with Amy and the few hours with Queenie this afternoon, meant a formless time with nowhere to go.

Another sudden shower and umbrellas bounced open. But over before it began, the umbrellas were put away again. She checked her wristwatch, saw there was time to kill and pulled her copy of Primo Levi's *Se questo è un uomo* from her bag. Found where she'd read to with her bookmark and, despite the horrific nature of the events described, lost herself in the calm sobriety of Levi's prose.

The bench shifted. Jerking her out of the brutal world of barbed wire and hunger. A bespectacled man in a raincoat and brown trilby had joined her.

''Ow do, lass.' He doffed his hat and gave her an unwanted glimpse of the bald domed head beneath.

His voice was little more than a pious whisper and reminded her of the priest at her mother's old church. Not that she trusted it. The malevolence held in the narrow skull made her suck back her breath in alarm.

'Lovely morning to be out and about.'

She nodded without smiling and returned to her book. Shrinking beneath her hat and turning the pages, she didn't want to engage in conversation. But reading was impossible; the sentences careered into one another and she couldn't take anything in. The man had an unsettling effect. Sneaking a downward look at his feet, to check he was still there, she sensed his veined eyes wander the length of her. Her coat had fallen open beyond the last button. Exposing her knees where her skirt had risen up. She gathered it together and gripped it in her fist so he couldn't see her legs. It was odd: despite his gentlemanly conduct and neat appearance, there was something sleazy about him. Something of the murky underbelly of London held in the unlit alleyways and seedy bars she knew to avoid. The canvas shoes were a curious choice for a damp day in the park. She would say they were tennis shoes, except they were black. Creepy somehow, the rubber soles were why she hadn't heard his approach. And what was that thing he was playing with? Coiling it over his hands like a string of rosary beads. It looked suspiciously like a woman's stocking.

The stranger's hands, working as a source of fluidity on the rim of her vision, delivered an unwanted memory of the maiden aunts who'd towered over her as a child. As inaccessible and durable as lighthouses, these women were nervous with their virginity and their only enjoyment was the wagging disapproval of their ringless fingers – when the fingers weren't worrying the rosary beads that hung in the ravines of their long black skirts.

A wire-haired terrier bounded over and snuffled around Joy's feet.

'Ah, *mon chérie*.' She bent forward over her knees to pet it. Forgetting, for a moment, the man sitting beside her. Joy loved all animals and stroked the topknot between the dog's ears, melting into its button brown eyes.

'Judy, come. Come 'ere. Sorry if she's a nuisance to you, lass.'

The man tapped his thigh and summoned his dog. He was English, but he didn't have an accent she associated with London – it was more melodic. She wondered if the stocking was some kind of crude leash, but no, he stowed it away in a pocket and pulled out a leather strap that he clipped to the collar.

'Ah, well. Best be off. Good day to you, lass. Mind how you go.'

A doff of the hat and the man and dog were gone. But not the unpleasant feeling. A feeling that lingered along with his peculiar, almost disinfectanty smell.

'Dear me, whatever's the matter with you? You're white as a sheet.'

It was Queenie. Glamorous under the trembling green light pushing through the canopy of leaves.

'There was this man… he was odd.' Joy flapped a hand at the space beside her. 'He was sitting right there.'

'Did he say something to upset you?' Queenie twisted to look for the offending stranger.

'No, nothing like that.' She stood up to kiss Queenie's cheek. 'He was polite, actually… he just gave me a horrible feeling.'

'You and your feelings.' Queenie sighed. 'It's those books you read. They've given you an imagination. What are you reading about now? It's not even written in English.' She pointed at the paperback Joy was still holding.

'It's Italian. A memoir by a man who survived Auschwitz.'

'Dreary, isn't it? Not surprised you're feeling horrible.'

'I don't agree.' Joy tucked the Primo Levi away in her bag. 'I'd say it was necessary reading.'

'Come on, let's go; you won't come to any harm with me.'

'How was your lesson with Mrs Fricker?' She had clocked Queenie's dance shoes in their drawstring bag.

'Good, thanks. Oh, I am glad to see you're wearing my gloves.'

'I love them.' Joy grinned and shared nothing of her mother's silly superstition that giving gloves as a present was unlucky.

Linking arms, they fell into step. Queenie, done up to the nines in heels and fur collar, her hair styled beneath a perky red hat; Joy, in her old school coat and panama. The slow slop of the Serpentine when it found the concrete bank had them stopping to watch the bob of moorhens and swans, the geese clustering the path.

'When do rehearsals start? It's so exciting.' Joy, pleased with herself for remembering to ask. 'When do you go?'

'To New York?'

'Well, yes.' As they walked, Joy looked down at her feet inside their clumpy shoes. She didn't mean to be despondent, but when was life going to dish up something for her to look forward to? It was always Queenie riding the crest of a wave.

'January. It hasn't sunk in yet.'

'I don't know why, with a talent like yours.'

'You're a love.' Queenie, gripping her tight, swung them both along. 'Now, where should we try first?'

'First?'

'To get ideas for outfits.'

'For your father's wedding. I nearly forgot. I don't know, you're the one who's good with clothes.'

'I bought some fabulous crêpe de Chine from the market. I'll make you something, too, if you like? I've some shot silk going spare. Red.' A sharp glance at Joy. 'Maybe not. But I've some taffeta in a soft grey, that would be perfect. Just think.' Queenie giggled, still holding Joy's arm. 'The two of us there together, we'll knock this Norma right off her perch.'

'I'm not sure that's a good idea. She is the bride, Queenie.'

'Serves her right.'

'You are naughty. You haven't even met her and you've decided you don't like her.'

'I know, but if she thinks she can replace my mother...' Queenie ran out of steam.

'I'm sure she's not thinking that. Give her a chance if she's good for your dad.'

'I'm worried about what'll happen to me. I don't know if I can keep the house going on my own.'

'But you'll be off to America?'

A beggar reached out to them like a child. The sight of his pleading eyes grasped Joy's core and uncurled her spinal cord. Too close, she sniffed the sourness of him and saw what looked like the tattered remains of his army coat. She always felt rotten when she was safe and others were in danger. Sometimes she would go without lunch and put the money in the poor box. Not that she shared this with Queenie, but she would give away the clothes on her back if she thought it would make a difference.

'Anything you can spare, miss.' He shook his tin cup at their feet.

Joy hunted his face for the human beneath the dirt.

'Anything... anything you can spare.'

She reached for her purse.

'Are you mad?' Queenie smacked her hand away. 'Don't give them money, it only encourages them. He'll be moved along in a minute. These people, they're nothing but scroungers. Look, those two will sort him out.' She pointed to a pair of policemen in black capes parading the opposite side.

'But I want to give him something.' Joy ignored her and wriggled the last two farthings from her purse. Dropped them into his cup. 'What was the war for if it wasn't to make us all one?' She gave him her best smile. This man had fought for them, kept them safe from Hitler. She wanted to remind Queenie but knew it wouldn't change her mind.

'Thank you, sweet lady.' The beggar gave Joy the hard, flat blue of his eye: a startling gem shining amid the grime.

The young friends were unaware of the man who had followed them through the park. With his trilby pulled down over his eyebrows, he moved stealthily through the trees; his white terrier, tail aloft, pulling him along like a sail. He was careful and kept to the shadows; it would be silly to alert them to him if he didn't need to. He worried it might not have been his wisest move to join the girl on the bench but hadn't been able to resist seeing her sitting alone like that. But he had his dog with him; Judy was useful when he came scouting around in the daylight. Walking dogs in parks was what members of civilised society did.

When he witnessed the girl's tenderness towards the beggar – someone he would have kicked sideways into the gutter – it boosted his confidence that he would one day have his way with this delicate little flower. Someone in possession of such sensitivities would be easy to manipulate and bend to his will, unlike her painted friend. A raven-haired beauty she may be, she looked too much of a handful and more than capable of looking after herself. No good setting his cap at her, unless she came to him, of course… then he might have a chance.

'Would you look at that. It's Charles Gilchrist.' The down-and-out forgotten, Queenie pointed to a man in a black overcoat and fedora, leaning on a cane. 'He's a member of the Mockin'. He was there the other night; didn't you see him?'

Joy shook her head.

'*Really?* Oh, you do live in a dreamworld. You want to open your eyes.' Queenie swished her head. 'He'd be a difficult one to miss. Nice bit of homework. I call him Captain Blood.'

Joy pulled a face, not understanding.

'Errol Flynn? He's the ringer of him.' Queenie laughed. Too loud for Joy, who was fearful Charles would be alerted to them. Although, she suspected this was precisely what Queenie wanted. 'I wouldn't kick him out of bed.'

'Oh, Queenie.' Joy shrank under her hat, wanting to make herself invisible for the second time that morning.

'Don't "oh, Queenie" me… you think he's as lovely as I do. I'll call him over.'

About to raise her hand, Joy stopped her. 'Don't. He's waiting for someone; he keeps checking his pocket watch.'

'He noticed you at the club. He was asking me about you.'

'Why would he do that?'

'Because he likes you, silly.'

'I'm not sure.'

'Are you crazy?'

'He's married, look...' Joy saw the same stylish blonde woman who'd knocked her off the pavement earlier sashay up to him and plant a kiss on his cheek.

'So he is, the sly fox. And he's got kiddies,' Queenie muttered as they strolled past. 'You dark horse, Charlie boy. His wife looks a bit old for him, no wonder he's got his eye on you, dearie.' She squeezed Joy's arm to reinforce the point. 'You've no idea how pretty you are. It's part of your charm. I told you Buster's mad for you, didn't I?'

'Yes, you said.' Joy sighed. She wished Queenie would stop going on about it. She didn't like Buster; he frightened her with his mad-eyed stare.

'You've made such a hit at the club. Don't worry about Captain Blood. We'll fix you up with someone nice soon.' Queenie twisted away for one last look at Charles who, cane abandoned, was scampering through the trees with the children. 'God, he really is the ringer of Errol Flynn.'

'Can we please stop talking about him?' Joy, her voice small. As well as thinking about the beggar, she still hadn't shaken off the bad feeling the man in the trilby had left her with – a man she was convinced had been shadowing them through the park.

CHAPTER NINE

'Ah, there you are. Good of you to be on time. Come in, lass, come in. Mind you don't trip over rug.'

'Dear me!' The young woman slapped a hand to her nose. 'What's that dreadful smell?'

'Had a bit of trouble with drains, nowt for you to fret about. Landlord's sorting it. That's it, you hang your coat up, then go into kitchen. I'll put kettle on, we'll have a nice cup of tea. Just ignore dog... ooo, Judy, you're forever under my feet. Off you go, go on, out... out.'

'Is the kitchen through here?'

'Aye, end of passageway, go and make yourself comfy... We've house to ourselves today.'

'Oh, I thought you said Mrs Christie was going to be here. Isn't she home?'

'No, lass, my wife's visiting family in Sheffield. Right then, you have a little sit down. That's it, rope chair's comfy. No need to be nervous, I've helped out many a young lass like you in past. Now, just to ask... d'you know how many weeks it is? You know, that you've gone?'

'About nine.'

'Ah, that's fine. Should be straightforward enough. There you go, you drink your tea. Nice, is it? Good, that's good. Don't look so worried, it's a tricky procedure but you're in safe hands with me. Like I told you, I'm medically trained, I know what I'm doing.'

'I'm afraid it's going to hurt. It's not going to hurt, is it, Mr Christie?'

'No, you'll be fine so long as you relax. But you've to trust me. Right, have you finished your tea? Good lass. Now lean back in chair, that's it. Relax… relax. Now you're not to go minding when I pop this mask over your face. I've to give you a little gas to help dull pain of this procedure. All you need do is breathe it in, that's it… breathe… breathe. Nice and deep for me. Are you feeling sleepy yet? I'd like you to be sleepy.'

CHAPTER TEN

'Are you always reading?'

Joy looked up at the man whose eyes were as blue as the lido in Kensington where she occasionally swam. 'I suppose I must be. I seem to prefer fictional worlds to mine.'

'French... you're French.'

'Guilty as charged.' She giggled, suddenly shy.

'Whereabouts?'

'Arras.'

Tugging on his moustache, the man eyed her with interest. 'Robespierre's home town.'

'How clever of you,' she congratulated him.

'My mother's French. She's from Arcis-sur-Aube, not a million miles away from you.'

'That's Danton country.'

'Indeed.' A mock frown. 'Let's hope we get along better than those two gentlemen... I'm Charles, by the way. Charles Gilchrist.'

She shook the hand he offered her. It felt warm and she held on to it for longer than necessary.

'You're Joy, aren't you? Queenie told me.' He unbuttoned his overcoat. Something that looked too warm for the bright spring day. 'I've seen you around.'

'Y-you have?' she stammered, closing her paperback. A blush travelled up her neck and she slapped a hand over it; felt the heat through her fingers.

'At the club. Here in the park, too, sometimes.'

But you're a married man, you shouldn't be noticing me... Her thoughts tumbling over themselves.

'It's rather warm in this little spot you've found. Would you mind awfully if I joined you? They seem to have run out of tables.'

'Please do.'

Joy had seen that creepy little man in the tennis shoes out exercising his dog again and felt immediately safer when Charles removed his coat and perched on the seat beside hers. It unsettled her that the man always seemed to be in the park when she was these days, and the idea he might be following her was deeply troubling.

'Are you sure you don't mind?' He had sensed something was amiss.

'Not at all.' She gave him her best smile.

His coat, folded over his knees, lay there like a sleeping animal and she resisted the urge to stroke it. He bashed out his pipe and refilled it with tobacco. Lit it and shook out the match. The smell of toasted marshmallow and vanilla reminded her of campfires in the woods along the banks of the Scarpe, the air full of birdsong and the heady scent of the flowering sweet chestnut.

'Your English is impeccable – where did you learn to speak it so well?'

'I spent five years on the Tendring Coast during the war.' She avoided all mention of Queenie. 'My parents sent me there to be safe.'

'Sensible people. I saw rather a lot of your country during the war.'

'Was France where you had your injury?' She had spotted his cane.

'This old thing?' He swung it through the air. 'It's only a precaution. I take it when I go walking. Just a bit of shrapnel, it feels quite better in the warmer months.'

'That's good.' She nodded, pleased for him. Unlike many men who'd returned from the war, he seemed to be in top physical health.

'You're a fan of Thomas Hardy?' He pointed to the collection of stories in her lap. 'I'm not much of a reader, but I did like *The*

Three Musketeers as a boy. Not that I could read it in French, much to my mother's annoyance.'

Charles had a whiff of the seventeenth century about him. The moustache, the gleam on his thick dark hair. Something she was seeing in all its glory, now his fedora had been placed on the table beside her gloves. He looked like a musketeer. D'Artagnan. *That's what comes of having your head in too many books...* Her mother's voice, echoing Queenie's. Unwelcome, snaking into her mind. It was always the same, whenever something good was about to happen. Joy shook it away. She didn't want to be that girl who hid under her hair and shaded her mouth with her fingers. She was twenty, for goodness' sake; she wasn't a child any more. A child who needed to watch her every move fearing the burn of her mother's precipitous smack.

'Can I buy you another of those?' Up on his feet, Charles signalled to her empty cup. 'Or perhaps *mademoiselle* would prefer something stronger?'

'That is kind.' She couldn't believe this glamorous man had singled her out in the crowd; and what a crowd there was at the Serpentine Café on this beautiful May morning. 'I'll have whatever you're having.'

'Is that wise?' Mischievous, he touched her shoulder. The briefest of gestures, so brief she wondered if she'd imagined it.

'Probably not.'

'I tell you what...' He laid his pipe on the ashtray. 'I'll get us a couple of coffees to start with.'

To start with?

Charles left his cane leaning against the table and his coat snoozing on his seat. Joy, uncomfortable with him gone, followed his progress from the terrace to the darkened café interior, then scanned around for the man in the trilby. Was relieved not to see him. She dropped her gaze to Charles's pipe and saw the little grooves his incisors had made in the stem. It propelled her back to her eleven-year-old self aboard the bus to Paris. Wedged between her parents as the undulating patchwork of fields, then the tall green forests of northern France, were left behind, she had a bird's eye view of her father's pipe preparation. Not that the lighting of his Meerschaum was to everyone's liking. A fellow passenger, balancing a crate of chickens on his knees, shouted at him to put it out and a fight nearly ensued. It was her mother who saved the day. Handing over money they didn't have to waste. It was all that got them to the Gare du Nord and her seat on the Calais train. Where she sat, helpless, as her parents' faces dissolved into the crowds on the platform and she was left alone. The next faces that were for her were Queenie's grandparents – the two strangers who met her off the ferry at Dover. Fred, in his tweed knickerbockers and hair like a half-blown dandelion, and Mary, her face scrubbed smooth as a pebble. These were the people with the secluded farm in the dunes her father had told her about. A place where she learnt it wasn't normal to be woken in the small hours to the sound of her parents arguing and that, contrary to what her mother told her, Joy was loveable.

Charles was back. He placed the tray of coffees down and pulled up a chair. This time his knees touched hers beneath the table. It made her quiver. It made her nearly forget to breathe. He picked up his pipe and slotted it between his teeth. A series of small puffs got it going again. The dappled shade flickered patterns on the tablecloth and she noticed how he drank his coffee. How he sipped at it like a girl while the sun shone shyly through the leaves. Joy asked him about the war and the part he had played. She sat on her hands and listened to him talk. To his tone, the timbre of his voice. His hesitations and the silences that fell between breaths. Up close he smelled of pomade and tobacco. At some point, the green ribbon in her hair worked loose. Charles saw it and, leaning forward, retied it.

If time ticked by, neither was aware of it. Time, so it seemed, was going on elsewhere, and it was as if they had been left to whirl around each other on a deserted dance floor. There was something about him: a warmth that made her want him to shelter her from the world she wasn't sure she liked. He seemed gentle, kind, the way his eyes creased at their corners when he smiled. She was falling in love with him for this alone.

He closed one of his hands over hers and gently squeezed as if to test the ripeness of a plum. It stopped her jittering. It nearly stopped her heart. She told herself it was wrong to feel like this – Charles was a married man.

'Do I make you nervous?'

She nodded. There was no point pretending. 'I'm not used to being offered coffee by men I don't know.'

'And you have plenty of offers from men you do know?'

Joy felt the pressure when he removed his hand. Noticed the sun going in behind the clouds.

'Where's your family today?' She forced herself to ask about the blonde woman and boys she had seen him with.

'My family?' He darted a look of concern. 'How do you know about them?'

'I saw you in the park.'

'When was that?'

'A few weeks ago.' Deliberately vague. 'You've children, haven't you?'

'Children?' he parroted. 'Goodness me, no. *No.*' He put his pipe away in a pocket, took out a silver cigarette case. Opened it and offered her one. She shook her head. 'Those boys you must've seen me with…' He paused, lit a cigarette and took a protracted drag. 'They're my brother's twins.' He exhaled a grey ribbon of smoke. 'My late brother, Philip. He was killed in the war.'

'Oh, dear. I am sorry.' Joy gathered the collar of her jacket and balled it in her fist. Had she inadvertently pushed him into sharing something he wasn't ready to?

'Bobby and Samuel live in Kent. I don't get to see them often.'

'Was their mother the elegant lady you were with?'

He laughed. 'Their mother? No, that was *my* mother.'

'Gosh, she looked young.'

'I'll remember to tell her that.' He pulled on his cigarette again.

At that moment, something shimmered beyond the trees, snatching her attention. It was that sinister little man again. He was inching his way along the path, his white dog full-stretch on its lead. The shock made her sit bolt upright and, narrowing her eyes against the glare, she stared at what she could see of him until he had been swallowed by the dark recesses of undergrowth.

Trembling, it was as if a cold moth had landed on her heart, and where its icy dorsal tufts touched, she was left with a horrible feeling of dread.

'Are you warm enough? I could go and ask for a blanket.'

'No, I'm perfectly fine.' She rubbed her arms through her sleeves. 'I thought I saw someone I recognised.'

'Can't have been anyone nice.' He twisted his gaze in the direction she'd been looking.

'It's nothing. Don't worry.' She picked a corner of the tablecloth, hunted for straggles of thread to unpick. She would love to tell Charles about the stranger in the raincoat and her fears he could be stalking her. Would have done, had she not been wary of him accusing her of having an overactive imagination as Queenie had.

Joy and Charles's gazes collided, bold then timid: flickering shutters on a camera lens. She looked down on herself as doubts crowded in. How plain she was in her frumpy clothes, her sensible shoes. How she had barely bothered to pull a comb through her hair before coming out.

'I'd love to see you again.' His declaration swashbuckling through her perceived shortcomings.

That pensive look. She was coming to recognise it, falling as it did between his dazzling smiles. He took her hand and led her away from the bustle of the café, with its clatter of crockery and bursts of laughter. Under the cathedral-like nave of trees where they stood facing one another. Overhead, a patch of blue showed through a tear in the clouds.

'Joy.' His voice finding her.

'Yes.'

And he kissed her.

Lost in each other, they were oblivious to the danger loitering close by. Oblivious to the man who had the power to blight the perfect setting beneath the chestnut trees, the tables with their pretty gingham cloths that shifted in the breeze, just by being there.

CHAPTER ELEVEN

'Come on, Judy.' He tapped his thigh to beckon the dog to his side. 'Let's go and have a nose over here, shall we?'

He abandoned the shady nook among the trees where he had been keeping an eye on them and moved towards the café. Found their recently vacated table and sat down. The still-warm chair where her womanliness had been, causing a small thrill deep in his groin.

'Oh, aye.' He recognised the plum-coloured gloves he'd often seen the girl wearing. 'Careless to leave these behind, lass… but I suppose you had your mind on other things.'

A dry chuckle as he picked them up. Delicately. Between finger and thumb. Emitting a low groan of pleasure as he did so. The gloves still held the shape of her, and it was too exciting to think of the parts of herself she would have touched with the very hands they had sheathed only moments before.

He fondled them in the way he longed to fondle her. Losing himself to the exquisite softness of the leather nap, the silky lining, while his dog wandered around, trailing its lead, licking the crumbs from recent diners. He put one of the gloves in his coat pocket and lifted the other in both hands. Tugged open its throat and placed it over his nose and mouth in the same way he did with the gas mask he forced over the faces of the women… those desperate women he tricked into his rope chair.

He breathed in.

Deeply.

Finding her scent.

'Mm, such intimate things… and now they're mine.' He clasped the glove in his fist. 'Just like you're going to be, lass. I'll have my way with you soon, and when I do, I'll do more than just breathe you in.'

CHAPTER TWELVE

A burst of summer and London's streets were bleached of shadow under the hot late-afternoon sun. A heat-struck pigeon flapped up off the pavement. It alerted Queenie to a man with a stoop who was waiting for her outside the Mockin' Bird. A man old enough to be her father, with a headful of coarse grey hair. She scanned his face but couldn't recall his name. He presented her with a posy of hothouse flowers and she nodded and listened politely. Laughing at the dirty joke she didn't get. Then, waving a hand to excuse herself, she clipped along the side alley to the stage door. No need to use her key, it was open. A glance over her shoulder to check the man wasn't following and she swapped the sunny street for the shadowy interior of the club.

Airless and muggy, the Mockin' Bird had its own distinctive smell. One that was only identifiable when you came in from outside. Not at night, when it was packed with people, but at quiet times like this. She breathed it in, classifying the smell of cigarettes and booze along with something else, from nature, like leaf mulch and roots. She heard the piano first. Ringing out like a voice from the dimness while she made up her mind about the smell. Terrence, seated at it in a dish of light, looked up when he heard the door close.

'Hello, Queenie.' He lifted his hands from the keys. 'More flowers?'

She waved the posy through the air and giggled. 'Lord, it's hot out there today.' She made a detour to the bar. Nodded to Sammy, who was polishing the bottle tops.

'Not so cool in here either.' Terrence dragged the back of his arm over his perspiring brow.

'How did last night go? Did I miss much?' She found a suitable glass and filled it with water.

'Not much. Was your meeting with Herbie's people successful?'

'It was just the one guy, sorting the contracts. Not that I've signed anything yet.' She climbed onto the stage, dropped the posy into the tumbler and placed it on top of the piano. 'They're fixing flights and accommodation for me.'

'Fancy you going off over the Atlantic. You've the world at your feet, darling.' Terrence jumped up to kiss her cheek, then sat back down again. 'And such wonderful news about Joy and Charles too, isn't it?'

'What wonderful news? I thought you said I didn't miss anything.'

'Hasn't Joy told you?'

'Told me what?' Queenie frowned. 'I haven't seen her for days.'

'Oh, then I suppose it's up to me. Joy and Charles. Well…' Terrence tapped his fingers against his bottom lip. 'They're practically engaged.' He returned to the piano and picked out the tune for 'I Don't Want to Set the World on Fire'.

'You what?' Queenie gawped at him askance. 'Don't be silly. Charles is married. He's got children.'

Terrence lifted his hands from the keys again. 'Married? Whatever gave you that idea?'

'Joy and me, we saw him in the park. I just thought…' What she thought was: *Joy's my friend, not yours; how come you know about this and I don't?* 'Oh, it doesn't matter. But he's way too old for her.'

'The guy's only a year or so older than me.' She sensed him search her face but she refused to soften her expression: she was serious, deadly serious. 'He's perfect for her and you know it.'

'If you say so.'

'Dear me, Queenie, darling.' Terrence snorted. 'I never had you down as the jealous type.'

'Don't be ridiculous. It's just a bit of a shock, that's all.'

'I don't know why. You're the one who said he'd been asking about her.'

'All right then, maybe not such a shock. It's just… I'm worried for her. He's so…'

'What?' Terrence looked expectant.

'Stylish. Worldly.' It was hard to articulate the mix of feelings she hadn't had the chance to process.

'You're not to go interfering.'

'*Me?*'

'Yes, you. I've seen the way you boss her around.'

'I don't.'

The look Terrence gave told her this wasn't true.

'I don't mean to.' She unwrapped her headscarf, tossed it onto a nearby chair. 'I'm just trying to help her make the most of herself.'

Another snort. 'I don't think she's going to need any more help in that department.'

'Are we having a run-through, or what?' Queenie, keen to change the subject. 'Where are the others?'

'Buster's at the bar.' Terrence rolled his eyes.

Queenie raised a hand, used it as a visor against the glare of stage lights. Picking Buster out of the gloom, she saw him lolling on a bar stool. 'Is he drunk, d'you think?'

'Probably. He was down in the dressing room sleeping when I arrived.'

'Where's Eddie?'

'Running late. But Dick's here somewhere. Want me to give him a shout?'

'No, don't bother. You and me can make a start. What d'you want to open with?'

Terrence began playing the intro of another song by the Ink Spots when Buster bulldozed his way between them. Knocking over music stands, his face as dark as a thundercloud.

'Dear me, Buster.' Queenie took a step back to let him pass. 'Are you going to be able to play tonight?'

'Leave off, will ya?' He took his jacket off and revealed a dark triangle of sweat on the back of his shirt. 'You lot are always on at me.' He tottered forwards, nearly falling. Pint glass in hand, he slopped most of his beer over his shoes.

'You're in a bad mood.' A nervous giggle: Buster was a fuse that could blow at any moment. With his pale eyelashes and pinkish face, he epitomised many of the infantrymen who had come back from the war: physically unharmed but psychologically damaged.

'I said leave off.' He stumbled to the rear of the stage and took up his position behind the drums.

'Excuse me, Buster.' Terrence, unusually bold from his piano stool. 'Don't go taking it out on Queenie. It's not her fault Joy turned you down.'

'Now what's gone on?' It seemed that Queenie was the last to know about whatever this was too. It left her feeling stupid and insignificant.

'I've seen 'em together, ain't I?'

'Seen who together?'

'Joy and that bloody officer... smoochin'.'

'*Smooching*? What are you talking about?'

'Last night, I dunno. I've just seen 'em,' Buster grumbled, almost incoherent. 'What she 'ave to go and pick 'im for? I bloody hate officers... specially 'im. Bloody toff, splashin' the cash. Flash bastard's already got everythin'.'

Queenie had seen the way Buster looked at Joy and knew he was smitten. But was there any contest? Major Charles Gilchrist, with his looks and charm; everything Buster wasn't. Unlike Charles and Terrence – achieving officer status in the army and elevated in civilian life as they would have been on the patrol ground – men like Buster still had something to prove. Wasting their youth fighting in France, all they wanted was to settle down to a good life, to marry and have children.

'It ain't fair. I love 'er. I bloody love 'er.'

'Oh, pull yourself together.'

'Terry, stop it,' Queenie warned him. 'I'm sorry for you, Buster, I am. But I'm sure Joy let you down gently.'

'What difference does that make?' He spat out his anger. 'She still let me down.'

'Yes, but it's hardly her fault.' Queenie was at a loss to know what to say.

A grunt from their drummer before he glugged what remained of his beer, belched without apology.

'Look at him, he isn't up for playing.' Terrence talked about him as if he wasn't there. 'What are we going to do?'

'You shut your gob.' Buster had heard him. 'You're as bad as that Gilchrist bastard. Bloody officers, you dunno nuffin. I'd say you're worse than 'im. Least 'e comes from officer class – *you*, you're a bloody turncoat.' He twirled his drumsticks through the air then smacked them against his cymbals and seemed pleased with the crashing discord. 'You were just a squaddie like me, but you think you're better,' he shouted over it. 'You just jumped ship, pretendin' to be better than what you are.'

'Do I care what you think?' Terrence scoffed. 'And if I didn't think myself better than you, I wouldn't be fit for the gutter.'

'You bastard.' Buster staggered to his feet and lunged for Terrence, arms flailing like a windmill.

Terrence twisted around and bopped him one easily on the chin, putting Buster on his backside.

'Hey, come on, you two.' Queenie, from the sidelines. 'Hasn't there been enough fighting in the world?'

'I'll fuckin' 'ave you.' Buster, snarling, scrabbling to get up, jabbed a finger at Terrence. 'You ain't what everyone thinks you are. I've bin watchin' ya. I've seen what you do. I'll 'ave ya for this, I know you want rid of me.'

'Are you surprised? You can barely stand,' Terrence bit back.

'What's going on here?' Dick had joined them, pulling up a chair and arranging his music. 'Who's trying to get rid of you?'

Buster didn't answer. He had flopped against the wall and closed his eyes. Dick took his saxophone out of its case and, moistening the reed, secured it to the mouthpiece.

'Give us an A, Terry,' he asked, blowing into it, adjusting and readjusting the neck cork. 'We're going to have to do something about him.' Dick wiped his lips with the back of his hand.

'I've heard there's this great drummer on the circuit,' Terrence murmured. 'He's working at the Blue Note Bar in Soho.'

'I've heard good things about that place.' Dick looked interested.

'We should go check him out. Poach him, if he's any good.'

'I heard that.' Buster opened one eye, then closed it again. Dropped a drumstick with a clatter and tipped sideways off his stool to pick it up.

'Come on, you lot,' Queenie intervened with a clap of her hands. 'We're opening in less than an hour.'

'Hi there, pretty lady. You look happy.' Eddie, waltzing with his double bass, lumbered on stage. He took up his position on Queenie's left.

Queenie thought he was winking at her, but he wasn't. The wink was for Joy, who, appearing out of nowhere, collected Buster's empty pint glass from the stage. *Not another one*, she thought, sighing, and briefly adjusting the seams on her stockings, she stepped boldly up to the mic. Communicating, without the need to say, just who the important one was around here.

'I am happy.' Joy, bright-eyed. 'Charles is taking me to Dorset for the weekend.'

'Why Dorset?' Queenie saw Joy fling a concerned glance at Buster. As aware of his volatile, drink-addled hostility as she was.

'Because it's Thomas Hardy country.' She looked at her as if she was stupid. 'You know how much I love Thomas Hardy.'

'It's lovely there this time of year.' Terrence gave Queenie a reproachful look. 'My parents used to take me and my brother and sisters to Swanage when we were little.'

Queenie couldn't trust herself not to say something spiteful so took out her compact and set about reapplying her lipstick. Offered some to Joy.

'No, thank you.' A giggle and a flap of her hand. 'Charles says I'm beautiful just as I am.'

At this moment, there was a sudden and violent hammering at the club's main door. All six heads turned to it.

Bang. Bang. Bang.

'Is someone going to answer that?' Queenie, faintly alarmed.

Bang. Bang. Bang.

'I think you'd better go, Sammy,' she shouted to the barman. 'Before they smash the door down.'

Sammy, in his long white barman's apron, slipped from behind the beer pumps and unlocked the door. Threw it wide to the early evening street that had been made prematurely dark by the unexpected rain.

'Is Terry here?' a West Indian man hollered from the threshold.

Terrence leapt to his feet. 'What is it?' A hand fluttering at his mouth.

'Terry! Terry! You've gotta come quick, man. 'Tis bad... Malcolm. Rozzers got him... Der was a fight. Dey took him in.'

'Go. Go.' Seeing Terrence's face drain of blood, Queenie shooed him away. 'Don't worry about us. Eddie can play the piano tonight.'

CHAPTER THIRTEEN

Terrence dashed out into the warm evening rain and ran the length of Mayfair's Curzon Street, down into Piccadilly. A double-decker bus, heading for Charing Cross, slid past. Slow enough for him to seize the metal pole and jump on board. With his ticket from the conductor in his hand, he climbed to the top deck. Sat down with the spent breath and cigarette smoke of his fellow travellers. He usually liked riding the top of buses, but not tonight. Too nervous, his mind churning, the fibres of the seat cover prickling his legs through the damp material of his trousers. He realised he was sweating. That the shirt beneath his waistcoat was wet under the arms. This was what they called sailing too close to the wind. Men like him should steer clear of the law. But he couldn't leave Malcolm to rot in there; he needed to get him out.

The light dispensed by the fluorescent tubes hurt his eyes and gave a corpse-like tinge to the brightest complexions. A pretty woman clambered up the stairwell. Terrence saw the men with their expectant glances as she took up a seat beside him. He stole a look at his accidental travelling companion. Smoking her cigarette, her blonde hair secured beneath a scarf, she was lost in thought. He looked past her, out through the windows, at what he could see of the giant glass and steel structures that had been flung up amid the bombed-out wreckage after the war. Like false teeth in a ruined mouth, they were only supposed to be temporary, but now they were homes and places of work; people had grown dependent on them. The city was fast dissolving into the night, but recognising the Strand, then the Savoy hotel, he remembered Winston saying the police station wasn't far from there and tugged the bell pull. The bus responded by slowing to a stop.

The wide stone steps of Charing Cross Police Station were cornered by soaring Corinthian columns set high above the traffic. Intimidating enough, they threatened to crumble his resolve. Could he go through with this? On the verge of turning back, he took a deep breath and climbed the steps. He was doing this for Malcolm, he told himself, going through a huge set of storm doors and into a tiled vestibule. Noisy under his shoes, it announced his arrival before he was ready.

'Good evening.' Terrence sniffed the unpleasant combination of French polish and fish glue. 'I believe you're holding someone. A man called Malcolm Taylor.' Avoiding eye contact, he spoke to the desk sergeant's pencil that was twitching in readiness of crime.

'Can I ask your name, sir?'

Terrence gave it. Watched as it was written down.

The man whose complexion was as wobbly as a plate of chitterlings eyed him warily. 'Now, perhaps we could start again, sir. How can we be of assistance?'

'I understand the police broke up a fight earlier tonight. Somewhere around Soho… and the thing is…' Terrence looked out from beneath the brim of his homburg. 'It was Mr Taylor who was set on, not the other way around.'

'Is that so? And what's this Mr Taylor to you, may I ask, sir?'

'He's my friend.'

'Like the Blacks, do you, sir?'

'Er, no, not especially.' Terrence felt his pulse quicken and his breathing change. 'I'm just here to tell you there's been some kind of mistake.' His expression fixed; he didn't want to give this one any reason to apprehend him.

'A mistake, eh?'

'That's right.' Terrence, with his cultured, expressive voice, fingered the buttons on his waistcoat. 'I know you think Malcolm... I mean, Mr Taylor, started the fight, but I can tell you categorically—'

'Are you married, sir?'

'Married? I'm sorry, what's that got to do with anything?'

'Touched a nerve, have I, sir?'

Terrence, declining to answer, felt a fresh wave of sweat break out between his shoulder blades.

'What is it you do, Mr Banks?'

'Sorry, what was that?' His mind a whirl, his heart racing; he hadn't heard correctly.

'I asked you what you do for a living.' The look was menacing.

'Oh, I... erm, I...' Best not say he played in a band. 'I work in Fleet Street.'

'A muckraker, eh?'

'No, I'm not a reporter... I work in a bank.'

'Mr Banks works in a bank.' A scornful snigger.

Great. That was all he needed, a policeman with a chip on his shoulder who thought he was a comedian.

'That's right.' Terrence didn't rise to it. 'I'm a departmental manager at F. Lambert & Co. It's one of the top banks in London.'

'Is that supposed to impress me, sir?'

'I don't know? It impresses my mother.'

'You some sort of ponce, or what?'

'Sorry, officer, but does my enquiry really warrant such hostility?' Terrence's stomach flipped over. Did this policeman know what he was? What Malcolm was? He was in trouble; he knew it had been risky to come here. He'd heard the stories about these zealous officers of the law who, wanting easy convictions, would pick you up for something as harmless as smiling at a man in the park. *Don't provoke him. Don't even blink.* His forehead bloomed with fresh sweat and he prayed his hat hid him well enough.

'I was just asking a question, sir.' The voice perforated his contemplations.

'And what an extraordinary question it is.' Terrence tipped his hat lower, down over his eyebrows, and worked hard to keep the quiver out of his voice.

The desk sergeant twisted the lid off a tin of fruit drops. Put one in his mouth. Not once moving his eyes from Terrence. This was agony. A bead of sweat rolled down his face, bypassing his eye. It took everything he had not to dab it away.

The desk sergeant swapped the fruit drop to the other side of his mouth. 'Fight for your country during the war, did you, sir?' he said, crunching down.

'I did, yes.' Terrence, close enough to smell the orangey breath. 'I was a warrant officer in the army.'

He stood back and crossed his arms over his chest. Watched the sergeant's expression change. He hoped he hadn't misread the situation and that this man, like Buster, didn't despise him because he'd swapped sides. Because Terrence had swapped sides: he'd joined the officer classes to be safer – he'd never been safe as a squaddie.

'Take a seat, sir.' The policeman continued to stare and Terrence feared he could see right down to the guilty core of him.

He moved away from the desk. Too nervous to sit, he ignored the benches set out against the shiny walls and wandered over the squeaky floor on his equally squeaky soles. It couldn't be a less welcoming space. The pegs heaped with black police capes dripping rainwater onto the floor tiles. The peeling paintwork. The posters warning of 'Danger hours for electricity cuts' and 'The National Service still expects you to do your duty'. Funny to think it was acceptable for him to have risked his life serving King and country during the war, but to live as he truly was, openly and without fear, was impossible. That if it was ever discovered he loved a man, he would be branded a criminal and a disgrace to society. It was a strain having to act all the time. He thought of the white lies he told his colleagues at the bank when they asked about his plans for the evening or the weekend. He took the unfairness of it to the window that looked out over the back of the building. Outside, darkness ruled. The area beyond the night-blackened yard was a wasteland. A dead zone of featureless tarmac and a forest of spindly gas lamps. He stared out at the rain that was coming in sideways. Millions of silvery lines brought in on the gusts of wind and clarified by the amber hue of gaslight and vehicle headlamps circling the city.

The wall clock struck ten. Terrence turned when he heard a door wheeze open behind the main desk. There was Malcolm. Steered out into the lobby by another uniformed officer. The sight of his bloodied shirt was bad enough, but those raw-looking stitches tacked in a hurried hand along his cheekbone made his knees buckle. He looked like he'd gone ten rounds with Rocky Marciano. Who had dared to hurt him? The tears in Malcolm's eyes and his little-lost-boy look stirred something primeval and vital in Terrence's heart. He gulped the emotion in the back of his throat and resisted the urge to run and comfort him. They were being watched, the pair of them. This was a test. A test they could not afford to fail.

CHAPTER FOURTEEN

He exchanged the dusky interior of Albert's Cavern for the equally tenebrous narrow alleyway, buttoning his raincoat and positioning his trilby as he went. Softly, in his rubber-soled shoes, he moved along the abandoned night-time streets, smiling his secret smile. He was at home among the seedy back alleys and run-down parts of Soho, and it satisfied him to move around unseen, unheard… watching. Yes, he had a certain façade to maintain, and this was why he pretended this part of town was beneath him, but the truth was, Soho was his favourite hunting ground.

He would have liked a cigarette but realised he'd smoked his last and didn't have the money to buy more. He'd handed over all he had to Albert.

'Thieving gypsy,' he grumbled. 'That bastard would steal your eyes and come back for sockets.'

With nothing else to do with his hands, he shoved them inside his coat pockets and let his mind circle back to the evening he'd just spent in the company of Doreen, one of Albert's classier prostitutes. Not that the woman had been able to satiate him; he could still identify the gnawing need that drove him there, time and again. But what did he expect? He should know by now that paying for it didn't make the doing of it any easier. The reality was, he could never perform with a woman unless she was unconscious… or better still, dead. A shiver of excitement pulsed through him as he thought of this, and he luxuriated in his recollections of how it felt to look down on the motionless body of a woman, reduced as she was to nothing more threatening than an innocent little girl.

Returning to his recent memory of Doreen and her nubile, young body, he lifted his fingers to his nose for what remained of her smell. He still had that, for the time being at least. The smell of them was probably more thrilling than the sex, in the same way the activity of prowling the streets unobserved was. Because he'd never been any good at it, the business of pleasuring women had always eluded him.

'Reggie No Dick.'

He replayed the hurtful taunt that had plagued his youth. It was a name they'd stuck on him after a calamitous encounter with a more experienced girl with whom he'd failed to perform. The humiliation still dogged him all these years on and was at the root of his hatred of women.

'Oi, mister!'

A sudden shout rang out in the empty street. Enough to make him stop and turn, to listen to the unwelcome echo of it reverberate against the wet-bricked buildings that were bathed in gaslight. It was that scantily clad girl from a few nights ago. Not one of Albert's, but one of the whores who plied her trade from the disused doorways he liked to lurk within. Like a child who had raided the dressing-up box, she tottered after him in her ill-fitting heels.

'Oi, mister.' Her voice shrill, grating his nerves. 'You owe me money.' She caught up with him, panting at his elbow. 'And you tore my blouse.'

He stared at her. At the flimsy piece of clothing that was ripped at the throat and barely concealing the undeveloped and malnourished body beneath. His cold gaze wandering over her sunken cheeks, her lank hair.

It wouldn't take much to finish her; his plans, lethal, while his hand, a mind of its own, sought out the silk stocking he kept in his pocket for occasions such as this.

'So, you gonna pay me what you owe, or what?' she whined, leaning into his space.

He could laugh at the way she puffed out her pathetic little chest as if she stood a chance against him.

'Aye, lass.' He let go a sigh, his fingers continuing to coil around the stocking. 'But if you'll remember,' his voice gentle, reeling her in, making sure to string out the words to give him time to debate whether or not to kill the bitch, here and now, 'I didn't actually have anything off you, did I?' A quivering of his eyebrows beneath the brim of his hat.

'Not my fault you can't do what a proper man can,' she bit back, surprisingly feisty.

Stupid girl, didn't she know the danger she was in and how unwise she was to rile him?

'You dare to speak to me like that? You? A dirty little scrubber off street. I were a policeman during war, I could have you arrested just like that.' He clicked his fingers.

'Supposed to impress me, is it? Being a copper still don't make you a proper man. All a bit soft down there, aren't you, mister?' A hand, ghostly as her hair, was wafted in the general direction of his groin. 'What are you?' She laughed. 'Some kinda queer?'

A sudden dangerous anger spurted inside him. 'Shut your filthy mouth.' He pushed his face close to hers, close enough to smell the remnants of a recent cigarette on her breath.

The girl didn't make a sound when his fist smashed into her cheek. And when a trickle of blood from the soft young mouth ran down over her chin, into the bony cleft between her breasts, she just stared at him. Then, in the dangling seconds before trying to make her getaway, he punched her again. Harder this time. Enough to make her stagger backwards and drop to her knees on the wet pavement. Her piteous cry of pain meant nothing to him as he stepped around her and carried on his way.

CHAPTER FIFTEEN

This was how Dorset, with its wind-blown bluffs and sea views, was to become their place. In the same way the Serpentine Café had become their place. Smuggler's Cove was out of the way. Winding up from Swanage on unadopted lanes, its position beneath looming chalk cliffs came as a complete surprise to Joy. As did the fake wedding ring Charles slipped onto her finger before checking them in as Mr and Mrs Smith at the boarding house that faced the sea.

'But we mustn't,' Joy protested when the landlady went to fetch their key. 'It's unlucky to pretend you're married when you're not.'

'Don't be silly. That's just superstitious nonsense,' Charles gently chided, then kissed her cheek. 'What can possibly go wrong for us?'

'Sorry the weather's not better for you, my dears. It's supposed to cheer up nicely later,' the landlady, a hearty, jolly sort, said when she returned. 'Not that you young lovers will mind, I'm sure. If you're stuck in your room, I mean.' Her laugh was as brassy as she was.

Rain pushed its way along the headland. A grey curtain sweeping eastwards over the town. It crackled against her straw hat and slid down inside her collar. This was summer. It should be hot, but the salt wind coming in off the sea was sharp. Apart from the wellington boots she'd borrowed from someone at work with bigger feet, it seemed they had both brought the wrong clothes. Not that Joy cared. Pink-nosed and happy, she was having the time of her life. They stood holding hands at the lip of the sea, listened to the mesmeric *shhh… shhh* of the surf as it swept the shore. When they stretched their necks to watch a white-winged Cessna make its airy flight over the bay and head inland, Joy let her thoughts haul her back to her childhood on the Essex coast. She was remembering the German pilot and how his plane had crashed to earth.

'Penny for them?' His eyes were as shocking as a kingfisher's wing.

'They're worth more than that.'

She knew it was flippant, but she didn't know how to share what was in her heart. She had so much to thank the likes of Charles, Terrence and Buster for. It was why she tolerated Buster and forgave him for his clumsy advances, his coarseness and insobriety. Because without men like them, France would have been done for, as it so nearly was.

They turned and walked away from the sea's edge and headed for the town. Found a tiny, dark-beamed inn called the Bluebell, with leather benches that had been ravaged by time. She shrugged out of her blue wool jacket, worried it might have shrunk in the rain, and hung it on a peg by a rack of newspapers neither was interested in looking at. The walls were full of sepia photographs. Tiered rows of rugby and cricket sides. Men who'd never come home from the war with families who still lived in this parish. They made Joy sad. These men, no older than her, their faces full of hope and youth, oblivious of the horrors to come.

Charles left his wet umbrella and fedora with her and sauntered to the bar with his pipe between his teeth. Returned minutes later with two glasses of beer.

'Sorry, Joy.' He dripped rainwater onto the floor. 'It was all they had. Well, this and Guinness.'

'Oh, I quite like Guinness.' She picked up a beer mat with a picture of a toucan balancing a glass of the dark Irish stout on its beak, tucked it into her handbag.

'You do?' Charles brushed sand from his sleeve. 'Aren't you full of surprises?'

*

They drank their beer and watched the rain thrash the pub's windows. Her face glowed with pleasure as she studied the grooves Charles's comb had left behind in his glossy, pomade-dressed hair. She rested her head on his shoulder, felt the beer track through her. The press of his thigh against her own beneath the table as she breathed in his smell, his aftershave, storing it away for when she was back in London, alone in her basement room.

'This place is for sale.' The clunk of teeth against his pipe. 'We should buy it, now I've finally given up my commission in the army.' He lifted her hand and kissed it, the bristles of his moustache tickling her. 'We could stay here forever… be far from the madding crowd.' He laughed at his witticism. 'Be a great place to bring up our children.'

Joy went along with his daydream, furnishing and equipping the Bluebell's rooms in a way she'd have done had they been kitting it out for real. But she knew it could be nothing more than that. From what Charles had already said, he would never be allowed to break away from the family firm.

They finished their drinks and left the pub with the idea of exploring the town. Sharing his umbrella, they set off through the rain towards a row of stalls facing the shore. Despite the dreadful weather, the town was busy with day trippers and dogs on leads. Young men in tight suits and old school ties. People eating iced buns out of paper bags, others sucking sticks of rock. A dog, ownerless and self-governing, stopped to sniff their ankles, making them giggle before it trotted off to cock its leg against a lamp post.

'I want to buy you something.' Charles put his arm around her. 'Something to mark this special time we're having. This place looks nice.' Charles pointed to a window crammed with the razzle-dazzle of lavender bags and crystal glasses.

'Bit expensive. I'd prefer to go in here.'

From the moment they stepped inside the market, Joy loved it. The untreated floor, the artisan shops laid out as comfortably as the interiors of ordinary people's houses. The wooden rafters reminded her of the roof of Saint-Géry in Arras. The craftsmen's handiworks, proudly set out for tourists, were touching in their simplicity, and it was an enamelled brooch with red and green apples she liked best.

'Are you sure? It only costs pennies.'

'Oh, yes,' she enthused, and pushed the pin into the lapel of her jacket. 'I'll wear it always.'

They stepped out of the market to find the sun had come out and a band had struck up.

'I bet you'd like something to eat?' Charles asked. 'Come on, I know just the place.'

The sun was shining. They had seen Dorset at its worst and now they were seeing it at its best. Hand in hand, they weaved through the holiday crowd and the scrape of trams that circled the town. The tea terrace was surprisingly empty and, after ordering fish and chips, they sat listening to the tide scuff the beach below. Staring out through the huge plate-glass windows, Joy trailed the progress of a cloud sailing over the broken spine of a castle, romantic and melancholy, perched on its rocky promontory. Watched a distant sheepdog dart over the bracken-covered slopes gathering sheep behind the town.

'Did you come to Smuggler's Cove with your family?' She touched the enamel brooch.

'Most summers.'

Joy was imagining Charles and his brother as children splashing around the shallows as the tea terrace filled up around them. Raw-skinned men, sporting brick-red bands of sunburnt foreheads, escorted by wives and children, their hair hanging like seaweed down their backs. She smiled into the general cheerfulness and, reaching across the bottle of OK Sauce, took a serviette. It had the name of the establishment and a line drawing of the bay and rise of cliffs. She liked it and folded it away in her bag.

'What are you doing?'

'Just a little memento.' Joy took souvenirs from everywhere they went; it was as if she was squirrelling memories away because she couldn't believe something this good would last.

'You took a beer mat from the pub too.'

'I'm collecting things to remember our holiday by.'

'I wish you wouldn't talk as if we're never coming back.' His expression clouded. 'Because I promised you. This place is ours now.'

It was on their drive back to London the following afternoon that Charles asked her. His hand resting on her thigh as she breathed in the leather interior of his Riley. He talked of his precarious position in his late father's firm, the demands being placed on him by his mother as he swayed and hooted, cutting in and out of the stream of traffic.

The day was warm enough to drive with the hood down and Joy's hair flapped around her face, adding to the drama as they put the desolate headlands behind them and followed the route of the Viking Norsemen. Charles was explaining how the business was about to make a big push into the emerging markets of South Africa, and that his mother expected him to head up the new division there. Listening to his voice as she silently bid goodbye to the heaving waves along the chain of coastal roads, his agitation punctured by views of ancient abbeys and patch-eyed cows, she remembered his mother and her rudeness from the morning she had accidentally collided with her in the street – it came as no surprise that his move to Cape Town was non-negotiable.

'Marry me,' he announced brightly, his fingers still gripping her thigh.

'Marry you?' She gasped her astonishment.

'Please say you will. We could go to Africa together. I could bear it with you. I could bear anything with you.'

CHAPTER SIXTEEN

The swoop of a large bird flying low between the buildings made him jerk his head up. He wasn't spooked by it, he barely noticed it. In the same way he barely noticed the paring of moon swinging like a hammock between the stars he had never bothered to identify. A cold, clear night. Rare, falling as it did between the rain and thick smog that plagued this city.

It was the second time he'd done this. The idea finding him when he followed the girl home one night. Seeing her lighted window and positioning himself in the entrance of an abandoned shop next door, it was the perfect place to hide and watch her. Lucky for him, there was that large, front-facing window that gave an eagle's view of her ochre-lit life. Craving excitement and stimulation, it was not in his nature to sustain his humdrum existence with his wife as other men his age might do; the temptation to come here and spy on the girl was too strong.

He lit a cigarette and crossed to the railings to peer down on her basement room that was as transparent as a goldfish bowl and left nothing to the imagination. Tonight, the girl was in blue. Something homespun and man-sized. It did nothing for her. Too big, it fell down over her bottom and he couldn't distinguish where her breasts began and ended. He felt thwarted, having made the effort to come out tonight, not to mention the cost of the fare from Ladbroke Grove to Gloucester Road he could ill afford. She was heating something in a pan on a single gas ring. Singing to herself as she stirred it around, her face over the steam. Then her hand tugged at the neck of her pullover and she blew down inside her clothes.

'Go on, lass.' He willed her with his stare, safely concealed from the lights of any passing car. 'Take it off.'

Then, ''Eh up.' Eyes straining, shifting around in his hiding place, to his delight she yanked the pullover off and was wearing next to nothing underneath. Only a flimsy chemise that left little to the imagination.

He shivered, not from the cold, as she tipped forward and gave him a generous eyeful, down to the smooth cleft of flesh between her small yet beautifully firm breasts.

CHAPTER SEVENTEEN

The house came as a surprise. Positioned on a corner and sheltered from the bustle of the Bayswater Road by a row of trees, it looked too grand to be occupied by anyone they were friends with. What also came as a surprise was, instead of Joy, it was Charles, in black tie and dinner jacket, who greeted them. The last of the evening sun through the glass-panelled porch trickling over him like water. Handsome. The only way to describe him. And Queenie, arm in arm with Terrence, gobbled Charles down as if handsome was something she had been starved of.

'Oops, I think I may be a little underdressed,' Terrence said as they pushed into the shadow-filled garden.

'Don't be silly, you're perfect,' she assured, keeping to herself the idea he might be.

Queenie, on the other hand, knew she looked fabulous. Hadn't Terrence said as much when he'd met her from the Tube? Not that she needed his endorsement; she'd already caught people's appreciative glances. There weren't many who could carry off this fox fur stole, never mind the dress beneath it. Her best dress. A hot red in shot silk. Something that, like the fox fur, belonged to her mother and Queenie had skilfully enhanced.

'What an awfully splendid couple you make.' Charles beamed at them. He was right, they did. She could be herself with Terrence: he demanded nothing from her, unlike other men. There was a peck on the cheek for Queenie and a pat on the back for Terrence. 'How's your friend? I heard he got into a spot of bother.'

Terrence swallowed: a dry, anxious sound. Did Charles know about him and Malcolm? Queenie didn't think so.

'He was very shaken up.'

'The police can be awfully heavy-handed with our West Indian friends.'

'Heavy-handed with us all. I was worried they wouldn't release him.'

'But he'd done nothing wrong. He was the one who was set on.'

'Not how the police saw it.'

'God help us all.' Charles gave Terrence another pat on the back. Compensatory this time, or so Queenie thought.

When the matter was dropped, she was free to concentrate on Charles again. Could a man of his standing seriously be interested in a little doe-eyed innocent like Joy? The question, scythe-shaped, cut into her and made her wince. She didn't like thinking it, but surely Charles required someone with more sophistication. Someone to complement his stylish clothes, his poise, the fine cut of his jaw. Someone like her – was that what she was thinking? The idea shocked her. This was her best friend's fiancé; they were to be married before the year was out. It was why they were here; she and Terrence had been invited to celebrate their engagement. She hated herself for thinking these things, but they were out now and couldn't be boxed away again. A flush reddened her neck. She felt its telltale fingers spreading over her chest.

'Are you all right?' Terrence enquired.

'I'm fine.' She jollied him along. 'We're going to have a wonderful time.'

When, at last, they went inside, it was as if to step into another world. She heard Terrence gasp when he tilted his head to the ceiling. To the lofty hall and grand curve of staircase.

'Dorothy will take your things.' Charles nodded to a stout woman in a grey uniform, and Terrence obediently handed over his coat and hat.

'And you, madam?' A raw red hand shot out.

'Oh, no.' Queenie, wary of it, clutched the stole to her chin. 'I'll hold on to this.'

They followed Charles and his cane up to the first floor and into an elegant suite of rooms with fine views of Hyde Park. Loving the feel of the place, the subdued tranquillity infused with the chalky London light pouring in through the tall sash windows, Queenie, a little awestruck, circled the room. Her heels sinking into the plush pile carpet as if walking on sand. All the while keeping one eye on Charles, who was demonstrating the correct way to open a champagne bottle to the housekeeper. Terrence, meanwhile, was admiring the tiles around the fireplace. The whimsical blue-green peacocks, dragons and fishes he would later tell her had been designed by the famous William De Morgan. It seemed to delight Charles to watch his guests look about them with such apprecia-tion. To see them marvel at the oils and watercolours that hardly left a space for a hand between the frames, the rosewood cabinets sagging under the weight of silver trinkets.

'Do sit.' He motioned them to a couch and handed them coupes of champagne.

Queenie sipped from hers, felt the bubbles spread through her like sunshine. The opulent surroundings had the question she'd tried to bat away pushing forward in her mind again. Why had Charles chosen Joy? It was Queenie who knew what men wanted. Joy was charming, on many levels. Sweet, the way she always had her nose in a book and her appreciation for the smallest of things. She would be ideal for someone less polished, but falling short of what a man of Charles's calibre would want from a wife. It was why Queenie was making sure he got a good look at her beautiful legs, just in case he might have overlooked her in some way.

'A glorious evening,' Charles addressed her directly.

'It is, isn't it?' She crossed her legs again, pleased with the way he looked at her.

'And you found us easily?' A flash of his eyes – he was flirting.

'You live here, do you?' Terrence restless beside her; obviously not enjoying the experience as much as she was.

'Since the end of the war. Polishing a desk at Wellington Barracks until recently, of course. All finished now – I think the army having thirteen years of me is quite enough. Quite enough for anyone.' An awkward glance at the floor. 'I've been looking for my own place, but no luck so far.' Charles leant against the mantelpiece, smoking his cigarette and inspecting his cufflinks.

'I wouldn't be in any hurry.' Queenie pressed her varnished nails to her lips and gave Charles a coquettish smile he seemed to appreciate.

She didn't understand why he was having this effect on her. She knew lots of men, her life was littered with them and their proposals, they blew around her as insubstantial as paper bags. What was so special about Charles Gilchrist all of a sudden?

'Where's Joy? I want to toast the two of you.' She sipped her champagne and let the fox fur stole fall open, wanting to reveal the red dress beneath, in the hope of tempting him. 'Isn't she coming to her own party?'

'She'll be here. She's out shopping with my mother.' Charles snapped open a silver cigarette case and offered them both one. 'You women... although, Joy did take some persuading...' He broke off, looked thoughtful for a moment. 'No matter how much you do, it's never enough.' The opinion was furnished with a long pull on his cigarette.

She laughed. A false wheeze of a laugh; her throat constricting under the weight of her financial worries.

Below them, the front door banged shut.

Charles turned to the door. 'They're here.' And he strolled out to the landing to lean over the banisters.

'You're terrible, you are.' Terrence, his voice low.

'Me? *Terrible*.' She finished her drink. 'Why?'

'Come off it, Queenie. Flirting like that with Charles. What d'you think you're playing at?'

'Flirting? No, I'm not.' She put her empty glass down on a table. 'I'm just being friendly.'

'If you say so.'

It was the frenzied yapping of a white dog which announced the arrival of Heloise Gilchrist. A sound not only at odds with the dog's cuteness but also with its stylish owner.

'Mother.' Charles kissed the cheek of the woman who didn't look old enough to have a grown-up son. He ignored the dog. 'This is Queenie. And this is Terrence.'

'Pleased to meet you, Mrs Gilchrist,' Queenie and Terrence chorused and rose to shake the black-gloved hand.

'Oh, please... *please*. It's Heloise.' The woman Queenie recognised from the park – the woman she'd thought was Charles's wife – jiggled the barking puffball up and down in a way you might try to placate a grizzling baby.

'*Please, please, it's Heloise...*' Queenie's muttered amusement was fortunately drowned out by the dog.

'Hush now, *mon chérie*.' The coiffured blonde head nuzzled the dog's fluffy neck.

'Dear me, you are a noisy little one, aren't you?' Queenie reached to stroke it, then changed her mind, fearful it would bite.

'I don't know what's wrong with her. She's never displayed such awful behaviour before.' Heloise, provocative, eyes glinting. 'It must be that thing you're wearing. Fox, isn't it?' A haughty tip of the chin. 'I'd take it off if I were you, dear.'

'Bichon.' Queenie, ignoring the blatant put-down, brandished the word with a sudden flourish. 'The breed of your dog, it's a bichon, isn't it?'

'Bichon *frise*.' The curt correction.

She gave up. It was a waste of time trying to be friendly – the woman was as dry and unwelcome as dandruff. Queenie removed her stole and handed it to the hovering housekeeper.

Dinner at Heloise's swish Regency-style house began with canapés that were served by the red-handed Dorothy, who curtseyed in and out of the shadows with salvers of asparagus on toast and shavings of beef. Queenie took one, then another. She couldn't remember the last time she'd tasted beef. But it was like her father said: if you had money, you could have anything, even with rationing still in full swing. It irked her a little; the war didn't appear to have touched the Gilchrists.

'Thank you for coming tonight. It's so lovely to see you and Terry.' Joy had stepped into the room. With her auburn hair coiled high on her head – a style suspiciously like her future mother-in-law's – and showing off a milk-white neck Queenie never knew existed. The transformation was astonishing; Joy looked the most alluring she had ever looked. Fitted out in a figure-hugging bodice, worn over full satin skirts.

'I wouldn't have missed it for the world.' She gave Joy a peck on the cheek, breathed in her perfume. 'Look at you, all dolled up.'

'Do you like the new me?' Joy pirouetted on her tiptoes.

'You look lovely.' Queenie gulped a mouthful of champagne, the bubbles fizzing up her nose. 'Huge congratulations to you and Charles, by the way.' They clinked glasses. 'Where's the ring?' Reaching for Joy's hand, she lifted it into the light. 'I was expecting some huge rock.'

'Charles is having it altered. It used to belong to his grand-mother.' Joy pulled back her hand. 'It's beautiful, I can't wait for you to see it.'

'You've certainly landed on your feet.' Queenie's gaze skimmed the riches they stood within. 'Fast worker, isn't he? You've only known each other five minutes.'

'It's like Heloise says – you have to go with your heart. She said it was the same when she met Charles's father.' Joy finished what was left of her champagne. 'Do you mind if I leave you for a minute? I want to say hello to Charles, I haven't seen him all day. I'd hate him to think I'm neglecting him.'

'He looks all right to me.' Queenie pursed her lips. 'But if it's what you want, don't let me stop you.'

The dog was quiet now. Curled up asleep on Heloise's black silk lap. Perhaps it was the absence of the fox fur, or perhaps it had been satiated by the morsels Heloise had fed it rather than feeding herself. Queenie joined Terrence on the couch and, sipping from what seemed to be a bottomless goblet – champagne finished, they had moved on to red wine – Queenie was tipsy already. The discussion she wasn't part of bored her, and she looked around for Charles, but he had disappeared. To amuse herself, she held her glass of claret up to the spangled shards of the chandelier, admired its rich garnet blush. She didn't notice him walk into the room behind her.

'It matches your dress.' Charles bowed to deliver the same observation she had made, before rejoining Joy and leaving a trail of aftershave her eyes tried to follow.

There it was again. What he did to her hadn't gone away. It was the same whenever he chose to turn his attention to her. That flip of her insides. The sensation not unlike the one she'd experienced as a child, riding bareback along the sands at Goldchurch. The thrill with Charles was the same as surging forward into a gallop. An element of danger. The power rendering her breathless, much as he did now.

Queenie sank back into the couch and did what she had been dying to do since she arrived. She watched them. The betrothed.

Each subtly orbiting the other as if engaged in some strange ceremonial dance. Their love – for this was something Queenie was forced to accept – delivered through silent gestures and furtive glances. Charles couldn't stop himself from touching Joy. His hand seeking her out should she move too far away. Joy too, her fingers on their recurrent quest for the skin between the onyx dress studs of his evening shirt, leaning into him, planting kisses on his mouth. Picking a spot of fluff off his satin peak lapel. How exultant they looked, how effortless.

Joy moved around the room with the grace of a ballerina and, observing the confidence this new Joy oozed, Queenie wondered who had persuaded her to dress up, apply make-up and do her hair. Thinking how often she had tried and failed. Joy then moved to sit beside Heloise. They exchanged soft smiles and Queenie saw the tender way Heloise patted Joy's hand. The gesture provided the answer. As did the conversation in French they were having, setting themselves apart with their foreignness. She was hurt by it; hurt by Joy's sudden superiority to her.

'Joy looks stunning, don't you think?' Terrence barged in on her contemplations. 'Wonderful to see her and Charles so happy.'

Queenie nodded. Incapable of openly agreeing, she sipped from her glass. Why wasn't it good to see her friend had finally shed the little-girl look she was always teasing her about? What was wrong with her?

'Mirror, mirror on the wall…' Terrence, chinking his glass against hers. 'Why so glum, Queenie, darling?' The portentous weight of his hand on her arm. 'Is it because you have competition for the number one slot?'

She cracked a smile she knew didn't reach her eyes. Terrence was right: this shift of power was going to take some adjusting to. She had always been the centre of attention; it had been that way forever. Certainly between her and Joy. Queenie was the beautiful one, the one everyone noticed. Damn that Gilchrist woman, she'd done this. But what was the appeal? Failing to charm Heloise herself, Queenie couldn't imagine her taking to anyone. But she'd certainly taken a shine to Joy. Look at them sharing a joke and tittering together; it made her feel quite left out.

Terrence extinguished his cigarette. 'How's about us going and checking that drummer out? I've heard him, he's good. And if you give him the thumbs up, the band will too.'

'Drummer?' Queenie was only half-listening.

'At the Blue Note. You remember me telling you? Joy and Charles could come along, we'll make a night of it… *Queenie?* Have you heard anything I've just said?'

'What?' Focused on Joy, she squeezed her hands into fists, her nails digging into her palms.

'Dear me, darling, your eyes have actually gone green. Is it because those two are getting on so well?' He nodded over at Joy and Heloise. 'Ooo, you're really jealous. I know you've been like a big sister to her but you're not going to be around much longer, you're off to a totally new world.'

'Too clever for your own good sometimes, aren't you, Terry?'

With a flash of irritation, Queenie left the room and went upstairs. Found the bathroom with its cast-iron tub on shiny black claws. The contrast to her outside privy, the tin bath she needed to rig up in the kitchen – it made her feel worse. She stared at herself in the wall of mirrors, her image reflecting off into infinity. *Quite an improvement on your dreary basement*, her silent thoughts to Joy. Queenie could see why she would snap this up and doing a quick calculation – pricing up the house, their outfits, the food, the wine – concluded, yes, there was money here, all right. Plenty of it.

She turned on the taps. One hot, one cold. She washed her hands and, looking around for something to dry them on, spied a shelf of towels. Hothouse peach. She pushed her hands between the folds of Egyptian cotton to appreciate the sumptuous luxury before dropping her head to smell them. They smelled of money.

Queenie longed to be surrounded with lovely things; she was sick of being hard up, of having to make do and mend. It wasn't fair Joy got to have all this and not her. New York and all its promises couldn't come quick enough now. Drying her hands, she gathered saliva in her mouth, spat on the towel and folded it away again. Such a pathetic act, but it made her feel better.

She left the bathroom and went for a snoop along the corridor. Pushed open the door of a bedroom and looked at the bed. A large brass affair with a vermilion eiderdown and lacy pillowcases. It was quite the most romantic thing she'd seen. She stepped inside and sidled to the wardrobe, turned the key and opened it on to a row of clothes. Expensive things, she could tell by the deep hems and the quality of the fabric. She stooped to the shoes at the bottom and lifted one into the light. Turned it over to admire the hand-stitched soles, the elegant heel and deep red leather. Heloise's, she guessed. It was at this moment she finally identified the sensation that had been prickling her all evening. Terrence was right: she was jealous of Joy. There she was, thinking she could just click her fingers and Charles would come running… He was only a man, after all. Not that she had wanted him until now. Strange that.

A dangerous thing, jealousy. She'd seen what it did to others; others who were jealous of her. She ran her fingertips over the beautiful leather bow on the front of the shoe and the pearl button fastening. No, this was more than jealousy; what Queenie felt was hate, and pressing her thumb deep into the soft nap of the leather upper, she dragged it across, scoring it with her nail.

CHAPTER EIGHTEEN

Joy slept with an arm flung out to the side. Her basement room was chilly. When she woke, she opened her eyes and didn't immediately register where she was. Sounds of the city filtered through to her, throwing her back to the house of her childhood and the room where she would lie awake listening to her parents quarrelling. A house with a tidy garden and a woodshed filled with her father's tools. A house with crumbling walls and hissing draughts. Where every time it rained, they needed to rush about with buckets, and her only playmates for miles were foxgloves the height of twelve-year-olds.

On the other side of the glass, the *coo coo* of the woodpigeon she fed scraps to. Soothing in its monotony, it would be easy to drift back to sleep but she needed to get up. Setting a pan of water on the single gas ring, she brushed her teeth while she waited for it to boil. Looking around at the comfortless, damp-stained walls of her bedsit, she sniffed what remained of the onions she'd fried for last night's meal. Fitted with a frugal mismatch of her landlord's furniture, she wouldn't miss this place; it belonged more to the mice than it did to her.

She rinsed her mouth and looked out of her front window to see what the weather was doing. Where had summer gone? She hoped it would cheer up by the weekend, Charles was taking her to Dorset again.

Hang on. She flinched.

A blink of a silver button and like a magpie, she twisted to claim it.

Only part of him was visible: a chunk of boot to belt, trapped between the pavement and railings. A smoker, judging by the swirl of cigarette smoke. Were policemen allowed to do that on duty? Why was he hovering around out there? Strange, wasn't it – what was he doing?

She put on her dressing gown and scooped a handful of crumbs from the bottom of the breadbin, then unlocked the door that opened on to the small stone entrance area with its steps that led up to the street. Tiptoeing outside, quietly, making no sudden movements, she stayed close to the wall and looked up at him. He stood with his back to her basement railings, and what struck her was that he looked too small for his uniform, that the peaked cap drowned him. A wavering recollection of the policeman who had leered at Queenie the morning they'd met up for her birthday. Hadn't he been too small for his regalia too?

The *coo coo* at her shoulder reminded her to open her palm and let the pigeon peck the crumbs from her hand. She had only turned away for a minute, but when she looked back, the policeman had gone.

'*Tant pis*, my little friend.' She stroked the bird's soft, pinkish breast. 'Whatever he was here for, it can't have been to do with me, can it?'

The water had boiled by the time she went back inside. She used some of it to make her morning cup of Camp coffee, the rest to wash in. A purple dress bought by Heloise was today's choice. With little buttons from collar to hem, the flared skirt made her feel glamorous. Her friend Amy was back from holiday today and they were to walk to work together. She thought about how at odds they were with the others employed at the museum. The frustrated and heavily familied men, who hated working with women and only wanted automated machines. *You could kick a machine*, Joy thought, suspecting they would kick her and Amy if they could get away with it.

She made the bed and checked her correspondence from Charles – the letters written in his violet ink, that she would read and reread, folding and refolding until the paper grew weak at the creases – was stowed under her pillow and the keepsakes she was steadily procuring were safe in their shoebox under the bed. She drank her coffee black. Breathed out against the steam. Thought of the small gifts they had exchanged like the lock of her hair and the yellow rock rose she had picked for him in Dorset that he pressed between the pages of his Matthew Arnold poems.

Joy combed out the knots in her hair: hair that never did as it was told. It was another of her failures, so her mother said. Heloise was going to take her to have it cut soon. Did she mind being remodelled this way? No, she liked it and thought, as she had a few minutes to spare, she might as well apply some rouge from the make-up bought from Woolworths. When Heloise gave her beauty tips, it felt different to Queenie: less like a scolding and more of an encouragement. Joy put on the stylish raincoat Heloise had also bought her and pinned the apple brooch to the lapel. She put the diamante hair clasp away in a drawer. She only wore it when she was waitressing at the club to please Queenie; she didn't think it suited her. Then, collecting her handbag, she set off with a jaunty step, aware it was quite a different girl who locked up her bedsit today. One who trotted up the stone steps and into a world she couldn't wait to be part of.

Amy was there with her generous smile bunching her freckles.

'Hello.' Joy hugged her and cast around for the policeman. The sight of an officer of the law was usually reassuring, but there was something about him that hadn't felt right. 'Did you enjoy your holiday?'

'Never mind about me.' Amy clapped her hands. 'You look like the cat who got the cream. What's been going on?'

Joy did a little swirl. 'It's my new outfit.'

'It's not the clothes, although they're lovely. It's you. You've changed into this whole new person. You better tell me everything.' Amy fizzed with enthusiasm.

They were about to go when Joy's landlord emerged from the communal door of the house.

'You've had post. Pink.' He stated the obvious.

'Give it to her then.' Amy, bolder than Joy could ever be. 'Standing there like an idiot.'

'*Merci, monsieur.*' Joy took the letter.

'From your sweetheart?' His amusement followed them down the street along with the callous pale blue gaze of the man dressed up as a policeman who stood in the empty doorway opposite.

'Is it?' Amy bobbed alongside.

Joy tucked the envelope in her bag. 'No, it's not.' She groaned. 'It's from my mother.'

CHAPTER NINETEEN

'That's it, lass, you relax for me… just breathe.' He pressed the mask down over her face with his right hand, used his other to pull the stocking from his pocket. 'Breathe nice and deeply,' he clucked around her. 'Silly girl, aren't you, getting yourself in trouble like this. I'd say it's a good job I'm here to help you out.'

He fiddled with a length of rubber tubing he kept concealed behind a grubby flap of curtain. Then a hiss of gas as he adjusted the bulldog clip and opened the tap.

'It smells a bit funny, Mr Christie.'

'Well, it will do, lass. It means it's working. Are you feeling sleepy?'

'Yes, a bit.'

'That's good… you'll drift off in a minute. Keep breathing, we want you nice and sleepy, don't we? There, lass,' he soothed. 'You're doing ever so well… nowt for you to fret about.'

'I don't know if I want to do this.' Her muffled distress as she tried to pull the mask off. 'I don't like it, I don't… I want to stop. I've changed my mind.'

'Stop being silly. You've to trust me. Now relax.' The mask was forced back over her mouth and nose. 'That's it… just breathe. That's it. Breathe. It won't hurt… I won't hurt you.'

'No, please, I want you to stop… Get off. Get that thing off me.' She thrashed her arms and scrabbled to push free of the mask, to get out of the rope chair.

'Stay still, you dirty bitch. I bet you used to be all cocky and aloof, didn't you? Aye, I know your type. Before your belly was bulging and tongues started wagging. You bloody want it, and I'm going to bloody well give it to you.'

And as she opened her mouth to scream, he drove his fist full into her face.

CHAPTER TWENTY

Tuesday. Mid-August. The Mockin' Bird was closed for the night and Queenie, preening herself all day for this evening's outing, told Terrence that she, Joy and Charles would meet him at the Blue Note Bar in Soho at eight. Calling for Joy and Charles in Bayswater, the maid, Dorothy, opened the door and instructed her to wait in the hall. Absorbed in what she could see of her face in an oval mirror, Queenie was applying fresh dabs of Californian Poppy to her décolletage when the sound of voices drifted down the stairwell. Animated. Insistent. Enough to make her shut her bag and edge up the stairs, in time to see Heloise Gilchrist pacing the landing. Her hands clasped before her like an expectant father, the puffball dog weaving between her ankles.

'Is anything the matter?'

'Oh, it's you. You were told to wait in the hall.' Heloise scooped the dog in her arms.

'I heard raised voices.'

'Did you now? Well, it's Joy. She's not feeling well. She says she's not up for going out this evening.'

'That's a shame. What's wrong with her, poor thing? Where is she?'

'She's having a lie down. But, please,' a restraining hand was placed on Queenie's arm, 'that scent you're wearing. What is it? I've noticed it on you before. It's awfully strong. The poor girl's feeling nauseous as it is.'

'My scent? Oh, for God's sake.' Close to losing her temper with this woman, she pushed past and leant around the door. Found a pale-faced Joy propped on a throne of cushions. Queenie adjusted her diaphanous shawl, its embossed butterflies threatening to flutter free of her shoulders.

'Queenie.' Joy gulped her greeting. 'You look beautiful. Doesn't she look beautiful, Charles?'

Charles was perched on the end of the bed, his back to the door. He twisted to face her, then returned to Joy to nod his appreciation. How dishy he looked in his dinner suit and glacé shoes. The sight of him made Queenie clean forget to ask Joy what was wrong.

'I hope she'll be better by tomorrow; she's meeting her mother for lunch.'

'Sylvie's coming to London?' Queenie raised her eyebrows to Heloise.

'I'll be fine. I just need an early night.' Joy lifted a hand to her fiancé's face. 'I can't wait for Maman to meet Charles.'

'If he can get away from the office. He's a meeting with the African contingency he needs to prepare for.'

'Yes, but that's not until late afternoon,' Charles reminded his mother.

'And we'll be finished with Maman by two.'

'Two?' Heloise spluttered. 'But she's coming all the way from Arras?'

'She's not stopping in London, she's off to Essex in the evening.'

'Essex?'

'Queenie's grandparents live there.'

'She's seeing them but not me?' An indignant wiggle. 'How come she knows them?'

'From before the war. It's how Queenie and I met.'

'Has Joy told you much about Sylvie?' Queenie asked Heloise.

'No. I've said she's to bring her to tea. I'd like to meet her.'

A mirthless laugh. 'You wouldn't want to meet her, trust me.'

'Anyway, enough of all that.' Heloise, cuddling her dog. 'Joy's been telling us she still wants you and Charles to go out tonight. Is that what you'd like?' The tone, accusatory.

Queenie returned her stare. 'I don't mind.'

'Charles?' Heloise prompted him. The chill of her stare boring holes between Queenie's shoulder blades.

'It's only for a couple of hours, my love.' Casual, stroking Joy's wrist. 'Just to check out this new drummer.'

'Yes, you must go,' Joy chirruped. 'You're all dressed up now.'

Charles turned to look at Queenie again. Properly this time. A slow, protracted look as he pulled on his cigarette, his eyes cruising the length of her: forehead to neck, over the swell of her hips and down her thighs. Queenie felt he could see every inch of what she was, and the flowing material of her dress no more covered her than water. She fiddled with the string of glass beads around her neck and, in the way a woman might let a lover, in the tingling moments before allowing him to touch her, she let him drink her in. It was the most erotic of sensations, standing there, wanting him to touch her; quivering in anticipation. The intensity was enough to make her stumble backwards.

'Are you feeling unwell?' Heloise was on to her. 'You're not coming down with what Joy's got?'

Queenie righted herself and tightened her shawl. 'What Joy's got?' She eyed Charles again. 'No, I haven't got what Joy's got.'

Malcolm wasn't there to meet Terrence from the train. Not in the ticket office or the waiting room, with its pre-war décor. Terrence hovered on the platform and heeded the sombre silence, hoping any minute his love would appear, shamefaced and apologetic. But he didn't and, under the weight of the passing time, doubts flooded his mind. Was Malcolm in trouble? Had he been arrested again?

Enough pacing, Terrence sat down on a bench, his face the picture of despondency as he watched trains come and go. When were they last in touch? Not long ago. He checked his watch, then

the clock on the platform in case his watch had stopped. It was
getting late. Malcolm was never usually kept back at work, so where
was he? Had he changed his mind? Terrence slumped against the
bench, felt its wooden skeleton press against his own.

'Everything all right, sir?'

A man in a blue jacket with dusty hair was standing beside him.
Terrence hadn't noticed his approach.

'It's just that, well…' Obviously station staff, the man blew
his nose on a handkerchief pulled from a pocket of his uniform.
'I couldn't help noticing you've been sat here for some time.' His
complexion washed out by the fading day. 'D'you need a cab or a
bus? Cos there's a taxi rank out front. I can show you if you like?'

Terrence gave a small smile. 'Thanks, but I'm waiting for
someone.'

The man didn't budge, his gaze intensifying.

'It's not a problem if I wait here?' Terrence, feeling the need to
ask permission.

'A girlfriend, is it, sir?' He shifted around inside his uniform.
'The person you're meeting?'

'No, just a friend.'

'A friend, eh?' He winked.

'Not to worry, I can meet…' Terrence began, but the man
had sat down beside him. He blinked through a shaft of evening
sunlight that fell between them. 'You're quite right; I can't sit here
any longer. I'd best get going.'

A restraining hand was placed on his leg. Terrence gawped at
it in shock.

'There's no need to rush, sir.' Another wink, creepy this time.

Terrence slipped to his feet and moved away from him. The
ghostly impression of the man's fingertips still on his thigh. 'I think
you've got the wrong idea, mate.'

'You sure about that, sir?' The stare was unwavering, drilling
down to the tormented nub of him.

'Perfectly sure, thank you.' Terrence, his voice trembling. 'I have to get going.'

'If you say so, sir.' The man gave him a strange, lopsided salute. 'Goodbye. I hope you find your friend.'

Terrence heard his landlady's voice before he reached the top of the stairs.

'You've a visitor, Mr Banks.'

'I have?'

'I said he could wait for you in your room. I hope that was all right?'

'Depends who it is.'

'A dark fella.' Mrs Spencer slapped a hand to her face that was stained a peculiar yellow by the light in the hall. 'He looked perfectly nice. Very polite. My Bert gave him the once over... didn't you, Bert?' Her husband's muffled response from their downstairs quarters. 'Bin in the wars a bit though, ain't he?'

Terrence knew immediately who she was talking about and was eager to get to his bed-sitting room. But, as usual, Mrs Spencer wanted to talk.

'We're not like others round here. Me and Bert don't mind them West Indian fellas. Not when they're here to put poor Old Blighty back together again. What d'you say, Mr Banks?'

'I totally agree.' Terrence, itching to get away.

'I was only sayin' to Mrs Carter from across the way, I was sayin', she shouldn't be discriminatin' against 'em. I said I'd seen that sign she got up in her winda... "No Blacks, no Irish, no dogs". That's not very Christian, is it, Mr Banks?'

'No, it isn't.' He was doing his level best to be polite.

'I don't get along with them people who are suspicious. The Blacks are fine by me, like I said. No, I don't go along with them nasty names they've got for 'em neither. Cos it's only suspicion that makes 'em behave that way. Taking their jobs? I ask you – I'd like to see them do the sorts of jobs they do.'

'Was there anything else, Mrs Spencer? Only it's been rather a long day.' Terrence feigned a yawn, hoping she would get the message.

'Oh, sorry, Mr Banks. There's me, yabberin' on. Bert's always on at me, aren't you, Bert?' Another grunt. 'Only to say, well, how to put it? If this visitor of yours is in a tight spot, me and Bert don't mind if he stays the night... just the one, mind.' She raised a finger. 'Any longer, and I'm not sure it'd go down well with me other tenants, what with the limited facilities, an' all.'

'That's very decent of you, Mrs Spencer. Thank you, I'll let him know.'

'Well, it's like my Bert says, it's not like you've got a woman up there.' A forceful cackle. ''Cos we couldn't be allowing those kinds of shenanigans under our roof.'

They stood touching hands beside the iron bedstead.

'Mrs Spencer says you can stay the night if you want.'

'She said dat?' Malcolm shot him a look of disbelief.

'She's a good sort. Her and her husband. It's funny,' Terrence smiled, 'you being a man turns out to be beneficial for once. She'd never have agreed if you'd been a girl.'

They laughed.

'Can I really stay?'

'One night.' Terrence took his cigarettes and lighter from his jacket pocket. Placed them beside the novels by his bed. 'I wouldn't push our luck beyond that.'

He watched Malcolm scan the room. Saw how he took in the mock-gilded mirror, the washstand, the double bed, the tallboy, the pink-and-grey patterned wallpaper that reminded Terrence of the spilled intestines he'd seen during the war.

'Nicer than my gaff.' Malcolm grinned in a way that suggested he felt safer here than out in the balmy summer evening.

'It's not bad.' Terrence looked at him. He wanted to share it with Malcolm forever, until it became a home for them both. 'Why don't we look into getting a place where we can both live? Would you like that?'

'Wouldn't dat be difficult?' Malcolm's voice: a deep rumble that began in his boots.

'Not if we were careful. Are you afraid?'

'I'm always afraid, man. But... but dey won't let us do dat.' His eyes, expectant as a child's.

'Why not? We've come this far.'

Terrence looked at the long piece of sticking plaster fixed to Malcolm's cheekbone. The face beneath, still a little swollen. Terrence lifted his fingers to what remained of the damage but didn't touch.

'Poor darling.' He flinched from the memories of that night.

'Wrong place, wrong time.' A painful smile.

Terrence was troubled by the vulnerability he found in Malcolm's eyes. His stint in police custody had changed him.

'I love you. You do know that?' He lifted Malcolm's hand to his lips. Kissed it. He smelled of spearmint and aftershave.

Terrence dropped his gaze to the mauve eiderdown and pillows on the bed. All he wanted was the intimacy others had. The double bed, the sharing, the growing old together. Marriage. Yes, why not? Why couldn't men who loved each other marry? Because society would rather see you strung up and flogged in the street, that's why. He counted his own mother among them, and his mother professed to love him. But she loved her religion more, he reminded himself. It was a fantasy to think he and Malcolm could be secure, to live a life that did not require looking over their shoulders. But, oh, to make peace with himself. A faint nostalgia for the dark confessional box and the priest's voice. For what had been lost, forgotten or rejected. To be made safe from the eternal pain that was surely awaiting him when his time on earth was over. *Huh*, he thought, flinging his head to the ceiling and coming to his senses – that was the biggest fantasy going.

The little clock on the tallboy pinged eight and Terrence, mindful that morning was just a few hours away, pressed his mouth against Malcolm's with an urgency like never before. They had to live, live for the moment; it was all they were guaranteed. Tasting the sweetness of him, he shut his eyes against the world. This was heaven. You could keep your puritanical God if this was a sin.

'Oh, hell, I was supposed to be checking out that drummer tonight.' He pulled away, suddenly remembering.

'You go. I'm not in de mood. And us out together in de street?' Malcolm sucked air in through his teeth.

'Queenie's going to be there, she'd love to meet you.'

Malcolm shook his head. 'It ain't safe, man. I know you tink you can trust her but…'

'Don't worry.' Terrence squeezed his hand. 'We don't have to go. I'd rather stay here. With you.'

'And dat double bed.' Malcolm whistled his appreciation. 'We ain't never had no double bed before.'

The Blue Note Bar in Soho was a twenty-minute taxicab ride from his mother's house in Bayswater. By the time Queenie and Charles arrived – without his cane for a change – the party was in full swing. Deep underground and jam-packed with young men in turtleneck sweaters and girls in cocktail dresses and pointy heels, it was a new experience. But where was Terrence? He'd been going on about this drummer for weeks. Queenie scanned the stone walls and vaulted ceiling running with condensation, but there was no sign of him. Charles, meanwhile, enquired about their reservation and they were ushered to a table near the stage, where the loud freeform rhythm of the instrumental band – the gambol of the piano, the alarm call of brass, woodwind and drums – made conversation near impossible.

Queenie made a point of listening to the drummer. He was good. Easily as good as Buster, in the days Buster was sober enough to keep the beat. She could see why Terrence was interested in him: he looked just his type in his natty suit and beaming smile. Toes tapping to the rhythm, she sipped the whisky macs Charles had bought her. The more she drank the less she cared about Terrence. It was great here. The lively crowd, the vibrancy. Americans had a word for it. *Groovy*, that was it. She was going to have to swot up on slang like that before going there.

Queenie gave up trying to keep the shawl in place and let it slip from her shoulders, delighting in the way her skin took on the blush of the rosy-coloured table lamp. The Mockin' had lamps, but not like these. These turned each table into a mini spotlit stage. All you saw were hands. Moving in and out of cigarette packets, lifting tumblers, jewellery twinkling on fingers and wrists. Nothing of the individuals they were attached to. Whoever they were, they dissolved into the tobacco smoke. It created an intimate, illicit, clandestine feel. A sense of danger. Nothing like the club where Queenie sang. Compared to the Blue Note, the Mockin' Bird seemed more of an old boy's club with its blatant cronyism and private members' policy.

'Can I dance with you?'

The vibration of Charles's request found the delicate edges of her ear and surged through her like electricity. Already charged by the alcohol, she drained her tumbler and watched – as if this was something happening to someone else entirely – him lift her hand and lead her to the dance floor. They held each other close. Him positioning her. She could feel the power of him as he pressed her close to his chest, iron-hot and steaming through the sleek material of her dress. Shoulders, chest, hips, knees. The hardness of his thighs. The hardness of him. Her legs buckled beneath her, forcing her to cling tighter.

'Sing for me,' he purred into her hair. And when she did, her lips brushing the satin-smooth of his freshly shaven cheek, the edge of his moustache, he closed his eyes. What she knew, through the haze of alcohol, to be her mellifluous voice, dissolving into his aftershave and the scented patina of his hair.

The fresh air was a shock when they came up to street level and, aiming for the taxi rank, they hardly exchanged a word. Queenie, giddy from the half a dozen whisky macs, twirled along the pavement in the way she had done on the dance floor below. Her heels clattering beneath a hotchpotch of stars showing between the breaking clouds that, shiny as policemen's buttons, looked close enough to pluck free.

'I've had the most wonderful evening, Charles.' She shimmied towards him through the empty Soho street. 'I know it's late, but I'm not the least tired.' She giggled into her hands.

He stopped to stare at her. Taking what was to be a final pull on his cigarette before throwing it away. He drew her towards him and kissed her full on the mouth. The stiffened brim of his fedora colliding with the bridge of her nose. Beyond them, the flux of the city melted and merged: the rumble of traffic, the occasional glare of passing headlamps, the smell of recent rain on the pavement.

Then he flung her aside as he had only minutes before with his cigarette.

'This isn't what I want.' His expression fierce, it was as if he hated her all of a sudden. 'This is not what I do.'

With a thousand things to say, Queenie couldn't form any one thought into a coherent sentence. They swam around her head, slippery as eels, and her mind was incapable of pulling them free.

'Charles?' Queenie found her voice, at last. 'Don't go. I don't want you to go.'

Clouds bashed together. They covered then uncovered the moon. She tilted her head to them and wished the night sky would turn a blood-red and echo her mood. And what was her mood? Reckless, she told herself. Reckless.

'Don't let's go home yet.' She seized his hand.

'But everything's shut.'

'Follow me.' She led the way. 'I know just the place.'

CHAPTER TWENTY-ONE

Lucky the good-looking couple were too engrossed in one another to notice him: an unremarkable man in a trilby and raincoat, standing in a spill of gaslight, watching. One of his favourite hidey-holes, this narrow gap that fell between these two high buildings. He didn't speak, he didn't move. But his eyes were busy. The pale blue of them, sharp as daggers from behind horn-rimmed spectacles, ferreted them out of the dark. When he had finished looking at the elegant man in his expensive suit and fedora, a man he thought he recognised from somewhere, he twisted his attention to his female companion. It was she who was of real interest.

She was everything his wife wasn't: there was nothing homely and passive about this one. She was what he termed a seductress. *Look at her, manipulating and seducing that man.* There was no doubting she knew how to use her feminine wiles. He blamed his smothering sisters for the sense of sexual inadequacy he always felt in the presence of women, especially alluring and gregarious ones like this. Women like this mortified and ridiculed him, but there was no denying they were his darkest desires and what he fantasised about when he did what he did to the ones he could overpower. And it was with the idea of overpowering this woman taking shape in his mind that he decided to follow the glamorous pair along the labyrinth of deserted streets to find out where they were going.

CHAPTER TWENTY-TWO

Unaware of the murderous intent which prowled the shadows listening to their receding footfalls – the slap of his shiny shoes, the click of her heels – Queenie fell into step alongside Charles, and they left Soho and moved into Mayfair. When it began to rain, he removed his jacket and held it over their heads as they negotiated the maze of cobbled lanes and murky alleyways, passing under an archway just as a clock struck three.

'I know where we are,' Charles said when they reached the stage door of the Mockin' Bird.

She felt his eyes on her as she took the key from her bag and guided it into the lock. He held the door open for her. Close to her back, his breath on the nape of her neck, she shivered in anticipation. The club looked different. Smaller. Plainer. But she knew which lights to put on and did, reluctant for the mood to change between them.

Glad to be out of the rain, she dropped her shawl and Charles draped his jacket over a bar stool. She poured them each a whisky and put a record on the turntable. When she went to the lavatory, she leant her forehead against the cool mirror. She was drunk. Had she ever been quite this drunk before? She couldn't remember.

Back in the bar, she began to waltz. Slowly. Holding out her hands for him to join her.

'Dance with me.'

'I'm not sure that's wise.'

'Isn't it rather too late for that?'

He joined her. Reluctant. Shifting his feet, imitating hers. She kept her eyes on his and whispered, 'One-two-three, one-two-three.' Showed him where she wanted him to put his hands. Stopped when the music stopped. They waited, listening as the stylus crackled in the groove and the rhythm changed. Charles made an arch of his arm and Queenie passed under. His hand, too fast for hers, caught the string of glass beads around her neck. The string snapped and the beads bounced around the dance floor, into the darkened corners of the club.

'Leave them.' She didn't want it to break the magic. 'I'll find them later.'

She led him downstairs to the dressing room. Warm and dark as a pocket. She kicked off her shoes and slipped the bow of her dress and let it float to the floor. She felt him move towards her, wrapped in darkness. Close enough to feel his breath on her skin. She dropped down onto the chaise longue, where, without warning, she sensed his nakedness, tender and vital, moulding the length of her spine. Unable to resist him as he soundlessly sought her out from beneath the silky material of her camisole. She was giving him the something he must have read in her a long time before now. There was no need to question it, so she didn't. Not then. She simply turned onto her back and let him slide her out of her underwear, before directing him to where she needed him most.

When later came, Charles stooped to retrieve a glass bead on his way out of the club. Then he found another. He picked them up and passed them back to her, warm from his hand. She looked at the fragile lines of his open palm. All she needed was one small sign. One word and she would abandon everything and go with him. Be whatever he wanted her to be. But he didn't speak. He lifted his jacket from where he'd left it, put on his hat and, without turning back, pushed out into the damp, ash-grey dawn. Unaware of the skulking menace in raincoat and trilby, who, having followed them to the Mockin' Bird some hours before, had been waiting patiently for them to re-emerge.

CHAPTER TWENTY-THREE

A thin grey morning. Chilly for September. Inside the church, there were flowers, pink as seaside rock, and Eric Osbourne waiting for his bride by the altar. Smart, in his hired morning suit and smelling of Potter and Moore. Queenie waited for her father to turn and look at her, wanting to share a smile, but he didn't move, so the opportunity was missed. Queenie, Joy and Terrence loitered in the narthex, reluctant to take up their positions until Charles had arrived. Where was he? Queenie hadn't seen him since their night at the Blue Note over three weeks earlier and was eager to get the inevitable awkwardness over. She looked at Joy. Her hands were as fidgety as the birds fluttering in the branches of the churchyard's yews.

Joy wasn't wearing the dove-grey taffeta dress with a sweetheart swing Queenie had made for her. A dress she'd delivered in person to her bedsit two days before. She was in something soft and flowing in a midnight-blue chiffon that Heloise Gilchrist had bought her. And Queenie had taken it as a snub.

'You're funny with me today, Queenie. Is everything all right?' A strand of hair had loosened from its pin, enhancing Joy's beauty.

Queenie said nothing. Afraid of bursting into tears. She might be hurting because of Joy's perceived thoughtlessness, but compared to what she had done, it was nothing, and she had no right to be miffed about something this trivial.

'Is it because of the dress?' Joy gripped the beaded bag, another thing that woman had no doubt purchased. Queenie gnawed her lip, afraid of what might spill out of her mouth. 'You've every right to be cross, I know how awfully hard you worked on it.'

'How could I be upset when you look so lovely?' Conscious of Terrence hovering within earshot, the wedding guests seated around them, she stroked Joy's arm, saw how her little fair hairs stood up in the cold. She didn't want to hear it, but now she had, there was no unhearing it. To Queenie's dismay, along with the hair and the clothes, Joy had started to speak like Charles and Heloise. Her resentment reared its head again. Black and nasty. 'But I don't like that brooch.' She couldn't stop the words from coming. 'It's horrible.'

Joy's fingers flew to her left shoulder strap and she adopted an injured look. 'Don't you like it?'

'No, I don't. It doesn't go with anything.'

Someone in the congregation sneezed and the subject of the brooch was dropped. The sneezing echoed around them while the organ wheezed through a piece of music Joy identified as a Bach toccata. Time ticked on. They decided they had better take up their seats on the groom's side. Like Charles, there was no sign of the bride. Had Norma changed her mind?

The vicar, in his cassock and surplice, lifted his head to the doors that opened behind them. Norma was suddenly there, dressed in white and silent as a ghost. With no one to give her away, she walked up the aisle alone. Carrying her pink posy like a cup of tea she didn't want to spill. The vicar welcomed everyone and did not refer to the lateness of the hour. The ceremony was performed – only once did he stumble over the words – so before they knew it the vows had been said, and Queenie's father had put a plain gold band on the plain little finger of the new Mrs Osbourne.

Queenie, called as their witness, noticed the bride's hand shook as she lifted the fountain pen. Scratching sounds as the ink flowed onto the register. A spidery scrawl compared to her father's confident strokes as he signed his name alongside. Out in the churchyard, Charles was waiting in his ordinary suit and fedora, gripping his silver-topped cane.

'There you are, you missed the service.' Joy trotted over to him, stretched up to kiss his cheek.

'I'm sorry, I was delayed.' Queenie watched a muscle twitch along his jaw and tried to catch his eye. 'I trust it all went off without a hitch?' He turned to her briefly, but it was all she was getting.

He stepped past Queenie to curl an arm around Joy's waist, claiming her. They kissed before he steered her away to stand on the periphery of the wedding party. Queenie ignored them. Her face flushed and angry. What right did he have to blank her? He was as much to blame for what had happened. She moved to stand beside Terrence and tossed rice over the happy couple. Higher and higher, as the vicar's vestments shifted and fell in the stiff September wind. Rice blew over their feet, collected beside the listing gravestones made black with rain. Under the yew trees, Norma's veil quivered as her hands had done when she'd signed her new name.

Queenie would have liked to go home and change into her dressing gown and slippers and sit down with a nice cup of tea. Feeling tired and bloated this past week, she wondered if she could be sickening for something. But there was the reception to be got through first; she couldn't leave before the speeches. The bride and groom were hassled by the photographer. They were to stand there, and there. Immediate family were instructed to join them. Then the wider group of friends. Joy and Charles didn't step forward – deep in conversation, they didn't appear to have heard. The wind caught the hem of Queenie's dress and she pushed a hand to it to keep it down. Someone laughed at something the best man said. She looked over at Joy: she was a beauty in the dress she'd chosen to wear today. She heard Terrence tell her so. He said nothing to Queenie about how she looked. Joy was different these days. Since meeting Charles, it was as if she had been lit up inside, and Queenie still wasn't sure how she felt about this. She closed her eyes against the photographer's flashing bulb. Exchanged them for flashes of what she and Charles had been that night. The feel of his lips on hers.

His skin on hers. How it felt when he was inside her. She pressed the palm of her hand to her lower abdomen. To where the ache for him had begun again. She would make him talk to her, she would; she would not let him pretend what they had done hadn't happened.

Clouds cast strange shadows over the wedding guests. Then a shout went up. Probably the photographer, saying, 'That's it, folks. All finished here.' Norma lobbed the small bouquet high into the air. When Joy caught it, Queenie moved back to stand beside her. Did her best to ignore the way Charles stiffened and turned away. Looked instead at the spray of fine freckles on Joy's bare shoulder, the midnight-blue setting off the reddish-brown tones of her hair. It was a good choice, although she doubted it was Joy's choice. But what did that matter? All that mattered was that, for once, Queenie wasn't the belle of the ball.

'Are you two coming to the Hen and Chickens? Dad's paid for sherry and sandwiches.' She breathed her question close to Joy. Noticed her gold earrings glinting like tiny flares in the muted daylight.

'I'm sorry, Queenie, we can't.' Joy sniffed the petals in the bouquet. 'Charles has an engagement elsewhere.'

'Suit yourselves.'

'Don't be like that. We aren't doing it to spite you.'

'No?' Queenie's gaze travelled over the blue chiffon dress again, then she looked over at Charles to see what he was doing. He was smoking his pipe and talking to Terrence. She wondered briefly what he might be telling him, and if they were discussing her. *Don't be ridiculous, girl. The man's forgotten you already.*

'You know we're not, Queenie, you're not being fair. Big things are happening in Charles's firm. People from Africa have come over for talks and he wants me there with him.'

'Nice for you.' Queenie couldn't help it; she knew she was being given the brush-off. 'Well,' she shivered from the cold and made to go, 'don't let me hold you up. I'll see you at the club next week.'

'I've been meaning to talk to you about that.'

'Oh, yes?' She turned back to Joy.

'You're not to be cross.'

'Cross?'

Joy scrunched up her face. 'Heloise doesn't like me working there.'

'I knew it.' Queenie lifted then dropped her arms through the air. Charles turned to her for a second and, worried he would hear them, she waited for him to refocus on Terrence before adding, 'That wretched woman, she's really got her claws into you.'

'I knew you'd be like this. I've been dreading telling you. Look…' Joy reached for Queenie's hand but she threw it off. 'It's Buster too. Honestly, Queenie, I know you think I'm being silly, but he's getting worse. He won't leave me alone. I've tried telling him… he frightens me a bit.'

'Buster?' Queenie shivered again. 'If that's your only problem, I'll have a word with him, tell him to leave you alone.'

'It's not just that, it's… well, Charles. He says he doesn't want to renew his membership.'

'You what? He doesn't want to come to the club either?'

'Not once we're married.'

'You've fixed a date?' Queenie tried to keep her voice down, but it was difficult. What was wrong with her? It was as if she had an ants' nest niggling her insides. What she wanted to do was scream, throw something: do a real physical thing.

'The last Saturday in December.'

'A Christmas wedding?' She was imagining ermine and velvet… red berries and holly.

They fell into an awkward silence.

'About the club.' Joy broke it. 'I'm only there two evenings anyway.'

'It was good enough for you before you hooked up with him.' Queenie looked over to Charles again.

'Don't be like this.'

'What do you expect? You cast aside a dress I spent ages making for some shop-bought thing that woman buys you.' Queenie said what she had been determined not to say. 'I thought I was your friend.' A sob had invaded her voice. What was the matter with her? Teary one minute, angry the next; it was like riding an emotional roller coaster.

'What's wrong, Queenie? You're not yourself at all.'

Joy was right, she wasn't. Moody and irritable for days. Was she hormonal? She wasn't due on, was she? Queenie counted on her fingers, tried to work it out.

'You are my friend, silly. You're my best friend. And you're right, it was selfish of me to wear this.' Joy lifted the chiffon, then dropped it again. 'And, all right, if it's so important, I won't finish at the Mockin' just yet.'

Queenie nodded; it was all she could manage.

'Joy! We'd best get going.' Charles, jingling his keys.

Joy passed her the bouquet. 'You have this, it'll look nice in your kitchen.'

She accepted the flowers and the two of them hugged goodbye. Queenie averted her gaze, reluctant to see her friend and Charles disappear through the lychgate and drive away in his Riley. She strode over the damp grass to where Terrence was lighting up a cigarette.

'Give me a drag, I'm desperate.' She pinched it out of his hand and drew on it. 'God, that's better.' She gasped. 'You and Charles were deep in conversation. Have a lot to say, did he?'

'Not especially. The guy seemed to be pretty stressed to me.'

'Stressed. About what?' She didn't like the sound of that.

'How should I know? He's more likely to open up to you than me.'

'What makes you say that? What did he say?'

'Have you got cloth ears all of a sudden? I told you, he didn't *say* anything.' Terrence gawped at her. 'Honestly, Queenie, darling, what's got into you today? You're a bag of nerves.'

'I'm not.'

'You are.' He passed his cigarette back to her. 'Have another go on that. Are you going to tell me what's wrong?'

'Nothing's wrong,' she answered too quickly.

'I know you.' He gave her one of his steady looks. 'Come on, spill.'

'There's nothing to say.'

'Do you good to get it off your chest.'

'God, Terry, leave me alone.' She returned his fag.

'You weren't being particularly nice to Joy earlier. A little catty about her choice of jewellery, if you don't mind me saying.'

'I do mind, as a matter of fact.' The pink posy trembling at her waist.

'Ooo, something's rattled your cage. Go on, tell me, what's up?' He jostled her elbow.

'Drop it, Terry.'

'If that's what you want.' He raised the flat of his hand: flagged his surrender. 'But I'm here if you want to talk.'

She left him to finish his cigarette and stepped beside Norma. Stared down at the gleaming white line of her scalp where her black hair fell open like the pages of a book. The woman looked tranquil, happy, even though her hands were still shaking.

'Are you cold?'

'No.' Norma narrowed her eyes at Queenie. They were as dark and sour as apple seeds.

'You must be. I am.'

'I'm not cold.' Her new stepmother turned her head away.

'So that's how it's going to be, is it?' Queenie sighed.

She should leave right now, but she wouldn't. Norma's behaviour made her change her mind. She would stay – stay to the bitter end, just to spite her.

CHAPTER TWENTY-FOUR

Leaving Albert's unsatisfied with the prostitute he'd paid for – his inability to perform, yet again – had left him feeling frustrated. It also made him dangerous. He'd been using prostitutes since before he was married and it had marked the beginning of a lifelong addiction. Unlike other women, they didn't have to be won over and they didn't involve his emotions. He was able to make a straight bargain and pay an agreed price for what they had to offer. Yet even prostitutes failed to give him satisfaction, for they were no lesser than other women and could sometimes sniff out his failings and inadequacies. And across the body of every prostitute he lay with was the shadow of his overprotective mother and his four dominant sisters, the shadow of his tyrannical father. He had hoped that through the use of these types of women he might eventually find peace, but what he found, on the twisted road he'd started on, grew like a canker inside him.

He was in no hurry to return to Rillington Place and the screaming rows between Timothy and Beryl Evans in the flat upstairs, or his wife's nagging, wanting to know where he'd been. Life in that matchbox house where everyone lived on top of one another wasn't a happy one and it felt good to be out walking the streets. Although, he reminded himself, things weren't so bad. How could he mind someone as attractive as Beryl needing to pass his front room and kitchen several times a day to use the wash house and lavatory in the yard? In the past, his sex life had been conducted largely in the shadows with women of the shadows, and now there was this young, pretty girl who'd just turned twenty living under the same roof. Not that his desire could be gratified with her husband in the house. But, he smiled, there had been some development in that department. Ethel had passed on the news that Beryl was panic-stricken at finding herself pregnant again, the fact they couldn't cope with another mouth to feed and that she was looking for someone to abort the pregnancy.

He let go a jerky little laugh to think of the part in the proceedings he might play, having broached the subject with Beryl the other morning over a nice cup of tea when Timothy was out at work. Talking of his knowledge of medicine, sickness and disease, the gullible girl had readily believed he might cure her. Here was a priceless, heaven-sent opportunity of achieving what he'd desired for so long: to see Beryl Evans naked, of touching her parts with his fingers, and doing so moreover with her willing consent. *Dear me*, he thought, quivering with excitement, as darker, murderous thoughts flooded in.

It was with thoughts of murder that he looked up at the way ahead and saw her. The other thing he desired. The little fey one he'd been making it his business to keep tabs on, travelling to Gloucester Road to watch her in her basement lodgings. And now, by some amazing coincidence, there she was again, striding out of Mayfair towards Piccadilly and wearing a diamante clasp in her hair.

'Rather late to be out on your own, little girl.' He moistened his lips as he ogled her. ''Specially on these streets. You don't belong here, lass. Not in the way that painted friend of yours does.'

The girl's hair fell forward into her eyes and she stopped to tidy it off her face. Ah, her beautiful face, that lustrous auburn hair... so dazzling, she put him in mind of Jeanne Crain in the musical *State Fair* he'd so enjoyed when he had worked as a projectionist at the Electric Cinema in Notting Hill. This young woman, in his opinion, had the kind of understated glamour rarely seen in ordinary life; he had certainly never come across another to match her on his travels. He would say that perhaps this one was even more tempting than Beryl.

By gum, she walked quickly and – almost jogging along in his canvas shoes – he went over the plan that had been taking shape in his mind as he joined her in the queue at the bus stop. The plan he needed to map out carefully if he were to do to her what he had done to the two women buried in his back garden... what he intended to do to Beryl Evans when the time was right.

But there were a couple of major stumbling blocks to him getting this one back to Rillington Place, alone and undisturbed. One was the presence of Ethel, who was always waiting for him; the other was that this girl would be certain to resist any sexual advances. But, he reminded himself, cheering a little, the first problem might have solved itself with Ethel's announcement that she was again going up to Sheffield for a holiday with her brother. The second problem was more difficult; he was going to have to come up with some ingenious way if he was to have a chance with this one. But he was clever and confident that something would show itself.

And until it did?

Well, he would keep up the surveillance and bide his time. He sniggered to himself as he followed her aboard the bus.

CHAPTER TWENTY-FIVE

Blackness. Queenie woke with a jolt to it. The sound of her breathing bounced back to her while her hand, negotiating the objects littering the bedside table, switched on the lamp. She looked at her alarm clock. Twenty past three. What was the matter with her? Slick with sweat, she pressed her fingers to her forehead, then into the pool of moisture that had collected between her breasts; her nightdress and bedsheets were sodden. Feeling crummy since her father's wedding, she had been worse again before bed and, fearful of being sick, she had lain down and willed the sensation away. Now, clearing a path through the layering of nightmarish sequences that had been turning on a loop since her head had hit the pillow, the nausea was back and briny water gathered in her mouth. She needed to spit it out, but where? She barely had the strength to sit up, never mind push herself downstairs and outside to the privy.

She stretched for the glass of water by the bed. Spat out the saltiness, only for more to collect in its place. It tasted of the sea and she couldn't get rid of it fast enough. 'Got to get up... Got to get up,' she chanted, the words ebbing and flowing as she pushed her legs out from beneath the covers. Staggering like a drunkard, she groped along the landing and down the stairs in the dark. The kitchen sink would have to do. *Thank God my father isn't here*, her only thought when she held back her hair and purged herself. The violence of heaving was nearly enough to finish her off. What the hell had she eaten? The idea of eating made her retch again and the stinging after-effects were enough to make her cry out. Tears filled her eyes. Even now, with all she'd experienced since losing her mother, it was her mother she wanted. Her soothing hand on her back. Her calm voice telling her, 'There, there, sweetheart… there, there.'

Stupid fool, she scolded the blur of her reflection in the mirror next to the sink. *Pull yourself together – there's no one to help you through this, you're on your own.* And forcing herself to look away from the ashen-faced woman staring back at her, she dipped her sweaty forehead at the sink to vomit again. Swilled it away down the plughole and rinsed her mouth. Mint. She wet her toothbrush and dabbed it into the tin of Eucryl toothpowder and brushed her teeth. Then dragged herself upstairs again and slid between what were now damp, icy sheets. Calm. She dropped back on her pillows and closed her eyes to the sickly dawn light that was sliding into the room.

Drifting in and out of consciousness, dreaming she was back at Bugbrooke Farm and astride a Suffolk Punch. Her legs scarcely long enough to wrap around its girth and forcing her to trust the rolling rhythm of its generous bone. Joy was riding beside her. Laughing and screaming to go faster. Gripping the manes of horses free from the drag of the plough, they skimmed the foaming shallows, magical as mythical beasts. Sleeping soundly now, Queenie was making little puffing noises. She was inhaling the creeping rhizomes of the cordgrass fringing Goldchurch beach. Then the laughter stopped and the sun went in. Rain began to fall. Dropping like needles, spiking her legs. She couldn't keep up: Joy was galloping ahead, leaving her alone.

When she opened her eyes, night had become day. Cold beneath the bedcovers, she sat up to receive it. The realisation came like a slap in the face. She knew why her body felt alien and her moods were all over the place. Why she had been sick. And it was enough to have her charging downstairs to embrace the kitchen sink again.

'Happy birthday, Queenie.' Terrence knocked on the dressing-room door and breezed inside. 'Dearie me, darling,' he said when he saw her. 'Joy told me you were looking peaky – are you going to be able to sing tonight?'

'I wish everyone would stop fussing, I'm fine.'

'You don't look fine.'

'I've been sick, that's all. I feel better now.'

'She said you told her it was something you ate?'

Joy had given Queenie a hardcover volume of *Palgrave's Golden Treasury* edged in gold for her birthday. She opened the cover and reread the words Joy had written in pencil: 'With love.'

'What else can it be?' She gulped back sudden tears.

Finished fastening her stockings, she put on her slingbacks. Plonked down at the dressing table and stared at her face in the mirror.

'You shouldn't have come in. We can manage a night without you. We'll be managing without you all the time soon.' He moved to stand beside her, pressed the back of his hand to her forehead. Cool, she closed her eyes to it. 'Poor darling. Is there anything I can get for you? Do you want a cigarette? I always find smoking helps settle my stomach.'

'God, no.' She flapped him away. 'I can't stand the smell; they make me want to gag. Can't stand the smell of this, either.' She pushed her bottle of Californian Poppy away too.

He eyed her quizzically.

'What?' Her mouth was full of pins as she tried to gather her hair into a style that improved her.

'Are you sure it was something you ate? It's just I remember a sister of mine, when she, erm... when she was first married. If you're in trouble, you can tell me.'

Queenie blinked away the image she had of Joy and refused to dwell on the dreadful thing she had done. All she needed was a good night's sleep; things would feel better then. She hadn't slept properly for days and it was showing. People were commenting, asking if she was all right. Stupid question.

'Is it cold in here, or is it me?' She reached for her coat.

'It's you.' Terrence handed it to her, then sat on the chaise longue. He put his chin in his hands and gave her a look she didn't want to see. 'Queenie?' he began, and she steeled herself for what was to come. 'You're not ill, are you? Do you need to see a doctor?'

Silence closed its lid over them. The only sound was their shallow breathing and the ticking of the wall clock.

'I'm frightened, Terry.' Queenie was the one who severed it. 'I'm really frightened… I've done something terrible.' She broke down into floods of tears.

'Queenie, darling.' Terrence leapt to his feet to comfort her. 'Whatever's the matter?'

'It's… it's—' She hiccupped through her sobs, unable to catch her breath.

'I knew it, I knew something was wrong.' He hesitated then, bounding away like a hare, checked the corridor outside the dressing room was empty. Happy it was, he came back in and closed the door. 'Tell me, Queenie.' Beside her again, he lifted her hand, soothed it between his own.

'It's my birthday. I'm twenty-three.' She sniffed.

'Well, yes? I hadn't forgotten the date. Don't worry if you're not feeling up to it, we can celebrate another time. But, come on, there must be more to it than that. I've never seen you upset like this before.'

'All right, keeping on at me.' She snatched back her hand and turned from him. 'I'm up the bloody duff, that's what's wrong with me.'

Terrence's hand swung by his side. She wanted to ask him to bring it back. 'Okay.' He breathed through the tiny word.

'No, Terry, it really isn't okay.' She wiped the mascara that had run down her cheeks. 'It's not okay at all.' Her voice wobbling with emotion as fresh tears threatened.

'Explains why you've been so strange recently… what all that was about at your father's wedding.' He talked to himself, then stared her right in the eye. 'I should have guessed. How far gone are you?'

'Four or five weeks.'

'And you're sure? You're sure you're pregnant?'

A grim nod.

'Can I ask whose it is?'

'Charles.' She dropped his name between them like a hand grenade that was too hot to hold.

Terrence almost laughed. 'You are joking? I know you like taking risks, but that's madness. Christ, Queenie, what are you going to do? Are you sure it's his?'

Queenie gawped at him. 'What d'you mean, *am I sure*? 'Course I'm flamin' sure.'

'But with all your men friends, how would you know?'

'Men *friends*?' Angry at him. 'Yes, *friends*, Terrence. I don't sleep with them. What d'you take me for? Good God, I'm not like you.'

'Like me?' His turn to be offended.

'Yes, it's different for you. You men can do what you want. You don't have to worry about the—' She broke off, hunted for the right word. '*Consequences.*'

'I can't do what I want. What I *want* is illegal, in case you hadn't heard.'

'Well, yes,' she conceded, eager to return to the point she was making. 'So long as you don't get caught.'

'You make it sound like it means nothing to me. I resent that a bit.'

'I'm sorry, Terry, I didn't mean… I mean, I know how fearful you are, how careful you need to be. But I'm just trying to say, I know it might look like I put myself about – it's my fault, it's the impression I give – but it couldn't be further from the truth.'

'So why the hell did you go with Charles?'

'*Shh*, for God's sake, keep your voice down,' she hissed.

'All right, but why Charles?' he hissed back. 'Why him, of all people?'

'Because I'm stupid.'

'This is going to break Joy's heart.'

'Don't you think I know that?' Queenie started to cry again. 'It's why she can't find out. Why she must never find out... oh, Terry, I don't know what to do. How could I have been so stupid?'

'Do you want to keep the baby?'

'How can I? I want to go to America. God, this is an almighty mess.'

'I still can't believe you could do that with Charles. How could you, Queenie?' Terrence looked as upset as she was. Wringing his hands and pacing the dressing-room floor.

'I feel rotten about it.' Queenie's mood swung from insulted to feeling sorry for herself. 'But honestly, Terry, I don't sleep around.'

'So why sleep with him? Your best friend's man.'

'I don't know. It just happened. You've seen what he's like, all flirty with me.'

'That's just his way, Queenie. He's a friendly guy. You've read too much into him and look where it's got you.'

'Don't you go blaming me. This is your fault.'

'I beg your pardon?' Terrence glared at her. 'How the hell d'you work that out?'

'If you'd been there, that night at the Blue Note like you said.' Queenie screwed her mascara-muddied eyes tight. 'Then we wouldn't have been alone. Nothing would have happened.'

'So that's when you did it?'

She nodded, pointing a guilty finger at the chaise longue.

'On there?' His jaw fell open and he took a step backwards. Pressed his weight against the door. 'You brought him back here?'

'I'm desperate, Terry.' Tears welling again. 'I'm frightened. What if Joy finds out? I've got to get rid of it, it's the only way out of this. But how? You've got to help me, Terry. *Please.*'

'I'm thinking, I'm thinking. What you're asking is illegal, you do know that?'

'Yes, it's why I need your help. You know people that could help me, don't you?' She sensed him waver. 'Even if it wasn't Charles's, can you seriously see me handing myself over to nappies and safety pins? I've got plans.' She was sobbing again.

'*Shh*, Queenie, let me think… I've got to think.' Terrence, a finger pressed to his mouth. 'All right,' he said firmly, throwing her a reckless look. 'Leave it with me. I'm not making any promises but there might… there might…' His voice tapered off. 'Just leave it with me.'

CHAPTER TWENTY-SIX

'Hey, Christie. You seen that new girl Albert's got in for us? Marie, her name is. Supposed to come from Liverpool. Right dolly bird, real special. Yeah, reckon I'll be samplin' a bit of 'er before long…'

He could barely be bothered to engage with what his accidental drinking partner was saying. Having wandered along to Soho to seek out his usual haunt, he'd found Albert's Cavern was heaving and, standing up at the bar, sipping his half of mild, he was more interested in observing the people around him.

That rather dapper homosexual was here again, the one with the sandy hair who dressed like a banker. Canoodling with his black boyfriend against the wall by the side of the door.

'Filthy buggers.' He muttered his disgust under his breath, and yet he was unable to peel his eyes away. 'God, they are revolting – do they have no shame?' He should have a word with Albert; the place was crawling with them, it really wasn't acceptable. Professing to hate these men, they stirred something inside him he didn't understand; something he wasn't sure he wanted to.

'… Albert's got 'er in to replace that Doreen.' The man beside him was still wittering on. 'You used to like Doreen, didn't ya? Yeah, thought so. But she's gone and got 'erself a bun in the oven though, ain't she? Shame, cos I liked 'er 'n all. But you can't be livin' a tart's life if you're in the family way, can ya?'

Christie moistened his lips with the tip of his tongue and, turning away from the banker and his boyfriend, treated himself to a long, leisurely look at the pretty young prostitute in feather boa and black stockings. He liked the look of her too, not that he would admit it. He didn't like the types who frequented the Cavern; he saw himself as a cut above and made sure to set himself apart. 'I don't know how many times I've told Albert he's to send them to me,' he answered, at last.

'Send 'em to you. What you on about?'

'Well, I can help them out in that department, can't I?' He removed his hat and rubbed a hand over his bald, domed pate.

'Yeah?' The man paused, then frowned. 'Oh yeah, that's right. I heard about you. Is that why they call you the Doc?'

'I'm not one to brag, but aye, I've been medically trained.' A sly smile. 'Suffice to say I've helped a good few of them out in my time. These girls, well, they see me as their saviour when they get themselves into trouble like they've a habit of doing – I can do owt I like with them… putty in my hands they are.' The Yorkshire accent trailed off, only to circle back again. 'They come to my house in Notting Hill, you know. My wife's very good about it, she likes helping out in her way. Oh, aye.' A self-satisfied sigh. 'Them needing my help when they're desperate like that, well, it makes me feel—' He broke off to consider how it made him feel when he had a woman helpless in his rope chair, breathing gas through the mask he pressed down over her face; how it felt to render her unconscious, then strip off her clothes and have intercourse with her lifeless body before strangling her; how it felt to look down on the body afterwards… so quiet, so serene, so still. He knew how it felt, right enough, it was why he needed to do it time and again. Because only when the power shifted from them to him could he quell his crippling inadequacies, the bitterness and humiliation his fear of women caused in him – these were the only times in his life he could feel like a proper man. 'It makes me feel…' He cleared his throat to finish what he'd been about to say. 'Like I'm giving something back to community. You know, doing community a favour. Because there's enough unwanted little ones in world, wouldn't you say? Oh, aye.' Pleased with himself. 'I like to think I'm rather kind like that.'

CHAPTER TWENTY-SEVEN

Amid the indelible shadows thrown like ink stains over the offices of F. Lambert & Co, Terrence lifted his cup to his mouth and curled his lip against the cold film that had formed over his coffee. He looked away from the ships and fish he'd been doodling in the margins of his ledger and stared into a series of lithographs of Victorian London that hung on the wall beside his desk. Something in the dark outline of Trafalgar Square, with its pigeons and lions, made him think of Queenie. No joke what she had asked him for. It had been bothering him all day. Another thing that had been bothering him was the possibility she had deliberately set out to destroy Joy and Charles's happiness. But surely not, he challenged himself – he couldn't be friends with someone who was capable of doing such a dreadful thing, and was determined to banish the thought.

Extinguishing what remained of his cigarette, he swivelled his chair to look out the window. To the great-domed view of St Paul's. A dray laden with barrels clopped by. Already the slant of the early evening sun had crossed the roofs of the opposite buildings. He stroked the dark varnished wood of his desk. His fingertips travelling the ridges and scratches that told tales on past employees who, like him, would have sat staring out through the same windows onto a street that had remained unchanged for centuries. Fleet Street. His mother hadn't been able to get over it when he'd told her he'd been offered the job on the spot. 'My son,' he heard her boast to neighbours and friends, 'he's hit the big time.' But his job at the bank wasn't what Terrence was proud of. This was just a means to an end, a way to keep the wolf from the door. What he loved,

what he had a talent and flair for, was the piano, not numbers and
money-counting. Playing on stage with the band was the only
thing, apart from Malcolm, that made life worthwhile. Performing
at the Mockin' Bird was a cloak he could wear to hide the true
shabbiness of himself.

The clock struck five. Terrence closed the ledger and arranged
his desk in readiness for the morning. Put on his coat and homburg
and with a polite 'Good evening' to his smattering of colleagues
– men he had never discussed more than the weather with – he
left the building.

Striding down the grey street, keeping pace with the wind as
it went on its exuberant journey, Terrence stared at the sea of grey
suits and hats spilling out of buildings onto the pavement. The
wave upon wave of faceless men, of which he was one. A sinuous
mass, cascading down into the mouth of the Underground. London
meant living in the footprints of war. Holes where a V-2 had hit
or a bomb had landed. Half of the city where he lived and worked
was still rubble. Nobody had worked out what to do. Apparently,
Attlee's government – Terrence followed the editorials in the newspapers – didn't know where to start. Everywhere looked tired and
scruffy: even this supposedly smart part of town had been smirched
by war. It was another reason the Mockin' Bird appealed to him.
It was a sanctuary, a place he could forget himself and the losses
that had touched and changed the lives of everyone he knew. At
the club, he could forget the part of himself that had been broken
and would probably never be put back together again. He thought
of Uncle Fish, a man Queenie joked about looking like Humpty
Dumpty who, losing both sons in the war, couldn't quite be put
back together again either. Did Terrence want to be involved in
terminating the new life that Queenie had growing inside her? Surely
new life meant hope, and hope was in short supply these days. He
should ask her to marry him. They could help each other out. It
would take the heat off him. He would talk to her, try and make

her see sense. He could bring the child up as his, it wouldn't be so bad. They were friends, weren't they? He loved her like a sister... it might work. He'd always hoped to one day be a father and this could be his chance.

Later. Terrence was drinking in his usual sleazy backstreet bar. Driven to his hole like a hunted animal, he had gazed back on the bright and breezy world he could never truly belong to before pushing in through the anonymous black door. In the hole was murder, copulation, poverty, infidelity and sin – and he was part of it whether he liked it or not. Malcolm was with him, and others they knew. Smoking and drinking, playing backgammon, they could relax here. People knew them, accepted them as a couple, and there was some comfort in that. This may be one seedy joint, where the majority was unsavoury and of dubious character, but they were at least reasonably safe to be themselves among the prostitutes, the petty criminals and other homosexuals. Although the fear of reprisals and the heavy hand of the law and the social disgrace that would follow if they were discovered was never far away.

'I'll go get the drinks in.' Terrence sprang to his feet. 'Another for you?'

A nod from Malcolm and he wandered to the bar. While he waited to be served, he scanned the blood-coloured walls. Decorated with frescoes of nymphs twirling in moonlight, they spun him back to Bologna and one of the last battles of the Italian Campaign. When he, along with some of his troop, sought refuge from the enemy inside the Basilica of San Petronio in much the same way he hid from the enemy by coming here. This was just as colourful and distinctive a venue, albeit a little vulgar with its dubious activities on the floor below. Not that Terrence needed to concern himself with Albert's basement, which, so the rumours went, had the fiery feeling of hell. He glanced over at the row of prostitutes lined up for trade. The girls with bruised looks and sorrowful eyes who, after sharing drinks with scores of shifty men, were led away downstairs.

'Terry, my dear, what can I get you?'

Piggy eyes, puffy face. Albert's big body was draped in its usual velvet. Up close he smelled stale. His breath bad. Terrence put a discreet hand to his nose and reeled off his drink order.

'Can I have a word?'

'Fire away, dear heart.' Albert poured and arranged the glasses into a line along the bar. Terrence tried not to look at the man's filthy nails.

'You know everyone there is to know.' He was unsure, now he'd started down this route, if he should keep going. Ideally, he'd have preferred to talk to Queenie first. Share his idea about her marrying him and keeping the baby. But ultimately it was her decision, and she had asked him to find her the name of someone who could help. So that's what he had to do. 'I… I… erm…' He looked around to check no one was listening, then beckoned Albert to a quiet corner of the bar.

'Spit it out, dear boy.'

'A friend of mine, a woman—' Terrence, still looking around him, handed over the necessary money and scooped the glasses to one side. 'She's gone and got herself into a spot of trouble.'

'Trouble, eh?' Albert's hand made an exaggerated curve over his stomach. 'That sort, you mean?'

'Yes, that's right.' Terrence, awkward, heaved down air before plunging in with his question. 'You don't know anyone who could, erm, perhaps… you know, help her out, do you?'

'Help her out?' Albert took the request and leant further in. Terrence, trying not to recoil from his breath, watched him consider this as he cleaned his nails on the corner of a matchbox. The grubby crescent moons floating to the counter. 'As a matter of fact, I think I just might. It's interesting you coming here tonight and asking me this.' Albert stopped cleaning his nails and began stroking his beard that had been braided into a long single plait.

'Is it?'

'Yes, very interesting. You see...' Albert began, then took a breath, enjoying the power Terrence's need gave him. 'There's this quiet, well-educated fellow. People look up to him, they say he's medically trained. They call him the Doc.' Terrence opened his mouth to respond and found himself silenced by Albert's heavy hand on his sleeve. 'They say,' a dramatic sigh, 'he knows how to help young women in trouble, just like your friend is. He claims to have helped them out in the past.'

'Is he decent? I mean...' Terrence fumbled around for what he wanted to say. 'I know what we're talking is risky, but will my friend be safe?'

'I should say so.' The nodded guarantee as the kohl-dirty eyes raked over him. 'They say he's rather genteel, as a matter of fact. Very neatly dressed,' Albert added with a flourish. 'Oh, yes, quite the ladies' man, by all accounts, and very well respected.' Albert leant even closer to Terrence, who in turn tried not to flinch from his smell.

'Have you got his name? His address?'

'Not on me, but I can get it for you. A day or two should do it.'

'That's great, thanks. You don't happen to know anyone he's helped out, do you? Maybe I could talk to them.'

'Silly boy.' Albert peeled back his lips on his nicotine-stained teeth and gave him a fatherly smile. 'They aren't likely to go broadcasting that kind of thing, are they?'

CHAPTER TWENTY-EIGHT

'Shall we go out this morning?' Joy suggested to Queenie as they breakfasted on charcuterie and cheeses in Heloise Gilchrist's dining room.

She noticed Queenie had barely eaten anything and looked a little tired and drawn. Was she still under the weather? She hadn't been sick again, had she?

'Sounds good to me.' Queenie sipped her weak black tea and declined the offer of milk.

Sitting up at the vast dining table and looking out over Hyde Park with its fading trees, Joy doubted she would ever get used to being here. She was watching a lone white cloud sail over the azure October sky. A leftover from another day, she fancied, losing herself to it. Then something occurred to her. Maybe Queenie didn't know what to do with the array of cutlery, and that was why she hadn't eaten much. When Joy had first come here, she hadn't known what to do with the cutlery either. Until Dorothy. Dear, kindly Dorothy, with her poor red hands, whispered, 'Start from the outside, miss, and work your way in.' She should have passed this gem on to her friend before they had sat down to eat.

'You go and enjoy yourselves.' Heloise, eating very little herself, was feeding strips of ham to the dog in her lap. 'The wedding planner's coming to talk table decorations.' Joy watched her slide her eyes to Queenie, and the look she gave her was cold. 'Have lunch in Dominique's on the Strand. My treat. Just mention me, I've an account there.'

'Thank you. That sounds lovely.'

'And what are you doing today?' Joy heard Queenie ask Charles, who seemed to be hiding behind his broadsheet.

Joy didn't want to admit it, but things between her and Charles had been strained recently; she put it down to pressures at work.

'Me?' He lifted his glossy head and rustled his newspaper. 'Work.'

'Silly me. Just because it's a Saturday. You men, you don't stop, do you?'

Joy identified a twinge of sarcasm in Queenie's tone but didn't interfere. She read the front of Charles's paper instead. Saw how two hundred people had been killed on an express train travelling between Warsaw and Gdańsk. Poor Poland, hadn't the country suffered enough?

'Do you know, Charles,' Queenie again, 'I've never thought to ask what it is you actually do?'

'He assists in the running of the family firm. Real estate,' Heloise interjected as Charles licked a thumb and turned the pages of his newspaper. 'Don't you, darling?' She spread, with minute precision, a smear of butter on a triangle of toast, then bit it in half.

'Indeed, I do.' Charles folded his paper and laid it over his crumb-speckled plate. 'And that's exactly where I should've been twenty minutes ago. I'll see you ladies later.' He kissed Joy's cheek then pitched from the room.

Queenie gave what remained of her query to Heloise. 'You say Charles *assists* – are you the person he's assisting?'

'Me? Work? *Stupide*. I look after the home. I've always looked after the home.'

Joy wondered if Queenie was thinking about her poor dead mother. Comparing her existence to the privileged life of the woman seated opposite, with her perfect hair and nails. An image of Ellen Osbourne dropped down behind her eyelids. Her hands as they had been when she and Queenie were small. Red and coarse like Dorothy's: a woman who, up to then, hadn't reminded Joy of Queenie's mother at all. Poor Ellen, Joy doubted she had ever dipped a toe into the kind of luxury Heloise enjoyed.

Watching Heloise, Joy tried to see her through Queenie's eyes. She supposed the way she drank her coffee, dabbing her lips between each sip, then rolling her napkin away in its silver ring, could be considered irritating. Because despite the claim, that was about as much housework as Heloise did.

'Are you going to work with Charles when you're married, Joy?' Queenie asked.

'No.' The shrill reply. Not from Joy, from Heloise. 'She is to devote herself to her husband and family, as I have done.'

'But she hasn't got a family. Not yet.' Queenie looked confused. 'You are going to carry on at the museum?'

'You're not listening. It's preposterous for Joy to concern herself with work.'

'... Because Joy's already told me you don't like her working at the Mockin' Bird.' Queenie, projecting her voice above Heloise's, determined to finish what she wanted to say.

'Once they are married,' Heloise ignored her, 'she must leave that side of things to her husband. And anyway, Joy must've told you?' The arching of the perfect eyebrows. 'The firm wants Charles to set up a division in Cape Town. So, the matter of the British Museum will be irrelevant when they relocate.'

'South Africa? But that's on the other side of the world.'

'What do you care? I heard you were off to New York to sing, or whatever it is you do.' Heloise again.

'I'm not sure about that now.' Joy watched Queenie press a hand to her abdomen. 'But Joy, what about your job? You love your job... all those old books.'

Joy turned her head away and followed the rays of sunlight fragmenting the room, hoping they would show her a way out. Then she thought of one.

'Do you want to see my wedding dress?'

Queenie nodded and folded her napkin into a neat square.

'Come on then.' Joy, gleeful, dashed from the room and up the stairs.

She failed to see Queenie rise from the table to follow her. Or Heloise, viper-quick from her chair, clamp a hand on Queenie's wrist and squeeze it tight like a punishment.

'I know what you've done,' Heloise hissed, pulling her close. 'I could smell that cheap scent of yours on him when he came home.'

The world stopped turning. Queenie froze. She couldn't think past Heloise's icy stare and the pain where she pressed her fingers into the bones of her wrist.

'Joy must never find out. *Never*. Do you hear me?' Heloise shook her. 'If she does, I won't be responsible for my actions.'

The words shimmered. So double-edged they cut Queenie wherever they touched.

Joy emerged. Wedding dress, veil, tiara, shoes, all in place. She stood where a slant of daylight partitioned the room and waited for Queenie to stop rubbing her wrist and look at her. When she did, the expression in her brown eyes gave nothing away. They maintained a steady detachment. Joy watched her light up one of her white cigarettes and take a leisurely drag. Joy didn't think she had ever seen Queenie rush. Not for anything or anyone. Every gesture was deliberate and, enriched by her beauty, meant you had no choice but to look at her. Queenie crossed the room in silence, smoking her cigarette. Reached out to stroke the bodice of freshwater pearls, the sheen of the skirt.

'Oh, my,' she gasped. 'You look...' She scrunched up her face, then swallowed.

'You hate it, don't you?'

Queenie emitted a small, stale laugh. 'You look sensational.' The words, delivered cautiously, sounded as if she hadn't wanted to believe them.

Queenie wandered over to a vase of red roses. 'It fits you perfectly… the cut of the silk.' She was reading the card that accompanied the flowers. 'From Charles, eh?' Her mouth set in a hard, thin line. 'He either really loves you or he's guilty of something.'

Joy stared at Queenie while she finished her cigarette and screwed it out in an ashtray. What was wrong with her? She'd been in a foul mood for weeks.

'I'd better get out of this.' Joy bent her arm up behind her to unfasten the dress.

'Want a hand?' Queenie pulled off a rose petal, dropped it on the carpet. 'You don't want to damage it.'

Heloise's dog wandered into the bedroom, gave a couple of yaps then sat between them.

'What have you done to your wrist? It looks awfully red.'

'It's nothing.' Queenie covered it with her other hand and backed away.

'What were you talking about with Heloise?'

'When?' Queenie prodded the dog with her foot, and when it failed to move, she prodded it harder.

'Before you came upstairs.' Joy rescued the dog, carried him to the landing, out of harm's way.

'Oh, something and nothing. I can't remember.'

When their order for French onion soup had been given to the waiter, Queenie and Joy sat at a table among trees that had been planted in the pavement. They peeled off their leather gloves and unpinned their hats.

'They're not the gloves I bought you. Where'd you get them from? Oh, don't tell me – Heloise.' An irritated sigh. 'Don't you like mine any more? They cost me a fortune, you know.'

'I do. I love them.' Joy placed her hat beside Queenie's on the table. Watched its three white feathers flutter flightless in the breeze.

She felt dreadful about losing those beautiful plum-coloured gloves but was afraid to tell Queenie the truth. 'I didn't wear them today because they don't match my outfit.'

'Since when do you care? Is that another thing Heloise has trained you in – matching accessories?'

'What a glorious day.' Joy looked up at the canvas awning shifting above them and ignored the subtext. 'Sitting here reminds me of Montmartre. It was kind of Heloise to buy us lunch.'

'You shouldn't let her dictate to you.' Queenie seemed unable to delight in the world and it was so unlike her.

'She means well and she's an awfully kind heart.'

'I say you want to watch it.' Queenie lifted the lighted end of her cigarette, drew squiggles in the air. 'You even sound like her. And she's dressing you now, I see. Buying them new, or are they her cast-offs?'

'If I didn't know better, Queenie Osbourne, I'd say you were jealous.'

'*Jealous?*' A final pull on the cigarette before stubbing it out.

'It must have been a shock when Charles and I got together. Seeing how much better my life is. How happy I am.' The waiter had arrived at their table. 'Oh, *merci*. That smells delicious.' Joy breathed through the steam curling up from the bowl and poked the island of Gruyère-covered crouton.

Queenie was laughing at her, not unkindly. 'There was me, worried you might have turned into Heloise Gilchrist. But you're just the same.'

'I'm glad it reassures you.' Joy tore off a hunk of bread.

'I know I've asked before,' Queenie, spooning up her soup, 'but why d'you wear that brooch all the time?'

Joy's fingertips travelled the cool cluster of enamel apples fastened to her lapel. 'Because Charles gave it to me.'

'I'd have credited him with more taste.' Queenie dabbed at her scarlet mouth with the napkin: now who was copying Heloise?

'Charles has bought me other things.'

'Wear them then. They've got to be better than that.'

'I do.'

Joy lifted her left hand and flashed the diamond on the fourth finger. Sat back to enjoy the change that washed over Queenie's face. Happy to let the beauty of her engagement ring do the talking. And it did. Cutting between them as sudden and deadening as the blade of an axe.

They finished their soup in silence, and when they had, Joy signed the bill that would go on Heloise's account and put a bright new shilling on the saucer. Then they secured their hats and pulled on their gloves and headed into the Saturday crowd.

CHAPTER TWENTY-NINE

He had been following these two young friends all day. Not that he had any particular plan, just an idea it would be nice to keep an eye on them. It wasn't as if he had anything to rush home to Notting Hill for. No one was expecting him. His wife had gone to Sheffield and would be away for a good while yet.

He was careful, he kept his distance, even though the friends were too busy with themselves to notice him. Why would they? Middle-aged and unprepossessing in his trilby and soft-soled shoes, he blended into the background. It was how he could creep about unseen and ogle women in the way he was ogling these two now. Women excited and stimulated him, and he would have loved nothing better than to assert himself with them, to gain their love and admiration. But his fear of rejection and humiliation always prevented him from trying. It was why he hated women who tempted him and whom he knew he couldn't satisfy. Not that he went about publicising the fact; this side of his life, along with his need to use prostitutes, was his best-kept secret.

Trailing behind the young women, he wondered where they were going and if they could be lost. They looked as if they were lost, turning this way and that, uncertain whether to go left or right. Lost was good: it meant they were vulnerable and might need his help. He moved as close as he dared to the pretty pair: the bold brunette and her auburn-haired friend he'd been privy to such intimacies with. Spying on her in her basement room, seeing her in a state of undress. But looking at her now, he admired her with fresh eyes – quite the little lady in her expensive-looking outfit, heels and hat. Her glorious hair beautifully coiffured. It seemed the days of the imitation panama, baggy coat and ungainly footwear were well and truly behind her. And he thought again how she would make an interesting addition to his already considerable collection of pubic hair that didn't yet contain such a vibrant shade of auburn.

Don't be too eager, he warned himself. *Be patient.* The more despairing they were, the easier it would be. It was always better when they approached him; it never worked the other way around, not if he wanted them to trust him, which he did. He licked his lips with interest, and although physically disturbed by the sight of them and what he knew of their female magic, he couldn't stop himself from imagining the things he would do to them if he could get them home, inside his kitchen and seated in his rope chair.

He strolled along behind them, plucking things from their conversation – not that they were having much of a conversation. They didn't seem to be getting on particularly well and walked along in the kind of glowering silence that followed a stinking row. He recognised the moody aftermath that was communicated in their faces. A resentfulness not unlike his wife and him after they'd been tearing strips off one another. The idea these two had fallen out pleased him, and he hoped things would deteriorate to such an extent they would eventually separate off from one another. If they did, he might have a chance of getting his hands on one of them.

'Joy,' he murmured when he overheard the brunette using the little fey one's name. 'So that's what she's called, is it? Mm.' He caressed the stocking in his pocket. 'She could bring me some joy, I'm sure.'

He took her name and rolled it over his tongue. It tasted sweet. As sweet as she looked. There was something about her, the way she moved, that reminded him of Ruth.

His first.

'And look where she ended up.' A mordant chuckle.

Ruth Fuerst. Why he'd picked her he didn't know. Young and pretty, she had certainly done him no harm. Because, he answered himself, a lifetime of repressed masculine aggression had, at that time, come to its climacteric. He had been simmering towards explosion point for years. He was simmering now. He unpicked what he had retained of her. That poor, friendless foreigner. Not unlike this little one: he gazed at the auburn-haired beauty who was trotting along the pavement beside her painted friend. She was foreign; he could tell her accent wasn't from these shores. It was an accent not unlike Ruth's. Austrian, then? Or German? Possibly French? He could surmise all he liked, but he couldn't be sure; the only thing he was sure about was that this girl wasn't a prostitute. Not like Ruth. Which was a shame because they were always easier to manipulate. Their desperation made them grateful, less choosy, and a whole lot easier to get inside his home. In the same way, he could have his pick of this lot, his thoughts as he perused the sudden gaggle of street girls that had surrounded them. Ruth, lucky for him, had come from the same shadowy world where girls were always disappearing. Leaving one place one day, then popping up somewhere else. Especially during the war, when there were flying bombs and so many people were being blasted into anonymity.

'Aye,' he mumbled, as close as he dared to Joy and the dark-haired one. 'Things are certainly hotting up. What with the lovely Beryl in the flat above and now this little Joy to make plans for... he hadn't been this fired since he'd had Ruth, then Muriel, comatose in his special chair. Gazing down on their stiff, dead forms, it had given him such a strange and peaceful thrill. *I can't wait to do it again. It's been far too long.*

CHAPTER THIRTY

Queenie and Joy wandered along in sulky silence. On and on they tramped. The heels Joy was unaccustomed to wearing had given her blisters, but both were reluctant to admit they were lost. With the holiday atmosphere of the Strand long behind them, they had wandered into Soho. The atmosphere had changed and the city took on a dingy, seedy feel. Gone were the smart boutiques and coffee shops, traded in for a series of condemned streets and boarded-up outlets. Passing a succession of shady alcoves flanked by flaking paint and broken windows, they clutched their bags to their fronts as if shielding themselves from whatever depravity they imagined going on within.

They stopped when they reached a crossroads. On their left, a cluster of West Indian men stood around smoking in snazzy suits and striped ties. To their right, a pack of girls with dirty faces and flimsy dresses. Queenie said she thought they needed to take a right and, with no idea where she was, Joy could only follow. The girls dispersed. Some to kick through the gutters, others to lean against the dripping brickwork or the sporadic parked car. Each sharing the same hollow, hungry look. A look Joy had seen before. Years ago, separated from her schoolmates on a trip to Paris, she had accidentally wandered into Place Pigalle. Prostitutes. Joy knew what they were and was a little frightened of them. Emaciated, threatening, these girls were probably around her age but looked older. Victims of Britain's class-ridden society. The down-and-outs, the dispossessed, driven to the streets to sell the only thing they had. Joy avoided their gaze and strode past with a sense of purpose. Conscious of her tailored coat, her leather shoes, her shiny, sunny appearance. How fortunate was she, that this grim reality – the only choice for these poor souls – would, since meeting Charles and Heloise, never be her reality? To never need concern herself with money again, the days of scraping together enough to pay the rent and feed herself long behind her.

'Gis a shilling, love.' Up close, the broken mouth of a girl. It shook Joy out of her contemplations and she looked into the pleading eyes under the curtain of greasy hair. 'You look like ya can spare a few bob. What d'ya say, ladies?' A scrawny arm shot out. Mottled in purple bruises, it gathered the rest of her crew closer.

Joy sensed the menacing press of them and was reaching for her purse when Queenie seized her and tugged her away to a chorus of, 'Stuck-up bitches... think you're better than us, do ya?'

The sun went in and the way ahead darkened. They quickened their pace and took, what neither would admit, another wrong turn. This time into a dark, cobbled lane that reeked of stale urine. They clamped their gloved hands to their noses until they emerged at the opposite end.

'Look!' Queenie squealed and pointed to a suited man in a homburg striding ahead. 'It's Terry. Hey! Wait!' she called to him, but he didn't turn around. 'Let's follow him.' Eager-eyed. 'See where he's going.'

Queenie seized hold of Joy again and steered her purposefully across the street, down towards a section of pavement where they found a secret, narrow-bricked alleyway falling between two high buildings. But no Terrence; he had disappeared. Why would he need to sneak around here? Joy didn't like it and said so, but Queenie, determined to find him, clicked ahead on her heels.

It was Joy who saw the man in the brown trilby. She recognised him from the times she had seen him walking his dog in Hyde

Park. Secreted in the shadows, had he been following them? The possibility alarmed her and she ran to catch Queenie up.

'Where? I can't see anyone.' Queenie, snappish, hardly bothering to look.

'Over there.' Joy spun on her heels and jabbed a frantic finger into the gloomy spaces that dropped between the buildings. 'He was, I'm telling you.' She tried not to shriek. 'He's following us… he's following me. I've seen him before.'

Whoever this man was – a wisp of air, as soft as breath, a fleeting, floating shadow – he had undoubtedly rattled Joy.

'Don't be ridiculous. Who would bother to follow you? Come on, Joy, get a move on. I want to see where Terry's going.'

'Leave it. Whatever he's up to, it's none of our business.'

'Get you, little Miss Prude. Just because you don't want to know about the world he moves in, doesn't mean it doesn't exist.'

'I don't care.' Joy, firm, was still casting around for the stranger she believed was stalking them, but to her mounting unease, she'd lost sight of him. 'We shouldn't be here, it's dangerous. Please, Queenie, I want to go… I want to go home.'

'Oh, come on. Where's your sense of adventure?'

'I just want to get out of here.' Joy, frustrated at Queenie not taking her seriously. 'Terry must've heard you calling. He just didn't want to see us. Don't you get it?'

'You're an odd one.' Queenie eyed her with curiosity, then fished out a white paper bag from her coat pocket. 'Here, fancy one of these? You used to love them when we were nippers.'

'Pear drops.' Joy took a sweet, its sugary shell rasping against the roof of her mouth. Something about the flavour and the rush of memories it brought with it made her burst into tears.

'Oh, don't cry. Please don't cry.' Queenie put an arm about her middle and squeezed. 'Whatever's the matter?'

'You.' She sobbed. 'You've been horrible with me today. You've been horrible for weeks.'

'What? No, I haven't.' A softer Queenie tutted her concern.

'I'd love to know what I've done to annoy you.' Joy brushed away her tears and watched Queenie scrabble around in her bag. 'What's that?' She thrust a finger at a length of orange rubber tubing she wasn't supposed to have seen.

'Nothing. It's nothing.' The bag was snapped shut and Queenie passed her a handkerchief.

CHAPTER THIRTY-ONE

Queenie sat in the tin bath she had filled with water heated kettle by kettle. No hot running water here. She dropped her thoughts of the Bayswater bathroom and looked out through the kitchen window at a day that was as dark as the dusk. A flock of unknown birds flew over the sky. Autumn had well and truly blown in; the clocks would be going back soon. It was all downhill from here.

She stared at her tummy. At the slight mound that parted the bathwater like an island. It felt disconnected from her. Since first realising she was pregnant, she'd been feeling rather like a castaway, something the tide spat out. Ghostly, the translucency of her skin frightened her. Its blue-veined intersection, mapping across her body. She traced it, searching, but could find no clear route out of the mess she'd got herself into. Because there wasn't one. She had betrayed her childhood friend – how could that ever be put right?

She positioned her flannel at the nape of her neck and made a pillow. Eased her head back against the rim of the bath. Loops of vapour coiled over the near-scalding water. Scribbles in the steam. She breathed through them, trying to decipher what the scribbles meant as the coal fire crackled beyond the concertina of clothes horses, draped in wet washing and screening her off. Not that there was anything to screen herself off from. Her father had been gone for weeks. Often, alone in the dark after lights out, Queenie heard him coughing and needed to remind herself he wasn't there. He was miles away with his new wife, enjoying his new life on a smallholding in a Norfolk village she would probably never go to. She missed him, she missed his lavender smell, and thinking about the lack of him made her feel lonelier. Lying chin-deep in hot water, she counted up all she had lost… all she would go on to lose if Joy found out what she and Charles had done. Her world had capsized and she was irrefutably changed.

The shadows cast by the blustery trees threw stirring patterns over the ceiling. She watched them. Lost herself to them until she remembered the thing she must do. The Higginson syringe was ready and waiting on the edge of the bath. She eyed it warily. Spurred on by Heloise's threat, Queenie had nipped into the chemist along the Bayswater Road while Joy waited outside. Risky, it had her questioning whether she had wanted her to find out and for the pain that came with carrying a secret as deadly as this to end. The chemist wasn't one she expected to be recognised in, but she expected people to be suspicious. But no one was. No one blinked an eye when she went up to the counter to pay. The syringe was an everyday household gadget that anyone could purchase. Obvious, from the amount available on the shelf. Used by women to self-douche, she'd heard. Used by men and women to cleanse and regulate the digestive system through enemas. Mad, wasn't it? When Queenie considered the illicitness surrounding abortion, that this innocuous tube, when used with water containing carbolic soap and liquid disinfectant, as she intended to do, could be converted into a dangerous killing device.

Right, she steeled herself for what had to be done. Her hands, wet as fish, seized the syringe with a kind of baulked ferocity. She stared at it. Unsure how to use it, or what to do, she compressed the rubber bulb and filled it with the warm, soapy mixture she had set by in a bowl. Stand up or sit down? She didn't know. The thing hadn't come with an instruction manual. She stood up. Shaky. Naked. Needing to use both hands, she guided one end up between her legs. With a deep breath, she squeezed the ball-like bulb. But not with any conviction, so the warm, soapy water seeped down the inside of her thighs. She tried again. Refilling the syringe from the bowl with Heloise's warning whirling in her head. She directed one end of the tube up between her legs again and squashed the bulb at its centre. This time a spurt of the carbolic mixture surged inside her. She gasped in shock. Doubled over in sudden pain. Enough. She put the syringe down. It hurt too much, she couldn't do it. She wasn't brave enough.

'You coward.' She began to cry. Hating herself for failing before she'd even begun. What the hell was she going to do? She had to get rid of this baby.

A knock on the kitchen door and a voice rang out through the turgid air. She recognised it and shivered. Dropped down into the bathwater.

'Queenie, it's me.' Joy had stepped inside; the air changed when the door was opened then shut.

Why didn't I lock it? Today of all days. Bloody fool.

'Golly, it's like a Turkish bath in here.' An ebullient giggle. 'Queenie? Where are you?'

'I'm here.' She splashed the water.

'I'm disturbing you, I'm sorry. D'you want me to leave?' Queenie would have loved to tell her that now wasn't the best time, but before she could Joy added, 'Well, well. Since when did you get a cat?'

'A cat? What are you on about?'

'A black cat's having a warm on your stove.' The scrape of a chair and she imagined Joy going over to it. 'Curled up, happy as you like. He's purring his head off.'

'I don't think I want a cat.' Queenie wiped away her tears.

'Not sure you've a choice. Cats go where they want.'

'How did he get in?'

'A window, the door? Oh, he's handsome...' Joy's voice trailed off. 'I reckon he's turned up at just the right time.'

'What do you mean?'

'He knows you're on your own. Cats are such spiritual creatures.'

'But I don't have the first idea how to look after a cat.'

'I wouldn't worry, this one looks able to take care of himself. Shall I make us tea? Yes, I'll make tea,' Joy answered herself and Queenie sat with her knees up to her chin, listening as drawers were opened to the accompanying rattle of cutlery, the chink of porcelain. The rush of water as the kettle was filled and set on the stove. 'I only called over to tell you I won't be at the club Monday.' Joy talked to her through the screen of drying clothes. 'Charles is taking me to Dorset again.'

Determined not to cry, Queenie shoved a wet fist against her mouth. 'I hope you have a good time.'

'We've started calling it *Snuggler's* Cove.' Another giggle. 'Can you believe it's only weeks away before we're married? I'm going to burst with excitement,' Joy prattled on. 'I wanted to ask you about me giving up my bedsit. Do you think I should wait? Heloise wants me to move to Bayswater, but I'm not sure. Oh, I'm all in a quandary…'

The kettle sang when it came to the boil and filled the kitchen with its steamy breath. It saved Queenie from the need to comment. More rattling and stirring, then Joy's hand appeared between the end of the clothes horse and windowsill, holding a cup of tea.

'Ta.' Queenie whipped the syringe out of sight then took the cup in both hands. Noticed her fingers had puckered like the skin on a cooling milk pudding. Grateful for the warmth of the tea, with the bathwater steadily losing its heat, she wasn't sure how much longer she would be able to sit in it.

'I'm thinking I should invite your grandparents to the wedding.'

'I don't know, Joy. They've been weird since Mum died. Refusing to come to Dad and Norma's.'

'I wondered where they were. Never mind… I'll invite them, they might come. I'd love them to meet Charles.' Joy was talking nineteen to the dozen. 'He's the most wonderful man. I'm so happy.' Her friend's cheerfulness, finding her between the layers of damp laundry.

Queenie struggled to hold it together and was grateful Joy couldn't see her face. If she hated herself for her part in this, what kind of man was Charles? He was lying to Joy too. He didn't know Queenie was pregnant, but he couldn't have forgotten what they had done together that night at the Mockin'? So much of her wanted to warn Joy about him because he wasn't the man any of them thought he was.

Another scrape of a chair and the tap was turned on. 'I've been wondering how you'll manage the garden, but you're not going to be here, are you? Hang on, that reminds me…' Queenie listened to Joy take a breath. 'When Heloise asked you about New York, you said something about not being sure. What did you mean? Aren't you going?'

Queenie couldn't answer. She sipped her tea. The unforgivable thing she'd done tasted sour in her mouth and she clamped her jaw together to stop her teeth from chattering. However uncomfortable it was to sit in tepid water, it was better than facing Joy, especially with what she'd just tried to do to herself. She eyed the orange tube.

'Has something happened? You can tell me.'

'There's nothing to tell.' The lie burnt like hot embers in Queenie's mouth.

'If you say so.' Joy didn't sound convinced. 'But I've been worrying about you. Terry's worried about you too.'

'Terry?' He wouldn't say anything, would he? He wouldn't squeal on her to Joy?

'He was going on about Buster too. He was in a bad way again the other night.'

'Buster!' Queenie, sharper than she meant to be. 'I'm sick of hearing about him. Terry had the chance; we went to the Blue Note to check that drummer out… but he didn't show up.'

'Terry wasn't there?' Joy's voice faded to a whisper. 'Charles never said.'

Queenie swallowed the last of her tea. *Why did I have to go saying that? Stupid, stupid.* 'He probably just forgot.'

'So, it was just you and Charles that night?' Joy had worked it out and Queenie needed to be careful.

'That's right.' Her tone light. 'Just us.'

'Oh.' A rustling of something and the sound of a drawer being shut. 'You never said whether he was any good.'

'If who was any good?' Her heart thumped in her mouth and she put the cup down.

'The drummer.'

Queenie splashed around, pretending to wash. She was freezing, her teeth chattering. 'He was great. It's why I'm cross with Terry; he should've been there to sign him up.' Queenie needed to get into the warm. 'Anyway, it is sweet of you but there's no need to worry about me.'

'You're chilly. D'you want to get out? Let me fetch your towel. It feels odd, us talking without being able to see each other.'

'I'm not chilly, I haven't been in the bath long.' Another lie, but she couldn't bear to look Joy in the face.

'Oh, dear, is that the time? I'd better dash.'

'Have fun in Dorset. The weather's supposed to cheer up tomorrow.'

'We will. See you soon.'

Queenie hugged herself, her skin bobbly from the cold. She waited for the door to close and Joy to go before stepping free of the bathtub. She looked at the grey-green water and the Higginson syringe and had never felt so wretched and miserable and alone. Shivering, she found her towel and wrapped it around herself for the comfort that wasn't there.

'Hello, matey. Where did you come from?' She padded over to see the cat. Her wet feet cold against the flagstones. 'Cor, I wish I had a fur coat like yours to keep me warm.' She dried herself off while the yellow stripe of his eyes observed her with a steady resolve. 'I suppose you can stay.' She stroked him with her wrinkled fingers. 'Was Joy right, do you think I need a pal?' His purring was strangely comforting. 'I'll call you Dizzy,' she said to him. 'In honour of the great Dizzy Gillespie. How d'you like that?'

She added a couple of lumps of coal to the fire and repositioned the clothes horses in front of it. She would empty the bath when she was dressed but, halfway up the stairs, a loud banging on the kitchen door forced her to turn back.

Who the hell is it now?

More banging.

Dizzy scarpered.

'All right… I'm coming.' She adjusted her towel and tiptoed down through her shadow to answer it. With wet hair trickling into her eyes, Queenie opened the door a crack and felt the chilly wind curl over her toes. 'Oh, it's you.'

Terrence – urbane and elegant in dark coat and hat – on her back step. 'I waited until Joy left,' he rushed headlong into his explanation. 'You didn't tell her, did you?'

'Don't be stupid. Are you coming in or not?' She opened the door to him. 'Messing about… you're letting all the cold air in.'

The wind against her skin was almost human. She listened to it nudge through the dry-stalked honeysuckle.

'I think you've got one of your admirers outside.'

'What d'you mean?' She frowned and closed the door.

'Some bloke. Hanging around, watching the house. Hoping for a glimpse of the glamorous Queenie.'

'What bloke? What's he look like?'

'I don't know. Ordinary enough, trilby… glasses. Just standing there smoking, he is.'

'Where?' Queenie, clutching her towel around her, dashed into the front parlour and lifted the net to peer out to the empty street. 'I can't see anyone.'

'Oh, he was there a minute ago. He must've gone. Strange, he was sort of familiar. It's why I thought he was from the club. Not that I like the idea of men following you home. Let's hope he was waiting for someone else, eh?'

She gave him a funny look and padded back to the kitchen.

'I'm sorry, Queenie, darling, did I interrupt you?' Terrence had noticed the bath.

She crushed the edge of her damp towel into a ball. 'I'd finished.' She didn't know why, but seeing Terrence's kind face made her want to cry.

'Dear me, that's not what I think it is, is it?' He had seen the orange tube. 'Oh, Queenie, no. Please don't tell me you've been using that thing!' His face communicating his horror. 'My darling, you can't, it's too dangerous. I know you're desperate, but you'll end up poisoning yourself.'

She sat down at the table. Wondered about telling him what Heloise had said, then changed her mind. 'I tried to use it, but I couldn't go through with it. I lost my nerve.'

'Thank God for that.' He pulled up a chair beside hers. 'Come on, darling girl.' Terrence lifted her hand and pressed it between his own. At this small show of kindness, Queenie burst into tears. 'Oh, dear, you are in a bad way.'

'One minute I'm teary, the next I'm furious.' She gulped through her sobs. 'It's like I don't know my own mind.'

'Hormones, darling.' He put a brotherly arm around her. 'One of my sisters was the same. But it'll be all right, I promise.'

'How will it?' She sniffed and wiped her nose on the back of her hand. 'How will anything be right again? Joy's so happy, Terry. She can't *ever* find out what I've done.' She echoed Heloise. 'It would kill her.'

'You still want to go through with it?' His eyes searching hers.

'What choice is there? I can't have a baby… Charles's baby. How would I support myself? I couldn't keep a roof over our heads, never mind feed us.' She wrung her hands.

'Look…' He paused. 'I've been giving it a lot of thought, and you don't have to say anything right away, just promise me you'll think about it.'

'Think about what?'

His eyes were swimming with tears too. 'I could marry you. Say the baby's mine.' Terrence tightened his arm around her.

'Marry me?'

'Queenie, think about it. We could help each other out.'

'You're such a sweetheart.' She kissed his cheek. 'But wouldn't people smell a rat?' She was thinking of Heloise again. 'No, Terry, I've just got to get rid of it.'

'I said not to answer straight away. Why don't you think about it? You don't want to go rushing into anything you might regret.'

'I've thought of nothing else. But marry you? No, Terry.' She shook her head and water droplets showered her shoulders. 'Sweet of you to offer, but it would never work. You know,' she paused to rub her eyes, 'I always thought I'd be something wonderful in the world. How stupid was I? I'm not different, or special at all. I've ruined everything.'

'Come on, now. You're just feeling sorry for yourself.'

'Maybe. But it's true. I'm not fit for anything; I never deserved to have Joy as a friend.'

Terrence pulled away and the warmth of him was replaced by the chilly air.

'Right.' He held her in his gaze. 'Just so we're straight, the me-and-you-getting-married thing – you're saying that's never going to happen?'

'I can see it's a solution of sorts, but it's not what I want. I don't want a baby; I'm not cut out to be a mother.'

At this, he flopped back into his chair, head down.

'Terry?' She prodded him. 'Say something.'

'Well, if that's what you've decided. Oh, here... I did some asking around.' He pulled a square of folded paper from his coat pocket. 'It's the name of someone who should be able to help you out. I've written it down for you.'

'Help me out, what d'you mean?' Her insides cartwheeling with dread as she lifted the scrap of paper from his fingers. She didn't unfold it; unfolding it would make it real.

'They call him the Doc.'

'He's a doctor?'

'They say he was training to be a doctor before the war but had to give it up. An accident or something. Was hit by a car, so they say. But it's what they call him.'

'So, he's had some sort of medical training?' Queenie was encouraged by this.

'Apparently so. And they say he's clever... intelligent.'

'I see. And dare I ask who *they* are?' She hadn't expected an answer. Not because Terrence was secretive, but because of the shadowy underworld of sex and forbidden love he needed to exist in. Not that you'd know it to look at him: tall and suave; her well-spoken, gentle friend couldn't have liked living the way he did, mixing with the types he mixed with just to keep his secret safe.

'Apparently,' Terrence sidestepped her question as she thought he would, 'this man knows how to help girls in trouble. He's helped them out in the past.'

'A right Mr Fix-It, aren't you?' A watery smile as she stared at the square of paper in her hand. 'I'm ever so grateful, Terry. Thank you.'

'Thank me when it's all over.' He gripped his thin knees. 'The nearest Tube's Ladbroke Grove, it's not far from there. I'll write down the directions I've been given. I have to say, to warn you – I haven't been there myself, but I've heard Notting Hill's a bit of a run-down part of town. But that's where he lives.' His face was congested with concern. 'Do you want me to come with you?'

'No.' She was firm. 'If I decide this is what I want to do, I don't want you getting in trouble. You take enough risks in your own life.'

Queenie unfolded the note, her lips moving over the words as she read:

John Christie. 10 Rillington Place.

CHAPTER THIRTY-TWO

Joy woke up in the big boarding-house bed. She watched Charles, a towel wrapped around him, his chest bare, his damp hair looking darker. He kept smiling at her. Bobbing in and out of the bathroom to check she hadn't moved.

'We've probably missed breakfast.'

'It doesn't matter, we'll get something out.'

'But you'd like a cup of tea? I'll nip down and ask.'

She watched him dress and blew him a kiss as he backed out of the room. Hesitant, tapping his cane against the carpet, reluctant to leave her. When he did, she got up and drew the curtains, looked over the red-roofed town to the sea, then further, up to the bird-haunted headland that was as motionless as a dream. Could all this be a dream? A drowsy bluebottle, the last of the summer, struggled against the glass. She opened the window and guided it to freedom. Above her, the fast shadows of birds flying over in fleeting pairs. She tilted her head and marvelled at their speed, their skill. There was an energy in the air. It felt like anything could happen.

She washed and brushed her teeth. Stared at her face in the mirror lit with an electric bulb. Then, opening the wardrobe on the array of outfits Heloise had bought her, she opted for a wool dress in a rich beetroot colour that matched the flecks in her new winter coat. Different to the clothes she had worn when first here. She smiled an appreciative smile.

As she pulled the dress on over her head, she thought of Queenie and wondered if she felt better today. Her strangeness lately had been playing on her mind. Perhaps she was ill and was afraid to tell her. There wasn't the time to think much about it: the door opened, and Charles was back.

'You look wonderful.' Puffing from his climb up the stairs.

'Your mother bought it for me. She's so kind.'

'It's because she adores you.' The declaration seemed to trouble him.

'Was the landlady all right?'

'Fine.' His expression brightened. 'But we're too late for breakfast.'

Joy and Charles walked along Castle Row looking for the footpath their landlady had told them to take. Passing well-to-do villas that hung back from the cliff edge, they eventually found the sign beneath its hood of ivy. The path spiralled upwards between a high outcrop where the last of the wood sage and greater celandine still clung to crevices in the slabs of chalky cliff.

'This is steeper than I thought.' Charles, panting, prodding the way ahead with his cane while Joy looked down at the rock-strewn shore and envisaged calamitous shipwrecks and pirates.

'It's hot.' She tugged the neck of her dress and blew down inside. 'I hadn't expected it to be, it's nearly November.'

The track continued to climb, providing ever more spectacular views of the coastline. Charles talked of the Victorian fossil hunters who came to comb this rugged landscape as Joy stared out at the oaks and sycamores on the headland. Dwarfed by the wind, they were the only shelter for the castle, which in turn gripped the cliffs above the seashore. When they reached an elevated grassy knoll, they looked down on the bay hundreds of feet below, to where the low tide had exposed the beach with its bladderwrack and rockpools and families huddled in the dunes with picnics, making the most of this unseasonably warm autumn day.

'Want to stop for a minute?' Charles clasped her hand in his. 'Catch our breath?' His suggestion came just as a shaft of sunlight speared the dolphin-smooth skin of the sea and turned it silver.

'If you like,' Joy agreed.

To their left, a battered kissing gate with a sign saying 'To the beach'. They leant over it and gasped, thrilled by its terrifying steepness. Charles removed his coat and spread it over the grass for them to sit on. Careful to stay well back from the eroding cliff edge. He opened his shirt and took off his blazer and tie and she kicked off her shoes. Let her hair down. He put his hand into the pocket of his coat and, deliberately mysterious, conjured up bars of chocolate like a magician.

'Wherever did you get them?' She laughed in amazement.

'I've got my sources.' He winked: enigmatic, teasing. 'I've a sweet tooth; I like nice things.' It sounded like an apology. 'I'm sorry if I've been preoccupied recently.' Another apology, given with a flash of his blue eyes.

'I understand.' She broke off a chunk of chocolate and fed it to him. 'Work's been tough for you. There's lots to sort out.'

'Yes. Work.' He chewed and swallowed. 'That's it. Just work.'

They lay together. Her head on his chest as he smoked a cigarette, she listened to his breathing keeping rhythm with the suck and sigh of the tide. Charles closed his eyes and slept through the rippling call of a curlew. Joy dozed a little too. But aware of the dwindling time and their need to return to London, she couldn't relax enough to hand herself over to sleep the way he did. She counted down the hours, trying to hold on to time even though it was as impossible to stop as sand falling through her fingers.

CHAPTER THIRTY-THREE

The tunic, when he slipped it on over his shoulders, felt good. He felt good. The black thoughts that usually crowded his mind receded a little. The silver buttons were cold under his fingers as he did them up, methodically, one by one, his body tingling with anticipation about the night ahead and how the girl would look when he watched her moving around in her bedsit, when she took off her clothes.

You would have thought the wearing of a uniform would have thrust him back to the horrors of the First War and his experiences of the firing line thirty years before. On the contrary, a uniform of any kind gave him a persona, a camouflage to disguise the depravity of his true self. It set him up in his own and his neighbours' eyes. Dressing up, even though his duties with the force had long since ceased, not only allowed him to go on leading the shadow life that he loved, it encouraged him to do so. Dark alleyways and squalid cafés were his rightful province, and who knew what favours he could obtain from prostitutes and petty criminals anxious to keep clear of the law?

Before he took the Circle Line and travelled the eight stops to Gloucester Road to see if anything was worth viewing there, he'd have a stride around this locality now his tea had gone down, see what was up. Bouncing along the passageway in his polished police-man's boots, he put on his peaked cap that some might say looked too big for him and grinned at himself in the mirror. Reluctant to spoil his mood, he couldn't bear the pained look on his wife's moon-face whenever he said he was going out. But she could nag all she wanted; his jaunts to Gloucester Road were about the only pleasure he had these days. It wasn't as if he had work to get up for in the morning: he'd been back to Dr Odess complaining of nervous diarrhoea and he'd issued yet another sick note.

'See you later, Ethel, love.' And before a reply could reach him, he had slammed out the front door.

As he strode down Rillington Place, his neighbours waved and bid him good evening. He barely responded; bestowing one of his don't-try-sucking-up-to-me smiles as he systematically set about checking the tax discs and the state of tyres on the few vehicles that were parked against the kerb. Confident in the assumed authority his uniform gave him, he homed in on a cluster of children up ahead. Too raucous, he decided before he'd even heard them, and he summoned them over. He had no time for youngsters – as far as he was concerned, they were all up to no good and needed bringing into line.

'What d'ya want?' A boy of around eight, immediately on the defensive. 'We ain't doing nuffin'.'

'How'd you know? I haven't asked you yet.' Plumped up by his perceived cleverness, he stood facing them, his legs placed slightly apart.

'We're not, all right?' The children that had gathered around him began to disperse.

'Er, not so fast. You get back here.'

'What d'ya say? Speak up, grandad, we can't 'ear ya?' The gang leader cupped a hand to his ear.

'I said get back here.'

'Can't make us.'

'I think you'll find I can, laddie.'

'We don't have to do nuffin' you say, you're a nobody.' The boy, jogging on the spot, impatient to return to his game. 'It's what me dad says. You're only a joking copper.'

The taunt, thrown like a ball, hit him full in the stomach.

'You get back here. D'you hear me?'

'Sorry, mister. Like I said, you'll 'ave to speak up. Can't 'ear ya.' And he ran off to join his friends.

Skulking down the street under the cover of darkness, he made a grim silhouette in his black serge uniform. He looked as if he might be on his way to Albert's, but he wasn't. Tonight, he had other plans. He squinted through the vapour that was thick enough to draw his name in. Someone was out there; he could hear their footfalls. Their creeping emergence gave him a flutter of excitement deep in his stomach. Closer and closer, until the dark stain took on the shape of a young woman and child. He watched them with interest as they advanced towards him along the pavement. Saw how progress was slow, with the boy wanting to be carried one minute, walk the next. The mother set her child down and crouched to pull up his socks, arrange his curls under his cap while he played with the bow on her pillbox hat. A lone gull floated overhead. He listened to the heavy flap of wings, ghostly as it rode the equally heavy air. How still everything was. Softer than breath. The fog had draped itself over the city like a damp, grey blanket.

The woman shivered with unease. *Yes* – his silent thoughts in answer to hers – *we could be the only people in the world*.

They eventually passed one another. Her on her clicking heels, hand in hand with the boy; him with his right hand tucked inside the pocket of his tunic, his face hidden beneath his peaked cap. Slightly built, even dressed as a policeman, he knew he didn't look much, but whatever he communicated, it had her bundling her child in her arms, out of harm's way.

Then the child dropped his tin giraffe and it clattered to the ground. He ducked to pick it up and, returning the toy, he let his pale blue gaze scuttle over the boy's mother, rummaging beneath her clothes.

'Good night to you, lass,' he said, and strode away in his police-man's boots.

He had other fish to fry tonight. At least he hoped so. Hoped the girl was home after whatever jaunt she'd been on with that upper-class dandy and his flash motor, and that he wouldn't come to regret letting that pretty young mother go.

CHAPTER THIRTY-FOUR

Queenie was in no hurry to rise and face the day and dozed for another hour. Only when an arrow of afternoon sunshine burst and faded on the opposite wall did she sit up, pulling the eiderdown over her as if someone had unexpectedly entered the room. And in a way they had, although no one who could tell tales. It was the black cat with yellow eyes. He jumped on the bed and prowled along the mattress, startling her. There was something spooky about him.

'Do you want to say hello?'

Dizzy ignored her. But unbeknown to Queenie, he had been sussing her out from the floor all night. She tapped the bedcovers to beckon him, but he didn't budge until she made an involuntary noise, and he fled from the room as if he'd been shot.

'Scatty Catty,' she renamed him, listening to the *thump, thump* of his bounce as he descended the stairs.

Tuesday had come around again. The Mockin' Bird was shut. If she was going to visit that Mr Christie in Ladbroke Grove, it had to be today. She had tried and failed to use the Higginson syringe again and needed to do something; she would be showing soon. She had turned the scenario around in her mind through the small hours, her hands spread over the slight swell of what was growing inside her – it didn't matter she was frightened, she had to face up to it, she had to get it done. It was her punishment for what she had done to Joy.

It was the eighth of November. Her mother's birthday. That had to mean something. She reached across for the photograph of her she kept by the bed. The edges were blurry, echoing her receding memories. Someone had left it in direct sunlight and the right-hand side of her mother's body had been lost forever. Queenie pressed it to her chest, wanting her mother to look inside and read her thoughts. For her to steer her through her torment and show her what to do.

She got up and looked out on the garden that was dying in readiness for winter. A gibbous moon hung between the clouds. Queenie was someone who believed that seeing a moon in broad daylight was unlucky and dragged her gaze from its mesmeric pull to follow the snarl of pipes that ran over the exterior walls, the cracks and the mould that had invaded the light-starved parts of the house. Perhaps its spores had blighted her, and this was why she struggled to muster the enthusiasm to do anything; even performing at the Mockin' Bird, something she used to live for, was proving difficult.

The view swam before her. Her tears were for Joy, for herself… for her mother's best friend who couldn't afford to have another baby and had visited a backstreet abortionist, only to die four days later of septicaemia. This was the grim reality. It was risky. Everyone knew it was risky. But what choice did she have? Her mind groped limply for the alternatives and found none. When something was outlawed, this was what happened – it didn't make it go away; it drove it underground and put women in danger.

Queenie stood in her slip and stockings and looked at herself in the mirror. Her reflection was flyblown and tainted. She let the flat of her palm travel over the slight rise of her tummy and gulped back more tears. Curiosity had got the better of her, and she'd visited Merton library yesterday. Found a book with diagrams to see what a three-month-old foetus looked like. She had to stop making such elaborate plans for it and thinking of its heart beating in time with hers. Of dreaming it would be a girl. A girl who would grow up to be a fully formed, living image of her mother. With the same dark hair, the same expressions, the same laugh. She had to stop torturing herself. She couldn't keep it. Even if Charles wasn't the father and she hadn't betrayed Joy, it was impossible.

She buttoned herself inside a plain dress with a modest collar and hem. Applied a smear of lipstick and tied her hair under a triangle of scarf. Downstairs, she put the wireless on for the company and set the kettle to boil. Propped her elbow on the edge of the stove and pulled on her first cigarette of the day. When she'd made tea, she carried it out into what remained of the afternoon and opened the latch of her father's hen house. A blur of feathers, russet and gold, as they flew for the open air. She reached inside. Dipped her hands into the warm hollows they had left behind in the shredded newspaper. But there were no eggs.

With her back to the house, Queenie studied the hand-painted design on her cup. A birthday gift from Terrence. Something new for her kitchen, something that wouldn't keep reminding her of her father. She traced the straggle of bramble studded with blackberries and rosehips with a finger and was transported back to Goldchurch. Sniffing the imagined smell of hay, she saw the men of the village with pitchforks turning the rows of cut grass, and her grandmother striding from the farmhouse, out into the fields, flask and sandwiches in a basket looped over her arm. The men, laughing, eating their fill. Their laughter, carrying up to the yard, clear as birdsong. Queenie made a sound she was glad no one else could hear. She hadn't known it at the time, but those years with Joy were the most precious of her life. So keen was she to return to London, she had squandered them, in the same way she had squandered her friendship with Joy. And thinking about her complacency made her deeply ashamed.

Back inside, she couldn't sit. There had been enough inactivity, she needed to do something. With her insides heaving with butterflies, she placed her cup in the sink and put on her plain winter coat. No fur, no frills, no fuss. Not for this. She didn't want Mr Christie to look at her the way men usually looked at her. This was just something to be got through. And as if needing further impetus – to prove she had a future beyond the terror of the immediate one – she took out her passport and airline tickets from the sideboard. She looked strange in her photograph. Lost and sad, like her mother used to look when she thought no one was watching. She stepped over the cat, who was circling her ankles, and put the passport and tickets away. Checked her handbag for Terrence's note, even though she had memorised the directions and street names he'd given her. She saw her identity card. Took it out to look at the stamp with last year's date on it. How different things had been then. It was a good job you couldn't see into the future, or you probably wouldn't want to go there. She tucked the identity card away and opened her purse, looked at her rainy-day money. The five ten-shilling notes she had been saving for America, rolled up in a side pocket. Whoever this John Christie was, he would want paying; he wouldn't be doing it for free. She looked around the downstairs rooms as if to say goodbye to the fading rosebud wallpaper. The ceiling with its damp stain where the rain had come in before the tiles had been fixed.

'I'll be back,' she told the ghosts she shared her home with. 'In an hour or two it will all be over.' And she pushed out into the street that was washed a strange yellow in the dying day, the dread of what was to come making her heart beat faster.

CHAPTER THIRTY-FIVE

Early closing at the bank and Terrence was sitting in his work suit on the lower level of the double-decker bus, London's darkening streets skimming by on the other side of the smeary windows. With the Mockin' shut and no band to play with, he always felt a little lost on Tuesday nights. He was meeting Malcolm at Albert's later, but it was going to be a long wait. He supposed he could go to Camden Town; his mother was always pleased to see him. But it seemed sad, a grown man depending on his mother for company, for the supper she would be obliged to feed him. He closed his Penguin paperback and put it away in his pocket. He couldn't clear his mind enough to read. The words were jumping around, he wasn't taking anything in. After a tedious stint at the bank, receiving deposits and loan payments and dealing directly with customers, he wasn't in the mood.

He got off the bus two stops before he needed to. Ever careful, he checked behind him, ensuring he wasn't being followed. Hungry – he hadn't eaten much today – and spying a chalkboard sign advertising 'Good Grub', he scooted into a public house. There he drank two double whiskies in quick succession and ate a steak and kidney pie with fried potatoes. He left the pub, his stomach full, without ever learning its name. Turned his back on the three men in flat caps who sat up at the bar. Copies of their newspapers open next to their pints. Circling the fillies and talking the odds for tomorrow's races.

Picking winners was something his father had liked to do on Saturday mornings. Thinking of his father evoked a memory of the day he died. Something that was never far away. Tied in a knot, it swung close to his heart. That faceless teacher who sidled up to him and Colin during their music lesson to say the headmaster wanted to see them. Standing in the corridor and picking each other's brains for the bad thing they had done. It was their sister, Susan, who filled them in. Over a tin of Heinz Cream of Tomato. Eyes shiny with tears as she explained that their dad had suffered a fatal stroke and they mustn't be upset because Uncle Alan was on his way. And sure enough, their favourite uncle was there by the time they got up the next morning. Big and broad in his merchant navy uniform. A uniform he wore to the funeral, holding Terrence's hand through a white cotton glove, so all he could think of as his father's coffin was lowered into the ground was the discomfort of those reinforced seams digging into his fingers. His uncle made promises through his seafarer's moustache to take him fishing and took him to buy a rod and reel set at Woolworths. Terrence had it somewhere, in the spare room at his mother's, unused and still in its wrappings.

An engine backfired. Loud as gunshot. Then a bright clap of laughter and someone slammed a car door. It jolted him out of the memories he was happy to tuck away again. The alleyway leading to Albert's was up ahead. He was early. There was still a sliver of light in the sky. He pushed his weight against the familiar black door and found the place surprisingly packed. A churn of faces through the usual screen of smoke. It could be any time of day or night in here, or any time of year. He yawned, looking around at the gas lamps burning like a row of mock suns. It always surprised him to see this place full of people. Where did they all come from? How did they get to hear of it? And if they'd heard of it, wasn't it only a matter of time before the law came to hear of it also?

As he carried this thought and the frisson of fear it brought with it to the bar, he became aware of a scuffle on his periphery. A young prostitute in a flea-bitten feather boa and torn black stockings came charging up from downstairs, clutching her neck. She looked distraught: knocking into people, spilling their drinks, her mascara streaming in muddy rivulets down her cheeks, into her cleavage. The person she was running away from thumped against Terrence and he spun on his heels to confront whoever it was. The unwanted contact released that smell again. Jeyes Fluid. Along with something stronger, like industrial drain cleaner. It was that man in the horn-rimmed spectacles and trilby again.

'Oi, you!' Terrence loped after him, following him outside into the darkness that had dropped down over the city like a trap door. 'Stop!'

But the man didn't stop. Nimble in his plimsolls. By the time Terrence reached the end of the alleyway, the stranger had vanished.

CHAPTER THIRTY-SIX

A brisk breeze had come up since Queenie had left the house, and lazy clouds rimmed in gold gathered to the west. It would be dark soon; the city would only be identifiable by its lights. Slowly, the distance growing between her and home, her fear of what was to come dissipated a little. In its place, a queer kind of relief settled inside her. Yes, this was ugly and shameful, but she could do this, she could make things good again, for her and for Joy. Already, she felt, the terrible burden of her secret was a little lighter. Terrence said this John Christie she was on her way to see had trained to be a doctor. That he was intelligent and well respected. He did say respected, didn't he? Terrence might not have used that precise word, but she was sure it amounted to the same thing. Yes, this man would sort her out, in the way he'd helped others in trouble like her. She was sure she remembered Terrence telling her that.

A rag-and-bone man pulled up on the opposite side and Queenie did something she never did: she crossed the street to stroke the muzzle of his tired, old pony. A flash of Joy, feeding her apple to a horse on her birthday. The memory, bringing a pang of remorse for what she had done to her friend, had her blinking back tears.

'Don't you be feedin' him nuffin'.' The man in charge, gruff at her shoulder. 'No sugar lumps, miss.'

Sugar lumps? Chance would be a fine thing. She dabbed her eyes and searched the face scored by the weather for the irony that wasn't there. The man was craggy like a fallen bough that had been left out in all seasons. He dumped what he'd been given into his cart and swung up into the seat, and with a click of his tongue, the horse moved off down the street with a clip-clop and a rattle of iron in the load at his back.

Queenie put one foot in front of the other and moved along the pavement. The choke of coal smoke silting her nostrils as she listened to mothers calling their children in for tea. It seemed that suddenly there were children everywhere, babies and mothers with prams – they had never been of interest before. She passed the open doorway of the newsagents and ducked into its darkened innards. Chose a copy of *Woman's Weekly* and a quarter of liquorice twists ahead of her Tube journey. Not her usual read, but *Vogue* was too heavy to carry to Ladbroke Grove and back. This one fit nicely into her handbag. She never used to like the taste of liquorice but had recently found she couldn't get enough of the stuff. She put a piece in her mouth and was leaving the shop when Emily Boyd, from three doors down, nearly ran into her with her pram.

They exchanged silent nods and Emily disappeared inside the shop. Left her pram on the pavement. Queenie peeped in on the infant and, moved by the baby's supine stare, imagined him search-ing hers for answers about the universe. Queenie put a hand on her tummy and felt the sting of fresh tears. A tear was rolling down her cheek when Emily Boyd reappeared in the shop doorway with two cooking apples and a brown loaf. Embarrassed, Queenie made her excuses and turned away but was blocked by an image of her own face. Captured in one of the publicity fliers advertising the Mockin' Bird and fastened to a lamp post. She barely recognised the woman with the carefree expression. How changed she was. And feeling fraudulent, she wanted to tear it down.

She watched Emily push her pram away down the street. Perhaps she shouldn't have dismissed Terrence's offer. Could they marry and bring the child up together? As well as Heloise's, she listened to the other voice in her head, the one that told her she didn't love him, not like that, and he certainly didn't love her. No, it told her, she couldn't keep the baby, it wouldn't be fair on either of them.

It wouldn't be fair on Joy. *Get a grip*, she told herself and blew her nose. Her moods were all over the place: she was up one minute, down the next. How could she seriously think she could bring a child up on her own? What woman could with no family and her own mother gone? No, there was no way she could keep it, and she needed to stop being so romantic.

She crossed the road, walked through the confusion of horns and glare of headlamps, and reached the boundary railings pinpointing the entrance to South Wimbledon Underground. Her mind, whirling like a carousel she couldn't get off, made her knees give way a little.

'Are you unwell, miss?' One of the uniformed police officers standing guard at the entrance leapt to her aid. 'You look rather unsteady there.'

She felt the ominous weight of his hand on her elbow as she let herself be ushered inside the bustling ticket hall.

'I'm quite all right.' She forced a smile into her eyes. 'I just haven't eaten much today.'

'Well, mind how you go, miss.' The policeman backed away to his post.

A fleeting look at him and his colleague, before moving through the ticket barrier and down the steps. If only he knew what she was on her way to do: her thoughts sobering ones. If only he knew.

CHAPTER THIRTY-SEVEN

Terrence abandoned his search for the man in the trilby and returned to Albert's. A blast of noise and smoke when he pushed open the door and stepped inside for the second time that evening. At the bar, waiting to be served, he smoked a cigarette and looked around him, wondering where the girl in the boa had gone. Other prostitutes had gathered. Jittery as the house sparrows in his mother's garden. He feared for them. How was it right that any girl had to sell herself this way? Did none of them have families who cared about them? He supposed not, and it wasn't termed the oldest profession in the world for nothing: it would always go on. Legal, illegal – it mattered not. It seemed, or so Terrence had noticed, the only family these girls had was each other. And seated at the head of this unorthodox domicile, the one who was top of the dung heap: Albert. Albert, the velvet-clad patriarch.

Waiting his turn, Terrence took the opportunity to observe Albert. His self-imposed grandeur, the operatic hand gestures. He was a real showman and was certainly gifted at keeping his regulars entertained with his wild stories loaded in folklore and myth. In his elaborate clothes, strutting behind his bar like a peacock, the man could be considered appealing from a distance. And up close, too, if you ignored the bad breath and grime. Eavesdropping on conversations between His Girls, as Albert called them, Terrence learnt he was kind, that he treated them with respect. That his cut was fair compared to other brothel owners. Terrence supposed there was a modicum of safety working in the dungeon below stairs – it had to be better than plying their trade on the street and was, at least, inside in the dry and the warm.

'You're early tonight, my fine young fellow. What can I get you?' Albert's hand was on his arm. Encrusted in rings.

'Scotch and a splash, please.'

'Didn't I see you come in, then disappear out again? Is anything the matter?'

Terrence watched the progress of the lace-fringed sleeve, the grubby hand beneath as it reached for the optic.

'There's a man who comes here... I've seen him a couple of times.'

'Oh, yes?' Albert eyed him kindly.

'Small, quite insignificant. I'm not sure why I noticed him. He just gives me a bad feeling.'

'A bad feeling, eh?'

'He wears a raincoat and, erm, a trilby.'

'Small, you say? Insignificant?'

'That's right. Round-rimmed glasses... oh, and...' Terrence squinted through the sting of smoke that hung between them, remembering something else. 'He wears these tennis shoes, sort of plimsoll things.'

'Ooo, I know who you mean.' Albert gave a theatrical shiver. 'He's a dark one, he is. A right queer fish. There was us, thinking he was this nice, well-educated fellow.' A heavy sigh. 'It seems we got him quite wrong, Terry, old boy.'

'*We?*' Terrence shook his head; he didn't understand.

'Oh, yes.' Another shiver. 'He practically strangled Marie tonight, poor lamb.' Terrence followed the direction Albert pointed and saw the girl with the boa again. Saw too how she was still gripping her neck.

'Strangled her? Dear God.' Terrence, horrified. 'I saw her running away from him. It's why I went after him, but he'd disappeared.'

'They're so defenceless, aren't they?' Albert gave Marie a fatherly wink. 'I try and look after them, but I can't stand watch.' A smile

slid over his mouth. 'My clients would never allow that. But him…
it seems he's a dangerous one. You want to ask Marie to show you
the marks on her neck?'

Terrence pulled a face. 'The bastard doesn't look strong enough,
but—'

'You're right, it wouldn't take much to snap their girly bones.'
Albert read his thoughts.

'She should tell someone… report him.'

'Who to?' Albert looked at him as if he was stupid. 'Who gives
a damn about these lost souls? No one. We are, all of us, on the
fringes of so-called decent society. None of us… well, some of us,
maybe, but most of us, the likes of you and me, Terry, we don't have
that kind of recourse. We're on our own. Vulnerable to the world.'

Terrence nodded his agreement. Who could they go to? Who
could any of them go to? The police weren't a help to the likes of
them, they were a danger.

'Don't look so concerned, my dear. Marie won't be going near
him again, will you, duckie?' Albert called over to her. 'Apparently,
he was in here the other night, boasting about some young couple
living in the flat above his. Saying how he's taken a shine to the
young mother. Beryl, her name is. I only remember it because that
was my dear mother's name… Oh, yes, he's a dark one, all right.
Saying all these ghastly things he'd like to do to her. I do wish I hadn't
given you his name, Terry. I am most terribly sorry about that.'

'You gave me his name?'

'Yes. I heard he was a decent fellow, but as things have turned
out there's something altogether nastier going on with him. Was
your friend all right? I'd hate for her to have come to any harm.'

The penny dropped. The name and address Albert had found
for him. The one he'd written down and given to Queenie.

'Did she go along to see him?' Albert cringed, as if not wanting
the answer. 'Did he sort her out?'

CHAPTER THIRTY-EIGHT

Deep underground, somewhere between South Wimbledon and Ladbroke Grove, Queenie sat with her lush dark hair and handbag. Her legs crossed, an elbow propped on the dividing armrest, she smoked a cigarette without letting any single thought dominate her mind. Inhaling and exhaling in rhythm with the swaying of the train, she barely noticed the crowd of commuters and only vaguely acknowledged her luck at finding a seat. The carriage glowed dimly under the rows of lamps and was littered with discarded newspapers. The air was thick with the expended cigarette smoke she was adding to. Whenever the Tube lurched to a stop, she watched the doors pull apart, equating the exaggerated hiss to the industrial laundry she worked in when first back from Goldchurch after the war. A job she was relieved to jack in as soon as she could. The carriage emptied and refilled itself with passengers before the lips of the doors kissed closed again. A man in a dodgy suit caught her eye and smiled. She looked away and took out her copy of *Woman's Weekly*, leafed through the pages.

The train lurched again.

She consulted the map above her head. Nearly there. The man opposite was on his feet. His briefcase collided with her knee.

'Sorry, love.' He leered in close before steadying himself upright.

The substantial copper bangle on his wrist chinking against the handrail made her look up and into his bloodshot eyes, the threaded capillaries mapping his face. She didn't answer him and was glad to see him get off.

The train surged forward and clattered on. Queenie put her magazine away and looked at her reflection in the window opposite. The train's rocking, a lullaby rhythm: *Keep the baby... keep the baby... keep the baby*. She closed her eyes to it until the sudden cry of a baby had her opening them again. A mother, cuddling an infant on her lap, had sat beside her. She didn't smile at the child. She couldn't. She was too taut with anxiety.

Ladbroke Grove. Her stop. Queenie swallowed the last of her liquorice sweet and, rising to her feet, she adjusted her handbag and squeezed out past the row of knees and groans of protest, onto the platform, through the ticket hall and out to the street.

Daylight had been exchanged for a textured orange miasma, as gas lamps quivered against the encroachment of night. The wind had dropped and a cold, syrupy fog now shrouded the city and obscured the moon. Thickening into a soup, it had swathed the buildings like a living, breathing thing.

Queenie was in unfamiliar territory and it made her nervous. All around, the disjointed rise and fall of voices merged with the blare of horns and growl of traffic. Hurrying along, across the busy intersection with Lancaster Road, she fastened her coat and retied her headscarf. Abiding by Terrence's directions, she ducked down into a side street and left the main thoroughfare behind. This was a shortcut to St Marks Road. According to Terrence, Rillington Place was bounded by it on one end and the other end by the wall of Rickard's Transport Depot for Coaches and Vans. It should be easy to find.

The streets were stained by mustard-yellow gaslight that did nothing to brighten the shadows. She'd been warned that Notting Hill was rough, and it was, it was a slum. A battlefield. Half the houses in the streets were missing, torn up by bomb blasts, and despite the darkness, children were still playing on a steep slope of rubble. Grubbing around with pretend pistols. A girl with her leg in an iron brace bumped against her, making her look across at a section of fireplace showing where homes had been. The girl giggled and scurried ahead, the drag of her left leg carried behind her like an insult. A municipal notice had been pinned to a wooden stake and hammered into the torn asphalt. NEW FLATS, it boasted, but Queenie doubted anything new would help the dinginess of this area.

She stamped her feet and thumped her arms against her sides in an attempt to warm up. The agitated barking of a dog echoed around her and she looked sideways to monitor the progress of a young mother pushing a pram along the pavement. Hunched against the cold, the woman eyed her with suspicion. A van slithered past. In the bounce of headlamps, the perspective lengthened to the entire street and she walked past endless doorways shrouded in fog. Close up, the houses were shabby with flaking paintwork. Broken glass and bricks filled the tiny rectangles of scanty grass that grew between the bay windows and kerb.

A lamplighter was clanking along the street behind her with his ladder. His job was done for the night. Not that his efforts were effective: visibility was still poor and the undesirable feeling of this part of London frightened her. As she walked, she scanned the abandoned streets that yawned off into obscurity. The rows of dark-fronted houses, their curtains drawn against the world. Then a shadowy pub doorway came into view. The Elgin. Flanked by two black pillars, its sign, a cold eye, beckoned her through the gloom. A relief to see it, she trotted over and leant against the brick exterior, unsure if she should go inside. Alone in the dripping dark, she listened to herself breathing and pinched her cheeks that had gone numb from the cold. She checked her watch. Six thirty. Terrence had told her not to arrive before eight, that Mr Christie didn't care to be disturbed before he'd had the chance to digest his supper. She could risk a drink and a warm in here, couldn't she?

CHAPTER THIRTY-NINE

Fog. It rubbed itself against the high-sided buildings. Terrence left a note for Malcolm with Albert at the bar, saying he wouldn't be long and to wait for him, then stepped out into the night. There was no need to panic, he told himself, striding away in the direction of Piccadilly Circus. The chances Queenie had chosen tonight of all nights to go to Ladbroke Grove were slim. But it was best to check. He would never forgive himself if something happened to her.

The way ahead opened out into the bright lights of Piccadilly. A part of town that never slept, it was always lit up like Christmas and being here lifted his mood. A mood, because he'd started drinking too early, which had slumped. Remembering there was no point trying the Mockin' Bird – it was closed tonight – he looked around for a bus that was heading south of the river. If Queenie was anywhere, she would be at home. A glance to where a thin moon claimed its space in the dun-coloured sky. Colder now, a fine drizzle settled on his hat, on the sleeves of his coat. *Come on, come on.* He flapped his arms through the air. Where was a bus when you wanted one? He might not be in any particular hurry, but he didn't want this to take up his entire evening – he wanted to spend time with Malcolm.

A momentary lapse in concentration and a policeman on a bicycle whizzed past just as he stepped out to cross the road. His big black cape flapping out behind him. Dumbstruck, Terrence stared after it, aghast, adjusting himself in the aftershock, before aiming for the statue of Eros with its ceaseless roundabout of traffic. A memory of the sunny afternoon he'd borrowed Uncle Fish's

Kodak camera to take promotional pictures of Queenie to send to America. How beautiful she was, the sun picking out the tones of her hair, her bright eyes and tinkling laugh. It had been a while since he'd heard Queenie laugh. But given what was hanging over her, he supposed there wasn't much to laugh about.

Still no sign of a bus. If he set off towards Charing Cross, then on to the embankment, he might get lucky and pick up a bus along the way. Best to keep walking; standing here and waiting for one to come along was just wasting time.

At last. A double-decker sent up a spray of rainwater as it pulled to the kerb, drenching his already damp suit trousers. A hiss of brakes and the bus slowed to a stop to decant its passengers.

'Excuse me. Excuse me,' he called through the knot of people oblivious to anything but themselves.

Weaving through them, he saw a space on the lower deck and quickly, before the bus set off again, grabbed the metal pole and swung aboard. He couldn't be bothered climbing to the top. There probably weren't any seats and there wasn't much of a view tonight anyway.

Queenie's house, with its privet hedge and green front door, was locked up and dark. Reluctant to believe it, Terrence scampered down the side alley, crashing into dustbins. He let himself in through the garden gate to try the handle on the back door. Found this to be locked too. He shook it until the glass panel rattled in its frame.

Where is she? Where is she? Oh, God, please don't let her have gone there.

He nipped back around to the front, replaying Albert's words in his head: *He's a dark one, he is. A right queer fish... It seems we got him quite wrong.* And an image of the prostitute in her ripped stockings and boa found him as the tail of his coat snagged the thorns of a rosebush growing under the front window. Tugging it free, he stood on the red front step and hurled his voice in through the letterbox. Down into the dark empty hall and vacated rooms beyond.

'This can't be happening.' He flung a frantic look to the bow of the upstairs window. 'Queenie!' A cold panic slopping through him.

He charged out through the gap in the hedge and into the street again. Blinking through the fuzzy ochre light that was radiating from the gas lamps. The fog was thicker than ever. It hurt to breathe as he broke into a steady jog along the pavement, stopping whenever he saw someone. Black-clad, androgynous figures, fastened into winter coats. He didn't care who they were. Wild with worry, he accosted anyone and everyone, asking his desperate question: 'Have you seen Queenie? *Please*, you must've seen her.'

Then, someone he half-recognised from his frequent visits to this street, crossed from one side to the other as if to distance themselves from him.

'Excuse me, excuse me.' Terrence tried not to shout. 'Have you seen Queenie Osbourne from number seven? *No?* Are you sure?'

Met with little more than a series of befuddled faces, it terrified him; did they even know who Queenie was?

He circled back towards her house again. She had to be in. Maybe she'd gone to bed early. It seemed feasible; she had been complaining about being tired recently. Yes, that was it, hope rekindled. He retraced his steps, running one minute, walking the next and, reaching her door, he bent to pick up a handful of earth from the front garden. Was about to lob it against the upper window when a mousy-looking woman in curlers and floral wrap stepped out of the house next door.

'What's all the fuss?' she accused in her slippers. 'If you don't clear off, my husband's gonna fetch the police.'

'I'm looking for Queenie.'

'I'm sure you are, young man,' came the sour reply. 'Her and her gentlemen callers, a right dreadful carry-on, I can tell you.'

Terrence stared at her. Bolder, the urgent need to find his friend driving him on. 'Did you see her go out?'

'She's always going out. Keeps very strange hours, does that one.' The woman sniffed and scratched her nose.

'I mean tonight… have you seen her tonight?' Terrence tried again. The woman was so leisurely and sneery, it made him want to shake it out of her.

'I might have. What's it to you?' The languid reply and the neighbour crossed her arms. 'Friend of hers, are you?'

'Look, you've either seen her or you haven't. Please, I'm in a hurry, I've got to find her.'

'Don't go getting lippy with me, matey boy. I'll fetch my husband, and the police can be here in a minute. If that's what you want?'

'No, please. No police.' Terrence wafted his hand. 'I just want to know if you saw Queenie going out.'

'I did, as it happens. She in some sort of trouble, is she? Serves her right. Miss Hoity Toity. That one thinks she's better than everyone else round here—'

'Do you know what time?' Terrence, impatient, cut the woman off.

'It was just getting dark. I was putting tea on.'

'Getting dark, getting dark… about five, half five then?' God, this was like pulling teeth. The nosy old bat knew exactly when Queenie had left, he could tell.

'About then, yes.'

'You didn't happen to see what she was wearing?' He knew why he was asking this but refused to explain himself.

'What she was wearing?' A choked laugh. 'Bit of an odd question for a man to be asking, isn't it?'

'I just want to know if she looked dressed up to you or not.'

'Dressed up?' Another dry cackle. 'As it happens, no, she weren't. She looked pretty dowdy, to tell the truth. Come to think of it, she's been looking a bit under the weather lately.'

'Right, well, thank you very much.'

Terrence skidded out into Balfour Road. He veered off sideways and, turning right when he reached Merton Road, broke into a flat-out run. This was a race against time. She must have gone to see Christie. There was nowhere else she could be. His fears for her safety snapped at him like wild dogs as he hurtled down into the mouth of the Underground.

CHAPTER FORTY

The interior of the Elgin had a threadbare feel that echoed the streets around Notting Hill. Dimly lit and smoky, it was thick with the low murmuring of men who came to drink ale from pint glasses. She looked around at the etched mirrors, the stained-glass panels, the clock above the bar that was stuck at a quarter past four. This was a man's pub, no place for a woman. It was the sort of establishment her father liked, and what he would term a Victorian drinking house, with its formidable dark wood panelling and leather benches. Queenie didn't belong here, but it would have to do and it was at least warmer than outside. Horribly conspicuous, several pairs of eyes turned to her as she crossed the grimy floorboards, and every fibre of her wanted to flee. But it was still too early to call in on Mr Christie and she couldn't be seen to be hanging around in the street.

'Yes, what can I get you, love?' The barmaid, her hand on a brass beer pump, gave her a friendly smile.

'I'll have a port and lemon, please.' Queenie, relieved to see a woman, gripped the edge of the bar. She would just have one; it would steady her nerves.

The barmaid looked kind and Queenie had a strange longing to confide in her. To ask her advice. But there wasn't the time.

'I'm dealing with this young lady, if you don't mind, Millie.' And Queenie watched as the woman was bodily moved out of the way by a pair of large hairy hands.

'Suit yourself, Sid.' The barmaid backed away to serve a cluster of old men in cloth caps at the opposite end of the bar.

'Most unusual to see a young lady on her own in here, if you don't mind me sayin', love.' The man Queenie assumed was the pub's licensee leered at her.

She did mind him saying and pretended the nicotine-stained ceiling was of more interest than him.

'Don't want to talk, I take it?' Smouldering fag in hand, he dropped ash down his front.

A piano struck up somewhere in the far corner. Tinny and out of tune, it set Queenie's already frayed nerves on edge. Some of the men began singing along to whatever was being thumped out on the keys. Wet-lipped with toothless gums, now and again lifting their jars to their slobbering mouths; they were anything but jolly.

She stepped away from the bar and sipped her drink. Focused on the barmaid, who was now washing and drying glasses. It was probably best if they didn't get talking. What she had come to do was illegal and she couldn't be sure the woman wouldn't shop her to the police. Whoever this Mr Christie was, offering his services to desperate women like her, she doubted he would take too kindly to her blabbing to the staff at what was probably his local.

A man around her age limped up to the counter. Way shorter than Queenie, he was a little fellow with black eyes and shiny black hair that was plastered back off his long, thin face.

'Get you another, Tim?'

'Aye, why not, isn't it? My Beryl told me to go and make myself scarce for an hour or two, so best do as I'm told.' The man with the Welsh accent put his empty pint glass down on the bar.

'I hear Beryl's expecting another kiddie?'

'You bet she is.' The Welshman grinned: proud, fatherly. 'A little brother, I'm hoping, for Geraldine.' At this, Queenie saw a dark shadow cloud his face. 'Beryl's not happy, mind. Worrying we can't afford another babby… but like I say to her, where there's a will there's a way, isn't it?'

'I'm sure there is, Tim.'

Queenie tried not to eavesdrop on their conversation as she sipped her port and lemon, but she couldn't help it. The last thing she wanted to overhear was a discussion about the joy of parenthood and having babies. Fiddling with the damp corner of a bar mat advertising Guinness, she looked around at the pub's ruptured seating and shabby décor.

'Are you Italian?' the Welshman suddenly called over to her.

'Me?' A hand to her chest. 'I don't think so.'

She couldn't help but laugh at this. Cheeky and cocky, she liked this little fellow. So full of beans, his antics let her forget, for a minute, what she was there to do – now he had stopped talking babies.

'You look Italian if you don't mind me saying. My father's an Italian count, you know.'

Queenie stifled another laugh and bunched her lips. 'Is he indeed?' She nodded along with him, thinking how guileless he was. She didn't want to engage in any kind of chit-chat, she just wanted a quiet drink, but something about this chap made her feel a little sorry for him. Why? She didn't know. He was well-dressed and had a group of friends who all seemed to like him. But weighed down with her own problems, she didn't think too deeply about it.

'Take no notice of him, duckie,' the licensee advised her. 'This one's full of wild tales, aren't you, Timothy? The boy lives in a fantasy world half the time.'

'Oi, that thing I just said, it happens to be true, that does.' The Welshman laughed along, good-humouredly. 'It's you she shouldn't be taking no notice of.'

Queenie watched him return to his pals. Noticing again that he had a limp and wondered vaguely where he had the injury from. He looked too young to have fought in the war.

'Will you be wanting another, love?' The licensee drank from his tankard. Something, she'd noticed, he needed to frequently refill.

'Presently.' She swallowed the trepidation she held in her mouth and did her best to smile.

'You're not from round here.' He was trying to make conversation again, but Queenie wasn't interested. Too jittery to talk, she wanted to be left alone.

'That's right.' It was all she was prepared to give.

She caught sight of her reflection in a mirror advertising White Horse Whisky. How pale she was, the lipstick she had on made her look ghoulish. Turning away from it, she removed her gloves and coat, knowing she would need the benefit of them when she went back outside. It was a bitterly cold night. Time passed. But slower than she thought. She checked both the pub clock that never changed and her watch. Decided she had time for another.

'Go on then.' She waved at her empty glass. 'I'll have the same again, please.'

Head swimming. She knew she shouldn't drink on an empty stomach, but if she was going to get through this, she needed another one. She opened her purse and took out the necessary coins. Looked again at her rainy-day money. How rainy could it get? That day had come. Grim and bleak. That awful swirling in the pit of her stomach was back. She lit up a cigarette, hoping the nicotine would settle her as Terrence had said.

'You're waiting for someone, that's it, isn't it?' The licensee continued with his one-sided guessing game.

'That's always the time in here, is it?' She pointed to the clock on the wall, anything to divert his unwelcome questions.

'It is.' A tight laugh. 'The correct time is quarter to eight.'

Her second port and lemon arrived. She stared into her glass as if it could tell her fortune and read her doom. Then she swallowed it down in two. Was she prepared for what was undoubtedly going to be gruesome? She must be mad, going to this stranger's house and asking him to help her out of the mess she was in. No one knew she was here. Was she mad? No, she told herself for the umpteenth time – this was what desperation did, it made you take impossible risks.

She made room for her cigarette in the ashtray and stubbed it out. Put on her gloves and rebuttoned her coat. Without any kind of goodbye, she pushed out through the pub's swing doors and into the street again. And turning her collar to the cold and damp, she took off in the direction of Rillington Place.

CHAPTER FORTY-ONE

Terrence dashed from the train, onto the platform. A glance at the station clock as he ran towards the exit signs. He still might have time to stop her. He had told her not to go there before eight.

'I should have just gone with her… Why didn't I go with her?' he repeated, over and over, as he tore into the street. An image of the bruises on that Marie girl's neck bouncing along beside him. 'That Christie is one nasty bastard… If he hurts one hair on Queenie's head, I'll have him… I'll bloody have him.'

He charged out into Ladbroke Grove. Into the fog. Stopped. Was it left, or right? He couldn't remember the route he'd given Queenie. Right. He'd swear he'd told her to take a right when she left the station. A cold droplet slid down inside the collar of his coat, icy and shocking. He took off at a brisk pace. Pounding the pavement, splashing through puddles, his feet inside their thin socks chafed the frayed lining of his shoes. But he didn't stop, he kept on, half of him thinking it might have been quicker if he'd caught a taxicab. Except there were no taxicabs. There were no buses either. The street was dead under the ineffectual orange gaslight.

The drizzle slapped his face like a wet flannel. His skeleton, jarring against the pavement, made his jaw ache. But he refused to slow down, wouldn't stop to shake out the sharp stray stone swimming around in his shoe. Malcolm would be impressed with his surge of speed, his endurance; he was the athletic one, not Terrence. Except impressed was the last thing Malcolm would be. He would say it was irresponsible. Letting Albert find the name of someone, then passing it on to Queenie before vetting it himself.

He should have known it wasn't safe. Terrence should have gone and met this Christie bloke, not handed over his name and address to Queenie like that. What kind of a friend was he?

God, this place was awful. He'd been told it was run-down, but he didn't think it would be this bad. It was ruined street after ruined street. The display of poverty made him shudder in horror as he imagined the hotbed of depravity and vice going on beyond the cracked windows and rotting stucco-clad façades. Slums like this were a breeding ground for it. The people living here would think they had nothing to lose. They had already lost everything.

Panting his whisky breath, he reached yet another junction of Ladbroke Grove. He'd passed at least four. He recognised none of the street names in the directions he'd written down for Queenie. This was madness. He was lost, and because of it, he was going to lose her… he should have made her listen, made her marry him. They would have found a way. Anything but this.

He had to stop and, bending forward to catch his breath, he put his hands on his thighs and heaved down the soupy air. He watched a pack of stray dogs roaming a hummock of debris and, recovering a little, he lifted his head to read the street sign – St Charles Square – fixed to a shallow wall that fell away to rubble. Some irony there, he thought. This wasn't right. He tried to breathe past the burning sensation tightening in his chest. Where was he? He spun on his heels. All was quiet and still: a forgotten land of fog. He might have a chance if he could find St Marks Road – he knew Christie's was somewhere off there. But which way?

CHAPTER FORTY-TWO

Rillington Place was a mean, shabby cul-de-sac of ten houses on either side. Queenie thought they looked small, almost miniature, despite them having three floors. Each as ramshackle as the next, their most striking features were the peeling paint and the soot-stained chimneys. The light from the gas lamps barely penetrated the fog and the shadowy pockets that fell between them spooked her. But everything spooked her. Her nerves were shot and she was colder than she ever remembered.

She walked forward, dodging the oily puddles of pollution. Saw how London's flotsam and jetsam had gathered along this street that had no way out. The echoing bark of a dog started up, then stopped again. A rat scuttled past. Then another. This had to be the grimiest, most poverty-ridden part of London she'd ever set foot in. With purposeful strides, holding the collar of her coat to her jaw, she listened to the shuffle of trains that could only be a few streets away. The only other sound was her footsteps, and the only sign that anyone lived along here was a child's ball in the gutter.

Number ten was the last house on the south side, pushed hard up against the high transport depot wall and beneath the shadow of the black-skinned iron foundry chimney. Rearing up through the fog, the chimney's pear-shaped form dominated the street. Queenie walked to the foot of it and looked up. A redundant shell with no means to defend itself other than the sign of 'KEEP OUT' hanging like a necklace against its cold brick throat.

She hid in the dimness on the opposite side. Conscious of the rise and fall of her chest beneath her winter layers. Her heart fluttered like a trapped bird behind her ribs as she stared into the gas lamp squatting out front. Its tangerine flame flickering off-on, off-on. Pulse-steady. A dustbin had been blown sideways by the wind, its stinking innards spilled over the pavement.

Her stomach grumbled and gurgled and she feared she might be sick. Then a light went on in the hall of number ten, strong enough to pick out the edges of the curtains in the single ground-floor bay window. Did she dare risk crossing the street to look inside? No, she would smoke a cigarette first and gather herself together. She took out one of her white Sobranies and noticed the shake in her hand when she lit up. The burn of a match providing a brief respite against the cold night air. Then she was sick. She leant against the wall of the transport depot and retched until her insides felt raw. Only liquid, just the port and the splattering of the black sweets, nothing else. She hadn't eaten anything of substance. Woozy and light-headed, she berated herself for having that extra port. The alcohol, mixed with her nerves, had made her feel very queer indeed. Nervous all day, this was on top of a string of sleepless nights when she had tossed and turned, unable to make up her mind.

But she'd made it up now, and with Heloise's threat replaying in her mind – *Joy must never find out. Never. If she does, I won't be responsible for my actions* – she crossed to the other side of the street. A hand to her hair and a tweak of the headscarf, she glanced at the crumbling windowsill, the dead fern in its rusted can. Cigarette finished, she dropped it into the gutter and lifted her hand to knock on the filthy door. Failing to see the other hand that had pulled back the curtain of the downstairs window an inch. A hand that appeared to be quite detached from the eyes that peered out on her. Breath misting the glass.

CHAPTER FORTY-THREE

'Come on in then, lass. That's it. Don't look so worried. I'll put kettle on, we'll have a nice cup of tea before making a start, eh?' The softly spoken man with the Yorkshire accent beckoned her down inside his hall. 'That's it, you go through to kitchen, its cosier in there.' He adjusted the gaslight and blinked at her from behind his spectacles. 'That's it, you get nice and comfy, lass, make yourself at home.' He directed her towards his tatty rope chair. 'No standing on ceremony here. I know it's a serious thing we're doing, but I think it's best we're informal about it. Drop a milk in your tea, lass?'

'Just a little, thank you. I-I'm ever so nervous, Mr Christie... I-I don't really know if I should be here. I think perhaps I-I should go.'

'Ooo, no, no, no. You've come this far; you're doing right thing. I've helped out many a lass in your condition. I were nearly a doctor, you know, had it not been for my accident, so you're in safe hands with me. There you go, you drink your tea, lass. That's it... just, just, erm, one or two things I need to know... Have you popped off your, erm ... underthings, and prepared yourself for me? Oh, good, that is good. Have a little more of your tea. That's it, warm you up.' He rubbed his hands together. 'You ready for me to make a start now?'

'Y-yes, Mr Christie.'

Tea finished, he reached across for a cushion.

'Let's just pop this behind your head... that's it. And if you could lie back and relax for me.'

'Oh! What's that?'

'Just a bit of equipment I have to use, medical equipment... to give you a whiff of gas so you don't feel owt. That's way, good lass. Nowt to fret about. It'll soon be over. Just let me pop this mask over your face, and before you know it, you'll be asleep... Ah, that's it, I'd like you to sleep now...'

CHAPTER FORTY-FOUR

Terrence was still running. But at the end of his reserves, panting and sweating beneath his homburg, he'd undone his thick winter coat to let the foggy night air blow through him. Not that it did much to cool him down. With St Marks Road somewhere behind him and his desperation to find Queenie building street on street, he kept up the pace. Until eventually, looking up at a brick wall in front of him, a street sign read: Rillington Place.

'Thank God,' his murmured gratitude as he slackened to a jog and turned down into it.

He listened to the rasp of his breath as he looked around at the derelict houses on either side. How poor and sordid everything was. The squalor was even worse along here. The decaying façades, the litter that gathered in the gutters; his anxiety for Queenie's safety tightened its hold. These dwellings reminded him of the doll's houses his sisters had played with, and if there had been soft earth outside instead of concrete, Terrence imagined it would have been possible to jump from the top-floor windows without hurting himself. How could anyone live like this? And yet people evidently did. There were lights in the rooms beyond the blackout blinds and curtains pulled across mean bay windows. There were stilettos of chimney smoke.

He couldn't run any more and, slowing to a brisk walk, he put a hand to his mouth and coughed. Coughed again. His chest hurt and he thought he might be sick, but the feeling ebbed again. He listened to the fruitlessness of his cough reverberate along this forsaken dead-end street. When it faded, it was replaced by a ghastly silence that closed over him like the lid of a coffin. He dabbed perspiration from his brow with a cotton handkerchief, then pressed the handkerchief to his nose, reluctant to breathe any more of the filthy, coal-choked air. He hoped he'd got this wrong, that Queenie hadn't come here tonight.

He reached number ten. The last house, at the end of the street, and positioned up against a high brick wall topped with coiled barbed wire. The tall phallic finger of a disused foundry chimney skewering it to the sky. Still panting, he knocked on the grubby door. Used the seconds available to straighten himself out and smooth down his hair. There was no answer. But someone was in there. A chink in the curtains showed there were lights on inside. He lit a cigarette, took a good long drag and felt his heart rate slow. He knocked again, harder this time.

'Answer, why don't you?' he grumbled. 'I'm not going away until you do.'

He took a step back from the door, smoking his cigarette. Looked up at the front of the house and saw the upper floors were all in darkness. But whoever lived on the ground floor was home.

He was about to knock again when he happened to glance down at a white cigarette butt in the gutter. He bent and picked it up. Saw the telltale smudge of a lipstick's traces. Scarlet. Queenie's lipstick.

He chucked his cigarette aside and hammered the door with both hands. Harder and harder. Keeping on until his knuckles hurt.

'Open up!' he shouted, banging wildly. Flecks of paint came off on his fist and he brushed them away on his coat. 'Open up! I know you're in there. Open up… open up.'

He bit down on his lip and tasted blood. Queenie was in there, he knew it. He also knew he'd arrived too late. He buttoned his coat to the chin but not before the cold night had reached down into his stomach, making a little stale whisky return to his throat.

CHAPTER FORTY-FIVE

'Yes. What do you want?' The whispery voice from behind the partially open door of number ten was out of breath. 'You're making an awful lot of noise for this time of night... is there some kind of emergency?'

'Are you Mr Christie? Mr John Christie?' To Terrence's dismay, the man's accent reminded him of his late father's.

'I am, aye.' The clean-shaven face was sliced in half by the shadow of the door.

'My friend came to see you tonight. A young lady, dark hair?' He waited in the expectant silence.

'Your friend?' The one eye Terrence could see squinted from behind a horn-rimmed lens. 'No one's come here tonight. I don't know what you're talking about. Why a-are y-you hammering my door?'

Terrence could tell the man was nervous from the way he kept looking over his shoulder. It was as if he was fearful someone was about to come down the stairs behind him.

'Look, I know she was here. So, are you going to tell me where she is, or am I going to have to force my way in?'

Terrence tried to look past the man's slight frame, down into the gloomy hall. He watched him wipe an agitated hand over his high bald forehead and saw how his top lip glistened with sweat. There was no doubting it, he'd interrupted something and, taking a step closer, he shouldered his weight against the door, determined to get inside. But the door didn't budge. The man must have had his foot wedged against it.

'What are you hiding in there?' Up on tiptoes, peering over Christie's shoulder, Terrence saw a pram in the hall.

Then it hit him. Like walking into a wall. As corrosive as the industrial drain cleaner the landlord used when he came to unblock the drains at his mother's house. But despite its harshness, it wasn't enough to mask the rot beneath. A smell that thrust him back to Italy. To the German airstrikes of May 1944 and the putrid stench of decaying bodies trapped beneath the ruined streets of Pontecorvo.

'Uch!' he yelped and jumped back, clamped a hand to his nose. 'What the hell's that stink?'

As still as a post, Christie remained unmoved. The cold, hard gleam in the man's pale blue eye was pitiless. This was one sinister individual.

'My friend Queenie!' Terrence was shouting now. The white fag butt squeezed in his fist. 'She came here tonight; I know she did.' He shook it at him. 'You're to let me in, d'you hear?' He charged at the door again, rammed his weight against it. Christie was stronger than he looked. The door didn't move. 'Queenie! Are you in there? Queenie!'

'I don't know what you think you're doing, coming here and shouting. I've got no one here, you've no right. And another thing, you can't just… Hang on a minute… I know you, don't I? Aye, I know who you are now.' A flash of sharpness from the narrow-skulled man and, instead of cowering in the shadows, he leant around the door, emboldened and complacent all of a sudden. 'I know what you do. I've seen you.' The expression had mutated from fretful to indignant and was washed a strange curd-yellow in the guttering gaslight.

'Seen me?' Terrence gulped, holding the man's gaze. 'No. No, I don't think so.'

'Oh, I have.' Christie took his time. 'Aye, you're one of them dirty buggers.' The voice was no more than a whimper; the rat eyes scurried over him. 'I've a mind to call police and have you removed from premises. We don't want your type here. This is a respectable house, with respectable people. Your *friend*? Why would likes of me have owt to do with any friend of yours? I'm a decent citizen, I am. How dare you turn up here with your shouting. Who gave you this address? Supposing my wife had come to door?'

A glimmer of hope. A wife could mean Queenie was safe. 'Is your wife here? Can I talk to her? Maybe she's seen Queenie.'

'My wife, luckily for you, happens to be holidaying with her brother in Sheffield.' Christie snuffed out any hope. 'Not that it's any of your business.'

'Queenie! Queenie!' Terrence thrust his voice down into the dingy hallway Christie was protecting. 'Are you there? Queenie?'

'I said, didn't I?' Soft and slow. Terrence needed to strain to hear what the man was saying. 'I don't want your type here. I don't like your type. I know what you're up to. Filthy bugger… *buggering*.' A sickly smile. 'I've a mind to tell authorities about you. I've contacts, you know. Four years in London Police Force, I've two commenda- tions. One word from me, lad, and they'll pick you up in a jiffy.'

At the mention of police, Terrence's insides flipped over. This wasn't an empty threat; he knew all too well how easily and swiftly this could be made real.

'Go on. Clear off. You dirty bugger.'

Christie made to close the door. But before he did, Terrence heard the heart-wrenching cry of a baby.

CHAPTER FORTY-SIX

Joy loved the sensation of rubbing against the silky soles of Charles's feet. Pressed against his body beneath the bedcovers, this had become her favourite place. This wasn't Dorset, this was Bayswater, in the guestroom Heloise permitted Joy to use on the odd occasion she stayed over. Charles wasn't supposed to be in here. He was supposed to be in his own room. But with Heloise visiting her sister in Boulogne, and Dorothy at home, he'd crept along the landing and, without knocking, without any warning at all, she'd woken up to him climbing in beside her.

To sleep would be to squander these precious moments, so she stayed awake. Watched him sleep instead. Tonight, the splinters of gaslight seeping in through a gap in the curtains gave her parts of his face. How different he looked, vulnerable somehow. A rush of something maternal, coupled with the love she had for him, made her blink back tears.

'Blessed,' she mouthed her gratitude while focusing on his flickering eyelids. 'Blessed.'

This was how Joy considered herself to be these days, and the feeling was new to her. She turned over, onto her back, and counted the ways Charles had transformed her life in the few short months she'd known him. Hardly daring to believe she was to be his wife. That their wedding day was only weeks away, with all the adventures in South Africa that were to come. Breathtaking, the speed with which everything had changed, while at the same time, it was difficult for her to remember what life had been before it was filled with such colours and textures. She wriggled between the cool cotton sheets and thought she might explode with the anticipation of it all. The only fly in the ointment was Queenie. She had hoped she would be proud; proud that the geeky, awkward little Joy had finally fledged and found herself the most wonderful man. She couldn't leave things the way they were with her, she needed to try and make things right. She would call over and they could talk things through, get to the bottom of whatever it was. Joy didn't want there to be this strangeness between them, not when she was off to Cape Town and Queenie to New York. Despite their obvious differences, they shared too much history, and as far as Joy was concerned, their friendship was something worth saving.

She had so much to thank Queenie for; Queenie was why she had come to London in the first place. Her thoughts as she tucked the layers of blankets and eiderdown over them. Nuzzling into the generous sweep of Charles's back. She circled him with her arm and stroked the soft skin of his chest with the pad of her thumb. What a strange galaxy Queenie revolved in. She was about as far removed from Joy as the other side of the moon. What it took to stand up and sing at the Mockin' Bird night after night wasn't something she could imagine doing, but then she didn't have Queenie's talent. Charles was keen on the whole jazz scene, so, of course, it had to have some merits, but working there hadn't helped endear Joy to it. If she was honest, she found the smoky interior and patrons a little sleazy and was relieved to be finishing soon. She had only agreed to work there at all to please Queenie.

Joy still couldn't believe Charles wanted to marry her but supposed she never was any good at reading men; she'd not had the experience. Unlike Queenie, who understood how to play them. Before she'd met Charles, Joy knew she had frustrated Queenie by her seeming lack of interest, by preferring the company of books. Her mother used to warn her that men didn't want women who involved themselves with higher things and that what women thought would never be of importance. Showed how much she knew. Joy smiled, cuddling Charles tighter.

There had been a boy in Arras. They were in the same class at school. Everywhere she went, he was there – before her years in England and when she returned to France. It was something her mother actively encouraged. Recognising his interest, she would invite him for tea. But only because he came from an esteemed family that boasted established connections in the town – a family any self-respecting parent would wish their child to marry into, Joy heard her mother telling her aunts. But the idea of marrying someone she didn't love and ending up as unhappy as her parents frightened her.

Unbeknown to anyone – Joy, never speaking of it – the boy would regularly expose himself whenever the two of them were left alone and force her, by threatening harm, if she didn't touch him the way he instructed her to. Disgusted with herself, her hand weighted down by his, she would stroke the offending part, feeling it stiffen beneath her fingers most alarmingly. What he made her do was alien and repellent, and it was her shame that prevented her from seeking help. Coupled with a fear she wouldn't be believed, that people would take his side, saying he was a lovely boy and calling her a cheap little *salope* who must have led him on. One day the boy decided Joy's touching wasn't enough, and it was within the cobwebby confines of her father's woodshed that he yanked up her skirt, tore down her knickers and raped her. Bruising and cutting her little girl frame against the sharp work surface, he jammed himself inside her until purple-faced and eyes popping, he let go of an agonised groan and tossed her aside like a piece of rubbish. Refusing to cry, she had watched him casually return the flaccid member inside his trousers, wipe the spittle from his mouth and disappear down the garden at a sprightly gait while she fell to her knees on the filthy floor and vomited.

Fearing the reprisals the boy assured her she would get if she breathed a word of what he'd done, she did everything she could to ensure she was never left alone with him again. But unable to guarantee this possibility – her mother had a peculiar way of removing herself whenever the boy was around – she took to carrying a penknife found in the woodshed. Pressing her palm to the sharpness of its blade for reassurance whenever she saw him, she was calmed by the security it gave her. Half of her wished he had given her the excuse to plunge the knife in and then she could have had her revenge by quartering him up in the same way she'd seen her father pare fruit and vegetables.

But the boy grew up unscathed, didn't he? Joy recalled the conversation over lunch with her mother in the summer. He became high up in the town council and was rewarded for his repulsive ways. He was part of the reason she could never go home. Why she had left Arras. And the memory of that day, growing septic as it had, was another reason why Buster frightened her. She might not be any good at reading men, but you'd have to be stupid not to be able to read him. It was obvious what he wanted to do to her. And drunk, as he so often was, there wasn't much to stop him. It was another reason why Joy was glad to be finishing at the Mockin' Bird. Buster was dangerous and she wasn't sure how much longer she would be able to fend him off.

CHAPTER FORTY-SEVEN

Having spent the day fretting about Queenie, unable to concentrate on anything, as soon as he could get away from work, a rather dishevelled Terrence dashed over to the Mockin' Bird.

'Boy, am I glad to see you.' He charged inside the dressing room, panting for breath. 'Are you all right?'

'Hi, Terry. Yes, I'm fine.' Queenie turned coolly from her reflection. 'Uncle Fish says you've been ringing the club for me. What's up?' She frowned. 'You look done in.'

'Did you go?' An anxious hand up through his thick sandy hair, making it stand up in tufts. 'Did you go and see that Christie bloke last night?'

'Yes, I did.'

'You did?' His jaw dropped open. 'Are you all right? Wouldn't you need a couple of days off?' He winced under the weight of his question.

'I couldn't go through with it. I went there but it was so horrible... that street, that house.' He saw how she trembled beneath her gown. 'I couldn't even knock on the door.'

'You couldn't?'

'Don't be cross, Terry.' She bunched her lips, looked on the verge of tears. 'I'm grateful to you for getting me his name and everything, but there was a badness there, it oozed it. I'm not joking, it was evil... Don't look at me like that, I can't explain why, it was just—'

'You don't have to, darling.' Terrence, anticipating what she was going to say. 'I felt the same about it too.' He didn't say that he'd met Christie and the man had threatened him with the police.

'I didn't know you'd been there.'

'I went last night, looking for you.' He dropped into an armchair and rubbed his legs that ached from running.

'How did you know I'd gone?' Queenie kept her voice low.

'You weren't at home, so I sort of guessed. You said you couldn't be putting it off much longer.' Terrence glanced over at the red curtain, drawn across and partitioning the room, then got up to check the basement corridor was clear before closing the door. 'But I had to stop you going to him.' He sat down again. 'I'd heard these awful things.'

'About Mr Christie?'

'Yes. Dreadful things. He's not what we thought he was. He's bloody horrible. Dangerous.' A flash of Christie's pitiless stare that had been haunting him.

'Dangerous? What does that mean?'

'It doesn't matter, not now I know you're safe.' He was reluctant to scare her more than she already was.

'Yes, I'm safe.' A ghost of a smile. 'But I'm still in trouble.' Terrence followed the journey of her hand, saw it hover about her midriff. 'I'm going to be showing soon.'

'The thing is, Queenie, darling. These people…' He fumbled for the word he couldn't bring himself to say. 'They don't advertise, they have to work below the radar. It's illegal what they're doing. It was a fluke I found you Christie's name.'

'I should've let you come with me. Perhaps it would have been all right with you there?'

'No way.' He flinched. 'I'd rather you told Joy than go to him.' His mind, leapfrogging over the images he'd kept of John Christie: his weird waxy sheen, his thin lips, that strange sucking thing he did with his mouth. Terrence never wanted to set eyes on the creep again. 'But you're right, you are going to have to do something. Joy's been asking questions; she knows something's up. She's bound to twig soon, and when she does, she's going to want to know who the father is.'

'You're right. Oh, God, Terry, what am I going to do?'

'I know I sound like a broken record, but if you let me marry you, bring the baby up as mine, it would save Joy ever finding out it is Charles's.'

'You don't sound like a broken record.' Queenie walked and planted a kiss on his cheek. 'You're the kindest friend, but...'

'But what? I'm sorry to have to push you, darling, but you're running out of options.'

'Then I might just have to come clean.' She swivelled back to the mirror to check her make-up.

'Tell Joy? Oh no, Queenie, you can't. She's built her world around Charles. Oh, God, you can't, you can't tell her.'

'Keep your voice down. I know all that.' She propped her elbows on the dressing table, held her face in her hands. 'This is such a mess.'

A knock at the door and it burst open. 'Come on, you two. Chop-chop, you're on.' Uncle Fish filled the threshold, twizzling the ends of his white moustache.

'Are we? Just give me a minute.' Queenie snapped to it and applied her lipstick.

'Full house again tonight, my dears. So, off you go and do your stuff. And Buster?' Uncle Fish thrust his voice between them. 'You still there? You sobered up yet?'

At this, a rattling of curtain rings, and the red velvet drape was drawn aside.

'Yeah, I'm 'ere.' Buster appeared from behind it, rubbing his eyes and wearing a large, self-satisfied grin. 'I've been 'ere all the time.'

CHAPTER FORTY-EIGHT

Buster was different tonight. Instead of his usual inebriated, morose self, slumped over his beer at the bar, his movements were deliberate, measured. It was as if he was carrying something big: a bowlful of liquid he was fearful of spilling. He was entertaining people with his stories and Joy eyed him warily as he manoeuvred the club inch by careful inch.

'Hi there.' Buster strode in front of her, blocking her way. 'You're lookin' extra pretty tonight.'

'Thank you.' She nodded politely before stepping away to serve a tray of drinks to a nearby table. Despite the obvious improvement in his mood, he still frightened her.

'Aren't you gonna ask me how I am?' He stayed close on her heels.

'Excuse me, miss.' A man at another table beckoned her over.

'Yes, sir? What can I get you?'

'We'll all have martinis.'

'Very good, sir.'

Buster was at her elbow when she relayed the order for drinks at the bar.

'Do us a favour, Joy.' Sammy, with more orders than he could cope with, looked flustered. 'We've run out of olives. Nip down and fetch a couple of cans from the stores, would you?'

'No problem.' Joy smiled and placed the empty salver on the bar.

'You still ain't asked me how I am.' Buster, his bulldog face, close at her side.

'Haven't I?' Joy lifted a nervous hand to the diamante clasp fixed to her hair.

'No, you ain't,' he shouted above the music.

'I am rather busy.' She set off at a brisk pace, cutting between the tables in front of the stage. 'We'll talk later, yes?'

She hoped the empty promise would buy her some time and scooted away, aiming for the door at the back of the club that led down to the dressing room and stores. A fleeting look at Queenie: spot-lit and wooing the microphone with her red-painted lips. A shimmering showgirl in her shimmering dress, she owned the stage in the same way she owned the band. Didn't Queenie say she would have a word with Buster and tell him to stop harassing her? From the way the brute was behaving, it didn't seem as if she had.

'I look loads better, wouldn't ya say?'

Buster was proving difficult to shake off. 'Well, y-yes, I suppose you do.' He wasn't going to follow her down to the storeroom, was he? She scanned around but there was no one to help her; she was going to have to find a way to get rid of him on her own.

'Aren't you gonna ask me why?'

'Like I've said, Buster, I am rather busy. Can we talk later?'

She reached the back wall of the club and put the flat of her hand against the door that led down to the basement. Hoping he would get the message, she pushed against the door and left him behind. Trotted down the shadowy stairs. A burst of laughter rang out above the music before the door swung shut, the laughter ending in a wheeze.

'Oi, you listen to me. I'm sick of you ignorin' me.'

Buster. Close at her back. He had followed her downstairs. The suddenness of him made her jump. She spun to face him.

'I'd like some fuckin' respect.'

Joy touched the apple brooch pinned to her dress and threw a desperate glance over his shoulder. The door that led to the safety of the club looked a long way off.

'I think it's about time I got what I want. What I've been waitin' for since you started workin' 'ere.'

She gaped in shocked disbelief at his round, bare face beneath his sparse ginger hair. Having identified the malevolence in the snarl of his lip, in his bulk, she knew she was in big trouble.

'I've bin keepin' an eye on you.'

'Keeping an eye on me? What do you need to do that for?'

'Watchin' you flirtin' with Dick and Eddie... with Sammy.' Buster's indignation – a cerise sunset – bled up and over his neck and face.

'No, I haven't.' Her voice sounded as if it was coming from a long way away.

'You don't even know you're doin' it. Right little tease, ain't ya?' Stepping closer: insidious, intimidating. 'You're up for it with everyone... everyone but *me*.' He blocked her only means of escape.

'Go away, leave me alone.' Joy, blunted by shock, tried to reason with him; tried harder to keep the terror hammering behind her ribcage out of her voice.

'*Go away. Leave me alone*,' he mimicked. 'No way, it's my turn now.'

She couldn't speak. The basement was suddenly too small to stand up in, too small to think.

'Your turn? It's not anyone's turn... I'm engaged to be married. Get away, Buster, I don't know what you're talking about.'

'Oh, I think you do. And if you don't give me what I want, then I'm just gonna have to take it, aren't I?'

She stared into his face: a face that had been prematurely scored by the war and a lifetime of cigarettes and booze.

'I've seen ya, you're free and easy with everyone else, what's the matter with me?'

'Please leave me alone, you're frightening me.' Joy ducked away. But too quick, too strong, Buster seized her wrists and slammed her against the wall.

'Shut your mouth.' He shook her. Fierce. The spurt of movement released a puff of stale cigarettes, the reek of unwashed armpits. It fought for room alongside their tall shadows that had bent in half against the wall. 'You don't have the first idea what it's like for me. My life's been ruined by that fuckin' war... If it weren't for the likes of me, you and the rest of them Frogs would be goose-steppin' round Paris.' He loosened his grip a fraction, but pinned to the wall by his big, broad body, there was no escaping him, nowhere to go. 'You've a cheek, bloody lookin' down your nose at me.'

Charles? Where are you? Hardly daring to breathe, Joy made her voiceless and frantic plea. But Charles hadn't been to the Mockin' Bird for weeks. And even when he did, he never came down here.

'I hate my life... I've got nuffin. All I want's a girl, someone who'll love me. I wanted you to love me. Why can't ya love me?' He shook her again.

Chest tightening, mouth dry, Joy felt a portion of her brain constrict in panic. Buster was too strong. She was trapped. She had been in this situation before, in Arras. Buster wasn't going to hurt her, was he?

'Please, Buster. Stop. You're frightening me.'

'Not good enough for ya, am I?' Impervious to her pleadings, he growled from beneath a set of eyebrows wet with sweat. 'You're the same as the rest of 'em, lookin' down your nose.' Then he forced his face against hers. 'All I want is a kiss... one measly kiss.'

She twisted her head away. 'Stop it. Stop it. Leave me alone.'

His eyes narrowed, angled at the floor, measuring what he was going to do next. Then he nodded at the poster of jazz musician Gene Krupa, one of the many the band had fixed to the wall.

'That's who I shoulda bin.' Buster was like a bull: raging and angry, hell-bent on destroying everything around him. 'If it weren't for the bloody war... I'm as good as 'im on the drums.' He head-butted the words. 'You'd 'ave me then, wouldn't ya? If I was rich and famous. It wouldn't matter about not talkin' posh or me ugly face. *Bah*, you women, you're all the same. All ya want's money, a man to look after ya.'

'Why are you doing this? I've not done anything to you,' she cried, wincing under his grip.

'Who the fuck d'you think you are?' She felt his spittle land on her cheek. 'You're gonna be sorry for this.'

Helpless under the weight of him. He was insane and she knew he was going to strike.

'I've got the goods on everyone, I 'ave. And I'll tell you, you're gonna be on your own for the rest of your life.' A cruel laugh. 'Who's gonna want that toff's leftovers?'

'Get off me, leave me alone. I've told you, I'm with Charles. We're getting married.'

Another cruel laugh. 'Oh, yeah, *Charles.*' He spat out the name. 'I'll tell ya somethin' about Charles. Shall I tell ya somethin' about Charles?' Buster cocked his head, ugly in the sickly electric light. '*Charles* and Queenie, oh, yeah, *Queenie,*' he responded to the look Joy was giving him, then hurled her aside. 'You don't know 'em as well as you think, do ya? You haven't a clue what's goin' on.'

'What do you mean? What are you saying?' A hand to the wall to steady herself.

'That Queenie, *ha*! She ain't no friend of yours. And Charles? Marryin' 'im? *Ha!* Who are you fuckin' kiddin'?'

'What are you saying?' Joy backed away from him, afraid of the truth she hadn't consciously sought.

'Queenie's pregnant. Yeah, pregnant. And 'ave a guess who the father is?' He put a hand to his withered tie then adjusted his jacket over his shoulders. 'They've done the dirty on ya. The pair of 'em.'

At this, the door at the top of the stairs burst open. Light from the club dripped down into the gloomy passageway. Joy looked up at Terrence and let out a cry. A raw, base, animal sound so full of anguish it made both men recoil in fear.

CHAPTER FORTY-NINE

Albert's Cavern continued to perpetuate its twilit mood. The foetid atmosphere, dominated by tassels and drapery, all added to its disreputable feel. The low ceilings pressed down on the busted couches and wingback armchairs, condensing the heat, the reek of stale booze, body odour and tobacco, while lamps glowed dully and candleflames flickered. The kind of place, or so Terrence thought, that had been assembled from people's cast-offs, leftovers from the last century.

He pushed his way through the crush of bodies to get to the bar. He could see Malcolm seated with four men at a table to the side of the door. Engrossed in a card game, their glasses full. Terrence would join them in a minute, but first, he needed a drink. Something to steady his nerves. Buster had a screw loose and, as far as Terrence was concerned, his time with the band was up. What he'd done tonight was unforgivable. A flash of his pig-pink face. Terrence should have smacked him one there and then. What right did he have to be so casual with Joy's feelings? It had frightened him to see her so distraught. He had tried to offer comfort, but there was no consoling her. She had pushed him away, accusing him of keeping Queenie's filthy secret – which he had – before grabbing her coat and rushing out into the night. He trembled a little at the recent memory, trembled a little more when he thought about having to break the news to Queenie. Something he hadn't been able to bring himself to do tonight. Cowardly? Maybe. But telling her at the club wouldn't have been the best idea: she would hate for anyone else to find out what had gone on. Although it was probably only a matter of time, now Buster was in the driving seat.

Terrence stood at the bar waiting his turn. He took off his coat and hat and passed the time by watching Albert. The bulge of his nose, the thick body beneath the layers of lace and velvet. The flesh swag of his chin. He thought what an unyielding presence Albert was in his life, and with no hope of the law changing any time soon, the idea of nights like this stretching off into eternity depressed him. Unlike many who frequented this establishment, Terrence didn't suit it here. He didn't fit. Made sure he didn't fit. Most of the people he was forced to rub shoulders with in this place disgusted him.

'Good evening, my dear. Same as usual?' Albert turned his big face to his.

'Please.'

'I've been meaning to ask you.' Up close, Terrence saw Albert was wearing a woman's foundation. The pores of his skin pitted like an orange and clogged with powder. 'Was your friend all right? Because when you were last here you ran off into the night.'

'She's fine. She didn't go in the end.'

'That's a relief. That dreadful man was in here again yesterday.'

'You should ban him.'

'Rather difficult to do that, my dear. I can't keep tabs on every-one, and there's no one manning the door. But rest assured, none of my girls will be going with him again, so I'm hoping that will work as a deterrent to him coming here.'

Terrence glanced over to the usual gathering of prostitutes. There was no sign of the girl in the black feather boa. 'At least it'll mean they're safe.'

'From him, yes. Although…' Albert rolled his eyes. 'Another of my girls has gone missing. No one's seen her for days.'

'Oh, dear.'

'Oh, dear, indeed. Bella, do you know her? Fabulous redhead. Curls.' Albert flapped a ringed hand at his thinning mop of greasy hair. Terrence shook his head; he didn't think he did. 'I tell them not to go off, that they're to stay here. But do they listen?' Albert scrunched his pulpy mouth and pushed Terrence's tumbler of whisky towards him. 'No, they do not.'

'Does anyone know who she went with?' Terrence paid for his drink and did his best not to breathe in Albert's staleness.

'There's a few suspects. Not that we can do much, you understand.'

Terrence did understand. Involve the law, and the illegality that went on here would be blown wide open.

'All we can hope is that she turns up safe.'

A group of youngsters in polo necks jostled between them. Terrence picked up his drink and left them to it. Pushed back through the crowd to join Malcolm and his friends at a table that had been ravaged by cigarette burns and candlewax. The varnish that had once been applied, worn away in flaking patches.

'Terry, man.' Malcolm beamed. 'Come and join us… Seamus, deal a fresh hand, we'll start a new game.'

'Don't worry on my account.' Terrence kissed him then draped his coat over the back of the chair. Sat down with his hat on his knees. 'I'm not in the mood.'

'What's up, man? You looking tired. You sick, or summit?' Malcolm put his arm around him.

'A spot of trouble at the club, I'll tell you later.'

He downed his whisky and gasped. Better. Malcolm was watching him. Terrence touched his boyfriend's face and a tender moment passed between them. He tried not to look at the scar. The ugly, thickened snake across the bridge of Malcolm's nose that twisted down past his eye. He'd been lucky not to lose the eye. Terrence cringed at the memory and saw again the blood that wouldn't stop… the shiny white walls of the police station. Wanting to forget the trauma, he moved his hand to Malcolm's thigh and squeezed. A frisson of excitement fizzed through him.

'I've missed you, Terry, man.'

'I've missed you too.'

'Want me to get you another?' Malcolm pointed at Terrence's empty glass.

'Go on then.'

They kissed again and he sat back to watch Malcolm melt into the crowd. It never failed to shock, the lowlifes and crooks he was forced to rub shoulders with in this place. Seated at a table opposite, tipping ash into the candle bowl, was someone he knew to be an eminent cabinet minister, balancing a teenage boy on his knees. Head against head, drinking, giggling, oblivious to the swill of activity around them.

'I've not been to police. *Yet*.' The threat was little more than a puff of breath on the nape of Terrence's neck.

He jolted upright in alarm. That smell again. Industrial drain cleaner. Strong, but not strong enough. Terrence could still identify the rot beneath: the rot it was supposed to conceal.

He whipped his head around to confront him.

Christie.

Leaning close to his shoulder. The narrow face beneath the hat was half-hidden in shadow.

'That's not to say I haven't been considering it,' the whispering continued: soft and reasonable, as if he was telling Terrence it was going to rain tomorrow. 'Let's go and have a little chat, shall we, lad? Find ourselves a nice quiet corner. See what we can sort out.'

'I've nothing to say to you, and I think you'll find you're not welcome in this place after what you did.'

'Oh, dear. Is that right? Let's just say I think you'll find it were in your interest to do as I say.'

Something in Christie's expression made Terrence think he best just get whatever this was over with. He left his hat behind on the table, made his excuses to Seamus and the others, and followed the prim little man in plimsolls through the throng of revellers, into an empty booth that fell between a pairing of plaster pillars.

'I don't enjoy coming to these kinds of public houses. I abhor public houses. They are such ungodly places.' Christie, his nose in the air.

Terrence watched the man sit and arrange his raincoat around him, prissily, so nothing else of him made contact with the grimy upholstery.

'Do you mind telling me what this is about?'

'No, it's not my kind of place at all.' Christie ignored him. 'I've rather refined tastes, truth be told.'

'I asked you what this was about. What do you want?'

'All in good time, lad. All in good time.' He was doing that sucking thing with his mouth again. 'The name's Reginald, by the way. I know you were told my name's John, and it is, but my friends all call me Reginald… well, Reg, actually.' A small pale hand was extended from under the cuff of his sleeve.

'Friends?' Terrence refused it. 'I'm not your bloody friend.'

'Oh, now, don't be like that, Terry, lad. May I call you Terry?'

'Er… w-what?' Terrence spluttered his protest. 'How d'you know my name?'

'I know all sorts about you, lad. And me knowing your name's the least of your worries.' A nasty chuckle.

Terrence gawped at him, mindful of his beating heart, as he did his best to control his breathing.

'Anyway, where were we?' Christie continued in his whispery way. 'Ah, that's right, we were talking about this place, weren't we?' Another chuckle. 'Well, I can see why the likes of you come here. Nice and secret, isn't it?'

'I don't know what you're being so sniffy about, I've seen you here often enough.'

Terrence had been forced to sit beside Christie in the booth. The man spoke so softly, he needed to lean close to hear all he was telling him. His was a voice that would be lost among others and it made him wonder if it was a deliberate tactic on his part. A clever one if it was, as it forced him to listen, to give more attention than he ordinarily would. But that would make this man very calculated and cunning, wouldn't it? *All the more reason to watch yourself and not underestimate the bastard...* Terrence's warning to himself.

'Needs must. You of all people should know that.'

'Yes, but just because you pay them, it doesn't give you the right to hurt them. Albert said you tried to strangle Marie.'

'Maybe I did, but it's not like I hurt an innocent woman.'

'You're not denying it then?'

Nervous in this creep's company, Terrence was desperate for a smoke but he'd left his fags behind. Fidgety, he lit the candle on the table instead, positioned it between them. Saw how far it threw its light. Not far. The room around them dissolved into obscurity and their shadows flickered like giants against the walls.

'I don't like naked flames.' Christie tipped forward: a dark-winged moth drawn to the candle flame. 'I don't trust 'em.' He smothered it.

'I don't trust *you*,' Terrence mumbled. 'Anyway, enough of this shilly-shallying. Are you going to tell me what this is about?'

As alarming as he was compelling, Terrence couldn't peel his eyes away from this noxious little man. His hypocrisy was stunning, as was his sanctimonious manner. Despite the smell he carried on his person, the man was obsessively neat in his appearance and this puzzled him too. He'd seen where this man lived. He'd seen the squalor.

'Don't be testing my patience, lad.' Christie pressed a hand to the small of his back and grimaced. 'I'm in a great deal of pain tonight.'

'You look all right to me.'

'I've a bad back.' The eyes glistened. 'I've a certificate from my doctor saying I'm unfit for work.'

'What's that got to do with me?'

Christie gave him a black look that made Terrence shrink under his clothes.

'I suffer with headaches too, and flatulence, diarrhoea and piles...
oh, yes, I'm a martyr to my piles.'

'*Nice*.' Terrence pulled a face. The man's seemingly never-ending
list of ailments was as revolting as he was. 'Am I supposed to feel
sorry for you, or something?'

'I'm just explaining,' the Yorkshire accent tiptoed over the
words. 'If you'll do me courtesy of listening... it's why I'm a bit
short this week.'

'You want money?'

'Ah, now, there's no need to be vulgar. Let's just say I need a
little something to help tide me over.' The quiet voice continued
with its despicable demands. 'Unless you'd rather I went to police,
told them what it is you and that darkie get up to.'

'You want me to give you money so you don't go to the police?'

'Aye, why not? The likes of you should be locked up.' The
expression hardened; the mouth set in a thin, grim line. 'Letting
you roam streets, it's disgusting... you're not safe. Aye, I'd be doing
community a favour by reporting you. But I suppose...' Switching
back to his slimy self and rubbing the side of his nose with an
outstretched finger. 'I could be persuaded for right kind of fee, if
you catch my drift?'

'Hang on, let me get this straight. You want me to pay you to
keep your mouth shut? But that's blackmail!'

Christie narrowed his eyes. 'Ah, now, blackmail's such an ugly
word, Terry. No, this is just a little way for you to help me out
now and again, and in exchange... well, I'll keep quiet about your
filthy habits.'

Terrence noticed the shake in his hand when he took out his
soft leather wallet. 'And if I give you this – if I give you what I've
got on me – then you'll leave me alone?'

'Well, now, we'll see about that.' Christie smiled and snatched
the money.

'What d'you mean, we'll see?'

'I don't think you're in any position to be ordering me about, do you, lad? I'm one in charge, wouldn't you say?'

'Terry, man. I've been lookin' all over. What you doin'? Who's dat?'

'Malcolm!' Terrence jolted upright. 'It's nothing… nothing for you to worry about.'

'Dat not nuffin', man.' Malcolm pointed at Christie's fist curled over the wad of notes. 'Dat look like a load o' dough. What you be payin' him for?'

'Honestly, it's fine. Everything's under control.' Terrence leapt to his feet and placed what he hoped was a reassuring hand on Malcolm's shirtsleeve. 'He's got what he came for and was just leaving, weren't you?'

Christie stuffed the money into a pocket and rose to his feet. 'Goodnight, both.' He doffed his hat. 'I'm sure we'll be bumping into one another again, Terry, lad.'

CHAPTER FIFTY

There was only Dizzy, purring and circling her calves, to welcome Queenie home from the dance class she'd had to duck out of halfway through. Before she could do anything, she had to give him the attention he craved.

'Good boy.' She stroked his fur and was soothed by him. 'I'll make us something to eat, presently.'

Her morning sickness had eased, but she was just as tired and achy. Dulcie Fricker's concern had come as a surprise. The way she had put her arm around her and led her aside, asking, in a motherly way, if there was anything wrong. At this show of kindness, Queenie had wanted to come clean, to share her guilt and the dilemma she was in. Desperate to talk and unburden herself, she just wanted the fear and uncertainty she was lugging around to stop. She wanted an end to this misery. It was the same feeling she'd had when she was last in Joy's company. But in the same way she did with Joy, she resisted telling Dulcie. Recognising it to be nothing more than a tapering moment girdled in gold like a sunlit cloud, that although it had the potential to offer some temporary respite, it would only slide her into a different kind of trouble.

As she hung up her coat and dance shoes, she wondered what would happen if she did take Dulcie into her confidence. If she told her about the baby. How she was as frightened about her best friend finding out what she'd done as she was about her future. But she and Dulcie had never been friends and Queenie couldn't go back on that now. So instead, and without pulling on her Marigolds as she usually would, she washed every part of the house. Knelt on the flagstone floor, the cold against her legs, scrubbing and scrubbing, until her hands grew red and sore. She cleaned out the fires. The stove. Pushed the Ewbank carpet sweeper over the bumpy rugs in the hall. Dusted the windowsills, polished the windows, the cabinet of her father's trophies. Things he had won before Queenie was born that Norma said they didn't have room for in their new Norfolk home. Cleared the matted strings of her dark hair from the plughole and polished the tap on the kitchen sink. Went outside and poured disinfectant down the toilet, swilled it around with the brush. Thought, *I should never have gone near Charles Gilchrist, I should have known it would end badly...* So why had she? She hadn't been interested in him before he was interested in Joy. Was that it? Had she been driven by a sense of loss for the friend she had thought would always need her, and jealousy towards the man she had lost her to? But he'd deceived Joy too, it wasn't only her. Not that halving the blame made her feel less dirty about herself.

She went upstairs to strip the bed. Boiled water on the stove and washed the sheets in the Belfast sink. Rubbed them in Tide washing powder and rinsed them under the icy water until her hands ached from the cold. This was life, her life. And life was grim. Unless you were Heloise and could afford the latest mod cons: a fridge, an electric cooker, a maid at your beck and call. What business did Queenie have in thinking there could be anything better for her? A sideways glance at the envelope on the kitchen table as she wrung out the sheets and passed them through the mangle. The contract from the record producers, the pages of typed text she flicked through, reaching the section she was supposed to sign but couldn't; the nibbling teeth of her conscience putting paid to that. Panting from the effort, she shook out the heavy sheets and folded them over the clothes horse in front of the fire. *You had the chance to do something different from the class you were born into, but you've blown it.* Queenie's thoughts were bleak ones. She could no more be part of the chorus in a Broadway show than she could sign that recording deal.

Her sudden frenzied activity made Dizzy scarper off upstairs, but she didn't stop. Carrying her block of beeswax and duster, she moved into what her parents had always called the front parlour. Circling the heavy leather furniture, buffing the top of the dark wood sideboard with its musty-smelling insides. The arms of the leather chairs that always sat on either side of the fireplace. Paused to stroke the antimacassars her mother had embroidered during the final bedridden months of her life. Turned on the stand lamp with its red silk shade and bobble fringe. The pinkish light glowed on the metal frame of a wedding group photo that she was just about to pick up and look at when someone knocked on the back door.

'Queenie? Are you there?' A man's voice filtered through the glass panel. A voice she recognised.

'I'm just coming.' She dumped her beeswax and duster and, with the cat tiptoeing behind her into the kitchen, she rubbed the soot off her cheek and opened the door.

'Terry! Oh, it's good to see you.' She was kissing his cheek when Dizzy jetted out between their feet and into the garden.

'Was that a cat I just saw?'

'Yes, that's Dizzy. He's as crazy as me, as it turns out.'

'Great name, but since when do you have a cat?'

'He just turned up.' Queenie shrugged. 'It's nice to have the company. It's lonely without Dad. Come in, I'll make tea.'

'Good heavens, Queenie, darling.' Terrence, as if only just noticing her. 'You look like you've been shovelling coal.'

You don't look so hot yourself. He did look tired, his eyes sore like he hadn't been sleeping and – what was unheard of for Terrence – day-old stubble on his chin. Dead leaves skidded in across the floor tiles.

'I've been cleaning.' She shut the door behind him then turned to put the kettle on to boil. 'I'd not given the place a thorough going-over since Dad left.'

'Sorry for calling round unannounced, but I didn't want to wait until you got to the club.'

'No?' She thought he looked as troubled as she felt. 'Why's that?'

'Queenie, darling…' Terrence coughed into his hand. 'She knows.'

'You what?'

'She knows.'

'Who? Who knows?'

'Joy. She knows about you and Charles. She knows you're carrying his child. Buster told her last night at the club.'

Queenie turned away from him. Began spooning loose tea out of a caddy her mother had bought. A battered tin with a faded portrait of Earl Grey stamped on its sides. It was something that had always been an object of mild family mockery but Queenie loved it. She'd grown up with it. Her father liked to fill it with Taylors tea. *Earl Grey, no disrespect to his lordship* – she replayed her father's voice, anything other than listen to Terrence, who was pestering her for a reaction she wasn't ready to give – *was for toffs and women.*

Her hand shook as she poured boiling water into the teapot. Chose two of the pretty porcelain cups and saucers Terrence had bought her. With automatic movements, she closed the lid of the caddy and put it away into its cupboard. Gripped the teapot by the scruff of its tweed cosy and transported it from work surface to tabletop: a she-cat with a kitten.

'Queenie? Say something…' Terrence filtered through to her. 'Are you all right? You've gone terribly pale. Sit down, darling, sit.'

She let him steer her to a chair. 'I'll pour tea. Oh, I forgot the milk. It's on the windowsill, can you get it?'

'Never mind the bloody tea. Did you hear what I just said?'

Queenie stared at her hands. The chipped nail varnish, the raw knuckles. It was as if the world had stopped, but looking out through the kitchen window, at what was left of the November afternoon, she saw black clouds sliding over the rooftops, threatening rain.

'I should have been the one to tell her, not Buster. I've got to talk to her,' Queenie spoke, at last. 'It's not too late, she'll be at work.'

'Is that wise?'

'Probably not, but I can't leave it like this.'

'What will you say?'

'I've no idea, but she deserves an explanation.'

'Do you want me to come with you?'

'Would you?' Queenie looked up and into Terrence's warm, kind eyes. Then, reaching out for his hand, she gripped it in her own.

They left the pot of tea to go cold on the table. Queenie grabbed her bag and coat, and without checking her face or applying the merest smear of lipstick, she put an arm through Terrence's and they head off out into the blustery street.

They walked as far as Wimbledon Broadway, where they boarded a bus. Terrence wanted to climb to the top deck, so they did. Sat side by silent side, smoking cigarettes throughout the journey. Queenie could tell he was preoccupied, that it was something more than the trouble she was in. There was a heaviness about him that showed in the purple half-moons under his eyes. Did he hate her, was that it? Hate her in the way she hated herself for what she had done to Joy? She didn't dare to ask, fearful of his answer, so she let whatever was bothering him sit beside them like another passenger as they turned their heads to look out through the bus windows at the lowering sun bleeding red over the city.

They got off the bus when the British Museum's tall black railings came into view. Queenie, her insides knotted up with nerves, felt the cold finger of wind push through her coat buttons as they bumped up against the traffic sounds along Great Russell Street.

'Are you all right?'

'Not really, but come on, I don't want to miss her.'

They took a right turn down into a side street squashed between the high walls of the museum. A route the staff used, which Joy had shown her. An old woman sat on the cobbles. Queenie could see the rotting and discoloured face. It was as if to look into the face of damnation. Beggars made her nervous with their visceral demands for help she couldn't afford to give, so she shifted her attention to a gang of pigeons. Watched them swoop down on the overhanging roofs and dump their load, streaking the Portland stone with grey.

'Help me, sweet lady. Spare me a penny?' the woman called to her.

Queenie's mind curved back to the beggar she and Joy had seen in Hyde Park that showery spring day. Telling Joy off when she had given him money. What right did she have to do that?

'Hang on for me, would you?' She left Terrence and retraced her steps. Back to the woman whose head and shoulders were wrapped in a soiled blanket. 'Here you go.' She took out her purse and dropped coins into the filthy folds of the woman's palm, watched the wrinkled fingers fumble over them.

'Since when do you give to beggars?' Terrence asked her when she returned to him.

'Since I ruined my best friend's life.'

It wasn't Joy who came to meet Queenie in the grand marble foyer of the museum, it was Amy. Amy with her cloud of curls and freckle-filled face.

'Where's Joy?'

From the girl's hostile expression, Queenie wished she'd asked Terrence to come inside with her.

'Are you mad, coming here like this? Joy doesn't want to see you ever again.'

'But I want to explain.'

'There's nothing to explain. You slept with her sweetheart and broke her heart. You've ruined everything…' Queenie followed the trajectory of Amy's gaze, saw it hover over her stomach. 'You've even managed to ruin yourself by the look of you.'

'Please? I want to tell her how sorry I am.' She moistened her lips.

'To salve your conscience, more like. You just don't get it, do you? This isn't about you. God, you're unbelievable.' Amy crossed her arms. 'Who d'you think you are, turning up here? You're beyond selfish.'

'But how else am I going to put this right?'

'Put this right?' A sneer. 'You really are brazen. Can't you see how impossible that is? It's your fault about that Buster bloke in your band, too. Joy wanted to finish at that sleazy club of yours, but you wouldn't let her. She only agreed to work there to please you. Everything she did, she did to please you.'

Queenie looked blank.

'You don't know about Buster, do you?'

'Know what?'

'That the brute forced himself on her.'

'*What? When?*' Queenie slapped a hand to her mouth. 'What happened?'

'I've told you what happened, and I told Joy she should have reported him.'

'Please let me see her,' Queenie implored. She was thinking, *If I hadn't persuaded Joy to stay on at the club, she might never have found out about me and Charles.*

'No. Clear off and leave her alone.'

'You can't speak to me like that.'

'Do you want me to have you removed from the building?' Hands on hips, mildly threatening. 'Because I will. You don't realise, do you? The damage you've done to Joy… it's… it's beyond repair. Call yourself a friend?' Amy flung back her head and Queenie saw there were tears in her eyes. 'You're no friend. You never deserved her.'

CHAPTER FIFTY-ONE

It was as if Joy had strayed into another narrative altogether. Nothing made sense any more. She couldn't believe the two most precious people in the world had betrayed her. There had to be some mistake. Except there wasn't. She'd been a fool. How could Charles have ever been hers? A man like him, a girl like her – who was she kidding?

She had found an empty window seat. A quiet nook under the vast vaulted ceiling of the Reading Room. Sat with her feet tucked under her, turning page after page of a book, unable to take anything in. A break in the rain and a November sun blinked in through the permanently closed windows, throwing bands of gold against the walls of books. There one second, gone the next. They were as elusive as the wedding ring she had been promised but would never now wear. The light had gone from her since the night Buster had told her the truth. The core of her nothing more than a shrivelled, ruined kernel as black as her father's compost heap when he would push his garden fork into it. Her father's compost had fertilised and fed; what was she fit to nourish? Not even herself, from the way she was shrinking inside her clothes. She knew it and knew her colleagues saw it also. Taking her gently by the elbow to question her mental state in the shadowy recesses of the museum. Buttonholing her in hollow corridors, in the deserted stairwell that led to different floors.

'Charles is in reception. He says he needs to talk to you.' Amy was suddenly beside her. Her earnest expression cut in half by shadow. She must have come up three flights of stairs to find her.

'Tell him there's nothing to say.'

'If you're sure?'

'I'm sure.'

Amy disappeared again and Joy flopped back against the window. There wasn't anything to say. What could he say that would put this right? He'd shown her who he wanted, he'd made his choice – she didn't need to see him to know that. Part of her wanted to remember what the two of them had been, not for everything to be sullied, which it would be if she listened to his ham-fisted explanation.

'Stuff him.' Amy was back. 'Let him think you're coming, the stupid sod. I'm not going all the way back down there.'

'I'm not surprised he's come here. He keeps turning up at my lodgings.'

'Does he?'

Joy closed the book. 'Banging on the door, waking people up. He's going to land me in hot water with my landlord if he keeps on.'

'Cruel sod. Why can't he leave you alone? Her too, turning up here like that; who does she think she is?'

'I am right not to hear what he has to say, aren't I?' Joy picked at a bobble on her blue wool jacket. Strange to be back in her old clothes, for the new Joy to have been put back in her box before she'd had the time to enjoy her. 'Maybe there is an explanation? Maybe it was something I did. Do you think?'

Amy picked up Joy's hand. 'This is not your fault; you've done nothing wrong.'

'Queenie sent me a letter.'

'What?'

'I haven't opened it.' Joy reached for her bag and took out the envelope that had arrived before she'd left for work that morning. 'Will you read it to me?'

'I will do no such thing. That bitch doesn't deserve anything from you.' Amy lifted the letter from Joy's fingers and ripped it in half, then half again.

Joy laughed a little at this. At Amy's boldness. She was glad to have her as a shield. Sitting shoulder against shoulder, they stared out on the rain that had started again.

'November.' Amy groaned. 'Such a dark time of year. Hang on in there, Joy. You've had the most terrible kick in the teeth. You don't have to see either of them again, they're no good for you. You have to do what's best for you. You're always thinking of everyone else.' Amy put a protective arm around her and pulled her close. 'Who is there to ever think of you?'

'You're always kind to me.' Joy couldn't stop the tears. They spilled over her cheeks like the rain against the window. 'Thank you.'

'You don't have to thank me, silly.' Amy gave her another squeeze. 'I'm here for you, you're here for me, it's what friends do.'

Sadness held like a ball in the fist of that dreary afternoon. Joy waited for it to be thrown to her before speaking again.

'I can't get beyond him.' She sobbed. 'I don't know what to do with myself.'

'We used to play this game when we were little.' Amy, taking their conversation in a different direction. 'Do you want to play?'

'We?' Joy, a glimmer of interest.

'Me and my sister. Pick a raindrop.'

Joy put her finger to the windowpane. 'I didn't know you had a sister.'

'You can meet her if you like. My lot are all coming to London fortnight Saturday. We always get together for a nosh-up before Christmas. Same place, it's in Putney. Views of the bridge. You'll love it.' Amy bumped against her, jollying her along. 'I can draw you a map so you'll be able to find it?'

Joy looked at her and nodded blankly into her enthusiasm; she didn't have it in her to think that far ahead.

'Right, this is mine.' Amy tapped the glass. 'We'll see whose raindrop goes the fastest, shall we?'

CHAPTER FIFTY-TWO

Terrence stood in the middle of F. Lambert & Co's impressive trading floor and looked around him. Operating as a private bank for over three hundred years, to enter this building from a crestfallen Fleet Street was to step into a bygone world. A world of exquisite architecture, antique portraits and furniture, untouched by the war. But he didn't fit within the rich warm hues of the oak-panelled walls, the gentle lighting and muffled sounds of money-counting, and couldn't care less that the bank's collections included records from former customers such as Samuel Pepys, Lord Byron and Jane Austen. That it offered a unique insight into the minutiae of their lives.

He had been lucky to get this job. His mother was always telling him and he was always telling himself. It was the only way he could drag himself in here day after day. To join the troupe of obsequious men who guarded the cash boxes and shared the etiolated look of creatures kept under stones.

I dunno how you stand it with dem stuffed shirts, man. Terrence played Malcolm's voice in his head. How did he stand it? These faceless men in suits weren't his kind of people; always the outsider, all they did was make him feel inferior. *You wanna be playin' piano... that place is killin' you, man.*

Turning, he saw how London's light filtered through the high glazed windows and magnified its stateliness, its glamour, but not glamour like the Mockin' Bird. And unlike the Mockin' Bird, this place didn't want him. A kind of dizziness afflicted him; he'd been experiencing it for several days. He wondered if he might be ill but refused to dwell on it, sensing it to be more of a realisation of his insignificance. A small cog in the mists of history he wouldn't make any impact on. Fearful of falling, he propelled himself forwards, shoes clicking against the marble floor. Took up his position behind the curved walnut cash desk with its ornamental brass railings and removed his coat and hat, pegged them on the stand. He looked at the clock on the opposite wall and sighed at the prospect of another monotonous day stretching ahead.

'Good morning, sir.' Sensing the eyes attached to the scribbling hands of his colleagues, he greeted his first customer with a cheery smile. 'What can I do for you today?'

And so it went on. Well into the afternoon. Serving customer after customer. Receiving account transactions, deposits, loan payments; cashing cheques, issuing saving withdrawals. Nothing unusual. Nothing to concern himself with.

'Don't worry, madam, we'll sort it out for you,' he told one elderly lady who was fussing with his method of recording her mail deposits.

'But it seems stupid—'

'Stupid?'

'Well, illogical.'

Terrence tried to manufacture a convincing smile. 'Please be assured, madam, it will be fine, absolutely fine.'

'If you're sure?' the woman kept on.

'I'm sure.'

When the woman walked away, Terrence turned to file the relevant forms in a cabinet made up of tiny drawers. Then turned back to serve the next customer in the queue.

Christie.

Conveying the same deadly stare. The cosmic coldness it communicated travelled the length of Terrence's arms.

''Ow do.'

The hat was doffed and then removed. Held upturned like a begging bowl. Under the bank's subdued electric bulbs, the man's forehead glowed, giving his skin a strange, synthetic sheen.

Sick with fear, Terrence was rendered silent.

'Aren't you pleased to see me, lad?' the gentle voice enquired while the eyes bored through him.

'What the hell d'you want?' Finding his voice, at last, Terrence was frightened his colleagues would hear. He lowered his face and hissed at Christie through the thin brass railings. 'How the hell did you find me? Find where I work?'

'I've been watching you, Terry, lad. You and your friends. Especially that lovely Joy. Such a sweet little thing, isn't she?'

'Joy!' Terrence slapped a hand to the sudden clamminess that had broken out on his forehead. 'You know Joy?' The bubble of panic in his throat grew bigger and it took everything he had not to shout. 'How d'you know her?'

Christie tapped the side of his nose and Terrence could tell he was enjoying himself.

'You're to stay away from her, d'you hear?'

'I know about that club you play piano in, too.' Christie dismissed his concern with a nauseating smirk. 'I bet they don't know what you get up to in your spare time either. Like your friends here, because there's no way they'd employ you in a place like this if they knew about your dirty little ways.' That accent again, that sickening, gut-churning whisper. 'Aye, I've been following you.' Conceited and haughty. It was while fearing the damage this man could do to him, Terrence – not usually violent – had an overwhelming urge to punch him to the ground. 'You want to keep your eyes open, lad. I know all there is to know about you.'

Terrence studied him. He had the kind of face a nark might have. A man who grassed people up for fun. The kind of person who would squeal on him to the rozzers in a heartbeat.

'I want you to clear off. Clear out of here.'

'Dear me, that's hardly polite, is it? I travel over here to see you, and you speak to me like that. Does your boss know what a dirty bugger you are? Standing there in your nice smart suit, earning your big fat salary. I wonder what he'd say? Shall we ask him?'

Terrence could do nothing. In a kind of muted wonder, he watched Christie step back and raise his chin to scan the row of tellers, then further, his beady eyes searching through to the back where other colleagues of his sat working at desks.

'Are you going to tell me which one your boss is, or do I have to shout to get his attention?'

This man meant to destroy him, ruin him; with his colleagues, with the police. He had to do something – he had to get rid of him.

'What do you want?' Terrence lowered his head to the brass railings again. Felt his heart thrash like a netted bird behind his ribs. The bastard, how dare he come here, threaten him here. 'Just tell me what you want.'

'What I want… is for you to pay this.' A rent demand was pushed under the counter. 'I'm rather short this month, you see. My fibrositis has flared up again, and my enteritis. It's like I were saying other evening, the doctor's signed me off sick, it's why I've come to you.'

'I've already given you a walloping load. I'm not made of money.'

Christie pressed the shiny end of his nose close to the bars and slid his eyes to the cash box at Terrence's elbow. 'You dare to say no to me, lad?' The deadly murmur made sweat break out between Terrence's shoulder blades. 'I'm one with all cards, in case you'd forgotten.'

'But please, I haven't any more, not until the end of the month.'

'Don't give me that. You work in a bank, lad. You've access to loads of stuff. You deal in it all day long, passing it through your hands all time. I can't imagine they'd miss a bit.' That smell again: Terrence flinched from it in the same way he flinched from Christie's cold blue stare. 'Go on,' the simpering continued. 'We're not talking much, who's to notice? You could cover it if you wanted to.'

Terrence stared down on the trays of notes and coins and contemplated doing what this repulsive specimen had asked of him.

'Oh, well, have it your own way,' the soft voice started up again. 'And there was me, thinking you cared about Joy.'

Terrence, on the verge of losing it, snapped back his neck and raised his voice a notch. 'I've said you're to stay away from her, do you hear me? That poor girl's suffered enough without you adding to it.'

'Is that so?' The cold eyes shone with merriment. 'Well then, I'd say it were up to you, lad. If you'd see to paying me what I ask for, then I won't need to go bothering your little friend, will I?'

A thought occurring. 'That was you hanging around outside Queenie's house that day, wasn't it? I thought I recognised you. You're to stay away from them, both of them, do you hear me?'

'Excuse me, sir. Is there a problem here?' One of the senior clerks stepped up beside Terrence to address Christie. He had spotted that whatever transaction was going on, it wasn't banking business. 'Do you need further assistance, something Mr Banks can't help you with?'

'No, thank you.' Christie's curt reply and Terrence thought he saw the man's mask slip a little. 'We're all done here. I'm just going.' The rent book was whipped away and returned to a pocket in his raincoat.

'Jolly good, sir. Lambert's look forward to welcoming you again soon.' They waited for Christie to scuttle away, out into the street. Then Terrence's superior turned to him. 'A word, if you wouldn't mind.'

It wasn't a request; it was a demand. He followed the man he had never bothered to learn the name of into one of the small offices.

'I've been meaning to talk to you for a while.' The door was closed behind them.

'You have?'

'It's been noticed things are slipping, Terrence. There have been complaints. Is there anything I need to know about? You're not unwell, are you?'

'Just been feeling a bit run-down.' He pushed a hand up through his hair. 'Things getting on top of me.'

'Do you want to tell me what that business was about just now? Was that rather odd little gentleman a customer of ours? I really can't believe he was.'

'He was asking about opening an account.'

'An easy enough procedure. What took you so long?'

'I don't know. He was just awkward.'

'But you're experienced enough to deal with awkward customers, aren't you? Dear me, Terrence, you do need to take a good hard look at yourself and make some choices. I'd say you were burning the candle at both ends.' The senior clerk eyed him then turned briefly to pick up his pipe. Lit it with quick, inky fingers and the smell of tobacco filled the small space they stood up in. 'Something's got to give and I don't see why it should be the bank.'

'Oh, right.' Terrence shifted his feet. 'I hadn't realised there was a problem.'

'Well, there is.' A hard glare. 'They tell me you play at a West End nightclub.'

'Yes, I play the piano.'

'*Jazz*.' The pronunciation was given as a lazy zed of a word.

'Yes, along with other genres.'

'Black music, isn't it?' The clerk touched the knot of his tie. 'American?'

Terrence cocked his head, disinclined to educate the philistine.

'Mm, well, speaking for myself, I don't much care for *music*, and just to warn you, neither does the board. In fact,' he puffed on his pipe, 'I'd go so far to say the top brass here at Lambert's wouldn't approve of you being part of that scene at all.'

'And what is that scene, exactly?' *Careful*, Terrence warned himself, *you're skating on thin ice here.*

'Good God, must I spell it out?'

'I suppose you must.'

'Mixing with Coloureds and those other types.'

'Other types?'

'Well, yes, I imagine all sorts would frequent such places… even those *homosexuals* we hear about,' the senior clerk said darkly.

Terrence and Malcolm left Albert's Cavern and followed the progress of a ginger cat, tail aloft, slinking between the dustbins along the wet alleyway. In the Soho streets beyond, the lamps were out, and the perpetual darkness enclosed within the walls of Albert's seemed to thin out across the city. Terrence could make out basement railings, an empty milk bottle on the front step of a gramophone shop and, above, the illuminated front of a clock tower and the entrance to the public lavatories.

Dawn was a strange place. Made up of milk floats and foxes sloping through empty streets back to their holes. Nobody was about. He and Malcolm were alone. They were rarely alone. Without the fear of prejudicial eyes, in this envelope of time before the rest of the city woke up, Terrence felt Malcolm relax a little, heard it in the steady rhythm of his breathing. The air was fresh like country air. Terrence could believe they had escaped to a better place and, letting himself go with the fantasy for a moment, he put his hands into his coat pockets for the warmth, deciding, in time, it was always too risky to hold hands on the street whatever time of day it was.

They reached the corner where they were to say their farewells and were adjusting themselves inside their coats for their onward journeys when a black shape snagged the corner of Terrence's vision.

He spun to receive it. Saw a policeman in full uniform complete with peaked cap lurking in the shadows.

Panic flared behind his ribcage and he froze.

Impuissant.

The street had shrunk into some kind of hell and he and Malcolm were trapped in it.

'Hello, hello, hello.' The police officer emerged from the gloom. Straight-backed and shiny-chinned, his confident strides snatching the pavement. 'And what, may I ask, are you dirty buggers up to? Pair of you should be horse-whipped.'

What Terrence could see of the policeman's stony stare made it difficult to breathe.

'Dis is it, Terry, we're bloody done for. We gotta run, we gotta get outta here, man… I can't do dis… I can't.' Malcolm let go a frightened cry then spun on his heels.

Terrence couldn't move and a feeling like icy water sloshed through him. This was dangerous.

'Oh, dear. Was it something I said?'

Terrence recognised the accent. It found him through his fear. This was Christie. Dressed up in his old wartime special constable uniform, and not a real policeman at all. He wanted to shout after Malcolm, to call him back, but he'd already fled to the top of the street.

'What are you wearing that for? Like dressing up, do you?' Terrence felt his blood slow. 'You don't frighten me, you little weasel.'

'Could've fooled me, lad. I can see whites of your eyes.'

'What do you want, following me around? I've nothing to say to you.'

'But there's matter of our little bit of unfinished business. I don't like leaving loose ends.' Christie fixed him with his gimlet eye.

'Bloody hell, man, I'm not paying your rent; I can barely afford my own.' Terrence made to go. He felt this man's anger, his hatred. He was evil.

'Oh, no you don't, lad,' the voice whispered from the shadows. 'Not till we've settled our business.'

'I've already said, I haven't got that kind of money.'

'Right, well, don't say I didn't warn you.'

Terrence spun back to face him. Horror-struck. Was Christie's threat about Joy or reporting him to the police?

Kill him. Kill him.

It was the only way to stop this torture. How hard could it be? Just a hand around the throat. Snap his scrawny neck. He'd killed worthier men in the war. Men who would have been missed, who were loved. Who could love this wretch? Words of violence burst in his mouth. He held them there, bloody, like loose teeth, while he sized Christie up, measuring how small and narrow he was.

A clock chimed. Tuneful in the tightening seconds. Terrence took out his cotton handkerchief and dabbed his mouth. Looked at it, as if expecting to find blood there.

'Are you going to give me my money, lad, or am I going to have to report you to police?'

Terrence stepped back, his mind turning. 'I'm thinking I might just go and report you to the police myself. Impersonating a police officer is a very serious offence.' *Not to mention blackmail.*

'Aye, maybe. But not as serious as buggery, wouldn't you say?'

There was no way out of this. Terrence took out his wallet and handed over half of what was inside.

'All of it.' Christie stepped forward, his palm opening and closing like a clam. 'I'll take all of it, if you don't mind.'

Terrence handed over everything he had. Tried not to touch the revolting pale hand.

'I suppose this'll do for now.' The wormy fingers flicked through the banknotes: everything Terrence needed to pay for his mother's rent and his own. 'But it isn't enough… it's nowhere near enough.'

CHAPTER FIFTY-THREE

Snow. Joy woke to the shock of it pressing its cold white face up against her basement window. She couldn't remember when she'd last seen snow. She sipped her Camp coffee and watched it fall. Big, fat flakes, large as francs, settling ghost-light and transforming the drab London street into a dazzling Christmas card scene. It would be Christmas in a few short weeks. Not that it would mean anything to her this year. Last year she and Queenie had spent it together here; it had been fun. But she didn't want to have to think about Queenie; she didn't want to think about anyone. She just wanted the days to roll into nights, then days again. Some days were better than others, but perhaps it was just that she was too tired to think, and instead of diving into the depths of herself and harpooning the skin of her memories, she bobbed around on the surface.

Charles was there again. Calling to her, demanding she let him inside. Why couldn't he understand that for her to get over him, he needed to stay away? Upstairs, a door slammed and the skitter of raised voices, Charles's among them. Then heavy boots descending the stone steps, the crunch of snow in her entrance area.

'Miss Rivard, are you in there?'

Joy opened up. Her landlord, bristly-chinned and out of breath, was the angriest she'd seen him.

'That flamin' man's here again. Making a right rumpus. I thought you told him to stay away.'

'I did. But he won't listen.'

'Well, you're going to have to make him listen. This is a quiet house; we can't have this kind of disorder. Let this be a final warning to you, Miss Rivard. If this nonsense carries on,' he wagged a fat finger, 'I'll have no option other than to terminate your tenancy.'

This was a man who liked to throw his weight around – she'd seen him doing it with his other tenants. What he lacked in stature, he made up for with aggression. She nodded. Scrunched her lips together to stop herself from crying.

'Perhaps if you had a word with him?' Joy raised her eyebrows. 'He might listen to you.'

'I won't be having a word with anyone. This is your mess to sort out.' He glared at her. 'And while we're at it, you're to stop feeding that thing, d'you hear?' He jabbed his thumb at the woodpigeon roosting on its usual perch. 'Bloody thing shits everywhere; it's not hygienic.'

She didn't want to add homelessness to her lengthening list of problems, so when her landlord had gone, she shouted up at Charles, who was still hovering on the pavement. Shouted at him to go away, to leave her alone. Which he did. Eventually. She watched his dark shape disappear along the snowy pavement. His expression, whatever it had been, was hidden beneath the brim of his hat.

'Don't worry, little friend.' She wiped away her tears and talked to the pigeon before going back inside. 'You stay there. This is just as much your home as anyone else's.'

Joy had arranged to meet Amy and her family today. Not that she had the energy for making conversation but she couldn't let her down, not when she'd been so kind and careful with her over these past few weeks. She dressed in her plain blouse, blue wool jacket and nylon skirt. Ignored the beautiful clothes Heloise had bought her, deciding some days ago that she would pack them away and donate them to the Salvation Army and do some good. She counted the coins in her purse. She needed to be careful and hoped this restaurant in Putney wasn't going to be expensive.

Wanting to wear her apple brooch, she checked the collar of the dress she had worn to work yesterday. But it wasn't there. She picked through the items that were on top of the bedside cabinet and rifled through the chest of drawers. Then, getting down on her hands and knees, she searched beneath the bed.

Nothing. Where was it?

Please don't say I've lost it. I don't think I can bear it. In danger of spiralling down into a deep panic, she got up off the floor and paced the room, picking things up and putting them down at random. *This is hopeless.* She burst out crying. *It could be anywhere. I could've dropped it at work, or out on the street.*

She scrubbed her hands across her face: a frantic gesture to clear a way through her tears as if hoping there might be a better truth concealed beneath them than the one she feared.

A glance at her wristwatch. She was meeting Amy and her family in just over an hour and, knowing it would take longer to walk in the snow, she needed to get a move on. Promising herself she would have another search for the brooch just as soon as she came home, she laced her feet inside her shoes, put on her trusty green coat and slung her bag over her shoulder.

Without bothering to check her reflection, she closed the door of her bedsit, and with a handful of crumbs and a word or two of greeting to the pigeon, who was shaking snow off its back and settling inside its feathers, she hurried up the steps and into the silent, snowy world. Too wrapped up in her troubles to notice the danger hiding amid the black shadows across the street, waiting for her to leave so he could follow her.

CHAPTER FIFTY-FOUR

Safe in his hideout, he watched the girl moving around in her basement room. Silly thing, why didn't she draw the blind and stop prying eyes? He'd seen her do everything from washing and changing out of her calico nightdress to leaning out of her door and shouting at her boyfriend, who turned out to be the same elegant man in a fedora and big dark coat he'd seen gallivanting around Soho with her painted friend.

And what a carry-on that was. No wonder she told him to clear off. His snorted amusement as he smacked his hands together for warmth. It really wasn't the weather to be hanging around, but the promise he had made to himself to follow her and get her on her own was enough to keep him warm.

It was fortunate he had so much spare time, that he was no longer gainfully employed. And didn't need to be, so long as he could extort money from that filthy bugger, Terrence Banks. He was enjoying himself taunting him: it was fun making the pervert suffer. *Idle hands are the devil's workshop.* One of his father's favourite sayings elbowed its way inside his head. *Isn't that the truth?* he answered it and, brushing snow from his lapels and hat brim, he looked down on her window again.

What was the girl doing now? All in a flap. She seemed suddenly agitated, circling her bedsit, a hand clamped to her face. He continued to gaze down on her, his mouth agape, absorbing her in the way he used to do with Beryl Evans... except Beryl Evans was no more. He'd done what he'd wanted with her and now he was going to do what he wanted with this one.

He was glad the man in the black coat and fedora had finally got the message and cleared off. Talk about persistent – didn't he have any pride? It was obvious to an imbecile that the girl wanted no more to do with him. But he had to admit, it had been an anxious twenty minutes thinking the man would never go, and he would have to move on, to come back another day.

But Joy is alone again now, isn't she? His thin lips curving into a smile. *Oh, aye, completely alone, and there's no danger of me being interrupted this time.*

Not long now, he thought. Any minute… any minute… and his patience would be rewarded. He stuffed the stocking away and, rolling his tongue around in his mouth, lit a cigarette and smoked it. Looking down on himself, he wished he'd made more of an effort with his appearance. His faded raincoat had been looking rather shabby for some time.

Then, a flurry of activity he nearly wasn't ready for, and the door of her basement swung open. He watched her pause to feed that filthy pigeon from the palm of her hand with such tenderness and devotion. How could she? He realised how it angered him. To see her giving affection to vermin when she should have been displaying that affection to him.

When she emerged at the top of the steps, her drab choice of clothes surprised him; it seemed she had reverted to her loose-fitting coat and inelegant footwear, but there wasn't time to think much about it as she took off at speed.

Dear me, she is in a hurry. Come on, quick, quick, you're going to lose her if you're not careful. He chivvied himself up and, drawing on the last of his cigarette, screwed it out against the wall of a house and lobbed it into the garden. 'Wait for me,' he croaked, sliding along the snowbound pavement, his feet already wet inside his plimsolls. 'Wait for me.'

CHAPTER FIFTY-FIVE

Joy tried to smile and make polite conversation, but all she could think of was Charles and how much he would have enjoyed this. The food, the lively company, the sense of occasion. He always loved an occasion. Things got so bad, when the waiter finally came to take her order, she couldn't speak. She could only hide behind her menu card and cry while she listened to Amy making excuses for her.

When the food arrived, Joy couldn't eat. She stared dumbfounded at the epergne of flowers. The petals dropping like tears. Mournfully forking up mouthfuls she didn't want; what should have been delicious, turning to ash in her mouth. Torturous, this business of conducting herself as if her heart hadn't cracked in two. Lonely amid the company, the scrape of crockery, the air thick with voices and cooking smells. Joy saw Charles's face everywhere. In the whorls of the wooden floorboards of the restaurant floor, in the deep dish of buttery potatoes she couldn't bring herself to spoon onto her plate. In the rise of Putney Bridge through the windows. His personality entangled in a gesture that was inadvertently given by a stranger, or in the sound of laughter from a nearby table.

Her fingers, automatic, drifted to the lapel of her jacket for the assurance her little apple brooch always gave her. But it wasn't there. Like her love, she had lost this too. And the stark realisation of this triggered the same panicky feeling she'd been experiencing in the confines of her bedsit when she thought the walls were going to fall in and crush her. She needed to get out of this place. Out into what remained of the snowy afternoon.

'I'm sorry, Amy. All this, it's too soon,' she explained to her friend, wary of causing a fuss.

'No.' Amy took her hand. 'It's me who should be sorry, expecting you to be able to cope with my raucous lot.'

'It was kind of you to include me, but I need to be on my own.'

'Where will you go?' Amy, frowning.

'I'll have a walk. I'll feel better outside.'

'But it's cold, Joy, and it'll be dark soon. Do you want me to come with you?'

'No, don't worry.' Joy kissed her cheek and took out her purse. 'I don't want to spoil things for you. You've a lovely family, please tell them I'm sorry.'

'Stop saying sorry. Just promise me you'll take care of yourself. I'll see you Monday?' Amy waved away Joy's offer of money. 'Look, before you go, I bought you a little something. Don't worry, it's only small.'

'A present? But it's not my birthday or anything.' Joy, puzzled, took the tissue paper parcel.

'I know that, but, well, think of it as an early Christmas present.'

'Oh, Amy, thank you. It's beautiful.' Joy unwrapped the pretty patterned silk scarf and, liking the way the green and orange swirls brightened up her drab old coat, knotted it around her neck. 'You're so kind to me.'

Out on the street, gulping down the freezing air, she decided, as there was enough daylight left, to head home via Fulham, that the walk would do her good. It had stopped snowing, but the air was bitter and, fastening her coat to the throat to keep out the icy fingers of wind, she followed the puff of her breath along the slippery pavement.

She recognised the grand stone entrance of Brompton Cemetery from the time Charles had brought her here to show where his father and brother were buried. Joy sidestepped the offer of a map the guard wanted to thrust on her – she didn't need it; she knew where she was going. She was here to retrace the steps of that summer day. After all, she told herself, sweeping snow with a gloved hand from the tops of tombstones, she hadn't been able to find the origins of where he'd stopped loving her anywhere else.

A sudden rush made her look up to what must have been a thousand starlings. The green-black oiliness of their wings, each bird a unit of sound making a whole, they unfurled like a huge dark sheet shaken out by the breeze on her mother's washing line. Settling again, the birds, momentarily pinned to bare branches, their silhouettes cut sharp against the sky, dressed the trees like macabre Christmas decorations. Around her, the place was deserted. A hushed world of snow blanketing the land of the dead. Joy let go of a sigh that floated up to the amorphous grey sky. A sky that yielded nothing of the deep cobalt of that summer day. There was nothing of the green-leafed awning she and Charles had walked beneath either. Laughing, touching, their way ahead gilded in sunshine.

Winding along the maze of snowy paths that portioned up the cemetery, she took the gentle hill that led to the upper, grander section with its towering sepulchres and elaborate mini chapels. Some well-tended, others abandoned, spreading out like a romantic forest. She found the rather grand crypt dedicated to the family Gilchrist: its pink speckled marble standing proud and erect among its slanting neighbours. She walked up to it and swept the sharp edge of polished stone free of snow. A robin redbreast flew up from the undergrowth and sang to her, the anguished song of winter in its throat. She watched it, captivated by its boldness, until it flew away.

Left alone in the spooky hush of the enveloping gloom, she shivered and blinked away an image of Charles holding his bunch of chrysanthemums that had been as sunny as that afternoon.

'This is where I'll be one day.' He laid his flowers. 'You too. You'll be a Gilchrist when you marry me.'

It had been a strange and surprisingly comforting idea through the tumbling pennies of sunlight. One that buzzed in her head like summer insects as she stood in her cotton sundress and sandals, her white cardigan tied about her middle. Strange, that on such a glorious day she should be asked to look upon the spot where she would end up when she died. With the sun warm on her shoulders, death was the last thing on her mind, despite the setting he'd brought her to. All there had been was their future: a land of dragonflies and bumblebees under the blue dome of a perfect sky.

And now?

She stared at her hands and hunted the creases of her gloves for the answer. Now, she replied to herself, she was doomed to live life shut out in the cold with the wind biting her ears for company. Its torturous almost indecipherable whisper reminding her every second of every day how much she had lost.

Then there was another whisper.

''Ow do, lass.'

It was the man she had met in the park on that May morning. The man she thought had been following her around London ever since. Stepping out from behind a stone-faced angel, he startled her, and she slapped a hand to her quickening heart.

'I seem to have lost my dog. You haven't seen her, have you, lass? A little terrier? White as snow, she is.' The man pushed his round, horn-rimmed spectacles up his nose and emitted a soft chuckle. '*White as snow…* it's no wonder I can't find her.'

He must have been following her along the path and yet Joy had had no idea he was behind her. The expression beneath the trilby made her toes curl inside her shoes.

'Look at you, you poor little mite, you're shivering.' He stepped closer and, turning his wedding ring behind the knuckle, stared off into the middle distance as if trying to work something out. Then he snapped back, the cold blue of his eyes seeking hers. 'If you'd help find my Judy, I'd be happy to buy you a nice cup of tea somewhere so you can have a warm-up. What d'you say?'

Despite the polite request the susurrant voice was making, she didn't trust it, and felt a pinch of terror.

'Oh, I... I...' she stammered into the frozen air. 'I couldn't possibly.'

'Why ever not? There's no need to be nervous of me, lass, I don't mean you no harm.'

Watching his stiff little movements, the way he poked out his tongue as he twisted his gaze to search, or so she imagined, between the tilting gravestones for his missing dog. Something about him reminded her of an antique toy at her aunt's house: a monkey automaton she was not permitted to play with unsupervised.

'I'd say you could do with cheering up, lass.' She shrank from the smile that slithered and settled about his lips. 'I'd say you've had your heart broken.' He held her in his gaze. 'I think I'm right, aren't I? Aye, thought so.' Gentle-sounding and persuasive, he answered himself before she had the chance. 'But you really mustn't go blaming yourself, lass. There are some bad men in this world and, well, they draw women to 'em like dead bodies draw flies.'

The analogy, as chilling as it was unexpected, swung between them as haunting as an echo. He couldn't possibly know about what had happened between her and Charles, could he?

'I'm a good listener. You can talk to me. I trained in medicine and part of it were understanding people's predicaments, to develop... oh, how to say it? A good bedside manner.'

She stared at his chin. At the thatch of bristles that had escaped the razor. She wanted to believe he was harmless. She wanted to give him the benefit of the doubt. But she was as suspicious of the blade-sharp creases running vertically down the front of his trousers as she was of his motives. *Where is his dog? Where is its leash? Why isn't he calling for it?* She remembered his white terrier from the park that morning, but she didn't believe the dog was with him today. The unwanted thought was accompanied by images of Buster and the things he had tried to do to her in the basement of the Mockin'.

The remembered horror of it fought for attention through her billowing anxiety. She inadvertently tipped back her head to the sky, exposed the white curve of her throat. Then, sensing his gaze and her own defencelessness, she dropped her head again.

An unwelcome thought occurring, sharpening: no one knew she was here. She had come walking alone. What had she been thinking? *Stupid, stupid.* Not that admitting her foolishness did anything to help her. Hemmed in by the pink marble tomb and this troubling stranger, she knew she was in grave danger and was on the brink of something bad, but had no idea how to get herself out of it.

'Why so sad, little girl?' The man's face twisted horribly and looked hideous in the fading daylight. 'Don't be sad. Shake it off… shake it off.' And he tossed his head around as if to demonstrate. 'That's it, there's a good girl.' All friendly and light, yet Joy was aware of something deadly taking shape behind his eyes.

'I really should be going.' Her mouth wobbly, trembling against the cold. 'It'll be dark soon.'

The man smiled; he didn't appear to have heard. 'You do have the most beautiful hair.' He shuffled closer, his breath hot on her cheek. 'Such a vibrant shade. I were telling my wife about it.'

'Your wife?'

'Oh, aye.' He nodded and, as if requiring clarification, picked up a strand of her hair then dropped it again. 'I could tell you were special, moment I laid eyes on you.'

'Laid eyes on me?' Panic, a galloping horse she couldn't rein in. Joy cast around for someone to help her, but there was no one.

'Oh, aye. I've a very good instinct for people.'

A spike of fear through her gut. She needed to get away from him. *Run… run…!* the voice in her head screamed.

If she was to make a break for it, might she have a chance? A quick downward glance at the small feet in their peculiar canvas shoes. But how quick was he in those? How far could she get?

CHAPTER FIFTY-SIX

November went and December came. Queenie had never seen such rain. It didn't fall from the sky but swirled down on the wind and washed the snow away in an instant. She had ventured out nevertheless. Her hair damp from the gap between collar and hat. It was Friday. She had walked to the newsagents on Wimbledon Broadway, not for her usual women's magazines but for a bag of liquorice twists and the free sheet of classified ads she was making it her business to check each week. Passing women taking dead fir trees and sprigs of bright, berried holly into their houses. Balancing in slippered feet on stepladders to pin mistletoe under the weatherboards. She envisaged their children, sitting around kitchen tables, putting pen to paper, sending letters starting with, *Dear Father Christmas.* Quilp, the postman, was rushed off his feet, but the only cards Queenie had been given were by hand. The boys in the band, Uncle Fish, Sammy. Nothing from her father. No invite to spend Christmas with them on their smallholding in Norfolk. Not yet. *Don't hold your breath, girlie.* After writing to tell her father what had happened, could she seriously imagine Norma entertaining her – pregnant with no man in tow – around the table? Paper hats, pulling crackers, passing the buttered parsnips. The only post she'd had was a letter reminding her to sign the recording contract. Something she tore up, in the same way she had torn up the original contract. Burnt it on the fire. She was letting Dulcie Fricker break the bad news to Herbie Weiszmann.

To add to the sickening uncertainties about her future, Queenie was finding it difficult to sing. She couldn't make her voice work in the way it used to and she'd lost the buoyancy she needed to stand up on stage and perform. Riddled with guilt about what she'd done to Joy, she couldn't even apply her make-up properly. Unable to bear herself in the mirror for long enough, hating her face, what she found behind her eyes.

She scanned the sheet of classified ads taken from the newspaper rack, found an advert for psychiatric nurses to work at the Friern Mental Hospital in Barnet. Read about the training they were offering young women who wanted to work in this area of care. It seemed as if they were offering a decent wage with accommodation too. Queenie had decided some time ago that it was important to spend what was left of her life being useful to others. It was the only way to atone for what she'd done to Joy. She circled it with her pencil and folded the sheet into quarters, put it in her coat pocket. The rent on the house was running out soon and even if she was able to carry on singing at the club, she couldn't afford it on her own. She would send for an application form; it was worth a shot. She could start in early June. Yes, June would probably be about right. After the baby was born. Because she'd decided she would have it, then give it up for adoption. It was her only option now. There was enough in her Post Office savings account to stretch another month or two on the rent.

She moved down inside the crepuscular cavern of the shop to wait for a break in the rain. Although why? Her feet were wet inside her shoes and rainwater dripped from her hat; she couldn't get any wetter. The shop bell tinkled and suddenly it was a hive of women's voices up at the till. Queenie turned her back to them and worked her way along the shelves, pretending the meagre array of tins, jars and packets of Kellogg's cereal were of interest.

'She's only gone and got herself pregnant.'

'Someone else's man, I heard.'

'Don't see no ring on her finger.'

'She's a disgrace. It's a good job her father's not 'ere to see what a mess she's made of everything.'

'You seen that gentleman caller of hers?'

'He's no gentleman, he's one of them homo-sex-u-als.'

Were they talking about her? No, she mustn't be paranoid. No one knew the trouble she was in. Or did they? The waistband of her skirt under her coat was digging into her tummy and she hadn't been able to fasten it to the top. Was she showing? Always an object of curiosity to the women around here, it wouldn't be much of a surprise if they'd put two and two together.

'Little better than a prostitute.'

Ouch. Queenie smarted as if she had been struck in the face. She knew they resented her; she'd been a fool to give them the ammunition. She had played right into their hands.

In the old days, she would have marched up to the till and given them a piece of her mind, but not now; she was changed now. And plumping for a packet of custard creams, not because she wanted them but to satiate the eyes she imagined were boring into her, she steeled herself to go up to the till.

'A quarter of liquorice twists and a *Standard*, please.' She ignored the tittering at her elbow. Turned her head to the rain that sluiced down the shop's windowpanes. Nearly dark. Not that the day had ever got properly light.

'Don't you want a copy of *Vogue*? It's just come in this morning,' the shopkeeper asked.

'Not today, thank you.' And she took out her purse, paid for the sweets and the evening paper.

She was about to step out of the shop when the shocking blackened banner – 'Man with Two Bodies on His Hands' – stopped her dead.

She stared at the photograph of the man they were calling a murderer. He looked familiar. This startled young man caught in the flashbulb of the waiting reporters at Paddington Station. It took her a minute, then she remembered where she'd seen him. He was that Welshman in the pub in Ladbroke Grove that night. The

Elgin, that's right, she was remembering more. Timothy. Tim. She read his name and that too rang a bell. He was nice, cheery. Black eyes and shiny black hair that was plastered off his face. Joking with the barman, with her.

'This can't be right?' she muttered, snatching at the storyline. 'Arrested… Strangled his wife, Beryl, and his baby daughter…'

This was shocking enough. But not as shocking as seeing where Timothy Evans had been living and where he was supposed to have committed these murders. An address she knew, a house she had nearly stepped inside. A place in her memory that chilled her to the bone: 10 Rillington Place.

CHAPTER FIFTY-SEVEN

'Dear me, Reg, what in heaven's name are you doing out here? Digging garden? Not like you to be bothering.'

'Oh, you're home, are you? I weren't expecting you till tomorrow.' Working in shirtsleeves, his cuffs turned back to the elbow, he straightened his spine and dragged the back of an arm over his sweaty forehead. 'I'm just giving things a tidying.'

'Don't you go overdoing things, making your back bad – you know how you suffer with it.' His wife stooped to pet the white terrier that had trotted over to see her.

'Give over with your mitherin', woman.' He pressed a foot to the spade, forced his weight against it and sliced into the earth. 'Go and put kettle on. Do something useful. I'm about ready for a nice cup of tea. Go on.' Sensing her dither. 'And take Judy with you, blasted dog's been under my feet all day.'

'I can't have you coming in house dressed like that, Reg.' A worried frown. 'You'll have to get cleaned up first, you're filthy. What possessed you to wear your best trousers to do a job like that? You are silly.'

He flung her a look, pleased to see her flinch in fear. 'Have a nice Christmas in Sheffield, did you?'

'Aye, I did. Nicer than if I'd stayed here, as you don't celebrate it.'

'And how's that no-good brother of yours?'

'Oh, you know, same as always.' She shifted awkwardly from foot to foot. 'So,' her voice small, 'what've you been up to while I've been away?'

'*Up to* – what d'you mean, *up to*? I don't get up to anything.' He moistened his lips and resumed his digging, determined to finish the job by sundown.

'I think you know what I mean, Reginald.'

'No, I don't think I do.' He scowled, a little out of breath. 'I think you're going to have to spell it out for me, Ethel.'

'Well, for a start, I don't think this is yours, is it?' She flapped a brightly patterned silk scarf at him. 'And it certainly don't belong to me. I found it stuffed down back of rope chair in kitchen.' She heaved down a lungful of air, but not before he'd noticed the quiver in her throat. 'So, come on, Reg, are you going to tell me what's been going on?'

'I'll tell you, all right. Not that you're going to want to hear it.' He stopped what he was doing and leant on the spade. Gave her one of his horrid smiles. 'One of them young women that you arranged to call round turned up. Oh, aye.' Eyes glinting. 'Dead pretty, she were… beautiful hair. And what choice did I have? Poor little mite, I could hardly go turning her away, now could I? Not when she'd come here desperate for help.'

'I never arranged for no one to call round. I don't know what you're on about.'

'*No?* Perhaps she were waiting until you went away on your holidays.' A cruel laugh. 'All over me, she were, making a right nuisance of herself. Begging and pleading with me to do it to her, little hussy.' He kicked the dog that was taking an unhealthy interest in something buried beneath his feet. 'Get out of it, Judy. Go on, bugger off.' He waited for the dog to slope away before returning his attention to his wife. 'I did tell her, I said, "I'm not like that, young lady," and I were rather annoyed with her, truth be told. But no matter how many times I told her I weren't interested, she wouldn't have it. Kept insisting she stayed, even though I said it weren't proper, what with the lady of the house not being home.'

'I don't understand, what are you saying, Reg?' His wife, nervous, bunched the scarf into a ball and pushed it against her face as if to sniff the remnants of the other woman's perfume.

'What I'm saying is, a man has needs, Ethel. You of all people should know that. I'm saying, I fought her off for as long as I could, but...' A shrug. 'You and me, well, what we do don't satisfy neither of us, not when you won't even try. And, well...' Another shrug. 'What with girl being so pretty, I suppose she just wore me down. I had no choice but give in to her in end.'

'End?' His wife hugged herself, the scarf still balled in her fist. 'Oh, dear God, Reg.' She gasped, her eyes pulled wide. 'What have you done?' The question darkened and condensed to a cloud above their heads and she raised her eyes to it as if expecting it to burst and cause havoc. 'What have you done?'

'*You?* You dare to question me, woman?' He threw the spade down and strode towards her: threatening, frightening. He could throttle her here, this minute. 'You've no right to go questioning me about *anything*, Ethel Christie.'

CHAPTER FIFTY-EIGHT

Joy descended the six stone steps that, barricaded from Gloucester Road by a set of black railings, led down to her basement room. The pigeon was there, cooing its greeting from the dark.

'Hello, little friend.' Cheered by the sight of it tucked under the eaves and sheltering from the weather, she reached through the rain to stroke its feathery breast. 'Are you hungry? I'll bring you something in a while.'

The meagre gaslight from the night-time street barely penetrated her doorway and she struggled to find her latchkey in the caverns of her bag. She dropped the key and got down on her hands and knees to grope the ground. Sensing something shift on the pavement above her, she flung her head to scan what could be seen of the street. Nothing. No one was there. Only the merest hiss of tyres on wet asphalt. Yes, that must have been what it was. She shivered under the creeping unease that crawled over her skin and, finding the key, she scrabbled to her feet. She had not forgotten about that sinister man in the trilby and their strange encounter in Brompton Cemetery before Christmas. It was frightening to think she might not have escaped him had that couple not turned up at that moment to lay flowers on a nearby grave. But she needn't worry about him – it wasn't as if he knew where she lived.

She shook out her umbrella and unlocked her door. Stepping inside, she flicked on a lamp and flooded the space in a yellow glare. Her coat was wet and she hung it on the peg by the door; there was little point trying to dry it out, she would be putting it on again in a few hours. The building was silent. The rain going on in the street was little more than a muffled whisper against the exterior walls. A glance in the mirror told her what she had already guessed. Damp hair plastered to her forehead, the skin around her eyes bruised and thin-looking; she looked worn out. The girl she had been before meeting Charles had disappeared; she was unrecognisable to herself. This wasn't what she'd asked for. To have him, then lose him. To be shown the top of the mountain only to be pushed to the bottom again was beyond cruel. She had been happy before him, muddling along in the foothills. The role of attention's sweet centre was Queenie's; Joy had never consciously sought the part.

A sudden and loud rapping on her window.

'I've got your post,' her landlord mouthed on the other side of the glass. He must have slipped out of the house and down the steps without her hearing him. She opened the door onto the amplified dripping sounds.

'Expensive paper.'

'From a friend.' She took the envelope, saw the violet ink had smudged in the rain.

'A friend, eh?' Then he was gone, his laughter trailing behind him.

Her room was cold but Joy didn't have the energy to light the fire. She placed the unopened envelope on the side, swapped her jacket for her chunky blue pullover and put on her slippers. The slippers, along with a pair of navy leather gloves, were the only things from Heloise she hadn't given away. She tied her damp hair back off her face and saw that her landlord had delivered the bookcase he'd been promising for months, and although pleased, she wished he wouldn't come in here without her permission. She spent a minute arranging her paperbacks on the shelves: de Maupassant, Zola, Flaubert, Dumas... long dead, but with no Charles, she had been forced to seek solace beneath their covers again. Thinking she was hungry, she opened a can of vegetable soup and put it to heat in a pan. A slice of wholemeal would be nice, but checking the breadbin, she found it was empty. Crackers then. She opened the tin. Only a few broken ones lurking at the bottom. They would have to do; they were all she had.

Needing the warmth, she leant as close as she dared to the gas flame on the hob and stared at the envelope. It was the first letter Charles had sent to her lodgings. His others, and there had been many, for whatever reason, had arrived at work. And at work, she had Amy. Sensible, kind Amy. Telling her not to read them, to rip them up; that nothing he could say would change what he and Queenie had done. She put the letter in the bin, determined not to give in to her feelings. When her soup started to simmer, she poured it into a bowl and pushed the unidentifiable vegetables around with her spoon. Why cook it if it was so unappetising? It wasn't the soup's fault – everything looked unappetising these days. Evident from the way she was shrinking inside her clothes. An image of her and Charles found her. A crisp, bright morning when they had woken to the crash of waves and seabirds singing in a room that overlooked Smuggler's Cove. It was so sharp it could have been yesterday and yet it was already a lifetime ago, she thought sadly. Things weren't supposed to have turned out this way. If things had gone as planned, she and Charles would have been married by now. She would have given up her job and left this dump and begun a new adventure with him. Joy listened to Charles's voice swim up from the depths of her chest, dragging the wreckage of her life without him. It tugged like the tide, tearing her heart like seaweed caught on a fishing hook. To stop herself crying, she concentrated on the broken crackers in the bottom of the tin. Whether or not to eat one. When she did, she regretted it. It was stale and soft like her. Because Joy wasn't getting much sleep either: sleep brought dreams of dappled sunlit days and picnics with Charles reaching out to her, and she could hardly bear to watch them. Or wake from them. For in those first few seconds, flanked by sleeping and waking, all was still rosy until the painful reality crept up over her and covered her like a shroud.

She remembered the pigeon and took the tin with its miserable remains out into the January rain. Stood with her back to the door and crumbled the crackers, let the bird peck them from her palm.

'Do you think I should read his letter?' she asked the bird and it cooed its reply.

Back inside, she fished the letter from the bin. Wiped off a spray of tea leaves, a blob of soup. Without Amy to stop her, Joy's resolve had crumbled away. Her mouth moved over the words penned in his confident hand.

My dearest Joy. I have tried and tried to talk to you, to tell you how sorry I am. I am at a loss to know what to say to make things right between us again, and because you refuse to see me, I'm not sure I can. I write to tell you that I am set to leave for South Africa in four days. It won't be the adventure we promised ourselves and I do not know how I will bear it without you, dear Joy, but it is all in train and impossible for me to back out of now. Please hear me when I tell you there is no way to express my regret and I am sorry I have hurt you. If you can find it in your heart to forgive me for that one moment of madness, it will be more than I can ever forgive myself for. I send you my fondest, deepest love. Your Charles.

Four days. He was set to leave for South Africa in four days. But when was the letter dated? She checked the top right-hand corner. Might there still be time? She needed to telephone the house in Bayswater. She had to talk to him before it was too late.

Grabbing her bag and umbrella, she charged out of her room, up the stone steps and into the rainy street, splashing through the filthy puddles in her pretty satin slippers. Inside the phone box, her teeth chattering against the cold, she lifted the handset.

'Number, please?'

She gave it to the telephone exchange operator.

'Just putting you through, caller.'

Joy waited for a voice to answer at the other end before shoving coins down its throat.

CHAPTER FIFTY-NINE

It had been raining since breakfast. Not drizzling or spitting, but streaming over the city in heavy, grey, slanting slices.

'God alive,' Terrence complained as he did battle with his umbrella along the pavement.

It was a relief to finally reach his mother's gate and, conscious of the twitching net curtains of neighbours, he ambled down the garden path to stand in the porch. A space he needed to share with dried-out paint tins, solidified brushes and cracked boots. The things no one had bothered to clear out after his father had died. Sounds of rainwater spilling along the guttering as he slid his latchkey into the lock and stepped onto the welcome mat. Terrence had known this door all his life. A door with a rusted knocker hanging by a single screw that bled each time it rained. He closed his umbrella and took off his coat and hat, was about to peg them on the hooks in the hall.

What?

His insides went cold.

He gawped at the things that were hanging beside his father's old fishing jacket. Things that shouldn't be there.

What the hell?

A brown trilby and a wet raincoat with what looked like a woman's stocking hanging out of a pocket. With it, a fleeting image of the prostitute, Marie, and the vivid bruises on her neck. He glanced at the *Madonna and Child* on the wall and held his breath to the faint chinking of teaspoons on china that were coming from the living room. Then voices that made the hairs on the back of his neck stand up. One was his mother's; the other, little more than a pathetic whisper.

'… did you say Halifax, Mr Christie?'

'That's right. Boothtown District. Chester Road.'

'By golly, I know Chester Road. My gran lived along there. We lived in Boothtown too, oh, I forget the name of the street, my memory, you know.' Terrence imagined his mother flapping a hand at her head in that way she did when she couldn't recall something. 'But I do remember the moors above, and the railway below. Smart houses. Oh, yes, very nice along Chester Road, not like our street… Hey, I bet your mother used to shop in Arkwrights.' A giggle. 'If she did, I'm sure I'd have known her. Do you remember All Souls Cemetery? We used to go playing in there.'

'A right dreary place, if you don't mind me saying, Mrs Banks.' Christie's smarmy ways made Terrence's skin crawl. 'Although, as a boy, I used to sing in church choir. I had quite a fine voice, as it happens.'

'Well, I never.' His mother sighed. 'It's a small world. When did you move to London?'

'January 'twenty-four.'

'A little later than us. Me and my Ernest came here in nineteen twenty.'

'Were that about time your Terry were born?'

At the sound of his name, Terrence's mouth went dry.

'Aye, getting on for three years after. Then I had our Colin, my youngest, eighteen months later.'

'Does he live in London too?'

'No, Colin, like all five of my girls, is in Yorkshire. They never settled in London. I'm the same, I'd go back in a heartbeat… or maybe Dorset, I do love Dorset…' More tinkling of spoons.

'So, Terry's got five sisters, has he? I've got sisters… four of them. They were always bossing me about, smothered me, they did. When I were a boy, I had to share a room with them, sometimes a bed.

Only got any peace when they were sleeping. I liked it best when they were sleeping.'

'Families, Mr Christie. Families. Do you and Mrs Christie have children?'

'No. It's one of my biggest regrets.'

The soft, doleful voice with its Yorkshire burr was enough to freeze the blood in Terrence's veins. He needed to see what was going on, to check his mother was safe, and inched down the hall to look around the living-room door. Careful to remain out of sight. The first thing he saw was the back of Christie's bald head, the puny shoulders. John Christie, the weaselly little worm, was sitting in his father's leather armchair.

'Oh, there you are, Terry. Your trousers are all wet. Where have you been?' His mother had seen him. 'It's a good job I've had Mr Christie here to keep me company. We've been having a lovely chat... It turns out he's from Halifax, can you believe it? He grew up near where me and your dad—'

'Never mind about all that, how did he get in?' Terrence glared at the dull, priggish figure in his father's old chair. His gaze travelling down to the plimsolls and the trail of muddy marks Christie had left behind on the carpet. 'Who let him in? You shouldn't be letting strangers in.'

'But Mr Christie isn't a stranger, Terry. The two of you are friends, isn't that right, Mr Christie?' Flushed and excited, his mother was obviously enjoying herself.

'That's right.' Christie nodded: his face pinched, his domed head gleaming like a corpse candle beneath the ceiling bulb. 'We've been having a little cup of tea together.'

Terrence gawped at his mother – had she finally lost her marbles? She usually had such a good instinct for people. Couldn't she tell what kind of man this was? He oozed badness like that dreadful smell he carted around with him. Couldn't she smell that either?

'But you never answer the door. I don't understand.'

'I went out the front looking for Tiddles and nice Mr Christie here helped me find him.'

Christie was making that odd sucking movement with his mouth again; he really was the most nauseating man. Just at this moment, the cat jumped into his lap.

'Look at that.' A clap of the hands. 'Mr Tiddles likes you.'

'I'm very good with animals. My Ethel says I've a real way with them. I'm the same with children.' Christie's voice died to almost nothing. 'I've a cat and a dog of my own.'

'I beg your pardon, Mr Christie, I didn't catch that?'

'I were saying, I've a cat and dog of my own... but do call me Reg. All my friends call me Reg.'

Mr Tiddles had changed his mind about Christie and jumped out of his lap onto the wide leather arm of the chair, where he proceeded to clean himself. Licking a paw, then wiping the paw around the back of his ear, once, then again. Leisurely, all the while eyeing this baleful houseguest.

'I could tell you're an animal lover. All the nicest people are.'

'Is that so?' Terrence strode between them and stood with his back to the fire. 'Hitler had dogs, does that mean he was a nice man?' He didn't give his mother the chance to answer and flung his head to Christie, the burn of the coal fire on the back of his calves. 'What the hell d'you think you're doing?'

Christie frowned. 'I'm having a nice cup of tea and a chat with your mother.'

'I can see that. I want to know what you're doing here.'

'Dear me, Terry.' His mother put down her cup and saucer. 'Where's my gentle boy gone? What's got into you? Have you left Mr Manners on the Tube?'

'I do have to agree with your mother, Terrence,' Christie whispered, forcing them both to listen. 'I would never have dared speak to my mother like that, and as for my father... oh, no, I lived in dread of him. One word out of line and he'd take strap to me.'

Terrence could hardly bear to look at the man. 'Excuse me, but who asked for your opinion? You still haven't answered my question. I want to know what you're doing here. How did you know where my mother lives?'

'There's a way to speak to your friend. I am sorry, Mr Christie, I don't know what's got into him.'

'Like I said, call me Reg.'

'Reg. Yes. Would you like a sweetie?' His mother offered Christie one of her precious fruit jellies. 'I've been saving them for a special occasion.'

Christie leant forward over his knees and took one.

Terrence saw red and snatched the box away. *I don't think so, the bastard's bleeding me dry as it is.* 'I want to know why you're here. I want to know why you're bothering my mother!' He put the box of jellies out of arm's reach on the sideboard.

'Terrence! What the devil's wrong with you? You don't speak to guests like that.' His mother made a huffing sound and crossed her arms. 'Mr Christie, I mean, Reg... he's a friend. We've been having a nice little chat together, haven't we? We've been talking about that Timothy Evans.'

'It's an unfortunate business, Mrs Banks.' Christie rubbed a hand over his shiny pate, his voice almost inaudible. 'A really unfortunate business.'

'Oh no, Reg, you must call me Peggy.' Terrence's mother wriggled around in her chair, acting the coy little girl.

Terrence wanted to shake some sense into her. How could anyone be charmed by this snake in the grass?

'As Terrence has decided we're not allowed my jellies, do help yourself to another biscuit, Reg.'

'Thank you, Peggy.' Christie slid his dead fish eyes to Terrence, making him squirm, then took a ginger biscuit. Bit it in half and chewed slowly. 'I'm finding these regrettable happenings all very stressful.' He dispensed a lengthy sigh.

'He's going to be their principal witness, you know?' His mother seemed to be under this man's spell and Terrence gawped at her. 'That's quite some responsibility, don't you think, Terry? A principal witness in a serious murder trial at the Old Bailey. They must think you're very important, Mr Christie... I mean, Reg. But I'm not surprised, what with you being a policeman and training to be a doctor before the First War. You're ever so clever.'

'Kind of you to say so, Peggy, but I could've done without fuss.' Christie dabbed crumbs from his mouth. Prissy and irritating, his assumed gentility made Terrence want to thump him. 'I'm not a well man. I've never been particularly robust and stress of it all has made my stomach trouble flare up again.' He licked his lips and spoke slowly, taking care of his consonants. 'I suffer dreadful with fibrositis.'

'Can't you speak up?' Terrence, strident from the sidelines; hating this man's supercilious manner.

'Terrence!' his mother snapped. 'Mr Christie's voice got damaged in the trenches. Mustard gas poisoning, isn't that right, Mr Christie... I mean, Reg? And I'm the same as you, any stress and it goes straight to my stomach. Shows a sensitive nature, we must be alike in that way.' She scowled at Terrence then rubbed her abdomen as if feeling Christie's discomfort vicariously.

He wanted to scream. He wanted to grab Christie by the collar and haul him out of there. But he didn't. Remembering in time how this man moved among the seedy strata of London society just as he did, and knew who and what he was.

'What a terrible thing, to have that monster living in your house, Reg,' his mother added.

'A monster, indeed. He was a horribly violent man, I'm sorry to say. His poor wife, Beryl.' A tight, dry cough into his fist. 'It's so sad. She were a lovely young woman. Not that it were what you'd call a happy marriage, not by any means. Two of them were forever arguing. I were always having to go up there to tell them to be quiet. My poor Ethel, her nerves are in pieces. It's taken a terrible toll on us both.'

'That's all very well,' Terrence interrupted. He'd had enough of listening to this bilge and it concerned him how Christie referred to Timothy Evans in the past tense as though he was already dangling from the end of a rope. He needed to take action and, moving away from the fire, he stepped up beside his mother's armchair. 'You still haven't said what you're doing here. My mother doesn't want to be bothered by you.'

'But he's not bothering me, he's my guest.'

'Your guest? You don't even know him.'

'And whose fault is that? You never let me meet any of your friends. He doesn't, you know?' She inclined her head to Christie. 'I can sort of understand it at the bank, but not the nightclub where Terry plays piano, it's very upmarket. They don't allow any old riff-raff in there. And Cyril Bream, he's the owner, such a gentleman. He's really taken Terry under his wing.' His mother always did this: appropriating his life as her own and rattling off authoritatively about his band and his nights at the Mockin' Bird as if she went there herself. Terrence had heard her doing it with her neighbours and it maddened him. 'No, I don't get to meet any of his friends.'

'I don't suppose you do.' A smile that revealed a crooked graveyard of teeth. 'He likes to keep them secret… his friends.' A sneaky squint at Terrence. 'But I know a few of them, don't I, Terry? Who's that chap you're especially fond of?' Terrence, stiffening inside his suit, watched helplessly as Christie turned his attention to his mother again. 'He's one of them darkies, Peggy.' At this, the hands shot up. Not that this was any kind of capitulation. 'I've nowt against them in principle, don't get me wrong. But, well, you wouldn't want to be associating yourself with them, would you, Peggy?'

'No, I don't like the sound of my lad mixing with the likes of them.' She placed a hand on Terrence's leg. 'Oh, he always was a naughty boy. It's been a struggle for me since his father's gone.'

She leant forward in her chair and lowered her voice. 'Now, Reg, what were you telling me earlier? Something about my Terry owing you money?'

Terrence opened and closed his mouth. Flabbergasted at the gall of this man, he couldn't speak.

'Oh, I've gone and embarrassed him,' Christie chimed in. 'Look at him, Peggy.' Terrence felt two pairs of eyes. Neither of them welcome. 'It was when you were a bit short, wasn't it, Terry? Don't you remember?'

Sickly sweet and soft like a girl, there was so much about this man, with his effeminate affectations, that made Terrence wonder if he wasn't a latent homosexual himself. Was this why Christie had such a problem with him? An idea occurring.

'A few weeks back, wasn't it, lad? It's not his fault, Peggy. I don't say these things to get him into trouble, you understand.'

'Of course, you don't.' His mother sipped her tea.

Christie's thin lips formed a smile as sinister as the wind that threw its lopsided weight against the walls of the house. 'Peggy,' he began, delivering her name like a parcel, 'the thing is…' He lifted his chipped blue gaze to Terrence, his smile sliding away again. 'Like I was explaining earlier, I'm on tablets for my stomach.'

'Yes, you poor thing.'

'And your Terry, well, he knows my predicament, I've told him all about sick note doctor's given me for my back.' Christie lifted his cup from its saucer and sipped his tea, his little finger raised to the ceiling. 'I'm unfit for work. It's why I need money he owes me.'

'But you didn't need to come here. Why did you come here?' Terrence clasped and unclasped his hands, fearful of what this man was about to say.

'You left me no choice, lad.' Christie pushed his spectacles onto the bridge of his nose. 'I had to do something.'

'You are a naughty boy, Terry. Whatever would your father say? Borrowing money, didn't we always tell you?'

'Mum, will you please stay out of this?'

'I will do no such thing, young man. And with Mr Christie being so unwell—'

'There's nothing wrong with him.' Terrence cut across her and raised his voice over her protestations. 'And now he's leaving. Aren't you?'

'B-but Mr Christie's not finished his tea.'

'He's going. *Now.*' Terrence bounced his fists against his sides. Made sure Christie saw what he was doing.

'Er, yes. I'm afraid so, Peggy.' Christie brushed biscuit crumbs from his tie, and with a wince and a grumble put an exaggerated hand to his lower back and got to his feet. 'Such a pleasure to meet you. Thank you for tea, most kind.' Grovelling and scraping, he backed out of the room.

'You must come again, Mr Christie,' she called after him. 'Any time, I'm always here.'

'I won't be a minute, Mum,' Terrence told her before charging out into the rainy street. 'You fucking bastard,' he snarled through gritted teeth. 'What the hell d'you think you're doing coming here? She's an old woman.' He heard the front door slam behind him.

'I don't care for foul language if you don't mind.' Christie positioned his hat and pushed his arms into his raincoat – the pain in his back miraculously gone.

'I don't give a fuck what you mind about. I want to know what you're doing here. How come you know where my mother lives?' Terrence lit a cigarette and smoked it furiously. The rain, he didn't seem to notice, dripped off his hair, into his eyes.

'I've told you before, lad. I know all there is to know about you.'

'You're to stay away from her, d'you hear?'

'Important to you, is she?' Christie poked out the tip of his tongue and licked his lips. 'I wouldn't have needed to bother her if you'd stuck to our deal. I'm not unreasonable, I just want what's mine. What we agreed.' The whispering voice, all but swallowed up by the rush of the rain and the stiff north-easterly that was whipping around their ears.

'We agreed nothing. And I've told you, you're wasting your time. I haven't much left after I've paid for Mum. You want to see her out on the street, do you? What I gave you the other day was my rent. I'm in the fucking red, thanks to you.'

Christie gave a mock shiver. Cold, or because of Terrence's choice of language? Either way, the man's pomposity irritated the hell out of him. All he wanted to do was punch him, to finish him here and now. For this torment to stop.

Terrence stood with his back to his mother's house and smoked his cigarette. It seemed as if things had reached some kind of stalemate, and because he wasn't going to be the one to break it, he stared at the incessant rain and the fading day. They had the street to themselves until a lamplighter, ladder tucked under his arm, came clanking along the pavement. Christie saw him and hurried backwards into a dark alleyway, where he adjusted his trilby down over his eyes. The scrape of the ladder against the pavement added to Terrence's nerves and he watched Christie light up and smoke his own cigarette. The way he held it tucked back in his fist between puffs, the smoke leaking between his fingers.

'What would your mother say if she knew what a dirty bugger you are?' Those dead fish eyes glinting from behind their spectacles. 'I'd say it would break her heart.'

Terrence took a swing for him. Christie caught his arm. The man was surprisingly strong.

'Just pay me what you owe me, lad, and we'll hear no more about it.'

'And if I don't?'

'Well, now,' Christie seemed to think about it as he finished his cigarette and threw it away, 'let's just say it would be terrible if something bad were to happen to your mother.'

Terrence watched Christie pull the stocking from his coat pocket and wrap it around his hand. Snapped it taut. Then, with a stomach-churning wink, Christie twisted through the rain and pointed his nose at Terrence's mother's front door.

CHAPTER SIXTY

He had only just positioned himself in the doorway at the side of her building when, to his amazement, the girl ran out into the rain in her slippers to use the phone box. Not that the girl's telephone call could have been about anything important – it was over in a jiffy and now she was nicely back inside her brightly lit basement room. The phone box was something he had been making use of too. Employing his detecting skills to source a certain number, he had taken to dialling it whenever it took his fancy. It was great fun, putting the frighteners on them by keeping quiet when they picked up at the other end, and certainly helped pass the time on the occasions he found himself waiting for the girl to show up.

The rain had finally ceased, and the moon, slipping its moorings and floating free of the scudding clouds, washed the rooftops in its cold vein of light. He had wandered over here from Camden and was feeling chilly inside his wet raincoat and plimsolls, but he wasn't ready to head home yet. What a stupid old fool Mrs Banks was. He chuckled into his neck. All he had to do was tell her about his wartime services as a police constable and his injuries during the First War and she was inviting him inside her house, making him tea. Anything could have happened. It nearly did. He lit up a celebratory cigarette and smoked it while continuing to congratulate himself on how well the visit had gone. It had been worth traipsing all the way over there if only to put the fear of God into that filthy bugger of a son of hers. Which he had. His face had been a picture, and smiling into the memory, he wondered how long he should leave it before popping in to see the mother again.

Women were such stupid creatures. Take this one. Never closing her blinds. Never imagining someone could be watching from the street. Someone who meant her harm. Such guileless innocence in one plainly exposed to the dangers of the world. He couldn't believe how easy it was to spy on her. Seeing her move around her bedsit, she appeared to be distracted again tonight. Teary too, he'd say. He had tried to get her to open up to him in the cemetery that time, but she had refused to engage, which was a shame. Not that it took a genius to work out things with that boyfriend of hers had soured. Soured between her and that painted friend too. Which was hardly surprising. A right pair of feckless good-for-nothings, betraying her like that.

So, here she is, his roaming thoughts while he sucked on the last of his cigarette and squashed it against the wall, *friendless and alienated and miles from home.* Just how he liked them. He rubbed his hands together – things didn't get much better than this. He grinned, and although he was shivering inside his damp clothes, he would stay a little longer. There must be something more to see and, with this in mind, he moved closer, leant against the railings for a better look.

'Bloody vermin… bloody filth.' The cooing getting on his nerves, he flapped the pigeon away. The thing was tame enough to pick up and strangle. To smack its head against the brickwork and silence it forever. If he had a mind to, and half of him did. But for now, he wanted to concentrate on the job in hand.

Quietly, tucked into the shadows, he didn't want to alert the girl to him. All he wanted was to look. And look he did. His bloodshot eyes exploring her with a deadly intensity as she undressed for bed. He assessed her perfect breasts. His eyes grazing over her throat, the length of her body. Marvelling at how beautiful she was.

Light off and lit by the moon, she was sleeping now… his sleeping beauty. So peaceful, so silent, so still. His sleeping beauties was what he called them, in the moments before strangling them. And with saliva shining at the corners of his mouth, he tugged the stocking from his pocket. Grubby and laddered from much fingering, he pulled it tight, flattening the length of silk and running it through his hands like a tapeworm. He imagined how it would feel to wind it about this one's slender neck and strangle the life out of her. Massaging his crotch and growing in confidence, feeling he was safely hidden from the lights of any passing vehicle, he delved beyond his trousers, his underwear and right down to the clammy depths of his arousal. Then, with the sensation peaking to something almost too much to bear, he risked everything and stepped through the gap in the railings, down the stone steps, to press right up against her murky basement window.

CHAPTER SIXTY-ONE

Back in her bedsit, Joy thought she was going mad. She scrubbed and scrubbed at her little satin slippers but couldn't wash away the stains that haunted the weft and warp of the fabric. Like rose-coloured phantoms, they bloomed and swelled with each fresh soaking. She shouldn't have worn them in the street; how many times had she told herself how precious they were? And now they were ruined, like everything else was ruined. And what made it worse was that it had been for nothing. Running through the rain to stand shivering in the phone box only to be told by a voice she didn't recognise, a voice that sounded as far away from her as the moon, 'He's gone, my dear. You're too late. Charles left for Africa this morning.'

She gave up on the slippers and sat on the bed. Pushed the flats of her hands against the walls that seemed to be realigning themselves, fearing they were about to topple forward and crush her like the grief she couldn't push through. Nights were always the worst. It was when it was dark outside that the splintered images of her time with Charles shoved their sharpened ends into the tender parts of her. Unhappier than she ever remembered, Joy brushed away a tear and undressed for bed. She just wanted the suffering to stop. Whenever she had been sad in the past, she had found a way to snap out of it. After all, she'd lived through enough disappointment and loss before. Look how depressed she had been when her father had died. But this was different: she didn't seem able to find a way through this and it frightened her.

With the anguish of another sleepless night ahead, she retrieved the bottle of port she took care to hide in her bedside cabinet. Bought on her way home from work the previous evening, it had cut into her weekly budget in a big way. With no more shifts at the Mockin' and no more Charles, Joy needed to start economising again; she couldn't afford to overspend. But she needed this, and poured some into her toothbrush mug and drank it down. Poured a little more and swallowed that too. She had to block out Charles's face somehow. She returned the bottle, its sides sticky under her fingers, then rinsed out the mug and lifted the blind as high as it would go. Not that she ever fully closed it; the basement tended to be gloomy even on the brightest of days and needed all the light in the sky there was. Since childhood, she had always liked to uncover the window whenever she was in bed. There was something comforting about watching a night sky with her head on the pillow. Nowadays, it gave her something to do when sleep wouldn't come.

The sheets were cold, and she lay down and listened to sounds of life filtering through the ceiling. Voices, taps running, a smoker's cough rattling along the passageway above. Sounds that made her feel lonelier and more removed from the rest of the world than ever. But hadn't she always been alone? Nothing had changed that much. Thinking back on how Queenie had been with her recently. Temperamental, snappy. That would have been her hormones. They must have been all over the place. It made sense to her now, the sickness and Queenie pretending she had a stomach bug. The way she kept touching her tummy that time they had breakfast at Bayswater. Joy could almost feel sorry for her. Almost.

She stared at the ewer on the floor. The soap dish bought from Woolworths during her very first week in London. The basin of grey water in which she had perfunctorily washed. She looked around the room, at the faded pink roses on the wallpaper.

'Goodnight,' she told it.

Light out, and the moon went on like a lamp. It pinched out the edges of her meagre furniture. The washstand and the open cupboard door where the chamber pot stood. The brass balls at the foot of her bed. Then, counting the seconds, she waited for the mice to start scratching behind the skirting boards…

Until she was woken an hour or so later by another scratching coming from outside.

Joy pushed back the covers and moved to the window. Tipped her head to the moon and gulped it down. There were stars too. Millions of them. Spooky policeman's buttons, sparkly and silver and rare for a night in London.

A face at the glass.

There one second, gone the next.

She screamed. Breath glazed the window. Inside or out? She couldn't be sure. Frantic, she swivelled to check over her shoulder. There was nobody there, and in the dwindling seconds, doubting her senses, she couldn't be sure she had seen anyone at all.

It was her imagination playing tricks and she told herself to calm down. Everything was fine, she was safe. There was no way that man was prowling around out there, waiting to hurt her. That time in the cemetery was just her imagination working overtime too. Yes, he was strange and she didn't like the way he looked at her, but what had he actually done? Nothing.

He wouldn't.

Would he?

CHAPTER SIXTY-TWO

Gone midnight. Terrence dragged himself up the stairs to his bed-sitting room at the rear of the house. He'd come straight home after performing at the Mockin' Bird – there was little point going to Albert's. The way things were between him and Malcolm, and having next to no money, it was best to stay away. Not that the Mockin' Bird was much fun any more either. Things weren't the same without Queenie fronting the band. Terrence missed her and promised himself he'd call round to see her in Balfour Road just as soon as he could. He needed to find a way to check on Joy too. Christie's cockeyed threat that time he'd come to the bank, the fact he knew her name, it had been playing on his mind.

Sensing the ghostly presence of generations past, he stroked the peeling wallpaper and imagined the souls of previous tenants pressed between the centuries-old colours and patterns. Thought the chipped gloss on the skirting boards and doors – showing layers of yellow, turquoise then finally brown – marked the passing of years like the rings on a tree. He had the sense he was losing his grip on reality. His life. He wasn't sure if he could go on. The strain of keeping Christie at bay, at keeping what he was a secret, was proving too hard.

His landlady must have heard the front door go and came out of her ground-floor rooms.

'There you are, Mr Banks.' Her cheeks bulging with a half-eaten sandwich. 'You've not been avoiding me, have you?'

'Not at all.' Terrence stopped halfway up and forced a smile down on the head wrapped in its chequered scarf.

'Good, that's good.' She swallowed. 'And you'll be sure to settle the rent you owe? Because you're a month in arrears now, remember.'

'Rest assured, Mrs Spencer, I'll be settling what I owe before the week's out.' *How?* His panicky thoughts.

'I knew you were sound.' His landlady bestowed a generous smile. 'I was only saying to my Bert how it's not like you to be behind. You're our best lodger.'

'Just a little blip, Mrs Spencer. I've had some extra expenses with my mother these past weeks. Unforeseen things, you know.' He continued with his lie. 'But rest assured, it will all be paid to you soon.' He patted the wallet in his pocket, fat with what he'd *borrowed* from the cash box at work and needed to hand over to Christie – the man was making him a thief as well as a liar.

'Is everything all right with you, Mr Banks?' His landlady picked at what was left of the ham in her sandwich. 'Cos you've been looking a bit peaky if you don't mind me saying.'

The telephone rang from its wall bracket in the hall. It rang and kept on ringing. It saved him from the need to invent a reason for his shabby appearance.

'If that's for me, just tell them I'm not here, would you?' He waved a hand in its general direction.

'Flamin' thing's been going all day.' His landlady put what was left of her sandwich in her mouth, chewed around the words. 'There's never no one there. I was thinking, if it carries on, I should tell the police. What d'you think, Mr Banks?'

Terrence pretended not to hear and went up to his room. Switched on the single ceiling bulb.

Police?

He didn't want them coming here asking questions. Supposing it was Christie making these silent calls, as it might well have been, there was no way of proving it. No, he needed to deal with whatever this was in his own way. And he would, just as soon as he'd worked out how to put a stop to that man for good.

CHAPTER SIXTY-THREE

Joy woke hours later. Opened her eyes to the lilac-streaked morning leaching in through the blind she had pulled down over the window. Despite the port, she hadn't slept well. Shaken up by the face at the glass – imagined or otherwise – it had haunted her dreams and still wouldn't leave her alone. Was it that leery man with his dog? To think someone had been out there watching left her feeling more exposed than she had done since arriving in London.

Yawning as she pushed back the covers, she dropped her legs down over the side of the bed, her toes groping for the ruined satin slippers. She left the blind where it was and switched on a lamp, then wandered over to what passed for a kitchen and pressed the tip of her nose to the small side window to see what the day was doing. Her breath misted the glass as she looked out on the brick-walled ginnel, then further up to the identical terraced houses on the opposite side. Tall, elegant, Victorian brick dwellings topped with sky-grazing chimneys. She could see families pushing prams along the pavement blown with the last of winter's leaves. Couples wrapped in scarves and linking arms. People who looked as if they were making the most of the morning. It made her sad. Rudderless and cast out on a bilious sea, what was she supposed to do with her time now she had no one to share it with?

The answer came sooner than she could have imagined. On her way back to the bed to tidy the covers, she trod on the little enamel brooch Charles had bought her all those months ago. The one she'd believed she had lost. It pierced the sole of her slipper, not enough to hurt, just enough to let her know it was there. When she picked it up, she saw the pin had buckled and spent the next few minutes trying to straighten it. But her fingers weren't strong enough, and no matter how hard she tried, she couldn't get the clasp to work again.

'Smuggler's Cove,' she murmured, her eyes strangely dry. Defeated, finding her treasured brooch broken was the final straw. She had reached a crossroads with no idea which way to turn. 'Smuggler's Cove.'

Then suddenly the way ahead cleared and she knew what needed to be done. It had been staring her in the face all along. Tidying her hair in a sloppy ponytail, letting wispy bits trail down her neck, she got down on her hands and knees to retrieve the shoebox holding Charles's letters and the treasured souvenirs from their time together. A box she kept her heart in. She tipped its contents, along with the broken brooch, into a large brown envelope she had once carried papers from work home in. Tore off a sheet of writing paper from a pad and scribbled the few sentences she'd been rehearsing in her head. Then she sealed the flap and wrote a name and address on the front in big black capital letters. That done, she took down her suitcase from where it had been gathering dust on the top of her kitchen cupboard and packed a few items of clothing and her wash-up bag, along with the paperback she was reading. Pulled on a grey skirt, blouse and cardigan, her stout black shoes and old green school coat that was still damp from the day before. She tied Amy's pretty scarf about her neck and took a sideways look at her diamond engagement ring on the bedside cabinet. Snagging the light, it glinted indolently among her reading matter. Too late to put it in the envelope with the other things, she picked it up and placed it beside the sink for whoever moved in after her. It would be a nice surprise, the thought cheering her a little.

She locked her suitcase, picked up the envelope she'd tied with string and opened the door. Before closing it behind her, she paused on the threshold to say farewell to the pigeon who had been keeping her company since she'd arrived here. But to her bewilderment, its perch was empty. Strange. She frowned at the space it had left behind, its column of droppings; her little feathery friend was always there to greet her in the mornings. Refusing to believe it had gone, she searched the entrance area in the hope it had opted for another perch, but no, it must have flown away. Gripping the handle of her suitcase, the bulky envelope under her arm, she followed the journey of a sudden beam of sunshine, gulping down its dazzle as if this was to be the last of it. And it was. The light she stood in changed. Everything was cast into a weird apricot as the sun slipped behind a curtain of black storm clouds.

CHAPTER SIXTY-FOUR

With a copy of *The Times* tucked under his arm, Terrence let himself into his lodgings. Quiet, he didn't want to alert his landlady and for there to be another awkward conversation about the rent money he still hadn't paid her. He climbed the stairs, avoiding the treads that creaked, his hatred for Christie building with each step.

Clever though, wasn't he? Christie's method of torture… psychological torture… it was working. It was grinding him down and making him think he was losing his mind. The snivelling little runt was steadily, but surely, driving him into the ground.

He unlocked the door of his bed-sitting room and switched on the ceiling light. The blackout blind no one had bothered to take down was half-drawn over the window. Shutting out the night but leaving a slice of the chimney pots opposite, the pale smoke rising into the chilly air. He looked at his empty bed with its iron bedstead and mauve eiderdown. He could climb beneath it, not bother to change out of his suit or take off his shoes, and drift off into oblivion and never wake up.

Since he had encountered the wretched Christie, Terrence's life had evolved in such a way that he had come to expect very little from it. He had, almost overnight, become the persecuted man. He thought of Christie with a sullen disgust. Terrence could fantasise all he liked but it took guts to kill someone. Yes, he'd killed in the war, safe from behind his gun; he hated himself for it and still suffered from nightmares. If he wanted Christie dead without a gun – which was something he didn't have – he would need to make physical contact, and the idea appalled him. But he had to do something; he needed to stop the man before he destroyed him completely.

Terrence wandered about his room, looking for inspiration as to how to finish Christie and end this agony, but was greeted by nothing more rousing than his two flat-faced windows, staring dark and cold onto an indifferent street. He switched off the overhead bulb in favour of two lamps, filled the kettle and set it to boil for the company it would give. He opened the door of a cupboard in his kitchen area, knowing that inside there was a bowl of cold potatoes and a shrivelled joint. Sticky-skinned from roasting and trussed with string, he could have it for his supper. Leftovers from a meal he had cooked that Malcolm had failed to show up for. He sliced the potatoes along with some strips of beef into a frying pan and set a place for one.

If he had been asked to describe what he and Malcolm were these days, he would say they were merely ships that passed in the night. Their lights barely distinguishable to one another, drifting further and further apart. He had seen him last Sunday. He usually did at weekends. Between Malcolm's shifts on the Underground and Terrence's work at the bank, then sessions at the Mockin' Bird. They had collided along the alleyway that led to Albert's. Malcolm in his zoot suit and two-tone shoes shining in the moonlight. Terrence in his overcoat and hat. Malcolm had stared right through him, and when Terrence had gone to sit down beside him on one of Albert's battered couches, putting an arm around his shoulders, wanting to talk, Malcolm had flung it away.

'I can't do it no more, Terry. I'm frightened we're gonna get caught. After that run-in with the rozzers I had last time… I can't do it, man.'

Waiting for his potatoes to brown, Terrence opened out his broadsheet. The trial of Timothy Evans had begun at the Old Bailey and the newspaper was full of the upsetting circumstances surrounding the murders of Beryl Evans and her baby daughter, Geraldine.

Terrence read how Evans had changed his initial statement – the one he'd given at the police station in Merthyr Tydfil, confessing he'd put his wife's body down a drain. A story that unravelled as soon as the Met examined the drains at 10 Rillington Place and found no body. A more thorough search of the property was conducted, and the bodies of Beryl and fourteen-month-old Geraldine were found in the wash house in the backyard. Both had been strangled.

Terrence closed his eyes to the dark, superstitious, Transylvania-type land this story evoked. A land of trees, for some reason. Their gnarled trunks rising straight and unnatural as of those a child might outline with crayons; soaring high as giants and multiplying off into a never-ending nothingness. Opening his eyes, the daydream broken by sounds of his frying supper, he saw what came next in the paragraph. Evans' claim that he'd only made his initial statement to protect his neighbour, John Christie. A man who had offered to perform an abortion on his wife, Beryl, who had been depressed at finding herself pregnant again. And that upon his arrival home on the night of Tuesday, the eighth of November, Evans was informed by Christie that the procedure had gone wrong.

'Christ!' Terrence slapped a hand to his forehead. 'Does Queenie know about this?'

That was the night she had gone there, the night Terrence had chased through the streets of Notting Hill desperate to stop her. This could be it; this could be what he'd been waiting for. He read on, his heart in his mouth. But to his crashing disappointment, it didn't look as if anyone believed Evans' accusation about Christie, and according to this, he had gone on to make yet another statement, confessing to both murders.

'By God, that Christie's got the luck of the devil. This poor man, this poor Timothy Evans, he's been damned by his own hand. This is an open-and-shut case,' he mumbled and turned his potatoes over with a spatula. 'Evans probably only admitted to it because he was under extreme duress.' Terrence knew all too well what that felt like, especially recently. 'Bloody police, this is how they work, they have all the tools to tighten the screws. It's probably where Christie got it from – he spent time in the police, didn't he? Probably watched their interviewing techniques, playing on people's fears, the steady application of pressure until you crack. And I bet the crawly bastard duped the court just like he duped Mum. Going on about how he received commendations for his wartime services as a special constable and his injuries during the First War... Oh, come on,' he talked to himself, spurring himself on. 'I've got to do something, he can't be allowed to get away with it and, really, how hard could it be to kill him?' He gulped, the thought of murder turning his stomach. 'But I haven't got a choice, I've got to sort him out... It's my life or his.'

His appetite gone, Terrence turned off the gas ring and lights and left the pan and its contents to coagulate in the dark. He undressed for bed. Scooping out his wallet and a handful of loose coins from his pocket, he made a neat stack on the bedside table. The sheets were cold against his bare legs and he knew they would keep him awake. After finally drifting to sleep, he woke with a start to the blackness and through it, the ringing of the telephone. He tipped himself out of bed, put on his blue flannel dressing gown and charged downstairs to lift the receiver. His heart: a fish, flip-flopping in his mouth.

No one spoke.

Terrence knew it was Christie. Who else would ring at this hour? He listened to him pushing his pure, clean hatred down the line to him. And when he could no longer stand it, he replaced the handset and sat down on the bottom step of the stairs, the wiry carpet fibres prickling his bare legs. His skin was washed grey in the cold gaslight seeping into the hallway and he stared at an imaginary horizon, feeling the most despairing and hopeless he had ever felt in his life. Then, because there seemed to be no way out of the situation he found himself in, Terrence dropped forward onto his knees, his head in his hands, and wept.

CHAPTER SIXTY-FIVE

Queenie lay in bed and watched moonlight flicker through the trees. It was always Joy who had liked to sleep with the curtains open on Bugbrooke Farm. Queenie doubted she had noticed the moon before going there, but since returning to London, she had made a point of following its phases. Her hands swam out across the slippery sheen of the eiderdown. Silvery-grey like the surface of the sea, the whorls in the stitching rippled across its surface. If she concentrated, she could smell the salty breeze rushing in off the waves, its fingers playful, finding her hair and lifting it high off her forehead. Her thoughts drifted to Joy and what she might be doing. Imagined her asleep in her little bed all those streets away. Queenie hoped her dreams were less disturbed than hers but doubted they were.

When she woke, she found the moon had swapped places with the sun. Dizzy was the first to rise and jumped down from the bed. Like her, the cat kept odd hours, and like her also, he ate little and infrequently. The two of them had a surprising amount in common, which was good, as Dizzy was about the only company Queenie had these days. She had seen next to nothing of Terrence since the New Year, and when she did, he was weirdly distracted and distant. Cagey when she tried to push him to open up and tell her what was wrong. She supposed it was because he couldn't find it in him to forgive her for what she'd done to Joy. It had to be – it was how she felt about herself.

She got up and put on her mother's old dressing gown, knotted the cord around her ever-expanding middle. Downstairs, she arranged the kindling on yesterday's ashes and lit the fire. Blew on it until she saw a spark and waited until the orange ribbon of flame multiplied and became a fire. The temperatures had dipped to below zero since the storms London had been living under had finally blown out to sea. She set the kettle on the stove and tidied the table. Found the half-completed application form for the Friern Mental Hospital she planned to finish and post today. Dizzy jumped up beside her, rubbed his furry black jowls against her hand.

'Aren't you the stylish one, in your black harem pants.' She stroked him from tip to tail. His deep rumbling purr filling the void. She was grateful to have his heartbeat living alongside hers in the house. 'You're the only one I've got to talk to, d'you know that?'

And whose fault was that? She caught a slice of her reflection in the mirror. It was all she deserved after destroying Joy's life. Friendless and lonely, she didn't even have the club any more. Forced to take a break from the Mockin' Bird and put her singing career on hold until the *problem* had been resolved – Dulcie Fricker's words, not hers. The table was littered with the failed letters she had begun writing to Joy but couldn't finish. She picked up a sheet she'd scrunched into a ball. Flattened it with her fist. Another attempt that had come to nothing, because there just weren't the words to put this right. She had repeatedly turned up at the museum, in the hope of catching Joy at lunchtimes or on her way home. But it was only ever Amy she saw. Amy, who had, on more than one occasion, threatened to have her removed from the premises. She was doing it to protect Joy, and although Queenie had never got on with the girl, she had to admit Amy was a far better friend to Joy than she ever was.

J O Y.

The three letters that made up her best friend's name were scattered now. Dispersed like pollen from forgotten flowers. Desperate to make amends but with no idea how, Queenie looked for them on billboards, in posters on the sides of buses and shop windows. In her evening newspaper. Gathering the letters together was harder than it seemed, but if she could pull them back from wherever they had been, she could make what she and Joy used to be whole again, couldn't she?

The kettle came to the boil and Queenie made a pot of tea. Sat down with it at the table without making anything to eat. She looked out through the window, saw the morning was fine, but fine was the last thing she felt. Her mood wasn't helped by the distressing story she'd been following in the papers and on the wireless. The trial of Timothy Evans. Not that she had time to dwell on it. A knock at the door and Quilp, the postman, was calling to her through the letterbox.

'*Cooee*… where are you?' The voice was slippery, groping along the hall as if meaning to molest her. 'I've a package for you, my dear.'

Queenie left her chair and padded along the hall in her dressing gown and slippers. She opened the front door just enough for him to pass her what wouldn't fit through the letterbox.

'Thank you.' Deliberately curt, she snapped the door shut, narrowly missing Quilp's investigative fingers. She had never liked the man; she didn't trust the way he looked at her. And in her current condition without her father to act as a safeguard, she felt acutely vulnerable.

The large brown envelope was heavy. Queenie frowned and carried it through to the kitchen. Scanned the hard-edged capitals of her name and address, not recognising the handwriting. She sat down and untied the string. Ripped open the flap and tipped the contents onto the table. It was as if to look at the vestiges of someone's life. There were picture postcards of an expanse of sea with a sandy shoreline. There were letters written in violet ink, beginning with, *My dearest love*… and ending, *Your loving sweetheart*. One was decorated with tiny red hearts that cascaded like waterfalls down the margins. There were tickets for bus journeys, cinema showings and theatre seats with the middles punched out of them. Fliers for a book fair and an art exhibition. A paper napkin with a line drawing of a bay and cliffs. A beer mat with a toucan balancing a glass of Guinness on its bill. A single wildflower pressed between the covers of a poetry book. Three pearl buttons. A length of green ribbon and a folded white cotton handkerchief with the monogram C P G embroidered along its edge.

Something else from the pile caught her eye. A brooch. These were Joy's things; Joy had sent them to her. But why? Queenie's fingers explored the little apple shapes, her nail finding a tiny shard of chipped enamel and the bent pin that didn't fit into the clasp any more. 'Smuggler's Cove' stamped into the metal on the back. This was where Charles used to take Joy. Smuggler's Cove was their special place.

'I was so mean to you about this, Joy. I had no right.' A memory of the day they had eaten onion soup under the October sky rushed at her. 'You didn't ask for any of this to happen... I'm so sorry.'

She put down the brooch and picked up the quartered sheet of notepaper, held her breath while she read:

My dear Queenie,

You little know how you have crushed me in breaking faith with me, but with it all, I do not wish you anything but your happiness. Be happy, Queenie, have the baby and let something good come from the ruins of my life. Please accept the enclosed. I won't be needing them where I am going. When I think of your beauty and grace, I feel what a fool I have been to dream that Charles could ever love me. C'est la vie.

Don't think badly of me, think only of the good times we once had.

Joy

CHAPTER SIXTY-SIX

Without looking up at Britannia bearing the torch of liberty, Queenie walked under the Victory Arch and into Waterloo Station. People huddled in behind her. It was bitterly cold and they, like her, were desperate to get into the warm. Not that the station offered warmth, with its grand Victorian glass-and-steel roof and old-soot smell, but at least it was out of the wind. It had been dark when she'd left the house, but now, over her back, the city was emerging into the blue shine of a winter morning.

She edged forward, into the crowd of hats and belted raincoats, the children and dogs, old men wheeling bicycles. She was going on a journey with no idea how it would end. The straps of her portmanteau, heavy at the end of her arm, carved into her hand as she aimed for the enquiries desk to ask when the next train to Dorset was. Neat, but perhaps not quite so slim, in her navy hat and the coat she'd altered to accommodate her changing shape.

She slipped her ticket to Swanage into her coat pocket and peered up at a sign to find the platform she needed. With time to kill, she bought a newspaper and a pack of cigarettes from a tobacconist and, thinking she was hungry, a warm penny bun in a paper bag from a young girl wheeling a portable stall. When she moved to stand in line behind the railings – there to bar travellers from the platform until the train had arrived – she put her bun away in her handbag and sifted its contents with her scarlet nails. Joy's note was in there, and thinking about her words brought another twinge of anxiety. The idea Joy had gone to Dorset was only a hunch and she hoped this wasn't some wild goose chase. The journey sounded torturous. The train to Swanage took over three hours and then a bus to Smuggler's Cove, with no idea where she was going to spend the night. Having called around to Joy's lodgings on the Gloucester Road to be told by her landlord, in his usual obstructive manner, that he had no idea where she was, Queenie needed to check the museum. For once she didn't need to do battle with that Amy girl, and although she managed to establish Joy wasn't at work, no one could confirm where she actually was.

Queenie withdrew her hand from her bag and looked at it. It was a well-maintained, pretty hand that suited the well-maintained, pretty woman she was. It bore a gold ring with a cluster of diamonds. A present from an admirer she couldn't remember the face of. It gave her a tiny flash of victory, but then her heart overtook her head and the victory faded to a miserable feeling. The diamonds were a decent size and she wondered if they had been dug out of the faraway depths of South Africa. Somewhere Charles Gilchrist had gone if his mother was to be believed; because Queenie had gone to Bayswater yesterday too.

'Is Joy here?'

Heloise had come to the door clutching the hem of a black silk kimono around her as if her stomach hurt. She looked a mess and Queenie wondered if she had been ill.

'Please?' Queenie tried again. 'Is Joy here?'

Neither had moved.

'Then I want to speak to Charles.'

Without a word, Heloise had stepped out of her house and shoved Queenie sideways. Padded down the path in her slippers to open the garden gate.

'You've a nerve coming here,' Heloise had snarled. 'How dare you, after what you've done? You've destroyed the lives of two people that I love.' The woman had pushed her fist against her mouth as if frightened of losing control. 'Joy was the best thing to happen to Charles, they had their whole lives ahead of them. She was precious and kind, she was… she was…' Heloise had gulped down her anger. 'Too good for a trollop like you. I don't know why, but Joy refuses to see me. I've tried and tried but I can't get near her. And as well as this, I've had to send my darling boy to Cape Town to get him out of your clutches. Charles was talking about doing the honourable thing and marrying you… over my dead body. This awful mess… You caused this, you greedy, selfish…' When she had run out of insults, she'd seized Queenie by the wrist and shaken her in the same way she had that morning all those weeks ago. 'Oh, you're not worth bothering with.' Then she'd thrown her aside. 'All I can hope is that you'll get your comeuppance one day. Now, clear off. Go on. Get off my property. And if you ever dare,' Heloise had wagged an irate finger, 'to come here again, I'll be calling the police.'

Queenie wasn't sure if it was reliving this painful episode that made her double over in sudden agony. But out of nowhere, it was as if she was being punched in the stomach. Hard, swift, violent movements that left her gasping for air. Three, then four. Then a hot, feverish sensation rippled up through her and her legs gave way. She collapsed to the ground, felt a cold wind sweep over her body.

The world went quiet for what seemed to be the longest time. Then a swell of commotion she wasn't part of as people circled her in their leather shoes. When the pain ebbed a little, she looked past them at the activity going on in the station beyond, thought how weird everything looked sideways up.

'Quick, get help. This woman needs help.' A shout, close to her head.

'Oh, dear, look… she's bleeding.' Someone else – Queenie didn't know who – reached down to scoop up her arm, snatching at her coat, pulling her upright.

'No. Don't move her. Don't touch her.' A man's voice attached to a pair of black boots advanced, authoritatively.

Dropped again, her face struck the floor and she was strangely aware of a small circle of cold where her cheek pressed against it.

She focused on this circle while her eyes followed a crack on the station floor.

This is it. She screwed her eyes against a fresh surge of pain she could hardly breathe past. *This is where I'm going to die.*

'At last.' Queenie sighed as the bright light of the ward was finally dimmed. Thirty-seven minutes past midnight. Her eyes, adapting to the unhealthy hue of the night-time corridor, made out the hands of the clock on the opposite wall. She had been admitted to hospital early that morning and nobody knew she was here. Careful not to knock the IV tube in her arm, she sank into the pillows to the accompanying crackle of starched sheets against her hospital gown. She had been thinking about her mother since the ambulance had brought her here. Thinking how swiftly her death had come at the end. It had appeared to be as easy as the closing and fastening down of a window and had left Queenie curious as to why no one had got around to closing it before, rather than letting the cold draught of her illness blow through their lives for as long as it had.

Bored with the ceiling, she twisted her head to follow a shaft of light that sliced free of the nurses' restroom, through the iron-mongery clutter beneath the beds and over the floor of the ward. She could smell the toast the nurses must have brought up from the canteen to eat. It reminded her of the kinds of breakfasts she would treat herself to when home from a night performing at the Mockin' Bird. Ravenous and still on a high, eating standing up at the kitchen window watching dawn push over the sky.

She yawned. Her eyes watering from the effort. She was exhausted but couldn't sleep; her mind wouldn't let her go for long enough. She wondered if reading the paper might help her and reached to turn on her bedside light. Grateful the painful stomach cramps had finally eased, she wriggled upright and, careful of her drip, arranged the pillows at the small of her back.

'How are you feeling, Queenie, dear?' A nurse appeared, the stiff material of her uniform brushing her arm.

'Much better, thank you. The painkillers have helped.'

'You be sure to rest.' The nurse set about testing Queenie's blood pressure. 'Oh, isn't that an awful business?' She nodded at the newspaper. At the anguished photographed face of Timothy Evans, who hogged the front pages yet again. 'They're saying he strangled his little baby girl with his tie. Can you believe that? The man's a monster. No punishment would be enough for the likes of him.'

'I can't believe he would do that to his wife and child.' Queenie shuddered; the story had a horrible grip on her imagination.

'My dear, you have no idea of the terrible things men do.' A matronly look.

'But you didn't hear the way he spoke about his baby girl, such fondness.'

'You met him!' the nurse exclaimed.

'I did, yes.' Queenie recalled the dreadful night in the Elgin. The Welshman with the limp who made her laugh. 'He was harmless, naïve. Too naïve to do what he's being accused of. So, no, I don't believe it. I don't believe it was him. What do you make of that Mr Christie?'

'Christie? Was he one of the witnesses?'

Queenie nodded. 'One of the principal witnesses.'

'Well, they wouldn't have called on him if he wasn't a nice, upstanding fellow. He's a retired policeman, or something, isn't he?'

'One with a criminal record, other reports are saying. Surely that has to mean something?' Queenie shuddered again.

'Oh, dear, are you all right? You're not in pain again?'

'No, I'm much better.' Queenie wasn't able to share the things that troubled her. Whatever this nurse said, she didn't like the look of John Christie in the photographs that had been in the paper and would be forever thankful she had not knocked on his door that night.

'It's a sorry business, all right. But justice must run its course.' The nurse punctuated her opinion with a sigh.

'Except they're going to hang the wrong man.' A voice – disconsolate, instructive – sliced between them.

'Terry! I can't believe you're here, it's so good to see you.' Queenie burst into grateful tears.

'Oh, now, young man, I'm sorry, but it really is far too late for our patients to be receiving visitors,' the nurse intervened, looking flustered. 'We do have rules, you know. Does Matron know you're here? I can't think she does, she's terribly strict about visiting times.'

Terrence smiled his charming smile. 'Please don't worry,' he told her. 'I've cleared it with Matron. She was happy to bend the rules just this once.'

'Was she? I am surprised.'

'Oh, Terry can charm anyone, can't you, Terry? And anyway, how did you know I was here?' Queenie interjected.

'Uncle Fish. Gloria's in the ward above this one.'

'Oh, yes, that's right. I forgot.' She dabbed her eyes with the edge of the hospital sheet. 'I've been meaning to visit her. Bad, aren't I?'

No one answered. The nurse busied herself around her silently, tucking in Queenie's blankets and checking her drip, while Terrence stared into the middle distance. She thought he looked distracted and awkward, and there were dots of dried blood on his cheeks where he'd nicked himself shaving.

'How's the patient?' he eventually asked the nurse and put the bag of grapes he'd brought with him on the table beside her bed.

'She's going to be just fine.' The assurance was given with a generous smile. 'But she's to rest, do you hear? No more of this gadding about. You're to take better care that she does, young man.' She gave Terrence a sharp look. 'That was a close shave she had today, she might not be so lucky next time.'

They waited for the nurse to go.

'She thinks we're a couple.' Queenie's observation made him smile: warm, kind – a chink of the old Terrence. 'I nearly lost the baby, Terry.'

'B-but… but wasn't that what you wanted?'

'No, not now.' She watched his delicate pianist fingers twist the buttons of his coat. 'The shock of it all, it's made me decide.'

'Decide what?'

She paused to think, to weigh up the importance of what she wanted to share. 'I've decided I'm not going to give the baby away; I'm going to keep it. Where there's a will, there's a way, eh, Terry?' She found herself echoing the very same sentiment the Welshman, Timothy Evans, had in the Elgin that night.

Terrence was oddly quiet. Queenie was hoping he'd be pleased with this news, her change of heart, but he didn't seem interested. Deeply preoccupied, he looked weird, wired somehow, and those tender bruises under his eyes were worrying. It was obvious he wasn't himself, that something was eating him up. Queenie wanted to ask him what was wrong, but she was afraid the answer might have something to do with her.

'It's not half bad in here.' Terrence turned to her. 'It's nice to know you're in safe hands.'

'Shame we didn't have the NHS for my mum. I might still have her.'

'Me too with my dad.' Terrence was about to sit but Queenie's portmanteau was on the only chair.

'Just move it.'

He set it on the floor and positioned himself beside the bed. 'Where were you going, anyway? Uncle Fish said you collapsed in Waterloo Station. He's been in to see you, by the way, but you were sleeping. He sends his love.'

'That's nice of him.'

'So, where were you going?'

'Dorset.'

'In January? Whatever for?'

'If you give me my handbag, I'll show you.' She watched him lift it from the back of the chair. 'Here…' She opened it and passed him Joy's note. Waited for him to read it. 'What do you think?'

'I don't know. What do you think?' he batted her question back and returned the note to her.

'She's gone there, Terry. To Dorset.' Queenie put it away in her bag. 'She's gone to that place Charles used to take her.'

'Has she? Well, that's good. At least it'll mean she's safe.'

'Safe? What are you on about?'

'Oh, nothing.' Terrence flapped away her query and presented one of his own. 'What makes you think she's gone there? It's hardly the time of year for a seaside holiday.'

'I just know. Call it feminine instinct.' She slumped back against her pillows, exhausted. 'Don't look at me like that.'

'Like what?'

'Never mind. Anyway, it's a little fishing village… Smuggler's something, I can't remember.'

'Smuggler's Cove, yes, I know it.'

'That's right, I forgot, you used to have holidays there, didn't you? Oh, Terry, I'm so cross with myself, I wanted to go and find her, I was going to beg for her forgiveness.'

'You were?' He looked mildly surprised.

'Yes, but I can't go now, can I? Not like this. And I'm wondering…' She broke off, dropped her eyes.

'What?'

'If you'll go instead. Just to make sure Joy's all right?'

'It's a long way from London, Queenie. I'll need to clear it with work, not that I'm sure they'll give me the time off.'

'But if you say it's an emergency. Oh, Terry, please say you'll go and fetch her home? You're my only hope. I'm frightened she's going to do something to herself.'

'Like what?' He jerked his head in alarm.

'I don't know.' Tears gathered at the corners of her eyes. 'I just know she's broken, but she won't ask for help.'

'You don't know that. You haven't seen Joy since Buster told her about you and Charles.'

'I remember how she was when her father died.' Queenie brushed a tear away. 'She feels things so very deeply, Terry, you don't know her like I do.'

'I'm sorry, darling, and this is going to be hard for you to hear, but you're the last person in the world Joy would come to.'

'You're right. But I feel so bad about what I've done to her. I never deserved her; I've been so selfish. All I want is the chance to make it up with her, to tell her how sorry I am. Please, Terry, you've got to help me put this right. I miss her… I miss her so much.'

'Don't cry.' Terrence, soft at her side. 'And try not to worry. It will be all right, I'm sure it will be all right. Look, I'll sort something with the bank and get a train first thing tomorrow morning. If she's there, I'll find her.'

'And bring her home?'

'If that's what Joy wants. But if she has gone there, she probably just wants to be left alone.'

'But you'll try? The only thing that matters now is that Joy is okay. Find her for me, Terry, please? Talk to her, tell her how sorry I am and that I'll do anything to make it up to her if she lets me.'

'I'll do my best.'

'Oh, thank you so much. You don't know what a relief that is. I don't know what I'd do without you. I've been missing you as well, you know.'

'And I've missed you too. The club's not the same without you. Are you sure you don't want to come back?'

She shook her head. 'I can't sing, not like I used to. This dreadful thing I've done to Joy, I just wish I could turn back the clock. I've ruined everything… everything.' Queenie burst into tears again.

'You've got to stop being so hard on yourself, d'you hear? You didn't deliberately set out to cause this.'

'Is that what you think, *really?*' she asked in a small voice. 'I thought you hated me, and that's why you've been avoiding me.'

'Avoiding you, darling? Don't be silly.' Terrence stroked the inside of her arm. The cool tips of his fingers finding a patch of skin between the IV and bandages. 'Things have been busy for me, that's all.' He had that faraway look in his eyes again. 'You couldn't see to lending me a few bob, could you, darling? I'm a bit strapped this month.'

'Sure, I can.' Queenie opened her purse, the troubled look on Terrence's face bothering her more than him tapping her for money. 'Oh, look, you'd better take this with you.' She passed him a small square photograph of Joy wearing a beret and a broad smile. The black skeleton of the Eiffel Tower rising like some grotesque scaffold behind her.

CHAPTER SIXTY-SEVEN

Another nightmare-choked sleep and Terrence woke in a sweat and a tangle of sheets. He'd been plagued by nightmares since returning to Britain from Italy after the war, long before the anxiety and distress he now had about Christie. He walked in the shadows and was haunted by the ghosts of the men he'd killed. But he couldn't think about it, not if he was to keep putting one foot in front of the other.

The rain had eased, but with no moon, everything had been devoured by inky blackness. It panicked him and he leant down to touch the Winchester flashlight he kept within reach on the floor. Reassured, he didn't need to turn it on; it was enough to know it was there. For a long time, he lay in the dark too tired to sit up, listening to the rain that had started again. It pummelled the exterior walls. Its ferocity waxing and waning, with several seconds of calm dropping between the violent surges.

Ultimately, his mind got the better of his weariness and he stumbled out of bed, fumbled for the light. Was momentarily blinded by the electric overkill. He squinted at his watch. The only thing he left on when he went to bed. He thought he'd slept for hours but his head had barely touched the pillow. Naked, he walked to the window and peeked around the blind. Outside, darkness still ruled. Only the merest hint of a pink dawn bleeding in from the east. It was time to go out and face the world, and he brushed his teeth and shaved up at the basin. Saw a smattering of coarse grey hairs at his temples. Hairs he would swear weren't there a month ago. The pimples around his mouth. His bloodshot eyes. He didn't know the man who was mirrored back to him.

At this moment, a banging from downstairs.

Christie? These past months, Christie was always his first thought.

He stepped away from the washstand and grabbed a towel, wrapped it around himself before opening the door and craning his neck to look down on the drop of the staircase to the tiny hall with its strip of linoleum. Saw the old-fashioned telephone on its bracket on the wall. Nothing. But as he stared at the telephone it began to ring. He ignored it and went back into his room, where he dressed and packed the items he imagined he would need into his canvas kitbag. Checked his pockets for his wallet of Queenie's money and the photograph of Joy, and slung it onto his shoulder.

*

Out in the street, the rain had stopped and the sun was rising, gathering strength over the rooftops. It was going to be a fine day, not that the idea cheered Terrence.

''Ow do, lad.'

'You!' He jumped back. 'What d'you want now?'

'That's not very polite.' Christie's neatly dressed figure slipped free of the shadows: his right hand shoved inside the pocket of his coat, the left curved around a smouldering cigarette. 'And where might you be off to on such a fine morning?'

'None of your business.' Terrence turned up the collar of his overcoat and made off down the street. He wasn't as surprised to see Christie as he should have been. The man had been making a habit of hanging around here and outside the Mockin' Bird, demanding money. 'Christ!' he shouted, unable to control his temper. 'I can't bloody move without you being there. I've said I'll get you the money, now clear off before someone sees you.'

'Don't be coming it with me, lad. I could have police on to you in a flash.' Christie trotted after him; no sign of the bad back he was forever complaining about.

'Look, how many more bloody times, I've got nothing.' He was thinking about Malcolm as well as the shocking state of his finances. 'You've bled me dry. I'm behind on—'

'Don't give me that – likes of you can always get hold of money.' Christie cut across him, needing to take two steps for every one of Terrence's strides. 'And if you don't give me what you owe…'

'Just leave me alone.'

'I'll do what I want, lad, and you'd do well to remember it. You're lowest of low so far as law's concerned, and if you don't pay up, I'll have police on you like a dose of salts.'

The black-edged threat he kept hearing prickled along Terrence's hairline, up into his scalp. He stopped at the top of the street and turned to face him. Terrence had to give it to the bastard, he was clever. Without needing to resort to violence or even raising his voice, he applied a steady pressure by pestering and threatening all hours of the day and night to get what he wanted. Forced to steal from his employer and living in abject fear every minute of every day, Terrence was near breaking point. He stared at the pale face beneath the trilby. The face of his blackmailer, who led a kind of Jekyll and Hyde existence. Jekyll being the respectable, neat ledger clerk, genteel, moralising and superior. Hyde came out at night, the frequenter of squalid cafés and the consort of pimps and prostitutes. Echoes with his own existence, his dismal thoughts.

'You think you're so bloody superior, don't you? Sneaking around in those shoes you wear and putting it about that you can help women in trouble. I know what you are.'

'You better not be threatening me, lad.' The cold, pit pony eyes bored into him. 'I don't take kindly to threats, not from a dirty bugger like you. You've a nerve, with a secret like yours?'

It was true, he was wasting his breath, so Terrence came at things from another angle: 'You look different. Getting to you, is it?' Terrence glared at him. He couldn't believe that a man who used prostitutes and was capable of blackmail could be deemed a suitable witness in a murder trial. It was sickening to think the life of another man was in the hands of this reprobate. 'Been giving your evidence in court, have you?'

'I have, as a matter of fact.' Puffed-up with his own self-importance.

'Why do you do that thing with your mouth all the time? Creepy, creepy. Coming all moral with me, you use prostitutes for fuck's sake.'

'I've told you before, I don't care for foul language. And aye, as you come to mention it, a man is about to have his head put in a noose on my say-so.' Terrence gawped at Christie in horror and put a hand to his neck. This man's callous conceitedness made his chest tighten. 'But I've not come here to discuss Timothy Evans. I want to know where my money is.'

How come it was always Christie who was indignant? Terrence couldn't believe the audacity of the man; the situation he was in was as maddening as it was frightening. It was as if Christie had his own moral code, and despite occupying the shadowy, sleazy world where everyone was guilty of something, he managed to elevate himself above the scum he mixed with after dark. It was like Albert said: morals and values and evil were a dung heap, and everyone stood on their own and shouted out about everyone else. This was Christie in a nutshell: full of snivelling hypocrisy.

Terrence watched Christie stoop to retie his plimsolls. 'It's why you wear those things, so you can slink about unheard.' This man was his own shadow in a world of shadows. Down among the city's gangland in the shady back alleys. 'You killed Beryl Evans, didn't you? A botched abortion, the defence said. I've been following it in the papers.' Terrence stared at Christie's puny back, measuring where the vital organs were. Thought: *It wouldn't take much.* A knife would go in smooth as butter. Why not? He had nothing to lose. With Malcolm gone, about to be kicked out of his lodgings, his job at the bank teetering on a knife-edge... killing this man who was slowly killing him was his only way out. 'You're going to stand by and let them hang an innocent man.'

'*Innocent?* Don't give me that.' Christie scoffed, upright again. Then, as if remembering it was something he should do, he put a hand to his back and grimaced, let go an amplified groan. 'You've not been following things as closely as you think, lad.' Another exaggerated grimace. Terrence ignored it; there was no way he was getting any sympathy from him. 'Is that all you've got? What it says in papers? I've been there, in court; a principal witness, I am. That Beryl were strangled, and her husband did it. Same as he did for their baby daughter.'

'You sure about that?' Terrence was remembering that awful November night, the gut-wrenching cry of a baby before Christie had slammed the door on him.

'What possible motive would I have for killing a child? You want to stop casting aspersions, lad. Dangerous for someone with your habits. Or would you like authorities to come round and ask for your opinion on it? Aye, you might find yourself up in court if you don't watch it.'

Terrence had to admire him for this bravura performance and suspected it was what he had done during Evans' trial when the defence counsel had tried to present an alternative version of events.

'Anyway, you don't know them like I did.' Christie was doing that sucking thing with his mouth again. 'Fighting like cat and dog, morning, noon and night.'

'Why do you whisper all the time? Can't you speak up?'

'My larynx got damaged in the First War. I had aphonia, it left me with an extremely quiet voice.'

'Got you out of the trenches, did it? You just do it for attention, in the way you're always complaining about your back. You're nothing but a bloody shirker.'

'I couldn't care less what you think about me, lad. Now, if you'd give me what I've come for, I'll be on my way.' Christie, enjoying himself. 'And you and that darkie can get back to whatever filthy business you get up to. I could have you sent to prison. Do you know what they do to your sort in prison?' A repulsive smile.

'How come you've got the time to be hanging around and bothering me all the time? Why aren't you in work?' Terrence was thinking about the struggle he'd had with his employers to get two days off.

'Why aren't you married?' Christie whacked back a question of his own. 'Decent men get married.'

'*What* – like you, you mean?'

'It's not normal.' Christie ignored him. 'The way you sorts carry on. What would your mother say?'

'You leave my mother out of this.'

'I will if you give me what you owe me, lad.'

'I'll get you it,' Terrence hissed, about to walk off.

'You make sure you do,' the soft voice threatened. 'It'd break your mother's heart if she got to finding out who real Terry were. Terry and his filthy ways. And she's a bad heart, I heard.' The wormy lips parted to give him a thin smile. 'You wouldn't want to be responsible for bringing about her untimely death, now would you?'

The Swanage train was almost empty. Fearful that Christie was following him, Terrence repeatedly checked the carriage in the same way he had sifted the crowds in the ticket hall for the man's horrid, glassy gleam. Trouble was, the crowd was mostly men in hats and coats, and he couldn't be sure. Safe for now, he breathed his relief. His only travelling companion was a woman with an impressive set of whiskers who sat across the gangway. He watched her, fascinated, as she gabbled vaguely to herself in a lilting voice. Her supposed insanity was strangely comforting; it drew him away from London's unstable heart and the things that troubled him. Christie's threats and Terrence's need to pay up didn't go away but, tipping his head against the headrest, they did, at least, ebb a little. Beyond the train were the tiled roofs and the high-rise buildings of the capital. It was still early, and the January sun hadn't quite burnt away last night's rain. The few trees that were scattered here and there seemed to hang around on street corners like tramps. Bleached and stale with the scoured look of winter on their flaking boughs.

It was stiflingly warm and wafts of unwashed parts drifted over from his travelling companion. He closed his eyes against the sharp sunshine flooding the carriage, felt the way it settled in warm bands across his body. Too edgy to sleep and unable to concentrate on the book he'd brought with him, he passed the time by scanning the colourless topography beyond the train windows. Searching it for freshness. For anything green. But there wasn't so much as a window box.

He was concerned about Joy and felt desperately sad for her, but he couldn't imagine her travelling to Dorset. Surely the memories would be too painful. He had agreed to this trip to help Queenie out; seeing how agitated she was at not being well enough to make the journey herself, it was the least he could do. What a mess everything was. Queenie had no idea that what she had done to Joy had impacted on him too. Terrence longed to confide about Christie blackmailing him but it wouldn't solve anything. But what Queenie had done to Joy – despite what he had been saying to her face to salve her conscience – it was unforgivable. She had spoilt Joy. Spoilt her like a flower growing wild that she had crushed with her hand for no other reason than she could.

CHAPTER SIXTY-EIGHT

Joy was almost there. Weaving through the usual trampoline of youngsters who today were fastened into thick winter woollies and breakfasting on chips out of newspaper parcels. The morning air was thick with the smell of them, of the hot fat and vinegar, rising from their fingers. Avoiding eyes, she kept her head low and left the curve of abandoned guesthouses, the shuttered fronts of souvenir shops fringing the strip of shore.

A rumpus of clouds slid across the headland. Wonky clusters gathering momentum out along the weather-beaten land. This walk had become as familiar as her handwriting over these past months and, pausing to button her old green coat as far as it would go against the bitter January weather, she noticed a cluster of snowdrops sheltering under a wedge of gorse. She stooped to touch the drooping white heads and tears pricked her eyes. Why the tender things in life were harder to bear than injury, she didn't know. No hat today and her hair, the colour of autumn bonfires – amber, red, gold – blew obliquely across her face. She looked different. Instead of her usual bouncing gait, now and again stopping to take in the view, she looked depleted; as if she'd run the longest race and now that race was over.

Her feet, in their stout leather shoes, took her higher, under a canopy of spinning terns she could almost touch. Then higher, to a steep flight of brick steps, which eventually opened on to a grassy clifftop pathway. Head bowed – a little boat navigating a rough sea – she followed the path away from Smuggler's Cove and out to the desolate and windswept bluff. Of no interest, the tiny granite seafarer's chapel with its jumble of gravestones and seal gargoyles, usually so fascinating to her. Pausing only briefly, she adjusted the bag she wore over her shoulder before continuing her climb to the top.

The dramatic arches of chalk cliff, when she reached them, were as vast as cathedrals. Carved out by storms and sea, the guidebooks said they were breathtaking whatever the season. But they were of no significance either. She was somewhere far away today. Remembering something Charles had told her the first time he'd brought her here: how Thomas Hardy had compared the cliff she stood on to an elephant dipping its trunk into water. Finding his voice, she tottered forward, wanting to grab it, but elusive, it was lost to her again. Dispersing like smoke, it stung her eyes and made the bruise of horizon, where sea met sky, swim before her.

Backing away from the edge, she dropped to her knees to listen to the crashing waves on the beach below. She pulled out the note Terrence had left for her the previous evening and, taking a minute on this mossy plateau with views of the sea, she reread his words. Kind of him to come all this way to find her but she didn't want to be found; she wanted to be alone. With the salty taste of the wind in her mouth, she tilted her face to the milky-diffused light where the sun should be and opened her fingers to let the note go. Watched it float like a bird, up to heaven. Terrence couldn't help her, no one could – whoever Joy once was, she had lost her, and there was no way to bring her back.

She waited. Not long now. Her mind crowding with disparate memories… a pink iced birthday cake with five candles… the *snip-snip* of her mother's kitchen scissors cutting her fringe… the feel of her father's bristles when she scrubbed her face against his… running barefoot along the sand at Goldchurch with her best friend… her lover's fingers winding her hair. His blue eyes beneath the brim of his black fedora. The eyes that said she could trust him.

She rose to her feet and stepped up to the lip of the precipice. Fragments of the cliff edge crumbled to the shore below. She looked down at the scuffed toes of her clumpy shoes and thought of the beautiful deep-red leather ones Heloise had given her. The hand-stitched soles, the bow, the pearl button fastening. Such pretty things until she'd managed to scratch one. Not that she had any idea how she had done it. She had expected Heloise to be angry, in the way she had been with herself for spoiling them when they were so precious. But none of that mattered now.

She lifted her gaze and, staring into the distance, trembled a little under her coat. The wind tugged her glorious hair off her face to reveal a neck that was as white and exposed as the chalky cliff beneath. Then, deciding it was time, Joy stretched out her arms as she'd done as a child playing the aeroplane game with her father among his fruit trees, and fell forward into the plaintive cries of seabirds, down to the unforgiving rocks below.

CHAPTER SIXTY-NINE

It was evening and a chilly Terrence, surprisingly rejuvenated after his overnight trip to Dorset, was back in London. Despite the awful circumstances that had taken him there, he supposed he had been looking for an excuse to return to that little town for years. Secret and sheltered between two hulking ridges of chalk downland, Smuggler's Cove had always held a special place in his heart and it was a relief to find it unchanged. Stepping off the train at Swanage, he had felt the same surge of excitement he had as a boy. From the bold heights of Ballard Down, the jagged chalk stacks of Old Harry, the distinctive vertical swell of Durlston Castle set against the steel-blue backdrop of sea: it was a jewel of a place and he could see why Charles had wanted to take Joy there.

Zigzagging through the multitude clogging the platform, he took off his hat and tipped his head to the filigreed ironwork and glass panelled roof of Waterloo Station. He was already missing the squall of shearwaters; seeing their wings cut against the sweep of the English Channel had lifted his heart. It certainly beat London. He could think straight there, away from the smog and the creeping Christie. Sitting on the seafront, watching the fishing boats coming in, was when he had made up his mind about Joy. Deciding he couldn't do much, that she was a grown woman, and if she didn't want to see him – and why should she? – then it was her prerogative, he couldn't force her. If she had wanted to talk, she would have come to him at the Bluebell that morning. The poor girl had probably just wanted to be left alone to lick her wounds. Bruised by a man who didn't love her properly, it would take time to recover from that if she ever could. He didn't want to push things by going back to her boarding house and pestering her. He'd given her plenty of time and then he'd had a train to catch. As much as he would have liked to duck out of society for a week or two, he couldn't. He had to come back to London, if only for his mother's sake. He couldn't abandon her, fearful of what Christie would do if he wasn't around. London needn't be forever, though. He lay awake half the night thinking about the Bluebell with its guestrooms, its dark-beamed bar and row of beer pumps he could envisage working behind, how well the back room would lend itself to musical evenings. Thanks to Christie, Terrence might have run out of money, but Lambert's would sort him a mortgage – they weren't asking much for the place – and he knew his mother would go with him. She'd always loved that stretch of coast. It could be the new start he craved because things couldn't carry on the way they were; it was a seedy existence.

But what about Christie? That dark spectre who was draining his very life's blood. Escaping to a new life in Dorset where he would be out of the man's grasp and free of his blackmail seemed the ideal solution. The more he thought about it, the more he believed that this was something he could do. Short of that, Terrence knew the only other option he had to get his life back and be finally free of that man was to take far more drastic measures than merely relocating. The only other way was to kill him.

Terrence chose a small bunch of flowers for Queenie from a stall on the way out of the station and hurried out into the London smog. Buttoning his coat to keep out the freezing air, he felt the slide of pavement beneath his shoes as ambiguous shapes emerged then faded around him. He joined a queue at a bus stop. Part of him wished he was just heading home, but he'd promised Queenie he would let her know, and although there wasn't much to tell, at least he could impart the news that Joy was safe. Tell her he had spoken with the landlady at the boarding house where she was staying and make her understand Joy had gone there because she wanted to be left alone. The city's damp had seeped through the seams of his shoes and he stamped his feet to get warm. The bus arrived, pulled into the kerb.

'Royal Brompton, please.' He handed his coins over.

'Take your ticket, sir,' the conductor reminded him.

The lower deck was full, so he clambered up the metal stairwell hoping for a seat at the top. Not that there would be much of a view tonight; the world beyond the steamed-up windows evaporated into the fog.

It was the top of his head he saw first. Without the trilby for once, the bald crown shone under the aqueous light.

Bloody hell, it's him.

The unexpected sight of his puny shoulders made Terrence's heart beat faster as he pulled his homburg further down over his eyebrows.

Don't let him see you… don't let him see you.

He swept past, breathing in the man's unpleasant disinfectant smell. A frightening moment when the buckles of his khaki kitbag skimmed the sleeve of his raincoat.

Safe.

He didn't move.

Terrence made a beeline for a seat at the rear, sat down beside an elderly woman with a bundle of knitting in her lap. Amid wet umbrellas and the smell of damp shoe leather, he kept Christie in his eyeline.

Beyond the windows, the Thames's rippling reflection under a thousand city lights and the perpendicular rise of Big Ben. The bus wheezed and juddered like an old-age pensioner, emptying and refilling itself with each stop. Unfamiliar with this route, he had no idea how long the journey would take, but at least there was no need to change buses. He stared at the back of Christie's neck and shuddered. Whoever this man was, there was something frightening about him. Christie put on his hat and lunged forward in his seat to pull the rope. The grind of the engine vibrated through the floor as the bus slowed to a stop. When he got up, Terrence did the same. Curiosity, like a fishhook through his gut.

Follow him. Follow him.

And finding himself out on an unknown street with a voice in his head telling him to see where Christie went – what he was up to – it was a relief to find he wasn't alone. That others were spilling off the bus too. Except these others were taking too long. Christie had skulked off by the time they had opened their umbrellas and put on gloves in readiness for their walks home. Reluctant to lose him, Terrence broke away from the crowd. The cold gnawed through his clothes. It was a filthy night. He followed Christie around one corner, then another, fearful the sound of his shoes against the pavement would alert him, but not once did he turn around. Breathing hard, he shadowed him over a road and through the thickening fog. Off around another corner, close enough to see the puff of Christie's breath, he tracked him down dark cobbled passageways and along empty streets. On high alert, not daring to drop his guard, he squinted through the cloying gloom. Visibility was poor: the only illumination was the sickly blush of gas lamps, and Christie's dark shape was reduced to a smudge in the murkiness.

What the hell did he think he was doing? This was madness. He wanted his bumps felt. He should have stayed on the bus and gone to see Queenie as planned.

The dystopian setting unnerved him. It was the same kind of feeling he'd had reading Orwell's book, *Nineteen Eighty-Four*, that Joy had lent him. The idea of a totalitarian state may only be fiction to other readers, but to him and his kind, this was London life. As he walked, he scanned the deserted streets, swapped the flowers to the other hand. He knew the Thames was out there somewhere, he could sense the steady pulse of the tide. It seemed as if he and Christie were the only two people in the world. There was something sharp in his shoe. He stopped to shake it free. When he looked up again, Christie was nowhere.

Where has he gone?

There.

A silhouette lit by the headlamps of a passing taxicab. It had to be him; it was the only other human shape around. When Christie turned in his direction, Terrence's brain shrank in fear. For one heart-stopping moment, he feared the man was on to him. But he wasn't. *Repulsive little bastard… repulsive little slimeball.* Terrence's major fear was that he couldn't afford to keep paying him off, that he was going to lose his job, his home, and then Christie would end up reporting him to the police anyway. His fears loomed larger than ever tonight. His visit to Smuggler's Cove had changed him: it had given him hope for a better future. But back here with the threat of this man, danger pinched at him again.

The way ahead suddenly opened out onto a busy thoroughfare. Pimlico? Chelsea? There wasn't time to worry about his bearings. Close on Christie's tail, Terrence couldn't believe he didn't look round, and followed him down into the mouth of the Tube, onto the underground staircase, eyes glued to the back of the brown trilby. Part of the creaking, jostling crowd of commuters, he let himself be pulled along on the tide of grey suits and hats. A mechanical swarm, like tin soldiers, their noses turned to home. He bumped against a young man with oiled hair and mumbled an apology.

The air was dry and dusty. Terrence had grit in his eye but no time to stop and rid himself of it – he needed to work hard to keep up. The warm, simulated wind of the Underground tugged at his coat and blew more grit into his eyes. Rubbing them to clear the way, he trailed Christie down tunnels and tunnels of gleaming glazed bricks, barely lit by the glowing lamps. He stepped behind him into a crowded lift and tried not to look into the hollow lift shaft as it surged downwards. The giant rolling steel ropes over the deeply grooved pulley, the blackness above and below, made him feel queasy. They pushed out, onto the platform. Passed a sign on the wall with its yellow loop of Circle Line and the notches of stations heading westbound.

A sudden rush of hot air from an approaching train. The scream of metal on metal. Terrence knew what he needed to do. It was the answer to everything. It was the only way he would ever be free.

Close at Christie's back, measuring where best to push. All it would take was a little shove against the shoulder blades.

This was it. This was his chance. Who would miss him? Terrence felt sure that the world would be a better place without John Reginald Christie.

And mindful of the crowd, swelling forward as one in anticipation of the oncoming train, crushing the flowers he was still holding, Terrence allowed himself a small smile as he lifted a hand, spread his fingers and touched the slightly greasy material of Christie's coat.

Then, bang.

Terrence was shunted sideways and nearly lost his footing. A man, big and burly inside his suit, barged forward to claim his space on the platform, wanting to be first on the train as it screeched to a halt.

The space between train and track was gone. Terrence had missed his chance. And little did Terrence know then that by missing the chance to end Christie's life, it would cost the lives of four more women: Christie's wife Ethel, Rita Nelson, Kathleen Maloney and Hectorina Maclennan.

THREE YEARS LATER

It was the maid, Dorothy, who escorted Michael to the door of the smart Regency-style house. Queenie was not permitted to enter the porch, never mind go inside. Michael toddled down the garden path to where she waited for him by the gate. As well as the wicker basket, she now had a smart set of beach toys to carry home: presents to Michael from his grandmother. The kinds of playthings she would love to be able to buy him but couldn't afford on her nurse's salary.

She scooped her young son in her arms, but before moving out into the hubbub of the Bayswater Road, she paused and turned back to the house.

'Say bye-bye to Heloise… say bye-bye to Grandma.' Queenie encouraged him to wave to the blonde lady at the window. Manoeuvring his arm up and down.

'Grandma,' Michael copied her, laughing.

'Your grandma loves you very much, doesn't she, sweetheart?' Queenie talked to him, then added, under her breath, 'But she hates me… She'll never forgive me any more than I will ever forgive myself. What I did to Joy, what I caused her to do… it is unforgivable.'

'Will we come again soon, Mummy?'

''Course we will, sweetheart.' She forced a smile for Michael's benefit. 'After we've had our holiday with your Uncle Terry.'

'And Malcolm and Peggy?'

'Yes, and Malcolm and Peggy.' She cuddled him close. At first Queenie struggled to understand why Terrence wanted to live in the place where Joy had ended her life, but supposed he had a long-standing connection with the town and although she still found it difficult to visit Smuggler's Cove, she had to agree it was the most beautiful stretch of coastline. 'They'll be there too.'

'The seaside.' Still laughing, trying out his new words. 'Bucket and spade. Bluebell… bluebell.'

'That's right, the Bluebell,' Queenie congratulated him. 'My clever little boy.' Michael wriggled in her arms. 'Do you want to walk?' she asked him when the garden gate was closed.

'No, Mummy. Carry… carry.'

The fog had cleared at last, and what remained of the evening was closing down over the city. They took a right and turned into Queensway, passed a street vendor selling newspapers from a little wooden booth. She stopped to read the headlines on the sandwich board. The headlines that had been sliced into diagonal chunks by the wire mesh:

'NEWS EXTRA'
KILLER CHRISTIE
ARRESTED ON PUTNEY BRIDGE

They've got him. They've finally got him.

A cold feeling scuttled up between her shoulder blades and across her back. They had finally caught the monster who had raped and strangled those poor women… women like her, who had gone to him desperate for help. The monster who had been blackmailing Terrence and making life so miserable for him, he had been forced to up sticks to Dorset.

John Reginald Halliday Christie.

She shivered and squeezed Michael tight. Folded his little foot in her palm. 'How close I came.'

Her memory dished up a chilling picture of that freezing November night when she had stood outside that shabby door in that filthy dead-end street. The hideous rise of the foundry chimney through the thick grey smog.

'How close I came.' The thought, a terrifying one, as she breathed her gratitude into Michael's curls and nuzzled his baby cheek.

POSTSCRIPT

By the spring of 1953, Christie realised the net was closing in. He had no wife, no job, no money, no furniture and had turned his ground-floor flat into a mortuary. On 20 March, he moved out of 10 Rillington Place after fraudulently subletting it, and four days later, the new occupant discovered the bodies of three women in the kitchen alcove. The subsequent police search uncovered another under the floorboards and two bodies buried in the back garden. The house had already been the scene of the double murder of Beryl Evans and her infant daughter, Geraldine, in November 1949 – crimes that Timothy Evans had been convicted of and hanged for in 1950.

The grisly discoveries triggered a nationwide manhunt for John Christie, who was eventually caught seven days later, on 31 March, on Putney Bridge Embankment, where he had been sleeping rough. Under questioning, Christie shared the details of his ten-year killing spree. He murdered his wife, Ethel, in December 1952, and in his final months of freedom claimed a further three victims: prostitutes Kathleen Maloney and Rita Nelson – each subjected to gassing treatment and their unconscious or lifeless bodies sexually assaulted then strangled – and Christie's last victim, Hectorina Maclennan. They were added to the bodies of Ruth Fuerst and Muriel Eady, murdered in 1943 and 1944 and buried in the back garden of Rillington Place.

Immediately after Christie was sentenced to hang for the murder of his wife, Ethel, Timothy Evans' mother called on the government to reopen her son's case and demanded a public inquiry. Christie had said during his trial that he had strangled Timothy's wife, Beryl, on 8 November 1949, but strenuously denied killing baby Geraldine. Timothy Evans' mother lived in St Marks Road, a few hundred yards from 10 Rillington Place, where Timothy and Beryl rented the top-floor flat. She insisted her son had known nothing of his baby's death until he'd arrived at the police station in Notting Hill. When the police had first searched the property at Rillington Place, they'd found baby Geraldine's belongings hidden in a cupboard in Christie's front room. Her clothes, her pram, even her feeding bottle half-filled with milk were there, but no one had mentioned these facts at Timothy Evans' trial. A trial at which Christie had been a principal witness for the Crown, where he had given detailed evidence about the arguments between Evans and his wife and denied the accusations put forward by the defence.

The idea there could be two stranglers operating out of 10 Rillington Place in the autumn of 1949 stretched credulity to breaking point. But it was to be another twelve years before the government ordered a re-examination of the case, and a posthumous free pardon for Timothy Evans was not granted until October 1966. A pardon that exonerated Evans of the charge on which he had been convicted: that of killing his infant daughter. Timothy Evans' remains were exhumed from Pentonville prison and reinterred in consecrated ground. The case was instrumental in the decision to abolish the death penalty in the UK.

A LETTER FROM REBECCA

Thank you for reading *The Girl at My Door* – I do hope you enjoyed it as much as I enjoyed writing it. If you did and would like to be kept up to date with my latest releases, just sign up at the following link. Your email address will never be shared and you can unsubscribe at any time.

www.bookouture.com/rebecca-griffiths

I have to say that I really love hearing from readers; it is one of the most pleasurable and rewarding parts about writing for me. So please do get in touch either through Facebook or Twitter and let me know how this book made you feel and what you thought of Queenie and Joy and Terrence… and, dare I say, the creeping Christie.

If you did enjoy *The Girl at My Door*, I would be grateful if you could find the time to leave a short review. You wouldn't believe how much this helps to spread the word about a book and encourages others to pick it up and read it.

Thank you and happy reading!
Rebecca x

Rebecca Griffiths (writer)
@RebeccaGriffit7

ACKNOWLEDGEMENTS

Special thanks must go to my lovely agent Broo Doherty for her guidance and enthusiasm. There are many people at Bookouture for whose knowledge and dedication I am grateful, particularly Laura Deacon, my wonderful editor, for her expertise and valuable advice.

Thanks must also go to my two trusty readers and friends. The top book blogger and reviewer Jo Robertson, and her fabulous blog site: mychestnutreadingtree.wordpress.com; and the researcher, historian and folklorist Beverley Rogers, and her fascinating website: bevrogers.co.uk.

But most of all my thanks must go to my husband, Steven, to whom this book is dedicated, for his indomitable belief, love and creative inspiration.